Here and Now

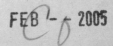

FEB - 2005

Here and Now

Kimberla Lawson Roby

DAFINA BOOKS
Kensington Publishing Corp.
http://www.kensingtonbooks.com

In loving memory of
Erick Haley, Ben Tennin, Jr., Derrick Horton,
and Derrick Jones

Acknowledgments

I am thankful to God for blessing me over and over, time and time again.

To my husband Will for eight wonderful years of marriage and for encouraging me to self-publish my first novel, BEHIND CLOSED DOORS. I love you from the bottom of my soul.

To my mother, Arletha Stapleton, for always being there when I need her to be and for having total confidence in everything I do. But most of all, Mom, thanks for just being you.

To my brothers, Willie Jr., and Michael Stapleton for their unconditional love and support.

To Peggy and Steven Hicks, Kelli Tunson Bullard, Aileen Blacknell, Keith and Shari Grace, Tammy Roby, Janell Green, Mary Carthell, and Ace Fehr for giving me their opinions, praises, and constructive criticism after reading HERE AND NOW.

To Dr. Ronald E. Burmeister, M.D. from the Department of Reproductive Medicine at Rockford Health System for taking the time to answer every infertility question I could think of.

To Evelyn Barmore of Evelyn's Hair Studio and Susan Saylor at Very Vogue for accomodating my sporadic traveling schedule. And to Pamela Sims of Braider One in Chicago for her braiding talent and amazing spirituality.

To Lori Whitaker Thurman, Veronda Johnson, Martha Moore, Vicky Pruitt, and Patricia Brown for calling me from time to time to see how everything was going.

To my incredible editor at Kensington, Karen Thomas, who is clearly one of the most pleasant persons I've ever worked with. You are simply wonderful.

To Christy Fletcher for introducing this novel to Monica Harris. And to Monica for believing in my idea from the very beginning.

And finally, to all of my readers everywhere, I thank you.

Chapter 1

A wave of depression settled over Marcella as she drove her beat-up Cutlass into the low-income housing complex. Pierce Commons had been her permanent residence for almost five years, but today the place looked different. It looked worse than ever before. Beer cans and liquor bottles thrown across the parking lot; trash spread over the sidewalks; and graffiti plastered across the once white, but now dirty-colored building. She couldn't help but wonder how she'd been so silly as to get herself caught up in this poverty-stricken situation. And Lord knows she was worn out from struggling to make ends meet by way of a seven-dollar-an-hour job, not to mention the child support Tyrone paid only when he felt like it. This wasn't at all how she'd hoped things would turn out for them. And never in her wildest dreams had she thought Tyrone, the so-called love of her life, would end up her worst nightmare. She regretted the day she'd ever laid eyes on him, let alone started dating him. And just thinking about how he treated her, and how he neglected Ashley and Nicholas, made her sick to her stomach.

She parked directly in front of her building, turned the ignition to the off position, and stepped out of the car. As she shut the door, she saw the children making their way off the school bus. She frowned when she spotted Ashley's bare head and Nicholas's pile-lined coat flagging wide open. No matter how often she lectured them about bundling up in the wintertime, it always seemed to ease through one ear and right out the other. Why did they always have to be so hard-headed? Didn't they know she couldn't afford to take off work when one of them got sick? If their sickness couldn't be helped, that was one thing, but if it was primarily because they were being careless and absent-minded, that was another. Of course, Nicholas was like most boys and just didn't have time to zip up his coat and put on his hood, but Ashley, on the other hand, was simply trying to be cute, and didn't want some knit hat messing up her little hairdo.

Marcella started fussing as soon as they approached her.

"Nicholas, haven't I told you a thousand times about walking around in zero-degree weather with that coat wide open? And Ashley, you know you're old enough to know better." The children just looked at her in silence. And it was obvious that they didn't have the slightest idea why she was so upset. She could see it in their faces, and that irked her even more. Marcella couldn't remember ever being that forgetful when she was a child, and couldn't understand at all where this particular generation had come from.

She shook her head and decided that maybe she was overreacting, which was possible since she'd had such a horrendous day at work. Right now anything would have stirred her nerves, and it wasn't fair to take her frustrations out on the children. Especially, since for the most part, Ashley and Nicholas were exceptional. They were obedient, intelligent, and had wonderful personalities. She loved her children, and most of all, she was proud of them. Proud because, even though they hadn't been born with silver spoons in their mouths or with the stability of a two-parent household, they were better mannered than some children who'd been blessed with all the financial advantages.

Marcella slid the key in the front door and opened it. They all walked in one by one; Ashley shut the door behind them, and they each kicked off their boots so they could dry. Marcella opened the hall closet, hung up her black wool scarf and charcoal-gray winter coat, and then reached for Nicholas's and Ashley's outer garments.

"You two have any homework to do?" Marcella asked, closing the closet door.

"I don't, Mom," Nicholas quickly offered, with a huge smile on his face.

"Good, then that means you can go work on those spelling words so you'll be ready for your test on Friday," Marcella responded back to him.

"Aw, Mom," Nicholas said, replacing his smile with a pout.

"Go on. I'll be in there to test you in a bit." Marcella knew if he didn't have anything constructive to do, he'd spend the rest of the evening glued to the Nickelodeon channel. Too much TV wasn't good for anyone, and it especially wasn't good for an eight-year-old little boy.

"What about you, Ashley?" Marcella asked.

"I have some math homework to do, but I finished everything else in class," Ashley answered and headed toward her bedroom.

Marcella smiled to herself, because at that moment she saw something in her daughter that she hadn't seen before. A ten-year-old version of herself. She'd been the very same way when she was growing up. She'd loved school from her very first day in kindergarten, and all the way through her graduation from high school. Ashley was a straight-A student, and was clearly following in her mother's footsteps academically. Which was fine. But when it came to falling hopelessly in love with some little boy—Marcella prayed that Ashley would find her own path to follow. Because the last thing Marcella wanted was for Ashley to end up pregnant, the way she had during the last month of her senior year in high school. It wasn't that she didn't love her daughter. Or both of her children, for that matter, because she did. But she could kick herself a thousand times for not being more careful when she started having sex with Tyrone. She'd loved him from the very first moment she laid eyes on him during their sophomore year. He, the school's top football star, and she, the girl voted most likely to succeed. The world had been theirs for the taking, but without even having the sense to know it, they'd ruined everything. Marcella had received acceptance letters from colleges and universities all across the country, but she'd had no choice except to decline each and every one of them. She'd tried hopelessly to overcome this irreversible mistake, but now that almost eleven years had passed and she was twenty-eight, her efforts to do so still didn't seem to be working.

Marcella dropped down on the leatherlike beige sofa, and leaned her head back. She closed her eyes and rested them for a moment. When she opened them, she gazed around her apartment. The desperately discounted furniture, dull-looking mini-blinds, and second-hand wall portraits were disgusting, and now she was even more depressed than she had been earlier. No matter how hard she tried, she was still barely making ends meet. Her salary alone just wasn't enough, and the few food stamps she received each month never seemed to last more than two weeks. And the only reason they lasted that long, was because of how conservative she was when it came to buying meat. If it hadn't been for her mother and sister, she wasn't sure what she would have done. They helped her out financially whenever she needed them and they went out of their way to show Ashley and Nicholas how much they loved them.

Marcella could ring Tyrone's neck. Sure, she'd been just as much at fault for not using the diaphragm, IUD, the pill or something, but he'd never made any attempts to use any form of protection, either. She could still hear him now: "Baby, I won't do it inside of you. I promise." *Hmmph*, some promise. Because the only thing that had resulted from his promise was her realization that the withdrawal method just didn't work. Somehow, though, she hadn't been the slightest bit upset when she'd first found out she was pregnant. If anything, she was thrilled. She loved Tyrone; he loved her; and they were going to have a beautiful baby girl that belonged to both of them. It was perfect. He'd go off to college on his football scholarship, marry her immediately after he graduated, allow her to work toward an accounting degree, and then she, Tyrone, and the baby would live happily ever after. And things just might have turned out that way, if he hadn't injured his knee two weeks before the start of his freshman year. Marcella could still remember that day the sports medicine specialist informed him that his football career was over;

that he would never play any sport on a professional or continuous basis ever again. Tyrone had cried like a baby, and for a while she'd been worried that he was going to experience a nervous breakdown. Because not once had he ever imagined life without playing football. The boy ate, drank, and slept it. It was his sole reason for existing.

Eventually his depression passed, but everything changed for the worst when he slipped into a horrible and unbearable mode of bitterness. He snapped at Marcella for just about everything, and was angry at the world. Her wonderful pregnancy had become a total nightmare, and she regretted the day she conceived his baby. By the end of her third trimester, he was barely speaking to her, and rumor had it that he was messing around with a girl she'd been friends with since third grade. At one point Marcella hadn't known whether she was coming or going. Her parents were completely put out by the fact that she'd gone to such extremes to disappoint them, and they proved it by not offering her one ounce of moral support. Partly because they spent the majority of their time arguing, but mostly because they each worked tons of overtime trying hard to make ends meet. All they saw when they looked at Marcella was an extra mouth they were going to have to feed, and they weren't at all happy about it. Which is exactly how it had turned out, too. They'd been stuck with a $2,000 hospital bill, and the responsibility of purchasing Pampers and formula for a baby they hadn't asked for.

Her sister, Racquel, had been wonderful throughout the entire pregnancy. She'd been away at school during most of it, but she always called to talk with her. And when she came home on weekends, she spent the majority of her time with Marcella. Racquel had thought having a baby was the most joyous and precious gift there was, and at the time Marcella had agreed with her. But now, she felt like a failure. Here, at the age of eighteen she'd had a child, and then gone on to have another child out of wedlock by the same man, who hadn't shown any interest in taking care of the first one. Things could have been so different had she gone to college, gotten married, and then took the time to plan for children. Children didn't ask to come here, and the very least a parent could do was make sure they could take care of them and give them the best possible life available.

A sadness engrossed Marcella, and she could feel the tears building as fast as the thoughts were twirling through her mind. She'd been sure that the children would bring her and Tyrone closer together. How could she have been so selfish? And so stupid? She'd had no right bringing Nicholas and Ashley into such a cruel world without the means to support herself, let alone the resources to provide for them. If only Tyrone would pay his child support, things would be so much easier. Their lives could be so much happier. If only he would spend more time with them. Didn't he know that little boys needed their fathers? Didn't he know that Nicholas needed him? How could someone simply walk away from the innocent little faces of his own children, and pretend they didn't even exist?

Marcella tried to blink back the tears, but she was unsuccessful at doing it. She placed her hands on each side of her head and looked down. "How could I have screwed things up like this?" she whispered softly.

"Mom, what's the matter?" Nicholas asked, walking toward her with a confused look on his face.

Marcella wiped the wetness from her face as best she could, looked up at him, and tried to smile. "Nothing, baby. Mom just had a hard day at work. That's all."

"Don't worry, Mom. Everything's gonna be okay. And things will be better when you go to work tomorrow because that's what you always tell me and Ashley when we have a bad day at school."

Marcella smiled, but the tears were still rolling. Nicholas was so considerate and so loving where she was concerned. Both of the children were. Especially, if they thought something was bothering her. Which was even more the reason why they deserved so much more than she was giving them.

She noticed a piece of notebook paper in his hand. "Is that your spelling list?"

"Uh-huh. You said you were going to test me on it, and I'm ready."

Marcella smiled, pulled him closer, hugged him as tight as she could, and then let him go.

"What was that for, Mom?" he asked, frowning like boys his age do when they think they're too old to be hugged by their mothers.

"It's because I love you."

Ashley had been listening from her bedroom and decided to come out to see what was going on.

"I love both of you so much. And don't either of you ever forget it," she said, reaching her hand out to Ashley.

Ashley looked at her, still trying to figure out why her mother was acting so strangely.

"We know that, Mom. We love you, too," Ashley said, leaning down to hug her mother.

"Come on, Mom, test me on my spelling words, so me and Ashley can watch Nick at Nite after dinner."

"Ashley and I," Marcella corrected Nicholas.

"Boy, I'm not even finished with my math homework yet," Ashley said to Nicholas and frowned.

"So what. You will be by the time Nick at Nite comes on."

"But that doesn't mean I want to watch TV with you."

"You just want to get on that phone with your friends. Mom, make her watch it with me."

"Okay, you two. That's enough. Ashley, you go finish your homework. And Mr. Nicholas, we'll see how many of these words you can spell before we discuss watching any television."

"I know them all, Mom. I promise."

"We'll see. You keep studying while I go change out of my work clothes, and I'll be back in a few minutes to start warming up dinner," Marcella said, rising from the sofa.

"Okay, Mom, but I'm telling you, I already know them all."

Marcella shook her head and smiled at him.

When she arrived inside of her bedroom, she shut the door behind her. It was so amazing how the children always managed to eliminate her depression. They were such a joy, and they were so special. All children were special to their mothers, she guessed, but hers were special because they were surviving a way of life that was barely one step up from living on welfare. They didn't live in the projects, but still, there were roaches, drug dealers, and gangs to contend with just the same. So, as far as she was concerned, it was the next best thing to being there.

Marcella pulled her black sweater dress over her head, hung it in the closet and walked toward the dreadful-looking wooden dresser. Then she slid off her black tights, stuffed them into the top right drawer, and slipped on the royal-blue jersey sweat suit she'd left scattered across the bed earlier that morning. She never liked leaving her clothing all over the place, but after pressing the snooze button on the alarm clock twice, she hadn't had any time to hang them up. Tomorrow, though, she was going to make time because she despised keeping a messy apartment. She hadn't been raised that way, and she made sure Nicholas and Ashley weren't, either. And even though the three of them didn't have any luxuries worth writing home about, they went out of their way to take care of what they did have. Ashley understood that no dinner dishes were to ever be left in the sink overnight, and Nicholas automatically took the garbage out without being told.

That's how it had been for her and Racquel when they were growing up. And she was glad her mother had taught them as well as she had. Her father had been the only messy one in the household. Walking across their off-white kitchen floor and their light-tan carpet with his filthy work boots had just about run her mother insane. But no matter how much she complained, he never stopped doing it. If they hadn't gotten divorced, she supposed he would still be tracking dirt. It was almost as if he did it just to get under her mother's skin. Her parents were at each other's throats constantly, and the only time there had been at least some peace in their household was when one or both of them were gone. They had had the perfect marriage, until she and Racquel became teenagers. Her parents seemed perfect for each other, and everyone said so. But, somewhere along the line, their father started staying out until midnight. And it wasn't long before midnight became one, two and even three in the morning. And finally when that wasn't good enough, the wee hours of the morning had become the next day's afternoon. It was obvious that he'd found someone else, but didn't have the guts to leave. Then one Friday night, when her mother decided that enough was enough, and that she wasn't in her own words "putting up with his shit any longer," she dragged every piece of anything that belonged to him out to the street, called the locksmith to change the locks, and flipped through the Yellow Pages until she found a reputable divorce attorney, whom she hadn't hesitated to call first thing that Monday morning.

Marcella could still see the look on her father's face when he'd finally arrived home that Saturday morning. She and Racquel had stared at him through the window from the moment he'd pulled up until the second he'd thrown the last of his things in the car and sped off. They'd wanted to help him, but their mother had promised each of them two weeks on punishment if they did. And they had no choice but to obey her.

As the weeks continued, their parents started seeing each other again, and it wasn't long before their father moved back into the house. Their mother stopped the divorce proceedings, and for the most part, they seemed to be enjoying each other's company. It was almost as if they couldn't keep their hands off of each other.

That lasted for two years, but then suddenly Daddy starting staying out during all hours of the night again. Their mother had wanted to kick him out for good this time, but her financial situation hadn't allowed it. She needed help with paying the household bills, Racquel's college tuition, and yes, supporting Marcella and her new baby. But it wasn't long before she realized that she couldn't take it anymore, and that it wasn't worth living with a man who spent all of his time with some other woman. So, again, their father moved out; and this time when their mother filed for a divorce, she went through with it.

Marcella shook her head as she reminisced about her past. Her unnecessary mistakes had caused financial problems not only for her, but for everyone involved.

And the more she thought about it, the more convinced she was that her situation had to change. She was born, raised, and still lived in Covington Park, a working-class suburb just south of Chicago, but her dream had always been to work for a prestigious accounting firm somewhere downtown in the Loop. Actually, part of the dream had come true, because she did work for an accounting firm, but not as a CPA, like she'd planned. Instead, she'd been hired as a glorified administrative assistant who spent the entire day greeting uppity clients and answering umpteen phone lines. She was capable of so much more, and each of the partners at the firm knew it. And they would have loved nothing more than to promote Marcella, but since she didn't have a four-year degree, their hands were tied, and there really wasn't much they could do to help her.

Marcella stepped in front of the mirror attached to the back of her bedroom door, pulled back her shoulder-length jet-black hair, and wrapped a beige rubber band around it. As she scanned her face, she noticed a pimple just under her right cheekbone. It took everything she had in her not to squeeze it. She hadn't had any problems with acne since adolescence, but this past year facial breakouts had become common. Of course, her medium-chocolate skin had never been babylike smooth, but at least it had always been above average. Maybe it was stress, but more than likely, it was because of her terrible eating habits. She was average height, but had lost close to fifteen pounds over the last six months. Which wasn't good, given the fact that most everyone she knew had always thought she was way too thin in the first place. She tried to make a conscious effort toward eating more regularly, but most of the time her stomach felt nervous. And it was obvious that it was because of all the worrying she'd been doing about bills.

Why were there so many bills? And how was she going to pay them?

Plus, she worried about everything else she could think of, too. Like, why she'd gotten pregnant at such a young age? And why on earth had she been crazy enough to make the same mistake twice? Why couldn't she have been blessed with a wonderful husband, like her sister, Racquel? Or even better, why couldn't she have married someone who earned a decent living? And most of all, why couldn't she have had the sense enough to go to college? Her sister had been blessed with everything any woman could ever hope for, and although Marcella loved her children more than life itself, she'd trade places with Racquel in a second. Marcella knew the grass usually appeared a lot greener than it actually was, but compared to her lifestyle, anything would be an improvement.

But she knew all this wishful thinking was nothing more than some far-fetched fantasy, and that no miracle was going to just happen. And that in order for her life to become better, she was going to have to take matters into her own hands. Make some very drastic changes in the way she viewed life in general, and the way she dealt with Tyrone James. No more feeling sorry for herself, and no more complaining. Her decision was made. She was going to give her children the decent life that they deserved. If it was the last thing she did.

Chapter 2

Racquel placed the phone receiver on its hook and slowly sat down on the side of the king-sized brass bed. She'd promised herself that she wouldn't cry this time, but as usual she just couldn't control it. She'd heard the nurse at her doctor's office announce enough negative pregnancy results to last a lifetime, but still, she wasn't able to handle it.

Tears rolled down her cheeks slowly at first, but it wasn't long before they began falling much more rapidly and in an uncontrollable manner. Her body shook, and her stomach raised up and down continuously. She locked her arms together in front of her and leaned her body toward her lap, rocking back and forth. She felt like the entire world was coming to an end.

One hour had passed when Racquel woke up and realized that she'd somehow fallen off to sleep. She lay there replaying what the nurse had said to her, "I'm sorry, Racquel, but your pregnancy test came back negative." It just wasn't fair, and for the life of her, she couldn't understand why God kept punishing her over and over again. She was a good person, and none of what was happening to her made any sense. The emotional pain she was feeling was worse than anything she'd ever felt, and she wasn't sure how much more of it she could take without cracking up. All she'd ever wanted was to have two beautiful, healthy children, and she couldn't understand why she was being cheated out of what rightfully should have been hers. If she'd done anything to deserve punishment, she wished He'd choose something else. Anything but deny her the right to have children. Because as far as she was concerned, nothing else was more important.

She'd fantasized about having children ever since the day Marcella had given birth to Ashley, and from that point on, she'd made the idea of getting pregnant her reason for living. She'd planned everything out so well. Graduated from college with a teaching degree, married a loving, intelligent husband, saved money for the future, bought a house. She and Kevin had done all the right things, and there was no doubt that they had all the love and financial resources it took to give any child a wonderful life.

Here, thousands of girls were running around having babies and then dumping them off on their parents because they had no way of taking care of them. And the ones who kept their own children were raising them irresponsibly on welfare. Not to mention, all the women who took their welfare checks and spent the money on some outfit, or even worse, gave it to the deadbeat father or some new lowlife they were trying to latch onto.

The thought of all this was enough to make Racquel sick. Even her own sister had gotten pregnant twice out of wedlock, still wasn't married, and struggled daily trying to take care of her children. And she didn't even want to think about that jerk Ashley and Nicholas called their father. Tyrone had to be the poorest excuse for being a father that she'd ever come in contact with, and she couldn't stand him.

She loved Marcella dearly, and there was nothing she wouldn't have done for her and the children, but it just wasn't fair that Marcella had been blessed with two adorable children, while she'd been blessed with nothing. She'd been raised with the understanding that she was never to question God and His actions, but this not-getting-pregnant business was going too far. In fact, it was becoming ridiculous, and her sadness and feeling of inadequacy were slowly turning to anger.

Racquel sat up on the side of the bed for a few seconds and then stood up. She dragged herself into the master bathroom and looked into the mirror above the double sinks. But to her surprise, she didn't see the attractive woman that everyone said she was. Her bobbed blackish-brown hair needed a serious trim, her deep-mocha skin had an ashy look to it, and her light-brown eyes looked depressingly dim. Her eyes were bloodshot red and severely swollen. She pulled a plush face towel from the rack, ran some cold water on it, squeezed it tight, and rubbed it across her face. When she was finished, she rehung the towel and headed back out to the bedroom. She felt like she was losing her mind. Like she didn't know Sunday from Monday. Like her whole life wasn't reality, but merely a bad dream.

She heard the front door shut and realized Kevin was home from work.

After removing his gloves, winter jacket, and boots, he headed up the stairs—the way he always did to greet his wife—and walked into the bedroom.

"How's my baby doing?" he asked, dropping his

blazer on the bed and moving closer to Racquel, who was now staring through the window.

Racquel opened her mouth to respond, but instead burst into tears and then fell into his arms.

"Hey, hey. What's this all about? Baby, what's wrong?"

Racquel still wasn't able to answer him.

"Baby . . . ," Kevin started to ask her again, but then paused when it dawned on him that she must have received the results from the pregnancy test she'd taken earlier that morning. How he could have allowed that to slip his mind for even a moment was beyond his understanding. Whenever Racquel thought she was pregnant, it was all she talked about. This morning he had begged and pleaded with her not to get her hopes up, but like always, she completely ignored what he was saying. He'd gone through this so many times with Racquel that he wasn't even sure what to say anymore. And although he loved his wife, he was starting to get fed up with this whole pregnancy obsession.

"Baby, I'm so sorry," he said, hugging and caressing her.

She hugged him back, but didn't say anything.

Kevin took a deep breath. "Baby, maybe it's time for us to accept the fact that you can't get pregnant."

Racquel released her arms from around him and stepped a couple of feet back. "What do you mean, I can't get pregnant?" she said defensively. "You make it sound as though it's all my fault. For all we know, it's you who's causing the problem. It's not like either of us have gone through any physical exams to find out one way or the other."

"What are you talking about?" Kevin asked in a state of confusion. "I wasn't blaming you for anything. But since you brought it up, you were the one who didn't want us to get evaluated. I wanted to be tested a long time ago. And why are you so pissed off at me, anyway?"

"Look, I'm sorry, okay? It's just that I'm so frustrated with all of this, and I'm having a hard time accepting any of it."

"I realize that, baby, but maybe we're at a point where we need to get on with our lives. We can always adopt a child. It's not the act of having a child that makes someone a parent, it's the love and commitment that make all the difference."

"Why are you still pressing me about adoption? I told you that I want to have my own baby. Our own flesh and blood. It just won't be the same raising a baby who belongs to someone else. And I'm not about to spend the rest of my life wondering when the biological parents are going to show up wanting to take their child back."

"Well, answer me this. How long are you going to keep this up? I mean, damn, Racquel, our lives haven't been the same since you had that miscarriage last year."

"I'm going to keep it up for as long as it takes. If only you could find a little more faith and patience, I know this can happen for us."

"As long as it takes? That could be forever. Look, I'm not going to keep arguing with you about the same thing over and over again. I've told you numerous times how much I love you, and whether you have a baby or not, my feelings for you won't ever change."

"I love you, too, honey, but if you could just hold on a little while longer, everything will work out. We just have to try harder is all."

"Racquel. We have sex almost every day of the week, and it's not even that great any . . . ," Kevin said, and then closed his eyes and sighed deeply. "Baby, I didn't mean that."

"Of course you meant it. Words like that don't just slip out, unless you've been saying them to someone else, or thinking about it awfully hard. I didn't realize making love to me had become so horrible."

"I didn't say that, but the fact of the matter is, we don't make love anymore. The whole idea of having sex has become more of a routine. Like some daily chore. It's not supposed to be like that, but you've become so obsessed with getting pregnant, that you don't seem to care about anything else. Much less about how I feel, or what's happening to our marriage."

"I do care about you and our marriage, but can't you see what I'm going through? I mean, Kevin, we're thirty years old, and we're definitely not getting any younger. We have to try as hard as we can now, before it's too late."

Kevin just looked at her and shook his head in disagreement. "I'm going to the 'Y' to work out. Do you need anything while I'm out?"

It was just like him to go running out to the "Y" when they were having an argument, and it really pissed her off. But at the same time, she knew if he didn't work out so diligently, there was a chance he wouldn't have such a tall, gorgeous-looking, muscular body. The same body she'd been attracted to when she first met him three years ago. Not to mention his thin, yet manly-looking mustache and cocoa-colored complexion.

"So, just like that, you're going to leave?" Racquel asked, folding her arms against her body.

"You're not listening to any of what I'm saying, anyway."

"I *am* listening to you, Kevin. But you know how strongly I feel about this."

Kevin didn't even bother commenting. He pulled off his suit pants, shirt, and tie. After hanging them up, he removed his dress socks and slipped on an athletic-gray sweatshirt and a pair of matching sweatpants. After he'd pulled on his thick white socks and tied his Nikes, he stood up. Racquel was staring out of the window again, crying.

He walked over to her and hugged her from behind. "I'm sorry that we don't see eye to eye about this situation, but I know we can work through this, okay?"

She nodded her head yes.

"You try to relax, and I'll be back in a couple of hours," Kevin said, kissing her on the side of her face.

Racquel never even turned around to face him, and as he left the room, she started to feel numb. She felt like that a lot lately; especially on days like today. She pulled the winter-white lamb's-wool sweater over her head and slid off matching pure wool pants and hung them inside the walk-in closet. She pulled her terry-cloth robe from the rack, wrapped it around her, tied the belt, and headed downstairs. Once she was in the kitchen, she opened the refrigerator, removed a can of pop, pulled the tab, and sat down at the glass table. She took a few sips from her soft drink and reached over to the chair next to where she was sitting and picked up her briefcase. She wasn't at all in the mood, but she'd promised her second-grade class that she would correct their math quizzes and return them the next day. And whenever she gave them her word on something, she followed through on it. The children trusted and depended on her, and she had a close relationship with all of them.

She'd worked at Covington Park Elementary for the entire eight years she'd been teaching, and she couldn't have been happier. It was one of the few careers that allowed a person to build a personal relationship with small children. In a sense, they were like her own, and she went out of her way to do special things for them. One month ago, just before Christmas, she asked Kevin to visit the class so he could tell them about Whitlock Aerospace, the company he worked for. He'd brought photos of the airplanes that the company manufactured parts for, and the children had been so impressed. As a matter of fact, two of the boys in the class said they wanted to be aerospace engineers, just like Kevin.

As Racquel pulled out the math quizzes, the phone rang. She reached up and pulled the cordless receiver from the wall. "Hello?"

"Hi, how are you?" the voice on the other end said.

"I'm fine, Mom. How are you?" Racquel said, crossing her legs.

"Pretty good."

"You must be on your break?"

"Uh-huh. I just thought I'd call you for a couple of minutes to see how you and Kevin were doing."

Racquel smiled. Corrine had been a second-shift mule driver at a local factory for almost thirty years, and still, she insisted on using her nightly breaks to call and check on her daughters. The same as she had when they were children.

"Not too well. We just had a huge blowup about me trying to get pregnant, and he left a little while ago to go work out. I got another negative test result, and he thinks we need to stop trying."

Corrine was silent on the phone because she was beginning to think the same thing herself. She'd seen Racquel's obsession growing deeper and deeper, and she was starting to get worried about her. "Well, honey, maybe it is time to accept things the way they are. And I know you aren't interested in adoption, but maybe you need to rethink how you feel about it. There are thousands of children that need a good home and the kind of love you and Kevin could give."

Racquel was already becoming pissed off. The last thing she wanted to do was disrespect her mother, but right now she was only an inch away from doing just that. "Not you, too? Sometimes it takes a little longer for some people to get pregnant than others. And it's not like I haven't been pregnant before. I was at the end of my first trimester when I lost the baby last year, but I know it will be different next time."

"But you've already been trying for three years, and I just don't want to see you and Kevin break up over something like this."

Racquel could no longer tolerate any more of these negative comments, and decided that it was time to end the conversation. "Mom, not every man is like Daddy. I mean, some men do stick by their wives until the end."

Corrine was silent at first, and it was obvious that her feelings were hurt. "Well. Maybe it will happen some time soon," she said softly.

"I know it will, Mom," Racquel said, feeling bad about the way she'd spoken to her mother. "All Kevin and I have to do is have a little faith."

"Well, I'd better get off of here, so I can check on Marcella and the children before my break is over. You take care of yourself. And try to work things out with Kevin when he gets in."

"I will. And Mom, have a good evening at work, okay?"

"Talk to you tomorrow."

"Bye," Racquel said and hung up the phone.

She couldn't believe it. Even her own mother didn't have any faith in her. And come to think of it, Marcella had made some of those same pessimistic remarks. Racquel was becoming fed up with all of them, and it was times like this that she needed her father. She hated him for messing around on her mother, for marrying that overbearing, facially challenged woman he called his wife, and for running off to Texas like some schoolboy ten years ago. But at least he believed in her and never doubted that she could do anything she set her mind to. If only she could lie in his arms the way she used to when she was still Daddy's little girl. She could still remember how safe she felt. As a matter of fact, she hadn't felt such a total sense of security ever since. Didn't he realize that his walking out was going to affect her for the rest of her life? Didn't he know that his leaving had forced her to live an unthinkable and totally unacceptable lifestyle during her college years? The kind of lifestyle that she'd never even told Marcella about, let alone anyone else like Kevin or her mother. And what if those mistakes were the real reason why she couldn't get pregnant? She'd wondered about this very thing off and on for some time now, but she kept telling herself that it just couldn't be. That there was no obvious connection between what happened then and what was going on now.

If only everyone would stop saying that she wasn't going to get pregnant. Because hell, what did they know? It wasn't like they were doctors or anything like that. But then, what the rest of them thought really didn't matter, because she was going to show all of them just how wrong they were. And it was only a matter of time before she did exactly that.

Chapter 3

Marcella blew out a sigh of frustration and shook her head when she realized the baby shower was less than three hours away, and still, she hadn't gone out to buy a gift yet. She and Racquel had known about Michelle's baby shower for over a month, but it hadn't been until this particular pay period that she'd managed to scrounge up the money. It seemed like somebody was always having a baby, getting married, or celebrating a birthday, and she hated it. Not because she didn't want to be a part of these special occasions, but because she simply just couldn't afford it. Racquel had offered to add Marcella's name to the gift she'd purchased, but Marcella had gone that route so many times before that she didn't feel comfortable doing it again. Not to mention the fact that they'd lived next door to Michelle since she and Racquel were five and seven. Michelle had been almost like a sister to them, so Marcella felt a certain obligation toward giving her a gift.

Marcella walked into the bathroom, plugged the bathtub drain, and turned on the water. As the water covered the bottom of the tub, she ran her right hand through it to check the temperature. It was hotter than she liked, so she turned the knob just a tad more clockwise to cool it down a bit. She checked the temperature again, and this time it was perfect. She stepped back out into the hallway, into her bedroom, and began browsing through her closet for something to wear. When she thumbed past the black pantsuit, she shook her head in disgust. She'd worn this thing to every "dressy-casual" event she'd gone to over the last twelve months, and she knew everyone was sick of seeing her in it. In all honesty, *she* was sick of seeing it herself. Just once, she wished she could buy something nice for herself. Whenever there was extra money, which was rare, she used it on the children. She didn't regret doing that, though, because she'd give her life for them if she had to. But she was human, like anyone else, and sometimes wanted to fulfill her own wants and needs.

She pulled the pantsuit out and held it away from her to check for closet wrinkles. She spotted a couple on each piece, and laid the entire outfit across the bed. As she stepped into the hallway, where the iron was located, she heard someone knocking at the front door. It was always like this on Saturday mornings. Winter, spring, summer, or fall. It was almost as if each of the other mothers in the complex had voted her weekend baby-sitter. They didn't seem to care where their children went, so long as they weren't in their hair, and it was really a crying shame. It was obvious that most of the children didn't know where their mothers were, and that was one of the main reasons Marcella usually let them stay. Unless of course, Ashley and Nicholas had homework to complete, chores to take care of, or like today, weren't at home. Corrine had picked them up early that morning, so they could go grocery shopping with her and planned to keep them until Sunday afternoon when they got out of church.

Marcella strutted to the door. "Who is it?"

"Tyrone."

Marcella rolled her eyes as far back in her head as they would go and frowned. What did he want? Unless he was about to pay this week's, last week's, and all of the other missed child-support payments, she didn't want to be bothered with his no-good behind. But she went ahead and opened the door reluctantly.

"Hey, how's it going?" Tyrone asked as he crossed the threshold and stepped inside the apartment without being asked.

How in the hell did he think she was doing? Here this fool had just arrived a couple of seconds ago, and was already sounding stupid. She felt like killing herself a thousand times over for ever getting mixed up with him. And the fact that he was dressed in an expensive pair of black jeans and an extremely costly-looking sweater wasn't helping the situation. And she hated him for still having that same smooth-looking dark-chocolate skin that she'd been so attracted to in the very beginning. "Ashley and Nicholas aren't here," she said, ignoring his question and heading toward the bathroom to turn off her bathwater.

"I see you still got that jacked-up attitude," he said, plopping down in the chair adjacent to the sofa.

Marcella stopped solidly in her tracks and turned around. "Tyrone, how do you expect my attitude to be? You pay child support whenever you damn well please, and then you show up to play Daddy whenever it's convenient. I'm sick of *it,* and I'm sick of *you.*"

"Look, girl, I didn't come over here for this," Tyrone

said in a hostile tone of voice and stood up. "All I want to know is where my kids are, and when they're going to be back home?"

What nerve. Marcella rolled her eyes at him and headed toward the bathroom. When she arrived, she reached to turn the water off, which had filled just short of two inches from the rim of the tub. Damn. She'd almost flooded her whole apartment by messing around with Tyrone. Her blood was starting to boil, and she'd had just about all she could take of him for one day. She went back out to the living room.

"You know, Tyrone, you are such a joke. While you're asking all these ignorant questions, where is my child support?"

"I don't have it," he said in a cocky tone of voice, staring her straight in her face. "My car payment is due, and my mom needs some help with the utilities."

"So what. Ashley and Nicholas still have to eat regardless of what you have going on. Whether you realize it or not, they are your first priority. Everything else is second. Your car payment wasn't due last week, so what happened then?"

"Marcella, I don't owe you any explanations on how I spend my money. Hell, I'm not married to you. I'll see what I can do next week, and that's that."

"What do you mean, you'll see what you can do? You're already two weeks behind, and I know you don't want me to talk about all the payments you missed this past year. How do you expect for us to make it, Tyrone? I mean, don't you care about what happens to your own children? And it's not like you don't make a lot of money at that electric company, because I know you do."

"From what I can see, Ashley and Nicholas are doing just fine. You always make it seem like they don't have food to eat or clothes to put on their backs, but I know better than that. I get so sick of you exaggerating about how you're barely making it. You get food stamps to feed them, the housing authority allows you to stay here practically rent-free, and your mother and sister are always buying something for them. So, don't even waste your time trying to make me feel guilty, because it's not going to work."

"You know, Tyrone, I'm doing the best that I can. You can criticize me and make all the excuses that you want, but it still doesn't dismiss the fact that you don't take care of your children the way you should. Hell, you don't even spend time with them. I didn't have them by myself, but for some reason you always act like I did. You should be ashamed to even say your children receive food stamps. Especially when they have a father who works full-time as an electrician. And worse than that, you still live at home with your mother. And as far as my mother and sister go, they aren't obligated to do anything for Ashley and Nicholas. They do it because they love them, but it's your responsibility."

Tyrone stood up. "Look. I'm not about to waste the rest of my Saturday afternoon listening to this shit. Can you just have Ashley or Nick call me when they get home? Damn. It always has to be such an ordeal every time I see you."

Marcella laughed sarcastically. "If you want to talk to them, I suggest you keep calling until you get in touch with them yourself, because I'm not going to have my babies runnin' behind you. As soon as Nicholas hears your voice, all he's going to do is beg you to come pick him up, and then all you're going to do is give him some sorry excuse as to why you can't. I'm sick of you disappointing them. And I'll tell you another thing. If you don't start paying my child support on time, I'm taking your ass to court so I can get it directly from your paycheck.''

Tyrone looked at her in total amazement. "Are you threatening me?"

"Take it however you want to," she said with her arms folded. She knew Tyrone would start to think twice, because they'd had this conversation before. He was well aware that if she took him to court, she'd get twenty-five percent for two children, which would end up being far more than that measly sixty dollars a week they'd agreed on eight years ago when Nicholas was born.

"You know what, Marcella? I hate the day I ever laid eyes on you, and I wish I had never allowed you to trap me the way you did. You'll get your child support. Don't even worry about it," Tyrone said, walking toward the front door.

"Good. Because that's all I want from you. And just for the record, a man can't be trapped when he knows what he's doing. When you were getting what you wanted, and I know you know what I'm talking about, you had a big smile on your face. But now that it's time to take responsibility for your actions, you have a problem with it."

"Whatever, Marcella," Tyrone said and slammed the door.

Marcella cringed. Why was he doing this? She'd thought she was making things easier for both of them when they'd made that verbal agreement concerning the child support. He'd pay sixty dollars a week and would help out with extras, like lunch money, birthdays, Christmas, and medical bills. And although she knew it was wrong, she'd be able to get a few food stamps to help out with their groceries, as long as the welfare agency never found out that she did in fact know where Tyrone was.

Before she'd found a full-time job, she'd been solely dependent on Aid to Families with Dependent Children. And while she wasn't proud of it, she'd told her caseworker that she didn't know where the father was, and that she hadn't seen him since the birth of her second child. When she'd given birth to Ashley, her mother had supported them, and she'd had no reason to apply for welfare, but after Nicholas was born, her parents had told her she didn't have a choice. If she told the agency about the sixty dollars a week, they would cut her food stamps off completely. But on the other hand, if she told them where Tyrone was, they would order him to pay child support through payroll deduction, and he'd be forced to give her at least one hundred twenty dollars a week. If she could get what was rightfully hers, though, she wouldn't need the food stamps to make ends meet.

The thought of going to court made her feel uncomfortable. But if Tyrone didn't start doing what he was supposed to, she didn't see where there was going to be any other choice. She owed it to her children, and that's just the way it was. She'd warned him, and now the ball was in his court. She was going to give him one more chance to improve his payment patterns, but if he was so much as one day late with the next or any future payments, she was going to take legal action.

After bathing, lotioning her body, and slipping on her underwear, Marcella stood in front of the bathroom mirror putting on her makeup. She plugged in her gold-tone curling iron so that it would be nice and hot by the time she was ready to curl her hair. This particular brand didn't take as long to heat up like some of the others she'd owned, and they seemed much more equipped to handle the kind of coarse hair that most Black people had been blessed with.

When she finished, she unplugged the curling iron and stepped back into the bedroom. She pulled on her pants and slid on the matching jacket. As she sat down on the side of the bed and reached for her shoes, she glanced at her watch and noticed that it was two o'clock. Michelle's shower started at four, and she still needed to stop to pick up a gift. She was starting to think that maybe it was a better idea to buy a money holder and place twenty-five dollars in it. That way she wouldn't have to rush, and she'd also have a little time to stop by and see the children at her mother's.

She lifted the phone from the receiver next to her bed and dialed Racquel.

"Hello?" Kevin answered.

"Hey, Kevin. It's Marcella."

"What's up, sister-in-law. How are you?"

"Good, now that Tyrone is gone."

"What did *he* want?"

"He came by looking for Ashley and Nicholas, but they're over at Mom's. But of course we got into it because he's two weeks behind with his child support."

"I can't believe that Negro is still playing games. He should be ashamed of himself. What you need to do is take his butt to court, so you can get everything he owes you."

"I know. And that's why I'm only giving him one more chance, but if he's late again, that's it."

"I hate to tell you this, but once a deadbeat, always a deadbeat. He'll pay you on time until he thinks you're happy, but you can bet he'll start messing up again. You might as well get ready for it."

"Well, all I know is that I'm not playing with him anymore. So, if he wants to hang himself, that's fine with me."

"Might as well get ready for what?" Racquel asked

in the background. She'd obviously walked in on the tail end of what Kevin had just said.

"Well, Marcella, since your sister is dying to get into our conversation, I'll let you speak to her," Kevin said and laughed. "I'll probably see you later this evening, though, when you guys get back from the baby shower."

"Talk to you later, Kevin." Marcella waited for Racquel to take the phone.

"Girl, what were you and Kevin talking about?" Racquel asked.

"That good-for-nothing Tyrone. Who else?"

"Please. What did he do this time?"

"You mean, what *didn't* he do."

"I can't believe him. He's still trying to slide by without taking care of his responsibility, huh?"

"Some things never change, but it's like I just told Kevin, he's got one more chance. If he messes that up, I'm taking him to court."

"Good for you, girl. You should have done that a long time ago, if you ask me."

"Yeah, I know. So, do you want to pick me up on the way to the shower, or what? I'm going by Mom's to check on Ashley and Nicholas, so if you want, you can pick me up over there."

"That sounds good. Kevin and I just finished eating a late lunch, but I already took my shower, so I should be ready in about an hour. I'll come by Mom's around three-fifteen."

"Don't even talk about food. I'm starved. What did you guys have?"

"Kevin made some spaghetti with ground beef, and of course I ate too much."

"Girl, you should be thanking God daily for giving you such a wonderful husband. You are so blessed."

"Oh, I'm thankful, but still, you're the lucky one."

"Please. How am *I* lucky?" Marcella asked, trying to figure out what Racquel could have possibly been talking about.

"Those two beautiful children. You have everything, and don't even realize it."

"I do thank God, but I'm far from having everything. It's hard raising two children all alone on seven dollars an hour. And even if Tyrone paid his child support like he should, it still wouldn't be the same as having a good husband by my side. Especially one who earns a decent income."

"I'm telling you, Marcella, having children is a blessing. And finding a good man is the easy part. I mean, look at you. You're beautiful. You're intelligent. And you're a good person. Any man would be lucky to find you."

"Not every man is looking to date, let alone marry, a woman with two children. And that's a fact."

"But at the same time there are a lot of men who don't have a problem with that. Especially when the children are as well-mannered as Ash and Nick."

By now, Marcella was starting to become slightly annoyed. She and Racquel were always going around and about when it came to who was lucky, blessed, and had everything they could hope for. It was definitely time to end the conversation before it stretched too far out of hand. "Hey, I'd better get off of here, so I can pick up a money holder at the drugstore."

"Okay, then. Well, I'll see you when I get to Mom's."

"See ya," Marcella said and hung up the phone. She took a deep breath. Partly because Racquel didn't have the sense enough to appreciate the life she'd been given, but mostly because her sister never seemed to understand where she was coming from. Whether she wanted to see it or not, Racquel was the one who had everything:

Kevin. A career that she loved. A semi-brick, two-story home. The girl needed to count her blessings and be thankful for what she had, and that was that. But Marcella knew that having children was the most important thing to her sister, and that she would have done just about anything to make it happen. But for the life of her, Marcella never saw what the big deal was, since she had the option of adopting as many children as she wanted at any time. Newborn babies—that is, Black newborn babies were being put up for adoption on a daily basis. Even White people were starting to adopt biracial babies, as soon as they realized they'd be waiting for all eternity to adopt a White one.

Marcella just couldn't understand it, and the more she thought about it, the more she hoped Racquel wasn't going to ruin their afternoon at the baby shower by becoming depressed. They'd gone to their cousin's baby shower last year, which had been a major mistake. Racquel had been fine until she entered the house and laid eyes on little Nathan. She'd stared at him on and off, but under no circumstances would she agree to hold him. As a matter of fact, when Marcella had brought the baby over to where Racquel was sitting, she'd gotten up and walked into the kitchen, totally ignoring him. But then, maybe today would be different, since Michelle's baby hadn't been born yet, and Racquel wouldn't have to physically see it. At least that's what Marcella was praying for.

After running into her best friend, Sharon, at the drugstore, Marcella hadn't arrived at her mother's until three o'clock. After locking her car doors, she walked around to the back door and knocked. After a few seconds, she knocked again, and her mother finally opened the door. Marcella opened her mouth to say hello, but paused when she noticed that her mother had been crying.

"Mom, what's wrong?" Marcella asked in a very concerned manner.

"That Tyrone has only got one more time to come in my house disrespecting me the way he did today."

A look of horror covered Marcella's face as she walked up the back steps into the kitchen. "Tyrone? What was he doing over here?"

Corrine wiped the last of her tears and swallowed hard. "I guess he figured out that the children were with me, so he decided to come by to see them. He wanted to take them to his house, and you know I don't mind that, because that's their father. But first I wanted them to finish their lunch, because they hadn't eaten since this morning. But when I asked him to have a seat until they did, out of nowhere, he starting rantin' and ravin'. Saying that he didn't have time to wait. That he'd already been by your house looking for them, and wasn't going to wait any longer. He told Ashley to go get their coats, and when I asked him why he was acting the way he was, he told me that I needed to mind my own business. That if I wanted to worry about somebody and what they were doing, I should have done that with you. He even had the nerve to say, that if I had raised you better, *he* wouldn't be in this situation. And that's when I'd had enough. I told him that if he didn't get out of my house right then, I was calling the police."

Marcella was speechless. She couldn't believe what she was hearing, because for as long as she could remember, Tyrone had always gotten along with her mother. Regardless of how she felt about him, he and her mother had never had any conflicts with each other. "Mom, I'm so sorry. I don't know what to say."

"Marcella, I don't know if Tyrone was having a bad

day or what, but what hurt me the most was when he said I should have raised you better. Lord knows, I did the best that I could with what I had, when it came to taking care of you and your sister.''

"Mom, don't pay Tyrone any attention. He's crazy. Just plain crazy," Marcella said, starting to get angry.

"Crazy or not, he still disrespected me in my own house and got away with it. And I won't ever forget that. Even though he never does anything for my grand-babies, and he's treated you like nothin' since you first got pregnant, I still gave him his respect. This doesn't make any sense at all, and it was uncalled for.''

"When is he bringing them back?''

"I don't know. He stormed out of here so fast, I didn't even think to ask him. Plus, I was too upset anyhow.''

As Marcella started toward the phone in the kitchen, someone knocked at the back door. Corrine went down the steps, peeped through the mini-blind, saw that it was Racquel, and opened the door. Corrine started back up the steps, and Racquel followed behind.

"Hey, Mom," Racquel said.

"Hi, honey." Corrine responded in a soft tone of voice.

Racquel looked around the corner and saw Marcella on the phone and waved at her.

"Tyrone, what is your problem?" Marcella screamed through the phone as soon as she heard him say hello. She wanted to say a whole lot more, and he had better thank his God that her mother was standing there listening to her.

Tyrone hung up the phone, and she could tell by the way it sounded that he'd slammed it down as hard as he could.

Racquel frowned and set her purse down on the counter. "Marcella, what's going on?"

"Tyrone came over here disrespecting Mom and then took the children."

"What?" Racquel screamed. "I just know he didn't. What's his phone number?" Racquel said, reaching for the phone.

"Racquel, don't even bother with him," Corrine said, sitting down at the breakfast table. "You know I didn't teach you girls to act this way. And just because he's acting ignorant doesn't mean the two of you have to stoop down to his level. I'm okay, and Tyrone will get what's coming to him one way or the other. We all have to reap what we sow, and there's definitely no way of getting around it. So it's best to just leave it alone."

"Mom, I promise you, this won't happen again. From now on, I'll make sure he comes to see the children at my house, and my house only. But I still can't understand why he did this. He and I had some words earlier, like we always do, but he had no right taking it out on you. I mean, this is so ridiculous."

Racquel didn't say anything because she didn't want to upset her mother any more than she already was, but she couldn't wait until she saw that Tyrone. She was going to give him more than a piece of her mind. She was sick of how he treated her sister anyway, and a much awaited confrontation with him was long overdue. Marcella had been playing games with him far too long, and it was time someone put him in his own pathetic little place. And if it had to be her, that was fine, too.

"That was a really nice shower, wasn't it," Racquel said to Marcella as she drove away from Michelle's northwest-suburban home, which was located about twenty minutes away from Chicago's city limits. "As a matter of fact, it was one of the nicest ones I've ever been to."

Marcella couldn't believe what she was hearing, and she was even more surprised at how pleasant Racquel's attitude had been throughout the entire afternoon. She'd participated in all the games, and she'd even went as far as holding Michelle's three-month-old nephew, little Joshua. Marcella didn't know what had come over her sister, but she was happy about it just the same. "Yeah, it *was* really nice, and she got a ton of nice gifts, too."

"And that little Joshua was about the most precious thing I've ever seen. Almost as precious as Nicholas and Ashley were when you had them."

"He's definitely a little cutey, and he's such a happy baby, too," Marcella said, gazing out the window at all the gorgeous homes they were passing. "My God. Wouldn't you just love living in this neighborhood?"

"Wouldn't we all? Michelle and her husband have definitely done well for themselves. That's for sure. And in a few months they're going to have a baby to complete the package," Racquel said, and then slowed down when she saw the green traffic light switch to yellow.

Marcella didn't comment.

"Some people have all the luck. I mean, why can't Kevin and I have a baby, so we can live happily ever after like everybody else? I know it's not right to envy what someone else has, but I just can't seem to help it. As a matter of fact, sometimes I hate myself for feeling the way I do, because I know how wrong it is. Sometimes I think I'm going crazy. And sometimes I can't help but wonder why having a baby is so important to me."

"Everybody has something that they want more than anything else. That's just the way life is. But instead of dwelling on our own self-defined misfortunes, what we need to do is spend more time trying to find satisfaction in what we *do* have. I know I've probably said all this before, but that's because it's the truth."

"I know, but no matter how hard I try to push the idea of getting pregnant out of my mind, it seems to haunt me more and more. It's almost like I'm on a mission to fill some kind of void in my life."

"What kind of void?" Marcella asked, obviously confused about Racquel's statement.

"I know it sounds crazy, but I've never gotten over the fact that Daddy started messing around on Mom the way he did. And even though he was still living in the house the whole time I was in high school, you know he was hardly ever there. Sometimes, it felt like we didn't even have a father. And even though I know Mom loved us more than anything in this world, it still wasn't the same as having both of them love us that way."

"Girl, what are you talking about? As far as I can tell, Daddy loved both of us just as much as Mom did. He may not have shown it very well, but I know for a fact that he loved us."

"Well, all I know is that my life, and yours, too, for that matter, might have turned out totally different if he hadn't started all that hangin'-out-with-other-women business. Sometimes I miss him so much, but at other times I despise everything that he stands for."

Marcella gazed at Racquel in amazement. She couldn't believe they were even having this particular conversation. Yes, her father had made some serious mistakes, and yes, he had remarried and moved almost a thousand miles away from them in the process, but that didn't mean he no longer loved them. And why was Racquel bringing all this up in the first place? She never had before, and Marcella couldn't help but wonder why she was so adamant on discussing it now. "Why are you all of a sudden blaming Daddy for the way our lives turned out?"

"I'm not blaming him. At least not totally, anyway.

But I do think that if he had been a better husband
and hadn't caused Mom so much pain, she could have
spent way more time concentrating on our emotional
needs, and not just what we needed to survive physically.
Food, clothing, and a home are fine, but what good is
any of that if a child still feels emotionally bankrupt?
And don't get me wrong, I'm thankful for everything
they did in that respect, but I still always felt like something was missing. It wasn't so bad when we were little,
but by the time I went to the ninth grade, things were
pretty bad between them. And I don't know how many
nights I cried myself to sleep after listening to all their
yelling and screaming at each other," Racquel said in
a trembling voice.

Marcella looked at her sister and saw tears building
in her eyes. She wasn't sure what to say, because she
had no idea that Racquel felt this way, or that their
parents' breakup had caused her so much pain. But she
knew she had to console her somehow. "Girl, that's all
in the past, but if it's bothering you this much, maybe
you should talk to Mom and Daddy about the way you
feel."

Racquel pulled into a CITGO parking lot, pushed
the gear in park, and then searched through her purse
for something to wipe her tears. Marcella turned her
body toward her and caressed the side of her arm, trying
her best to comfort her sister. After Racquel dried her
face, she took a deep breath. "Girl, I am so sorry for
taking you through all these changes, but sometimes
just thinking about their divorce really takes a toll on
me. And I guess I keep telling myself that if I have my
own child, I'm going to do everything I can to make
up for what I didn't have. And I'll finally have someone
in my life who won't simply just walk out on me just
because they feel like it. I want my child to know what

it's like to have a loving, stable, two-parent household. It might sound silly, but that's honestly how I feel."

Marcella wanted to tell her that there were no guarantees with any marriage, that no one knew what tomorrow was going to bring, and that her relationship with Kevin was no exception to the rule. But she decided instead that it was best not to say anything.

"Sometimes I get so angry at him for leaving us the way he did, and I get even angrier when I think about how much I still love him."

"It bothered me, too, when they got divorced," Marcella finally said. "But, based on my experience with Tyrone, I realize that not every relationship can work. And I'll tell you another thing, just because two people get divorced doesn't mean that they don't love their children."

"Then, why did he have to move so far away?" Racquel asked, looking directly at Marcella. "And why did he hardly call us? And why didn't he ask us to come visit him during the summer and on holidays? The man had a responsibility to us, and he acted like he didn't even care."

Marcella didn't like what Racquel was saying, but at the same time she knew her sister had a point. And a very good point, for that matter. He hadn't communicated with them nearly as often as he should have, and there wasn't any legitimate reason for his actions that she could think of. "To tell you the truth, I don't know why he didn't keep in contact with us."

"And he still doesn't now, either. And even worse, he's barely even seen Ash and Nick more than once, and they're the only two grandchildren that he has."

"Well, it's his loss, not mine. And to be honest, I really don't care, so long as my babies get to spend as much time as they want with their grandmother. Mom is there for them whenever they need her, and I'm just thankful for that."

"I know, Marcella, but it's still not right for him to just pretend like we don't even exist," Racquel said, pulling the gear down to drive and heading back out onto the street.

Marcella sighed deeply. She'd heard her grandmother say that a person's childhood could affect her for the rest of her life, and now she realized just how true that statement had been. She wished there were something she could say, or something she could do, to make Racquel feel better about this whole situation, but for the life of her, she had no idea what that something was. Sugarcoating her father's actions wasn't going to make things any better, and criticizing him the way Racquel wanted her to wasn't going to do a bit of good, either. But on top of all that, she wondered why their parents' divorce had affected Racquel so much more severely than it had her. Especially since Racquel was the oldest and always seemed to have everything in her life so nicely put together. Marcella had some other questions, too, but instead of adding more fuel to the fire, she decided to change this whole depressing conversation. "So, what are you and Kevin doing tonight?"

"As far as I know, watching some videos. What about you?"

"Girl, please. With Ashley and Nicholas spending the night with Mom, probably nothing at all. Which reminds me. Let me call Mom to see if that Negro has brought the kids back or not," Marcella said, picking up Racquel's car phone. She dialed the number and waited.

"Hello," Corrine answered.

"Hey, Mom. Did Tyrone bring Ashley and Nicholas back yet?"

"He just dropped them off a few minutes ago."

"Did he say anything to you?"

"He walked them around to the back door, and when I opened it, he said he was sorry for acting the way he had earlier, and that he was having a bad day."

"Yeah, right," Marcella said, pursing her lips together in disbelief.

"Well, whether he's sincere about being sorry or not, you know I'm not going to waste my time holding any grudges. Because like I said before, if Tyrone keeps treating people the way he does, he'll get what's coming to him. And I definitely don't want to keep a bunch of mess going on in front of these children."

"I know, Mom, but it's just that I feel so bad about him talking to you the way he did."

"It's over now, so don't worry about it. And anyway, how was Michelle's shower?"

"It was wonderful, and we had a good time."

"How did Racquel do?" Corrine whispered, and it was obvious that she thought Racquel might hear what she was asking Marcella.

"Fine," Marcella answered, hoping Racquel wouldn't pick up on the conversation.

"Good," Corrine said, and was clearly relieved.

"I'll probably come in for a while when Racquel drops me off to pick up my car."

"Okay, and tell Racquel I'll talk to her in the morning."

"I will. Bye, Mom," Marcella said, and placed the phone on its base.

"Why don't you come watch videos with us?" Racquel asked.

"Girl, the last thing you and Kevin need is a third wheel."

"Kevin will be offended if you don't show. You know

how he likes to have people over when we're watching videos."

"I don't know. Maybe I will."

"There's no maybe to it. You're going to my house now, and you can pick your car up later. Shoot, you can spend the night if you want to."

Marcella smiled. And was glad that she had a sister like Racquel.

Chapter 4

"**B**aby, I've got a good feeling about it this time," Racquel said, stretching both her arms up toward the brass headboard, with a confident smile on her face. It was spring break, and since she had the entire week off, Kevin had decided to take two vacation days.

"You think so, huh?" he said with an even bigger smile than hers. He'd just awakened, but his mind was already replaying every bit of what had gone on last night after they arrived home from dinner. They'd made love like they never had before. And for the first time in what seemed like years, it didn't feel like some job assignment. It was spontaneous, and Racquel had wanted him solely because of the pleasure he brought to her, and not simply because she wanted to conceive a baby. This is how it was supposed to be, and he was glad that the woman he married in the first place had come back. He had missed her more than he thought, and he'd been worried about what was going to happen to their marriage if she didn't start treating him like her husband again. But now things were finally starting to look up.

"I'm telling you, after we drop the urine off this morning, we may as well spend the rest of the day planning for the baby."

Kevin just lay there with his eyes closed, nodding his head in agreement. But he didn't say anything. He'd learned his lesson about showing any signs of negativity when it came to the subject of Racquel getting pregnant. He hated it when she got her hopes up so high, because whenever she did, she was never able to handle the disappointment. He hoped for her sake, though, that she was right this time. That it would be different from last month, and all the others previous. They needed some good news. And more than that, he wasn't sure how much more stress their marriage could actually survive.

"Kevin," she said. "Are you listening to me?"

"Yes, baby. I'm listening."

"Well, say something. I mean, since my period is at least five days late, I know this could really be it."

"I pray that it is. I really do," he said, pulling her closer to him. "I know you don't think I care about this as much as you, but I do. I want to have a child with you more than anything, because you mean everything to me. I didn't think it was possible to love another human being the way that I love you. Sometimes when I as much as think of you and the love that we have, my heart hurts, I mean it physically hurts."

"I love you, too, Kevin, and that's why I want to give you a child. I want to give you something that is a part of both of us. Something that can't be bought and paid for. Bringing a child into this world is the most beautiful thing. And it's so miraculous," she said, hugging him tight.

He hugged her back, and one thing led to another. The same way it used to when they'd first met.

After Racquel and Kevin had dropped her urine sample off at the clinic, they'd eaten breakfast at the nearby pancake house, and decided to ride downtown to do some shopping at Water Tower Place. This was Racquel's favorite mall, and if it had been left up to her, she would have shopped in Lord & Taylor's baby department until closing time. Three years ago, when they'd married, she looked forward to shopping for Kevin and herself, but over the last two years she seemed to spend the majority of her time shopping for the baby she was sure she was going to have. In the beginning she bought things that would have worked fine for a boy or girl. But when she realized that there were only so many diapers, bottles, receiving blankets, and bibs a person could buy, it wasn't long before she began purchasing anything that was cute. Dresses—just in case it was a girl, and little pant outfits—if it was a boy. She knew it was a waste of money, but she couldn't help herself. She wanted everything to be perfect because sooner or later the baby *was* going to arrive. And regardless of how many negative results there had been, she still believed it was all just a matter of time.

When they stepped up to the checkout counter, Racquel had each of her arms loaded with merchandise. Kevin wanted to tell her to put some of it back. To wait until they got home and found out the test results. But they'd been having such a wonderful time together, it wasn't worth breaking the mood. It almost felt like they'd fallen in love all over again. She hadn't overcome the pregnancy obsession, but at least she was making love with him again, and not just giving him sex. And she was happy. No, the last thing he wanted to do was piss her off and take the chance of her not wanting him tonight, so he decided to keep his mouth shut. He wasn't a wimp or anything like that, but he wasn't stupid, either.

"Aren't these cute?" Racquel asked Kevin, placing the three infant-sized dresses across the counter before the saleslady.

"Yeah, they are, but you better hope it's a girl, otherwise you're going to be returning an awful lot of stuff."

"I know, but it's better to have enough of both until we know for sure."

The saleslady, who was pushing middle fifties in age, looked at both of them like they were crazy. Like they needed psychiatric help.

Racquel never even noticed and continued to pass the rest of the items to her to ring up. After she'd handed over the last piece, she was shocked at all the things she had gathered up throughout the store.

"Your total is two hundred ninety-four dollars and ninety cents. Will this be on your Lord and Taylor charge?" the cashier asked, waiting for a response.

"No," Racquel said, pulling out her Visa card instead.

Kevin wanted to scream. This keeping-his-mouth-shut business was about to wear out, and fast. He couldn't believe she'd spent almost three hundred dollars on a baby she wasn't even sure she was going to have. And if she *was* pregnant, she didn't even know what sex it was going to be. He wanted to let her have it right there, but decided that this wasn't the place or the time; especially in front of someone they didn't even know. This was so unlike Racquel. She had always been so good with their finances. She was one of the most sensible women he'd ever met when it came to spending and saving money. But now she didn't even bat an eye when it came to blowing money on an infant they didn't have, or even worse, one they might not ever get.

"Baby, I'm going outside to get some fresh air. I'll be directly in front of the mall at the Michigan Avenue entrance," he said, and walked away without as much as glancing at her.

She watched him as he left the children's department until he was out of sight. He was pissed off at her, and she didn't know how she was going to change the way he was feeling. When the cashier passed her the receipt, she signed it, waited for her to place her copy in one of the two shopping bags, and proceeded toward the store entrance. As she stepped outside of the store and took a breath of fresh air, she suddenly felt better about the whole situation. She decided that there really wasn't anything to worry about at all. They'd be home in less than an hour, the nurse at the clinic would confirm that she was in fact pregnant, and Kevin would immediately forget about all the money she'd spent. She smiled when she realized everything was going to work out fine.

They'd argued almost the entire way to the interstate, but once they drove onto it, they'd rode the rest of the way in complete silence. Kevin was angrier than he had been in a long time, and Racquel's feelings were hurt. If only she could have gotten the test result before she purchased the clothing, maybe then he wouldn't have gotten so uptight about it.

As they drove into the subdivision, she turned to look at him, but he continued to look straight ahead, ignoring her. He was being stubborn, and she hated when he did that. It was almost like he was dismissing her and all that she believed in. All that she dreamed and hoped for. He was her husband, and it was his duty to stand by her through the good times and the bad.

And he was going to feel like a complete fool, once she made the phone call to the clinic.

Once they were inside the house, Racquel headed toward the off-white and black living room, dropped both shopping bags and her shoulder purse onto the carpet, and then backtracked toward the kitchen to pick up the cordless phone. Kevin proceeded up the stairs to their bedroom. She dialed seven digits and waited for the obstetrics and gynecology receptionist to answer.

"Obstetrics and Gynecology, how may I help you?"

"Yes, could you ring Dr. Mallard's nurse, please?" Racquel said, sitting down at the kitchen table. She could feel her nerves racing faster and faster by the second.

She never liked being placed on hold, but it was even worse when they played that irritating music. She'd only been waiting one minute, but it felt like ten. She was anxious, and she wished the nurse would hurry.

"This is Charmaine," the nurse said.

Finally. "Hi, Charmaine. This is Racquel Wilson, and I'm calling to check on my pregnancy test."

"Hi, Racquel. I just received the results from the group of tests I sent out this morning, but I haven't had a chance to review them yet. If you can wait, I'll pull yours right now."

"Fine." If she could wait? What kind of question was that? She and Charmaine had been on a first-name basis for over two years, and if there was anyone at all who knew how desperately she wanted to have a baby, it was Charmaine. She'd dropped off so many urine samples, that almost everyone in the department knew who she was, and most of them knew her personally. She could have easily taken home pregnancy tests, which she did occasionally on weekends when the clinic was closed, but it didn't make a lot of sense to spend that kind of money over and over when Kevin's insurance plan covered it.

"Racquel. I'm sorry, but your test came back negative."

Racquel didn't move and was speechless. She couldn't believe what she was hearing. How could this be happening again? She'd been so sure this time.

"Racquel? Are you there?"

"Yes, I'm here. Are you sure?"

"Yes. Again, I'm really sorry. Maybe you'll have better luck next time."

Racquel hung up the phone by reflex because her thoughts were too deep to realize any of what she was doing. How was she going to face Kevin? He'd doubted her all morning. And to think how stupid she was spending all that money at the department store. She must have been out of her eternal mind to even consider doing something like that. She closed her eyes, clasped her hands together, and prayed that Kevin would be more understanding this time than he had in the past. The last thing she needed to hear was his ideas on giving up and getting on with their lives. Because as far as she was concerned, there was no life for either of them without children.

A few minutes passed, and Kevin finally came back down to the main floor. As he entered the kitchen and saw Racquel, it was obvious to him that she'd gotten the news about her test. He was still upset with her for making all those charges on the credit card, but he felt sorry for her, as well. He walked over to where she was sitting and pulled her up from the light-tan wooden chair. He held her in silence. She laid the side of her head against his chest, and it was obvious that neither of them knew what to say. They were all talked out, and for the first time Racquel wasn't shedding any tears.

They held each other for a few more minutes, and finally Kevin broke the ice. "Baby, I know this isn't what you expected, but it's not the end of the world. We'll get through this. We always have, and this time won't be any different."

"I just can't understand what's wrong with me. I got pregnant last year, so I know it's not impossible. Maybe it's time we started thinking about some other options."

Wait. Was he hearing her right? After all this time, was she finally coming to the realization that maybe it wasn't meant for her to physically have a child? He'd been wanting to adopt ever since she had that miscarriage last year, and it was about time she realized that it wasn't such a bad thing, after all. "Well, you know how I feel because I've been trying to convince you of that all along."

"I'll call Dr. Mallard's office first thing tomorrow morning, so he can refer us to an infertility specialist. I'm sure the insurance will cover it. At least some of it, anyway."

Damn. After all that had happened, he couldn't believe she still planned to continue this pregnancy crusade. And from what he could tell, this new bright idea was going to be worse. Infertility drugs and the like were going to cost them a ton of money, and he wasn't at all sure that this was the right thing to do. "Do you have any idea how much this is going to cost us? We'll go broke trying to make something happen, something that obviously isn't meant to be in the first place."

"Why are you always so negative about everything?" she asked, releasing her arms from his waist and stepping away from him. It really got under her skin when he made comments like that.

"I'm not negative about everything, but after three

years of trying to have a baby, I've learned to accept things the way they are."

"Well, that's not good enough for me. For all we know, an infertility specialist could be the answer. So, the least you can do is go with me to find out."

"Are you ever going to give this a rest?"

"With the help of a specialist and all the new technology, the success rate of getting pregnant is a lot higher than it used to be. So, please, sweetheart. I'm begging you to do this one last thing. Not just for me, but for both of us."

"Fine, Racquel. I'll go. But only under one condition."

"What condition?" she said, scrunching her face together. She never liked ultimatums, but he'd sure been giving her a lot of those lately. And she could tell he was about to issue another one at this very moment.

"That if none of the treatments work after the period of time that they should be working, you'll give this up once and for all. We have the rest of our lives ahead of us, and I'm ready to get on with it."

"I promise you, baby, if this doesn't work, I'm through with it," she said, hugging him tight and smiling.

"I'm serious, Racquel," he said, hugging her back. "This is it."

He was right. This *was* it. She could feel it. Now she wished they'd gotten tested when Kevin had wanted them to. But she'd been so afraid that there was something wrong with her, that she decided against it. The last thing she wanted was to feel less than a woman. And if there was something wrong with Kevin, she didn't want to know that, either, because she didn't want to end up resenting him for something he couldn't help. But now, push was coming to shove, and she didn't have much choice. She still believed that with time, she'd get pregnant without drugs, artificial insemination, or whatever else medical researchers had come up with, but at least consulting with an infertility specialist would buy her more time. The kind of time Kevin wasn't willing to wait on.

Right now she felt more confident than she ever had before, and like always, she knew it was just a matter of time.

Chapter 5

No sooner than Marcella had sat down at her desk, the phone rang. It wasn't even eight yet, ten minutes until to be exact, and clients were already calling in. It was always like that on Monday mornings, and even worse when their business clients were preparing to pay their quarterly tax bills. Their firm dealt mostly with sole proprietorships and partnerships, but right now they were being flooded with calls and visits from individuals who were trying desperately to beat the April 15 deadline, which was only two weeks away. She never understood why people waited until the last minute to file. Employers were required to get W-2's and 1099's out to employees and independent contractors by January 31 of every year, so Marcella didn't know what the problem was. This annual rat race was stressful, and she avoided it like it was a deadly virus.

Come to think of it, Covington Park residents weren't much better when it came time to renew their vehicle stickers, either. And the ones who waited until the expiration date to make their purchases were the same ones who complained about how long they had to stand in line. This was total nonsense, and the reason why Marcella had completed and mailed her taxes by the first week in February. But then, maybe she was in more of a hurry than most people, since she was getting back a refund. Just about every dime she paid in, too, thanks to the government's earned-income credit. Which was the least they could do for a struggling mother who was raising her children all by her lonesome.

Finally at 8:01 A.M., she answered what she considered to be the first legitimate phone call of the day. "Good morning, Nicosia and Associates. How may I help you?" she said in a crisp, professional voice.

"Boy, don't we sound chipper for a Monday morning," Sharon said, laughing.

"Girl, please. It pays the bills."

"I know that's right. So what do you have up for lunch today?"

"Oh, didn't I tell you? I've got a hot date with this gorgeous guy I met over the weekend. I can't believe I didn't tell you yesterday."

"I can't believe you didn't tell me, either. I could just kill you. What's his name? Where did you meet him? What kind of car does he drive? And most of all, where does he work?"

Another phone line rang. "You are such a trip, Sharon. Hold on for a second," Marcella said and placed her best friend on hold.

"Good morning, Nicosia and Associates. How may I help you?"

"Good morning. Could you ring the auditing department, please," a female voice on the other end of the phone requested.

"Sure. One moment," Marcella responded, transferred the call, and then pressed the line that Sharon was waiting on.

"You still there?"

"Now, Marcella. Do you actually think I was going to hang up before you gave me the four-one-one on this guy you met? Please."

Marcella cracked up, but didn't say anything.

"Girl, why are you keeping me in all this suspense. I can hardly stand it."

"Gosh, you're really taking this seriously, aren't you?"

"Marcella," Sharon demanded.

"Girl, I was just messing with you. I didn't meet anybody. I don't go anywhere *to* meet anybody."

"I don't believe you. You got me all worked up, and now you don't have anything to tell? You know that's not right," Sharon said, sounding disappointed.

"I know. I'm sorry," Marcella said, still laughing.

"So, what are you *really* doing for lunch then?"

"Nothing that I know of. Why? You wanna meet somewhere?"

"We should. What about that rib place by your office?"

"You must be working at the Covington Park location today?" Marcella asked, holding the phone with her chin so she could sort through some filing while she conversed.

"I am, but I'll be going back to the main office downtown after lunch."

"Well, the rib place is fine with me," Marcella said, then noticed two phone lines blinking. "I've got to answer these calls, so I'll see you then."

"See ya," Sharon said and hung up.

Marcella answered ten more calls, and greeted seven

visitors before things finally started to calm down. This was going to be one of those days, and she couldn't wait for noontime.

As she stacked some of the tax files that needed reviewing, Thomas walked by and spoke to her. He had to have been the finest man she'd ever imagined. And he was as intelligent as they came. The man had a master's degree in accounting, and practically aced the CPA exam without the tiniest bit of difficulty. The partners at the firm had snatched him up without as much as even a second thought.

And he was smooth. Which was unusual, because most men graduating in the top five percent of any master's degree program from a school comparable to Northwestern University were dorks. She wasn't sure why, but they just were. Except Thomas wasn't like that. Now, why couldn't she ever meet men like him? The type of man who had it all? He was facially fine, intelligent, responsible, and well-dressed. And surprisingly enough, he was both book smart and street smart. Her grandmother used to say that when a person had too much book sense, they usually didn't have any common sense. But Thomas had loads of it. So, what more could a woman ask for? But then there was one downfall. He was married. The good ones were always married. That was the problem, and the reason why she only seemed to meet guys who wanted nothing more than to toss her into bed. The thought of it all was sickening. After Tyrone she'd learned her lesson and refused to be used by any man. She didn't have much, but at least she had her pride. And what if she did find a good man? He probably wouldn't be too happy about taking on a ready-made family, anyhow. Which is exactly how it would have to be if he wanted a relationship with her. She wasn't like a lot of these women who dumped their children wherever they pleased, whenever they felt like it, just so they could lie up with some man who couldn't care less about them. Every mother needed a break sometimes, but *all* the time was totally unacceptable. No, she, Ashley, and Nicholas were a package deal, and any man who couldn't accept those terms was better off moving on to his next victim.

Marcella had buried herself so deep in thought, she'd forgotten where she was. Five phone lines were blinking simultaneously. She hurried to answer each as fast as she could, but in the same professional manner as she always did. Two of the callers sounded irritated, but there was nothing she could do about that now. She transferred each of them accordingly.

It was only five minutes before lunchtime, so she grabbed her purse from her lower right-hand desk drawer. Most everyone had already left, so she decided to pull out her pressed-face-powder compact. She ran the sponge across the powder, and then across her face to remove the shine that had accumulated over the last four hours. Then she touched up her lip liner and Deep Raspberry lipstick. She liked this color a lot, but the name brand was already worn off the container. If it had been one of the better cosmetic lines like Fashion Fair, Flori Roberts, or Mary Kay, she would have recognized it by the packaging alone, but she'd purchased this from one of the many drugstores she frequented. And there was no telling which one she'd gotten it from.

Marcella drove three blocks from the accounting firm, pulled into the parking lot of The Rib House, parked near the entrance, and waited for Sharon to arrive. After about two minutes Sharon pulled her white BMW convertible into the stall next to Marcella. Which was a surprise, because usually the lot was so crowded by now that customers were forced to park on the street.

But then again, Mondays always seemed to be much slower than the rest of the days in the week.

"How long have you been waiting?" Sharon asked, shutting her car door. She was dressed in a navy-blue all-weather coat, a navy-blue business suit, and matching heels. Her hair was pulled back in a French twist. Her body was long and lean, but her behind stuck out just far enough to give her the perfect shape. That is, the kind of shape that was required by most Black men.

Marcella had on a two-piece, short-sleeved purple suit and a pair of off-white sling-backs.

"Just a couple of minutes," Marcella answered, strutting toward the entrance of the restaurant.

Once they were inside, Marcella ordered a barbeque shoulder sandwich, steak fries, and a large lemonade.

"Will this be on one ticket?" the cashier asked.

"Yes, and I'll have the same as her," Sharon said, removing a twenty-dollar bill from her navy Coach shoulder bag.

"You didn't have to do that," Marcella said, feeling semiembarrassed.

"Please. I asked *you* to go to lunch. Remember?"

Marcella smiled because Sharon was always making financial gestures, such as this one. She was the best friend she ever had, and she was thankful just to know her. Money was never an object to Sharon, but then why should it be? She earned over sixty thousand dollars a year working as a software engineer, and the girl was clearly living comfortable. Especially for a Black twenty-eight-year-old female.

They'd graduated high school side by side, and had every intention of being roommates in college. But when Marcella ended up pregnant, Sharon went to Spelman on her own. And when she finished her master's degree, she began working for a computer-information company downtown, and it wasn't long before she'd moved steadily up the engineering ladder. At least, one of them had made it to where they wanted to be, and Marcella was proud of her.

"So what did you end up doing yesterday evening after we talked?" Marcella asked, taking a seat at the table near the back of the restaurant. Sharon sat down in front of her.

"Marcus came by with some videos, and we sat around for the rest of the evening. That was about it."

"So, is he still pressing you about getting engaged?"

"Of course. And it's becoming harder and harder to say no. I mean, even though I love Marcus, I'm really not quite ready to get married yet. But on the other hand, all I have is my career, and sometimes it's hard being alone in this crazy world we live in."

"You're *not* alone. You know you have me. I'll always be here for you. You're just like my sister, and you know how Mom feels about you."

"I know, Marcella, and I appreciate that, but it's just not the same as having blood relatives. I feel like I don't have any roots. Every time I think about my mother dying while giving birth to me, it tears me apart. And who knows where my father is. No one ever knew for sure who he was, anyway."

"I know, but at least you knew your grandparents. They treated you as if you were their own, and nothing can ever replace that type of love."

"Yeah, but now they're gone. I guess I should be thankful that they were able to see me graduate from college, but still they're gone."

A heavyset almond-colored lady with a beautiful smile brought out their food and set it on the table. "Can I get you ladies anything else this afternoon?" she asked.

"No," Sharon said. "Everything is fine. Thank you."

"If you need anything else, just holler. Otherwise, enjoy your meal," the waitress said and strutted away.

Marcella couldn't understand why Sharon was so sad. She'd seemed so happy when they'd spoken earlier, but now she was sounding like her whole life was falling apart. "Well, all I can say is, you are blessed whether you believe it or not. I mean, you've only been out of college for four years, and look how much money you make. Most people don't even make that kind of money when they're in their thirties and forties," Marcella said, picking up her shoulder sandwich.

"Honey, let me tell you," Sharon said, dousing her fries with ketchup. "I'd give it up in a second, if I could bring my mother and my grandparents back. Having a family to love and to spend time with is the real blessing. You have a mother, father, sister, and two children. Not to mention your aunts, uncles, and cousins. My mother was an only child, so I don't even have that. Now tell me, what are the chances of that happening to a person?"

"Well, if you want my opinion, I think you should seriously consider marrying Marcus. He's a good man, and he practically worships the ground that you walk on," Marcella said, taking another bite from her sandwich.

"I don't know what my problem is, because I do love him. Maybe I'm just afraid of being hurt. I've always stood my own ground and taken care of myself. And I haven't depended on anyone for anything since my grandparents passed away."

"Marcus will still let you be yourself, and you know it. He's not the controlling type, and from what I can tell, he's the type of man that sort-of goes along with the program, not wanting to change the channel unless you say something better is on."

Sharon laughed for the first time since they'd taken their seats.

"He's not that easy. Believe me, he can get an attitude just as quick as the rest of us, if you cross him."

"But that's normal. Everybody gets angry or irritated every once in a while, but overall, you know I'm right about him."

"Well, there is one thing, and you know I've mentioned it before. The sex isn't that great. I mean, it's not terrible, but still it's not anything to jump up and down about, either."

"I'm sorry, but, girl, that is so hard for me to believe. Especially about a man that gorgeous," Marcella said, shaking her head.

"Well, believe it or not, it's true. And sometimes I feel so guilty for feeling that way because there's definitely more to a relationship than just sex."

"I don't know, Sharon," Marcella said, raising her eyebrows. "With a man like Marcus, I think I'd have to overlook that one little flaw."

"I keep trying to, but it's hard. But, enough about me. What's going on with you?" Sharon asked, taking a sip of her lemonade.

"Not much. I haven't spoken with Tyrone more than once since he clowned my mother a few weeks ago, but he has been paying his child support on time. And to tell you the truth, that's all I want from him."

"You know, I really hate that things turned out the way they did for the two of you. I can't help but remember how in love you guys were when we were in high school. Every girl that went to school with us envied you. Tyrone was the man back in the day," Sharon said, laughing.

"Maybe so, but now he's nothing but a low-down, conniving dog."

"I know what you're saying. I despise any man who tries to dodge his responsibility to his children."

"He's been working for the electric company as an electrician ever since he finished that apprenticeship program at the community college, so I know he's making decent money. But he still has the nerve to come up with every excuse in the book as to why he can't take care of his children. And the only reason he's doing it now, is because I threatened to take him back to court," Marcella said and bit into two fries at the same time.

"I don't blame you. That fool should be paying more than sixty dollars a week for two kids anyway. Plain old highway robbery is what that is."

"I know, but if he messes up one more time, and I do mean one more time, we're going to court."

"I know you would rather not go to court, but for Ashley and Nick's sake, I hope he does mess up, so you can finally get what's rightfully yours."

"Girl, what I really need is someone to hold me at night. You say you get lonely, but you don't know what being lonely is until you've had to sleep alone every single night for the last . . . I don't even know how many years it's been," Marcella said, laughing slightly. "And even though Ashley and Nicholas mean everything in this world to me, sometimes my life feels empty. Plus, I wish I could give them so much more."

"You'll find someone to fall in love with, you just have to be patient. But in the meantime, what you need to do is go back to school. Go get your degree, girl. You're too smart not to."

"I don't know if I can handle cutting my hours to part-time, because who knows when Tyrone will start acting scrappy with his payments again. And between working, going to class, and doing homework, I would hardly see my babies at all during the weekdays."

"I understand your point, but if you want to give them a better life, you might have to sacrifice some of your time. In the long run, you'll be glad you did. Maybe Tyrone will keep them in the evenings at his house. And you know his mother will do whatever she can to help you out."

"Tyrone? Are you kidding? He'll refuse to do it, just to spite me."

"Well, you do have your mother and Racquel. And don't forget me," Sharon said, smiling.

"I know. It's definitely something to think about, because Lord knows, I'm not getting any younger. And on top of that, I've got to find some way to make more money, so I can start saving for Ashley's and Nicholas's college educations. Because the last thing I want is for them to end up with some low-paying job."

"I'm telling you, Marcella, call and make an appointment with an admissions counselor at CU. At least, then, you can see what your options are and what they have to offer."

"Maybe I will. If I get a chance, I'll call this afternoon," Marcella said, leaning back in the chair.

They chatted a while longer and finally Marcella glanced at her watch. It was almost ten minutes to one. "Shoot, I'd better start heading back. Those phones will be ringing off the hook, if I don't," she said, pushing her chair away from the table.

"Yeah, I need to head downtown myself," Sharon said, standing up. Since she was between offices, though, she really didn't have a particular time to be back.

"I'll talk to you later on. I might stop by this evening to see what you found out from the university."

"Okay, I'll see you then. Oh, and thanks again for lunch."

"No problem," Sharon said, getting into her car.

Marcella turned her ignition, but nothing happened. She turned it again and again, and still, nothing happened. She groaned. "Come on. Not today. I need to get back to work." She calmed herself down, turned the ignition again, and breathed a sigh of relief when it started. Sharon was still waiting to make sure it did. Marcella waved at her and left the parking lot.

"That was a close call," Marcella thought as she drove down the street. If something went wrong with her car, where was she going to get the money to fix it? Money, money, money. Maybe Sharon was right after all. Maybe what she needed *was* a four-year degree, and she decided that this day would not end without her checking into it.

Chapter 6

The mere sight of Covington Park University's campus gave Marcella a warm feeling, and she could tell she'd made the right decision in scheduling a counseling session for possible admission. It was already the end of April, but if everything went okay with the application process, she'd be starting classes in less than four months.

She entered the building where the office of admissions was located, climbed two flights of stairs, and walked down the hallway, searching for Room 300. Once she found it, she walked in. A blond-haired girl, who looked to be in her mid-twenties, was sitting behind the desk. Marcella assumed she was the receptionist, and walked over to her.

"Hi, my name is Marcella Jones, and I'm here for a two o'clock appointment with Mrs. Harrison."

The receptionist searched through the appointment book, and Marcella looked on as she crossed through her name with a black-ink pen. "If you'll have a seat, she'll be with you shortly."

"Thank you," Marcella said, smiling.

After sitting down, she gazed around the room and noticed that three other women were already seated. If that's what you could call them. They didn't look to be much older than high-school seniors. Suddenly she felt uneasy. Almost embarrassed. Here she was, barely two weeks away from turning twenty-nine, and had the nerve to be sitting here with these young teenaged girls, who had their whole lives ahead of them. Just the sight of them made her feel like an old woman, and she didn't like it one bit. What was she doing here, anyway? She wished she'd had better sense than to let Sharon talk her into this, but four weeks ago it hadn't seemed like such a bad idea.

"Kayla Johnson?" a short, partially bald gentleman said, eye-searching the waiting area. The tall Black girl dropped what looked to be an old issue of *Seventeen* down on the table, stood up, and walked toward him. He introduced himself, shook the girl's hand, and they both proceeded toward his office.

Marcella looked at her watch and noticed that it was five minutes past her appointment time. She'd barely gotten there on time herself, but she resented with a passion the idea of waiting. She was already getting restless, and she wished this Mrs. Harrison would get a move on. What was the point of scheduling an appointment if the session wasn't going to start on time? If it hadn't been for all the White employees running around the department, she'd have easily blamed it on CP time. She sighed deeply with frustration.

After another ten minutes had passed, the second and third girls were called in by two additional counselors, but Marcella remained waiting. This was ridiculous.

Here it was 2:30 P.M., and still, she hadn't been called in. Had she known this, she'd have worked another half hour. Her nerves were already twirling every which way, and all this waiting was making things worse. When she finally couldn't take it any longer, she strutted over to the reception desk. "I've been waiting for almost thirty minutes now. Can you tell me how much longer Mrs. Harrison is going to be?" Marcella asked with no smile on her face.

"Let me check," the receptionist said reluctantly.

As she dialed the first two digits of Mrs. Harrison's extension, Marcella noticed a middle-aged, professionally dressed Black woman approach the waiting area.

"Marcella Jones?"

Well, it was about time. "Hi," Marcella said, forcing a smile on her face.

"I'm Mrs. Harrison," the counselor said, extending her hand to Marcella.

"Nice to meet you," Marcella said.

"My office is through this door, so if you'll follow me, we can get started."

Marcella followed Mrs. Harrison's lead, but something didn't feel right. This woman didn't seem too friendly, and she hoped this didn't mean trouble.

They walked until they reached the last office on the left side of the hallway. The office had a desk and chair that looked to be fifteen to twenty years old, and the carpet didn't appear to be much newer. Marcella had never been inside any university office, but she had expected a lot more glamour. But then, this was a state-funded university, and she was sure their tax dollars only went so far.

"So, Marcella Jones, you're interested in enrolling at the university this fall?"

"Yes, I am," Marcella answered, switching her behind from the left side of the chair to the right.

"Well, what I'd like to do first is find out a little more about you, review your entrance exam with you, and explain the entire application process. So, why don't you tell me a little about yourself."

Marcella didn't know what else she could tell her that wasn't on her application, but she decided to give her the basic intro. "I graduated from Eisenhower High almost eleven years ago in the top ten percent of my class, and I've been employed with Nicosia and Associates for the past two years as a receptionist."

"Are you married?"

What difference did that make? Those sort of questions were illegal when it came to job interviews, and she couldn't see where it should be any different with this. "No, I'm not."

"Any children?" the counselor asked, leaning back in her chair and slightly rocking.

This woman was crazy. Who did she think she was anyway, sitting there with her nose all stuck up in the air like she was God's gift to the world? Marcella wanted to ask her what her problem was, but her better judgment led her to respond differently. "Yes, two," she answered with no excitement in her voice.

"Well, the reason I'm asking you all of these questions is because I want you to be aware of how time consuming it will be going to classes and completing your assignments. And it will take even more determination for you than most because you've been away from school for so long and you have two children to take care of."

What did she think she was, stupid? This woman was really pushing it. "I'm aware of what it'll take, but this is still what I want to do. My employers have agreed to let me work part-time in the afternoons, and since my children are eight and ten, they're both in school all day."

The counselor looked at her doubtfully. "Your test scores were higher than most of the high-school seniors who take this exam," she said, skimming over Marcella's test scores.

Marcella had forgotten all about the entrance exam. At first she'd been nervous about it, but when she'd finished, she'd felt good about it. As a matter of fact, it had come pretty easy to her. "Thank you."

"That's unusual. I mean, you've been out of school since, what? 1982?"

"Yes," Marcella answered, trying to figure out what Mrs. Harrison was trying to get at. She hoped she wasn't insinuating that she'd cheated.

"And it says here that you want to complete a degree in accounting."

"That's right. I've wanted to be an accountant for as long as I can remember, and even more so after I began working for an accounting firm."

"Those are some pretty rough courses. They require lots of analytical thinking and strong perseverance. Have you had any accounting courses in the past?"

If she had, would she be sitting here going back and forth with *her* pompous ass? Why was this woman trying so hard to intimidate her? And she was a sister, too. She'd thought this whole meeting was supposed to be informative and encouraging, but instead it was turning out to be nothing less than total humiliation.

"No, I've never had any accounting courses, but I'm very good with numbers, and the partners that I work for think I would be good at accounting based on what I've learned on the job. Sometimes they give me some of the smaller projects when their junior accountants get overloaded with work."

"Going to class and taking exams are a lot different from on-the-job assignments."

"I'm aware of that," Marcella said, starting to lose her temper. "And I'm also aware that getting a degree doesn't mean anything, if you can't perform a job in the real world. I work at one of the most prestigious accounting firms in the area, and the guys that I work for think I'm the perfect candidate to pursue an accounting degree. And I tend to listen to them, because they're not just outsiders looking in. They're certified public accountants who have been in business for years and obviously have plenty of experience in the field," Marcella said and felt good afterward.

"Well, have you thought about the cost of tuition and books? College is expensive, and I suspect that over the next four years, the cost will climb even higher than where it is now."

"I earn seven dollars an hour, and I have two children. And from what I've researched so far, I should be more than eligible for some sort of financial aid. Grants, and even loans if necessary. I'll do whatever I have to. If the government is good enough to loan me the money while I'm going to school, I figure I'll be more than able to pay them back once I'm a CPA," Marcella said confidently.

The counselor didn't comment, and it was obvious that she was irritated.

Marcella continued. "Now that you have my application for admission and the results from my entrance exam, what else do I need to complete the admission process?"

"You still have to take the ACT exam, which should be coming up in a few weeks. Hopefully, there's still time for you to get your registration form and fees in before the deadline."

"Do you have any of the registration forms here?"

The counselor hesitated, and Marcella dared her to say she didn't have any. She pulled out the form from her left-hand drawer and passed it to Marcella without even looking at her. Without even the slightest comment. But Marcella didn't care, just so long as she'd given it to her.

"So, is that it?" Marcella said sternly.

"For now. However, *if* you pass the ACT exam, you'll need to come back so we can put together your first-semester schedule."

Hmmph. I'll be back, but I won't be meeting with you, Marcella thought.

"Well, thank you so much for your time," Marcella said, standing up.

"Thank you for coming in," Mrs. Harrison said, gazing down at her desk.

Marcella couldn't believe what had just happened. This woman had turned her first college experience into a total nightmare. She'd done and said everything she could to discourage her from enrolling at the university, and Marcella couldn't understand why. This sort of thing happened all the time when a young Black woman was trying to get ahead in White corporate America, but this was a Black woman she'd been talking with. She had a lot of nerve, and she'd obviously forgotten who she was. That expensive suit and classy hairdo didn't mean shit. And regardless of how educated she was and how much money she made, she was still Black, and nothing was going to change that. Instead of trying to intimidate Marcella, she should have been doing everything she could to help her, and then some.

As Marcella left the main entrance of the counseling

department, heading down the main corridor, she realized that she'd forgotten to ask for a college catalog. So, she turned around and went back into the waiting area. "I forgot to get a college catalog from Mrs. Harrison. Do you think I could run back to her office to get one?" she asked the receptionist.

"Sure, go ahead," the receptionist said, picking up the phone to answer a call.

As Marcella walked closer to Mrs. Harrison's office, she noticed that the door was closed halfway. She raised her fist and was about to knock, until she heard her talking on the phone.

"It really pisses me off when I see these welfare women getting over the way they do. I just met with one who thinks she's going to conquer the world. She claims to be working at some accounting firm, but I know she's lying. She's just like all the rest, laid up on welfare, collecting money and medical benefits that people like you and I are paying for. Now she's going to take it even further by using government grants to go to school scot-free. Nobody gave us any breaks like that. I worked my behind off while I was going to school, and it hasn't been that long since I paid all my student loans off."

Marcella bucked her eyes wide, shaking her head in disagreement and covered her mouth with her hand.

Mrs. Harrison continued. "And you should see the score she got on this entrance exam that we require all students to take. It was so high, that it doesn't take a rocket scientist to figure out that she cheated. No Black girl that I can think of, living on Covington Park's west side, could possibly be that smart. Especially if she was stupid enough to get pregnant in the first place. And you know she can't be too bright, if she made the same stupid mistake twice."

The deeper Marcella fell in thought, the more Mrs.

Harrison's voice faded. Marcella's heart dropped to her stomach, and her eyes filled with tears, which couldn't be controlled. Why was this woman criticizing her the way that she was? And why was she so bitter? Yes, she'd been on welfare a long time ago, and yes, she still received a small allotment of food stamps from time to time, but she worked forty hours a week like everyone else did. She didn't earn a lot, but it was honest work and the best she could do, considering the fact that she didn't have any education past high school. Which was the sole reason why she'd come here in the first place.

"Miss?" the short, bald gentleman she'd seen earlier said, standing behind her.

Marcella jumped and turned to face him.

"Are you okay? Is there something I can help you with?"

"Um. No. I mean, yes, I forgot to ask Mrs. Harrison for a college catalog, but now she's on the phone."

"Oh, I can get that for you from my office. Wait here," the man said, looking at her strangely.

Marcella pulled a tissue from her black shoulder purse and wiped her face during his absence.

When he returned to the hallway, he passed her the current catalog and a copy of the fall-semester course schedule. "Here you go."

"Thank you so much, Mr. . . ."

"I'm Mr. Dahl, another one of the counselors here. Are you sure you're okay? You seem to be upset about something," he said in a concerned and caring manner.

She didn't know whether to blow the whistle on this witch or pretend that she hadn't heard anything. And who was going to believe that one Black woman was trying to discriminate against another, anyway? "Mr. Dahl, could I have one of your business cards, just in case I have questions or need more information?"

"Didn't Mrs. Harrison give you one?"

"No. And to be honest, I'd prefer she didn't."

Mr. Dahl gazed at her, but then pulled a business-card holder from his shirt pocket and gave her one of his cards.

"Thank you," she said, sniffling as she prepared to walk away.

Marcella turned and headed toward the main entrance again, and this time continued all the way out of the building. She wasn't sure how a person could feel happy about attending college, excited about pursuing an accounting degree, pissed off at some snotty counselor, and sad about her low-income situation all at the same time, but she did know two things for sure. She'd be attending Covington Park University in the fall, and graduating with an accounting degree four years from now. And no one, absolutely no one, was going to prevent her from doing just that.

Marcella removed three, plump hot dogs from the portable electric grill, placed one each on her and the children's plates, and removed three hot-dog buns from a plastic bag. This wasn't at all what she wanted for dinner, but since the children had practically begged her to cook them, she decided to go along with their request. Plus with everything that had gone on at the university, she wasn't in the mood for fixing anything else. A few hours had passed since the incident had taken place, but her feelings were still pretty hurt. She couldn't wait to tell Sharon about it, and she was going to call her as soon as she finished her meal.

When they'd all finished eating, Ashley placed the dishes in the sink and started running the dish water, while Nicholas went to his room to begin his homework. Marcella went in her bedroom to call Sharon.

"Hello?" Sharon answered on the second ring.

"Hey, girl," Marcella said, sitting down on the edge of her bed.

"Hey. We must have been thinking on the same wavelength, because I was just about to call you as soon as I finished heating up Marcus and me some leftovers."

"Oh, I didn't know you had company. Tell Marcus I said hey. And you can call me back later, if you want to."

"Girl, you know Marcus doesn't mind. And you know I'm dying to know how things went at the university today, anyway."

"Well, to make a long story short, it went horrible."

"What do you mean?" Sharon asked, sounding serious.

"First of all, the counselor I met with gave me the third degree about my personal life, and pretty much did everything she could to try and discourage me from enrolling into the accounting program. Then after I left her office, I realized I didn't get a school catalog, so I went back. And when I stepped in front of her office door, which was cracked, I heard her talking to someone on the phone. And, girl, she was practically tearing me apart."

"Wait a minute. Did you know this woman?"

"No, but she was going on and on about how I must've cheated on the entrance exam because no one like me could have scored so high otherwise. And that she was sick of paying for welfare women like me who basically get everything scot-free."

"Pah-leeze! Why was she saying you were on welfare?" Sharon asked, totally appalled at what she was hearing.

"Because she said she knew I was lying about working for some accounting firm. And this is the best part. This witch has the nerve to be Black. Can you believe that?"

"You have got to be kidding, Marcella."

"No, she's just as Black as you and I, but you'd never know it, with the way she was acting toward me."

"So, did you confront her or what?"

"No, because the whole thing really caught me completely off guard, and before I knew it, I was in tears. But, of course, now I wish I had said something."

"Well, it's not too late, if you ask me. And to tell you the truth, if it were me, I would report her butt to the department head, university president, or somebody. Because there's no telling how many other times she's gotten away with treating people like this. What she needs is to be put in her little place."

"I know. My feelings are still hurt over this whole mess."

"Girl, I wouldn't pay her a bit of attention. You're the last person to try and get over on somebody. I mean, you're a decent person, you always try to do the right thing, and you treat other people the way you want to be treated, so what does that woman know, anyway?"

"Nothing. But with the way she was talking, you'd have thought she knew everything about everybody."

"Well, I hope she hasn't changed your mind about going back to school in the fall, because I know if you go, you'll do well."

"Oh, don't get me wrong. My feelings may be a little hurt, but I'm not about to let her or anyone else keep me from getting an education. I made that decision before I even left the campus."

"Good, because I'm telling you, this will be the best thing for you. Just wait and see."

"I know, and I can't thank you enough for being so supportive because it really means a lot to me."

"I'm behind you one hundred percent, and I'm here

for you whenever you need something. Regardless of what it is."

"I know, but hey, I'm gonna let you get back to Marcus, okay?" Marcella said, standing up.

"Alright, but call me if you need to talk, okay?"

"I will."

"I'm serious, Marcella."

"I know you are, and you know I'll call if I need to."

"Okay, then, I'll talk to you tomorrow."

"See ya," Marcella said and hung up the phone. She felt better already.

Chapter 7

Racquel pulled the seat belt across her stomach, snapped it down near her waist on her right side, and turned the ignition of the pure-white, gold-packaged Camry. As she headed out of the school parking lot, a feeling of nervousness took control of her. She'd been on pins and needles ever since she'd made the appointment with the infertility specialist one month ago, but now she wasn't so sure she wanted to go through with it. She still wanted a baby more than anything, but she couldn't help but wonder how she was going to feel if the doctor determined that she was unable to carry a fetus to full term. And as much as she hated herself for thinking it, a part of her wished that it was Kevin who had the problem. It wouldn't make things any better, but at least she wouldn't feel so much like a failure. But in reality, she knew it couldn't be him, because if it had been, she never would have gotten pregnant the first time.

She continued cruising down the street until she came to the first stoplight. As she sat there, an old woman pushing a cart crossed the street staring at her. It was the end of April, and while there was still a slight chill in the air, it wasn't cold enough for all that the lady had on. A pair of corduroy pants, which was clearly two sizes too large, a dingy-looking sweatshirt, and a plaid wool coat trimmed with fake fur around the collar and the end of the sleeves. The cart was filled with everything from empty milk jugs to worn-out dresses. Racquel felt sorry for her and wanted to help her. It was so sad how some people were burdened with the worst situations, while others seemed to practically walk on water. A person could be homeless or living comfortable in a mansion, struggling on welfare or employed as a CEO of some corporation, blessed with a house full of children or not able to have any at all.

She exhaled deeply. Why did everything always have to point back to her own situation? Why couldn't she just leave well enough alone and be happy with what she had? It seemed easy enough when she offered that advice to her sister and everyone else. But no matter how she weighed it, there could never be any real happiness for her without children.

As she drove into the parking lot of the infertility clinic, she spotted Kevin waiting patiently in their Ford Explorer. He was such a good husband. She didn't know how she would have gotten through the miscarriage and all the unsuccessful trying without him. All he seemed to care about was her, and she loved him for it, but their marriage alone just wasn't enough for her. She wished to God that it was, but it wasn't. She simply could not be content with the way things were. No matter how much she loved and trusted him, she always felt like something was missing. But maybe, things would start to look up after today. Maybe the specialist would have the answer to all her prayers.

"How long have you been here?" she asked, shutting the car door.

"About five minutes or so, not too long," he said, walking toward her.

He pulled the glass door open, waited for Racquel to step inside, and followed behind her. Racquel stepped up to the sliding glass window, wrote her name on the registration sheet, and sat down next to Kevin. Racquel was shocked when she noticed that no other patients were waiting in the reception area. She knew it wasn't because she and Kevin were the only ones having trouble with getting pregnant; she'd seen and read too many articles about it. Not to mention the women she heard talking about it from time to time. So, maybe this was just a slow day.

"Mrs. Wilson, since this is your first time, I need you to complete a medical-history form for us, and then, I'll need to get a Xerox copy of your insurance card," the young secretary said, looking in Racquel's direction.

Racquel walked back up to the window, reached for the clipboard, which had the medical-history form attached to it, and returned to her seat to fill it out.

On the first page were basic questions like what her name was, where she lived, what her phone number was, and who to contact in case of an emergency. When she came to the second, there were loads of questions asking about not just what she'd had as far as infections, diseases, and surgeries, but what her immediate family members had had or did have, as well. She checked yes or no to each of the ones she was sure of, and left the others blank. When she finished, she pulled her insurance card from her wallet, proceeded back up to the window, and passed everything to the secretary.

The secretary made a copy of the insurance card and returned it to Racquel. "The doctor will be with you shortly."

"Thank you," Racquel said and sat back down next to Kevin, who was thumbing through *Prevention* magazine.

"They've got some pretty interesting articles in here. I wouldn't mind getting this on a regular basis."

"Yeah, I've heard they have excellent information on health," Racquel said hesitantly. She didn't want to encourage him too much, because the last thing they needed was another magazine subscription. They already received more than they ever had time to read through: *Essence, Ebony, Ebony Man, Jet, Black Enterprise, Body & Soul, Better Homes and Gardens*. Not to mention every baby magazine available to man-kind. Some of these she'd subscribed to herself, but most of them had been ordered by Kevin from the various sweepstakes organizations. He wholeheartedly believed that there was a much better chance at winning the grand prize if you purchased the magazines they offered than if you simply returned the entry blank all by itself. Especially since one of the sweepstakes he'd entered last year came with two separate return envelopes. One addressed to Georgia if you weren't purchasing any magazines, and the other to some location in Florida if you were. And of course, ever since that day, he'd been convinced of his theory.

When Racquel noticed the words "Blessings Come In All Sizes" printed across an old issue of *Working Mother*, she picked it up and turned straight to the index to see what page the article was on. She scanned down the page with her forefinger until she found it, and turned to page 52. The article had been written by a thirty-seven-year-old woman who'd experienced a miscarriage about a year ago, and had finally come to the conclusion that instead of dwelling on what she didn't have, it was much healthier to pour all of her energy into what she did have, before she lost that. A beautiful three-year-old son, and a husband who loved both of them.

The story ended with the woman stressing how months and months of therapy had changed her way of life and thinking in general. She was finally at a point in her life where she no longer worried about what she didn't have, but instead showed thanks and appreciation for what she did.

Racquel closed the article with disappointment. Partly because she'd thought the article was something completely different from what it was, but mostly because this woman made it sound like there was no hope. That you simply had to give up and accept things the way they were.

But, Racquel wasn't buying into that. She'd come too far and tried too hard to even think on those terms, and wasn't going to. Regardless of what Kevin, Marcella, and her mother thought, she wasn't obsessed. She just knew what she wanted and had more determination than most people when it came to getting it.

"Mr. and Mrs. Wilson," an attractive-looking caramel-complexioned nurse called out. Kevin and Racquel rose from their seats and walked through the door behind her.

"I'm Dr. Reed's nurse, Vivian."

"Nice to meet you," Racquel said, smiling.

"Is it okay if I call you Racquel?" the nurse asked. "We like being on a first-name basis with our patients because it usually makes them feel a lot more comfortable."

"That's fine."

"The first thing I need to do is get your weight," the

nurse asked, pointing toward the scale. Racquel set her
purse down on the carpet, removed her brown leather
pumps, and stepped up onto the black rubbery plat-
form. She didn't know why she always took off her shoes
because if a person was overweight, shoes weren't going
to make that much of a difference anyhow.

"One forty-one," the nurse said, jotting it down
inside Racquel's newly created chart. "You can have a
seat in the second room on the right, and I'll be in
to review your medical-history form and to get some
additional information."

Once they arrived in the room, Racquel hopped up
on the tan table, which had shiny white paper running
down the center of it. Kevin sat down in the orange
plastic chair. They looked at each other, smiling, but
didn't speak.

"Okay," the nurse said, entering the examination
room. "You're here for an infertility consultation,
right?"

"Yes," Racquel said, sounding nervous.

"Actually, if you like, you can take a seat in the chair
next to your husband, because we won't be examining
you until after the consultation with Dr. Reed," the
nurse said, skimming through the form.

Racquel took a seat next to Kevin, and the nurse
leaned against the table facing them.

"Are you currently on any medications?"

"No," Racquel said, realizing she must have missed
that question by mistake.

"Is there any history of endometriosis in your
family?"

"No. Not that I'm aware of."

"Have there been any miscarriages?"

"Yes. Last year."

"How far along were you?" the nurse asked, looking at Racquel.

"Almost at the end of my first trimester."

"As far as you know, has anyone else in your family had problems with infertility?"

No, she thought. Just me. I'm the only one with this stupid problem. "No. My mother had two children, and so did my sister, but there were no problems that I know of."

"Okay. I think that covers just about everything," the nurse said, quickly scanning the form a second time. "If you'll follow me, I'll show you to Dr. Reed's office."

Once they were seated, Racquel's eye wandered around the entire office. It was simply gorgeous. It was more like a study, office, living room, and family room combined with all the books, office equipment, furniture, and exercise equipment. Dr. Reed's office wasn't much different from being at home. And it must have cost a fortune to furnish something so elaborate. But then, he was an infertility specialist who performed services that sometimes escalated into the thousands per patient. So, it was obvious that he could afford it.

Kevin sat in the chair looking straight ahead waiting for the good doctor to enter. He didn't seem the least bit excited, and Racquel wanted to ask him why he was so quiet. This could be the best day of their lives, and here he was acting as if it was some normal workday. She couldn't understand him at all. Especially after all they'd gone through. They were finally going to reap their reward. She was sure his attitude would be a lot different, though, once he heard everything the doctor had to say.

"Good afternoon. I'm Dr. Reed," he said, extending his hand first to Kevin and then Racquel. "Kevin and Racquel Wilson, correct?"

"That's us," Racquel said, smiling.

They both shook the doctor's hand one after the other. Then Dr. Reed, who was tall, broad-shouldered, and had salt-and-pepper hair, walked around his desk and took a seat in the burgundy leather high-back chair.

"I just reviewed your chart, and I think the first thing we need to do is schedule some testing to make sure there isn't some special reason why you haven't been able to conceive, or in your case, carry a child to full term." Dr. Reed looked at Racquel and Kevin, his eyes moving from one to the other. "Do you have any specific questions before we discuss some of the procedures you might be a candidate for?"

Racquel looked at Kevin. "Is there anything you'd like to know more about?"

"No. Not really, except how much all of this is going to cost," Kevin said with his eyes gazing in the direction of the doctor.

Racquel could just kill him. Who cared how much money this was all going to cost? She knew she didn't. And why did he always have to be so straightforward? Just couldn't beat around the bush or show some discretion like most people. And she didn't know what was wrong with him now anyway. He'd seemed perfectly fine this morning, and even appeared okay with all of this when they'd first arrived at the clinic. But now he was acting as if he didn't want to be there. She decided though, that Kevin Wilson was not going to rain on her much awaited parade, and it was better just to ignore him.

"Well," Racquel said, pausing. "I'd like to know how long it will take before the test results are back?"

"It shouldn't take much longer than six weeks after we've run them all."

"What sort of tests will you be conducting?" Racquel asked.

"First we'll do your initial examination, which will include a pelvic exam, and after that, we'll do a hystero-salpingogram, which is an X-ray of the uterus and the fallopian tubes. We'll also be doing some blood work to check for pelvic infections and to measure the levels of your thyroid, pituitary, and ovarian hormones. And if necessary, we'll do a vaginal ultrasound to check for proper ovulation and to make sure there are no fibroids or cysts. There are a number of tests we can do because there are a number of reasons why women have problems with getting pregnant. But at the same time you might fall into the category of women who have what we call 'unexplained infertility.' There's only a five to eight percent factor, but it's still a possibility," the doctor said, leaning back in his chair with his hands locked together, pivoting his chair from side to side.

Racquel felt comfortable with Dr. Reed. He was definitely knowledgeable in his area of expertise, and seemed to be very caring. She'd just met him, but she already sensed that she could trust him. Which was important, because she'd always felt that a doctor should be just as personable and caring as he was competent.

"How soon do you think we can schedule the testing?" Racquel asked.

"Probably as early as next week, but Vivian will check the calendar and let you know before you leave today."

Dr. Reed glanced over at Kevin, who was still sitting in complete silence. He'd nodded his head a few times to acknowledge what the doctor was saying, but that was about it.

"And to answer your question about cost," Dr. Reed said to Kevin. "It really depends on what sort of infertility treatments and procedures we're talking about, because there's a variety of options. Using infertility drugs is the least expensive, but if we consider something like 'in vitro fertilization,' the cost can be as much as ten thousand dollars. And you might want to check with your health-insurance carrier because the State of Illinois has a mandate that requires all group insurances and HMO's to provide infertility coverage to patients who work for companies or organizations that employ twenty-five or more employees. You may have to fight hard to prove that this particular procedure is what *they* consider medically necessary, and that it's not a pre existing condition, but it's worth it."

Kevin nodded in acknowledgment, and continued listening.

"It's hard to say until we know what we're dealing with."

"But there is a chance that the infertility drugs might do the trick?" Racquel asked hopefully.

"Yes, many of my patients have had success by using them, but then there's the chance of multiple births,' Dr. Reed said.

"After struggling this hard, I don't think that will be a problem. But if it did happen, we'd still be just as happy," she said confidently.

Kevin just smiled again, and he was making Racquel sick. As a matter of fact, she was downright embarrassed at the way he was acting. If she had known he was going to have such a messed-up attitude, she never would have asked him to come in the first place. And if he didn't cut it out real soon, she was going to let him have it as soon as they made their way back out to the parking lot.

"Also," Dr. Reed said to Kevin, "we'll need to do a semen analysis on you to check for sperm motility, which is the sperm's ability to swim; sperm count, which is the number of sperm per cubic centimeter of semen; and the sperm shape, to make sure the sperm has an oval head and a long tail, which is necessary to properly penetrate an egg.''

Kevin did his usual nod and forced another fake smile.

"So, if that's it, we'll step outside the office so Vivian can get you scheduled. I usually like to do an initial exam, but I think we can just wait and do everything next week.''

They all walked outside the doctor's office and waited for the nurse to check his schedule.

"We have an opening next Tuesday morning at eight A.M.''

"Let's see,'' Racquel said, thinking if that date and time were okay. "Do you know how long I'll be here?''

"I'd say at least two hours or so. Give or take.''

"That should be fine. I just need to make sure the school finds a substitute for my class during the morning.''

"Our lab will be doing some blood work, so you'll need to fast at least twelve hours before the appointment.''

Racquel didn't like the sound of that. She always had breakfast no matter what the situation was. Just didn't feel right throughout the day if she didn't. But then, she would have starved herself a whole week, if they'd asked her to. To tell the truth, she'd have done just about anything, if it meant they could help her with getting pregnant. "Sounds good,'' Racquel said.

As soon as they stepped outside to the parking lot, Racquel went off. "What was that all about?'' she asked in an elevated, salty tone of voice.

"What was *what* all about?'' Kevin asked, like he had no idea what she was talking about.

"You know what I mean. That attitude of yours. And that comment you made about the cost."

"He asked if we had any questions, and I told him what it was."

"But you acted as though you'd been forced here against your own will, and that made me look stupid."

"I told you I would come, and I did. I'm just not going to get my hopes up until I see something more concrete."

"How can anything positive happen with this, if your attitude stays like that? I don't believe you, because just a few weeks ago you said you were willing to try this, but now you're acting as if you couldn't care less."

"I haven't changed my mind, but I want you to understand that this is it."

"What do you mean, 'this is it'?" Racquel asked, squinting her eyes.

"If the infertility drugs don't work, we have to end all of this," Kevin said, noticing that the young couple who'd just stepped out of their car was staring, and he was slightly embarrassed.

Racquel felt total humiliation when she spotted the couple passing by them. This was ridiculous.

"This isn't the place for this, Kevin, so I'll see you at home," she said, walking toward her car without waiting for any response that he might have. Once she was in the car, she drove off without as much as even glancing back at him.

She hadn't gotten this angry since last year when she'd had the miscarriage, and Kevin kept insisting that everything happens for a reason, and that God didn't make mistakes. She'd heard it a zillion times from all their church members and most of her relatives. So by the time Kevin decided to bring those same two theories to her attention again, she'd had it up to here.

It wasn't that she didn't believe in God or that she was losing her faith in Him, but she just couldn't help but question why He allowed things to happen the way He did. And it wasn't just about her not being able to have children, either. What she wanted to know was why innocent people, especially children, were murdered for no reason at all. Why there was even such a thing as cancer, leukemia, and AIDS. And why on earth there were thousands of children starving and dying in almost every Third World country she could think of. It just didn't make sense. She knew it wasn't right, but she was angry at God. And anyway, who else could she blame all of her problems and shortcomings on?

As soon as that last thought passed through her mind, she regretted it. She wasn't by far Little-Miss-Holier-Than-Thou, and didn't go to church every time the church doors swung open, but she'd been raised to fear God and everything He stood for. She could still remember all the times it stormed, when she, Marcella, and their mother unplugged every appliance and anything that looked to be electric from its outlet. Just in case the lightning struck it. And after they'd all rushed through the house trying to take care of that, they would all huddle together in one room, sitting quietly until it was all over. Racquel and Marcella had thought it was silly, but Corrine had stressed on more than one occasion that it was their duty to remain still until God finished His work.

Racquel pulled into the driveway, pressed the garage door opener, and continued into the garage to park. When she slid her key into the door leading to the kitchen, she heard the phone ringing.

"Hello?" Racquel answered in a rushed voice, with her purse still hanging from her shoulder.

"Racquel? This is Vivian, Dr. Reed's nurse."

"Oh, hi, Vivian."

"I'm sorry to bother you, but there was another ques
tion that you missed on the medical-history form. But
I didn't want to ask you in front of your husband. So,
if he's there, you can just answer yes or no, and we'll
discuss the details when you come in next week."

Racquel felt like dropping the phone. And it took
everything she had not to fall to the floor. For years
she'd tried to forget that horrible day in December, just
two months before her seventeenth birthday, but now
it was being brought to the forefront, and there wasn't
a thing she could do about it.

The nurse continued. "Have you ever had any
induced abortions?"

Racquel's first instinct was to lie. Especially, since she
was sure that having an abortion had nothing to do with
her not getting pregnant. She'd proven that last year.
But she knew if these people were going to help her,
she had to be honest with them. Completely honest.

"Yes, I had one about thirteen years ago when I was
seventeen."

"Was that the only one?"

Damn. What difference did that make? An abortion
was an abortion, regardless of how many a person had
had. "No. I had another one three years later when I
was in college."

The nurse was silent at first, and then spoke. "Okay.
That's what I needed to know. You take care, and we'll
see you on Tuesday."

Racquel hung up the phone as best she could, but
her hand was shaking like a leaf on a tree. What was
going to happen if Kevin found out? He'd surely think
the worst of her if he did, and their marriage would be
over. She'd heard him on more than one occasion stress
his opinion of women who killed babies. And he'd be

convinced that this was the reason she wasn't able to have a baby.

She'd been young and dumb each time it happened, but she'd learned from her mistakes and paid for them. She'd thought.

She took a deep breath, stroked her hair from front to back with both of her hands, and rethought the whole situation. Maybe her secret was still intact, because from the sounds of what the nurse had said, this was strictly confidential. Something between her and them only. And since they weren't going to inform Kevin of anything, there really wasn't anything to worry about. Marcella knew about the first one, but she'd never even consider squealing on her own sister. Maybe she'd gotten herself all bent out of shape for nothing. In a few weeks they'd find out what the problem was, and figure out how to help or correct it. But then, what if the abortions *were* the problem. And what if Kevin found out how she'd gotten pregnant the second time around. If he did, she'd never be able to face him. As a matter of fact, she'd never be able to face anyone ever again. No. What she had to do was keep her cool and pretend that this subject was nonexistent. Because if she didn't, everything was going to be ruined.

Chapter 8

For as long as Racquel could remember, her family had always gotten together for a huge cookout on the Fourth of July, and today the tradition was continuing. Years ago it had always taken place at her mother's house, but ever since she and Kevin had gotten married, they became the ones who hosted it. Thanks to Marcella and Corrine, who literally fell in love with their patio the very first time they laid eyes on it. "There's so much more room at your house," Corrine would say. "Girl, just think how much more space we could have if we do it at yours and Kevin's," Marcella would add in. But really, Racquel didn't mind, because she loved entertaining in the summertime. There was nothing better than grilled brats, chicken, and steak. And sitting outside breathing in all the fresh air was so exhilarating. As far as she was concerned, summertime could have lasted twelve months out of the year, and she would have been just fine with it. But she knew that was wishful thinking for any city within a hundred-mile radius of Chicago. This wasn't Florida, and she had long since learned to live with it.

She opened the white plastic Wal-Mart bag sitting on the table, pulled out the red, white, and blue napkins, matching cups, plates, and silverware, and lined them across the light-beige cabinet. She knew her mother was going to die when she saw all of the colored eating utensils and decorations Racquel had picked up the day before. Corrine didn't see a reason to spend all that money for one day out of the year, and the white paper and plastic products suited her just fine. She'd said that every year since they'd started having the Fourth of July cookout, and Racquel knew this year wasn't going to be any different. And maybe it *was* ridiculously expensive, but all of the colors seemed to make the atmosphere so much more interesting, and Racquel liked that.

She pulled open the refrigerator and scanned through it to make sure she hadn't forgotten anything. The potato salad was there, and so were the macaroni, fruit, and pasta salads. Corrine was bringing all of the beverages, breads, and condiments, and Marcella was cooking macaroni and cheese, and barbequed baked beans. Kevin had purchased the meat yesterday evening, and was just about finished grilling all of it.

As she closed the refrigerator door, she noticed a small card attached by a magnet bearing their auto-insurance company's name. It was an appointment reminder for this coming Wednesday with her infertility specialist. A sadness engrossed her. Here she'd been taking this medication called Clomid for two months, and still wasn't the slightest bit pregnant. It was starting to seem like a waste of time, and a lot of unnecessary money. Dr. Reed kept insisting that it sometimes took a little longer for some patients than others, but she was sick of all this waiting, and her patience was starting to wear extremely thin. And of course, Kevin wouldn't even discuss any of the other methods like artificial insemination or in vitro fertilization because he said they were too costly. She agreed with him one hundred percent, and that was the reason why she suggested they take out a second mortgage, instead of spending their life savings, but he was still dead set against it. And it wasn't like she would forge his name or anything, so her hands were tied. If only their HMO would stop being so difficult. They'd approved payment for the medication, but when Dr. Reed had attempted to secure pre-approval for the other procedures, they'd flat out denied them. She and Kevin had filed an appeal, but so far, nothing had resulted from it. And she was afraid nothing was going to.

Racquel's emotions were high-strung. Sometimes she loved Kevin, but most of the time she hated the ground that he walked on. And she never knew when those feelings were going to come about. It simply depended on what day it was, and how she felt when she woke up in the morning.

She'd thought the medication would make a world of difference, since all of her test results had come back conclusive: There wasn't anything wrong with her, and there was no reason at all why she shouldn't eventually get pregnant.

And while it had only taken seven weeks to obtain the results, it had seemed like a whole year. For years she'd been in denial about the possibility of those two abortions being the problem, but it wasn't long before she convinced herself that maybe they *had* damaged her entire reproduction system. But when Dr. Reed confirmed that everything was kosher with both her and

Kevin, she'd been happier than she had been in a long time.

But, she wasn't going to think about any of this today, and she was going to keep things as cordial as possible with Kevin. Holidays were supposed to be a happy time, and it wouldn't be fair to spoil the day for everyone else. Especially since it seemed like they were having more people this year than they'd ever had before. Her mother, Marcella, Ashley, and Nicholas. One of the new engineers that Kevin worked with and his wife. Marcella's best friend Sharon and her boyfriend, Marcus. And her mother's only and older sister, Clara, and her husband, Leroy.

Including her and Kevin, that made twelve people, not to mention the few drop-ins who claimed they didn't want anything, but ended up eating more than the people who'd actually been invited. But Racquel never minded, because the more people that were there, the better time everyone seemed to have.

Kevin slid open the glass patio door, walked through it, placed some of the meat he'd cooked on top of the stove, pulled Racquel into his arms, and kissed her on her forehead.

Racquel was surprised. They'd had another falling-out this morning when she'd brought up the artificial-insemination subject again, and they hadn't spoken a single word to each other since. But she was glad he was making the first move, because that meant he wasn't nearly as pissed off as she thought.

"What was that for? " she asked, glaring straight into his light-brown eyes.

"Baby, you know I hate it when we argue like this. And I feel even worse when we're not speaking to each other."

"I don't like it, either, but it seems like we've been doing it a lot lately."

"We've got to work this out, but today isn't the day for it."

She'd just decided the same thing herself, and was glad to know that they agreed on at least something. "No. It's not."

"Baby, regardless of what you think, I do still love you," he said, hugging her firmly.

In all honesty, she wasn't sure if he did or not, but there was no sense in making any unnecessary waves. "I know you do, and I love you just the same," she said, laying her head against his chest.

He placed his finger under her chin, tilted her head up, and kissed her rough—the way she liked it. She kissed him back, and her heart became heavy. His beat so rapidly, that he was sure he was going to have a heart attack. They hadn't made love in over a week, and he wanted her right then and there. She wanted him just as badly. They kissed passionately, and cold chills ran through Racquel's entire body. Wild pulsations took control of his.

When he couldn't take it anymore, he tore off her white rayon shirt. See-through buttons flew all over the place, but neither of them paid any attention to it. He reached to pull his T-shirt off, and she quickly assisted him. Then he unzipped her black jean shorts and pushed them down her legs until they touched the floor. She stepped out of them. Now it was her turn. First she released the button of his pants, then pulled the zipper down as far as it would go. He slipped out of them without taking his eyes off her, pulled her toward him, and kissed her more passionately than he had the first time. She responded willingly.

He led her up the stairs to the master bedroom and

turned the covers back on the bed. She sprawled across it, he lunged on top, and entered her without delay. They each moved back and forth, but in opposite directions, and the moaning grew louder with every stroke. Then faster. And finally, so fast that they came simultaneously with loud groans, breathing deeply.

Tears flowed down each side of Racquel's face, and Kevin smiled at her, wiping them away. She'd thought for sure the passion between them was gone forever, and he basically felt the same. As of late, they'd only been going through the motions. Not because they longed for each other, but primarily because they needed to make a baby. And not only was there never any high-powered foreplay, like the kind they'd just given each other a short while ago, but it had gotten to the point where there was no foreplay at all. And they didn't hold each other the way they used to afterward, either. As a matter of fact, Kevin had become totally disgusted with Racquel lying on her back and pushing her butt upward, with her legs straight in the air, trying to help his semen make it all the way through to wherever it needed to be to get her pregnant. It had all become monotonous, and he'd become bored with it.

"Now, this is how it's supposed to be," Kevin said, still lying on top of her with his head lying to the side of hers.

"It was so wonderful, Kevin. We haven't made love like that since . . . Gosh, I can't even remember when," she said, kissing him on his shoulder.

They lay there for a few minutes in silence trying to recover from all the excitement. Kevin was exhausted, but he finally rolled over to his side, looked at Racquel, and shook his head. "Girl, I don't know what you've got down there, but I feel like falling into a coma."

"Please. It's no different than it's always been."

"Then, maybe I'm just getting old, because you've worn me completely out."

"At thirty years old? I don't think so," she said, laughing slightly.

"You might as well say I'm thirty-one. You know my birthday's next month. And come to think of it, so is yours."

"Don't remind me. You know how I feel about that subject."

Racquel glanced over at the digital clock on Kevin's side of the bed and saw that it was 12:15 P.M. "Oh, my God, everyone is supposed to be here at one," she said, jumping up from the bed.

"All we have to do is take a shower. We've got plenty of time," he said, closing his eyes, obviously not wanting to get up.

"Did you finish all the meat?"

As soon as he heard the question, he bucked his eyes wide open. He'd left an entire package of bratwurst on the grill before he'd come into the house. "Oh, shoot. I forgot about those brats," he said, pulling his robe from the chair, where he'd left it that morning. He slipped it on, and raced down the stairs as fast as he could.

When he opened the lid to the triple-rack gas grill, an enormous cloud of smoke forced its way out right into his face. He coughed uncontrollably for a few seconds and then looked down to see if the meat had been ruined. And it had. He turned each of the two flame controls off, and forked the brats into the pan lined with aluminum foil. Then he turned the knob on top of the gas-filled tank until it was completely closed.

They had more than enough meat to go around, so he wasn't going to worry about it. He walked into the kitchen, dumped the brats into the garbage container, picked up his and Racquel's clothing, and headed back upstairs to take his shower.

As soon as Racquel slipped on her full-length, sleeveless red dress, she went back down to the kitchen. When she arrived, the doorbell rang. "Goodness. We just barely made it," she said out loud to herself, walking to the front door.

"Hey, girl," Marcella said, walking through the door with a long, white baking dish covered with clear plastic wrapping. She was dressed in a rayon white summer jumpsuit.

"Hey, sis," Racquel said, already turning her attention to her niece and nephew. "How're my babies doing?" she asked.

"I'm good, Aunt Racquel. How are you?" Ashley said, following her mother with a medium-sized clear baking dish filled with macaroni and cheese.

"Fine," Nicholas said in a low tone, with a pout on his face.

"What's the matter with you, sweetheart?" Racquel asked, placing her arm around him. They walked side by side into the kitchen.

"Nothing," he lied.

"Marcella, what's wrong with Nicholas?" Racquel asked.

"I don't know, but if he doesn't get rid of that little attitude, there really will be something wrong with him."

"He's just mad because Mom wouldn't let him get a candy bar when we stopped at the store," Ashley said, laughing.

"Shut up, Ashley!" Nicholas yelled.

"Look," Marcella said, pointing her finger at him. "I'm not going to have this today, Nicholas. I told you, your aunt Sharon is bringing over two different desserts, and you can have some of that after you eat dinner. And that's that."

Nicholas changed his whole tune as soon as he saw the I'm-not-playing-with-you look on his mother's face.

"Now, you apologize to your aunt Racquel for acting like this," Marcella told him.

"I'm sorry, Aunt Racquel," he said.

"That's okay, sweetheart," Racquel said to Nicholas, and then turned her attention to Marcella. "Girl, he doesn't have to apologize for something like that."

See, it was exactly this kind of thing that pissed Marcella off. Racquel brushed off everything the children did, regardless of how serious it was. If it had been left up to her, the children would have never been disciplined at all. But instead of telling her to mind her own business, she decided to look over her. It just wasn't worth going into it.

"So, did you talk to Mom this morning?" Marcella asked.

"Actually, I spoke with her twice. She said she was going to be here by one, but maybe she decided to wait for Aunt Clara and Uncle Leroy, and you know they're never on time for anything," Racquel said.

"That's for sure," Marcella said, laughing. "Uncle Leroy is always saying how he's not about to rush his life away like the rest of us. And he doesn't."

"But it's kind of irritating when you're trying to keep the food warm. It's not so bad with the meat, because we eat that at room temperature anyway, but for the macaroni and cheese and baked beans, you have to keep reheating it."

"Aunt Racquel, how come all these buttons are on the floor?" Nicholas interrupted, picking them up one by one.

Racquel couldn't believe she'd forgotten about the

buttons, and she should have known Kevin hadn't thought twice about them, either. She had to come up with something quick, but she had no idea what. Maybe she could pretend she hadn't heard him. "So what kind of dessert is Sharon bringing?" Racquel asked Marcella.

"Buttons?" Marcella said in a confused tone of voice. "Let me see," she said, reaching her hand out to Nicholas.

"See," he said, showing his mother.

"Aunt Racquel, where did they come from?" Nicholas said, figuring that even though his mother *had* heard him, maybe his aunt Racquel *hadn't*.

"Oh, from my sewing box. I dropped it earlier, and a bunch of buttons fell out. I guess I missed a few," Racquel answered in a squirrelly tone of voice.

Marcella looked at her suspiciously, because these definitely weren't stray buttons, or the extras you got when you purchased something new from a clothing store. They were all alike. Something was wrong with Racquel's story, but at the same time she couldn't tell what the truth was, either.

"Ooooh," Ashley said, cracking up with laughter. "Look at all those brats Uncle Kevin burned up," she said, pointing at the plastic garbage container.

Racquel felt like running for her life. She loved her niece and nephew, but why did they have to be so nosey? Of course, they had no idea what was going on, but it was just a matter of time before Marcella put two and two together and figured out exactly what had really happened. "Yeah, he sure did," Racquel responded, laughing innocently.

Marcella could barely keep a straight face as it was, but when Kevin entered the room, she burst out laughing. "What's up, Kevin?"

"Hey, sister-in-law," he said, wondering what was so funny.

"Hey, Uncle Kevin," Nicholas said, hugging him.

"Hey, little man, what's goin' on?" Kevin said, grabbing Nicholas playfully in a headlock.

"Hi, Uncle Kevin," Ashley said, still laughing.

"Hey, Little Miss Giggles," Kevin said, hugging Ashley. "And what's so funny, anyway?"

"You burned up all that meat," Ashley said, looking at Nicholas, who started laughing right along with her.

"Oh, so you two are making fun of my cooking, huh?"

"Yep," the two children answered in unison.

Marcella looked at Kevin and thought, Yeah, right. She couldn't believe him and Racquel. Two grown people tearing their clothes off in the middle of the day like wild savages. Acting like they'd just met two weeks ago.

"Ashley and Nicholas. You two go outside and wait for Granny, so you can help her bring the pops in," Marcella said.

"Okay, Mom," Nicholas said, placing the buttons on the counter. "I think I got all of them, Aunt Racquel," he said, making a beeline toward the front door. Being outside was his most favorite place to be, so he didn't have any problem at all with waiting for his grandmother. Ashley followed behind him reluctantly. Unlike Nicholas, she wanted to stay and listen to what the grown-ups had to say.

"Don't even say it," Racquel said to Marcella as soon as she saw her opening her mouth.

"What? It's not my fault that you and Kevin got buttnaked in the center of the kitchen. And Kevin, did you have to tear all of my sister's buttons off in the process?" she said, smirking.

Kevin gazed at her in horror. And he felt like crawling under the table. He'd wondered where those buttons had come from when he saw Nicholas picking them up, but hadn't really given it much thought. He'd been so heated up, that he hadn't paid the slightest bit of attention to Racquel's buttons or anything else. But now, Marcella was calling him on it, and he could barely look her in her face. So, instead of acknowledging what she'd just said, he strolled out to the patio.

"Girl, why did you have to embarrass him like that," Racquel said, smiling.

"I didn't mean to. But you know it's funny. If it was the other way around, you would *never* let me live it down."

Racquel laughed. "I know, but you know how Kevin is."

"I'll apologize to him later, but not with a straight face."

"You're sick," Racquel said, shaking her head.

"Hey, where is everybody?" Marcella asked, glancing at her watch. "Where else? On CP time, of course."

"Well, I'm going to warm the macaroni and cheese, and the baked beans now, and if they don't get here soon, they'll have to eat it the way it is," Marcella said, turning on the oven. "Sharon said she had to go into work for a couple of hours, and that she might be a little late, but the rest of them don't have an excuse."

"I wonder what happened to Kevin's friend from work. He and his wife should have been here by now, too," Racquel said curiously.

Marcella sucked her teeth. "Are they Black or White?"

"If they're late, what do you think?" Racquel said, laughing.

"Should've known," Marcella said.

* * *

Shortly after 1:30 P.M. all the other guests finally arrived. And now they were all laid back on the patio chairs with their stomachs poked out. Racquel had always known that Aunt Clara and Uncle Leroy were big eaters, but they'd really shown out today. They'd each piled food on, not one but two plates on the first go-around, and then went back for what they called "seconds" when all of that was gone. They were both fairly large, but Racquel still couldn't figure out where they found the room to hold so much food. Steaks, brats, chicken, side dishes. You name it, they had it, and were already looking forward to dessert. It really didn't matter to her that they were overweight because she loved both of them like they were her second parents. However, Uncle Leroy had already had a slight heart attack last year, and Aunt Clara's "pressure" was sky-high every time you spoke with her. If they didn't start watching what they ate, both of them were going to be buried six feet under.

"So, can I get anybody anything?" Racquel asked.

"Noooo, honey. But we'll take a couple of plates home with us for this evening," Aunt Clara said.

Racquel wanted to say something. Anything. But she knew better. Plus, they'd never understand any advice like that, anyhow. Instead, their feelings would be hurt, and she didn't want that. "Take whatever you want. I'm hoping all of you will, because if all this food stays around here, I'll be tempted to eat it myself."

"That's what's wrong with you little folks," Uncle Leroy said. "You just don't know how to eat."

"Ain't that the truth," Aunt Clara said, chuckling.

Everyone laughed. Especially, Sharon and Marcus, who thought Aunt Clara and Uncle Leroy were hilarious. The rest of the family was used to it, and that was one of the main reasons they all looked forward to sharing the holidays with them.

"I do eat right, and sometimes too much," Racquel said, patting her stomach.

"Girl, get on away from here," Uncle Leroy said, fanning his hand to the side in disbelief.

"And this one over here *really* needs to put some meat on those bones right there," Uncle Leroy said, pointing to Marcella.

Oh, shoot. Everything was funny to Marcella as long as he wasn't talking about her, and this meat-on-the-bones comment wasn't making her too happy. Especially since she hated the fact that she'd lost so much weight without even trying. But she played the comment off by laughing right along with everyone else.

"And look at your friend," Uncle Leroy said, looking at Sharon. "She's in the same boat," he said, and cracked up at his own joke.

"Birds of a feather," Aunt Clara agreed, and then fell out laughing right with him.

Sharon laughed harder than ever before, and it was obvious that she wasn't offended in the least little bit. Which was fine, because everyone knew Uncle Leroy was a big jokester and didn't mean any harm. It was just that Marcella hated being reminded of what she already knew.

"Sharon, don't you mind my sister and brother-in-law," Corrine said, laughing. "They mess with everybody."

"I know, Mom," Sharon said. Since Sharon had never had the opportunity of knowing her own mother, she asked Corrine a few years ago if she could call her Mom. And of course, Corrine was honored, because she loved Sharon like she was her own.

"When are you two going to tie that knot?" Uncle Leroy said to Marcus.

"I'm ready right now," Marcus said to Uncle Leroy, and then smiled at Sharon.

"It must be you who's not ready," Uncle Leroy said to Sharon.

"Marriage is a big step," Sharon finally said.

"He seems like an awfully nice young man," Aunt Clara interrupted. "And handsome, too."

"You one of them career women, huh?" Uncle Leroy said, laughing.

"Yes," Sharon said, blushing. "But that doesn't have anything to do with it."

"You make some nice money, too, don't you?" Uncle Leroy continued.

"I do okay," Sharon said, laughing.

"See. I knew it. Career women don't need a man."

"That's not true, Uncle Leroy," Sharon said. "We need a man just like any other woman."

"Yeah, I bet," Uncle Leroy said, still snickering. "Tell me anything."

Everyone shook their heads and laughed again.

"Kevin, since your friend from work wasn't feeling too well, maybe you can take some of this food over to their house," Racquel said.

"I'll give him a call to see," Kevin said, and stretched out on the chaise.

"Where did Ashley and Nicholas sneak off to," Marcella said, realizing that they'd disappeared.

"Oh, they're probably upstairs playing that Nintendo," Racquel said.

"Did they ask you or Kevin?" Marcella asked.

"I don't think so, but I've told them before that they don't have to. Part of the reason why we bought it was so they'd have something to do when they stay over here, anyway."

Marcella had had just about enough of Racquel telling her what the children should and shouldn't have to do. Enough was enough, and she wasn't having any more of this backseat parenting. "Racquel, you know I don't like it when they do things without asking. It's not respectful, and I won't have it."

"Girl, leave those children alone. They're not bothering anybody."

"I didn't say they *were* bothering anybody, but when I tell them to do something, I expect them to do it. And they usually do, until they come around you," Marcella said angrily.

"And what is that supposed to mean?" Racquel said, becoming just as irritated.

"Exactly what I said. You let them get away with murder, and then they come home thinking I'm some sort of prison guard. And I'm sick of it. You know all the rules I've laid down for them, and it's your responsibility to enforce them, whether I'm around or not."

"No, my responsibility is to do whatever I feel like doing. Especially when it comes to anything going on in my own house," Racquel said, staring at Marcella.

"You know," Marcella said, laughing sarcastically and then standing up, "you're right. This is your house." Marcella gathered up her plate and cup.

"Marcella!" Corrine said. "I know you're not going to leave over something like this. You girls need to quit all of this arguing."

Racquel just looked at Marcella and rolled her eyes.

"No, Mom," Marcella said. "I'm sick of this. Those are *my* children, and I know what's best for them."

"I can tell you one thing, if they were mine, I'd raise

them a lot differently than the way you are," Racquel said nonchalantly.

"But they're not yours, Racquel. And from the way things look to me, you won't ever get the chance to raise your *own* children, anyway," Marcella said, walking toward the patio door.

"Marcella, that's enough," Corrine said, standing up. "You and Racquel are sisters, and you know this doesn't make any sense at all."

Racquel felt as though a bolt of lightning had struck her. How could Marcella have been so cruel? And in front of all these people. Everyone already knew the situation, so why did she have to put her down like that? This had gone too far, and Racquel wasn't about to let her humiliate her like that and get away with it. Sister or not. "At least I wasn't stupid enough to sit up there and have two babies by some no-good fool like Tyrone. Even the most ignorant person would have had better sense than that."

"You're just jealous. Always have been and always will be. Face it, Racquel. You're never going to have any children, and trying to criticize me isn't going to change that. And I'll tell you something else, you don't ever have to worry about Ashley and Nicholas coming over here anymore, either, because I'm through with you for good," Marcella said and stepped into the house.

Everyone looked on in amazement, but didn't say anything. Sharon finally stood up and went in behind Marcella, and Kevin pulled Racquel down on his lap, not knowing what to say, either.

"Lord, have mercy on these children," Aunt Clara said.

"Mm, mm, mm," Uncle Leroy said, shaking his head, obviously not believing what he was hearing. "I'm tellin' you the truth."

"Let me go in here and talk to Marcella," Corrine said, and walked into the house.

"Racquel, maybe you ought to go and talk to your sister, too," Aunt Clara said. "You girls know you weren't raised like that."

"I'm not apologizing for something I didn't do, Aunt Clara. She's the one that got upset about nothing."

"Baby, two wrongs don't make a right," Aunt Clara continued. "And I know you're not going to let something like this come between you."

Racquel didn't respond because she knew if she kept going back and forth with her aunt, it wasn't going to be long before she said something disrespectful. She loved her aunt, but she wanted her to mind her own business just as well.

Sharon's boyfriend, Marcus, was the only one left on the patio who wasn't a relative, and from the look on his face, it was obvious that he felt uncomfortable with all that had gone on. Racquel felt bad for him, and decided that she at least owed *him* an apology, if not anyone else. "Marcus, I hope you will accept my apology for what just happened."

"Oh, no, that's okay," he said, partially smiling.

"No," Racquel said. "It's not okay. You are a guest at our house, and you shouldn't have had to witness any of this confusion."

Marcus nodded his head, acknowledging what Racquel said.

When Marcella had finished scraping out her baking dishes, she went back out to the patio, said goodbye to everyone except Racquel, and then she and the children left. Sharon and Marcus followed right behind them. Then, Aunt Clara and Uncle Leroy fixed up their take-home plates, and went on their way an hour later. And when Corrine finished helping Racquel and Kevin with the dishes, she decided she'd better get home as well.

Kevin took a couple of plates over to his friend's house, and Racquel lay down on the chaise on the patio. Her whole body felt numb. Marcella had always meant everything in the world to her. She didn't know what she was going to do if Marcella was serious about keeping Ashley and Nicholas away from her. She loved them no differently than if they were her own. The cookout had started so perfectly and then ended in such turmoil. What she regretted the most was calling her sister stupid. And she never would have, if Marcella hadn't kept forcing that never-going-to-have-any-children business down her throat.

She breathed deeply, closed her eyes, and prayed— like she never had before—that all of this was nothing more than a very bad dream.

Chapter 9

Marcella was more excited than she'd ever been in her entire life, but at the same time she couldn't wait to find Messner Hall, the building her college-algebra course was located in. This was her first day at Covington Park University, and without a doubt, the hottest day of the year. When she'd watched the six A.M. weather report on television this morning, the temperature had already reached eighty-six, but now it had to be right around a hundred degrees. She'd worn her brown skort set, which had a sleeveless shirt, and still she was burning up. It felt like her whole body was on fire, and the humidity was so high that she felt like she was going to suffocate. And the reason why she couldn't wait for the month of August to be over with.

She strolled up the sidewalk slowly, skimming through the campus map that the admissions office had mailed to her two weeks ago, trying anxiously to figure out where she was. It would have been just as easy to ask one of the hundreds of students walking around from building to building, but she didn't want to sound like she was new. She was self-conscious as it was about being twenty-nine and just starting college for the first time, and didn't feel comfortable with asking some eighteen- or nineteen-year-old where her class was. She knew it was silly to think that way, but she just couldn't do it.

She stopped when she realized she was in a familiar area, and looked up at the building she was standing in front of. No wonder. It was the building she'd gone to four months ago for that counseling session with that witch-of-a-counselor, Mrs. Harrison. Just the thought of the woman pissed her off, and she was glad she'd finally gotten the chance to put her in her place.

When Marcella's ACT scores had arrived at the university, Mrs. Harrison had scheduled another appointment for her to come in and discuss her course load for the fall semester. Marcella's first thought was to tell her where she could go, and then reschedule with Mr. Dahl, the counselor who had given her the school catalog. But since she'd ranked well above the national test-score average, she decided instead to go and rub Miss High-and-Mighty's nose in it.

She could still remember that day so vividly. She'd gone into Mrs. Harrison's office, took a seat, and waited for her to start the conversation.

The woman had done just about everything imaginable to avoid any conversation relating to Marcella's test scores, and it was obvious that she would have rather died than compliment Marcella on her accomplishments. Finally, though, she didn't have a choice.

"I assume you received your letter of acceptance from

the university," Mrs. Harrison said, keeping her eyes on some irrelevant piece of paperwork on her desk.

"Yes, I did," Marcella said in an overly polite manner.

"So what we need to do now, is plan your schedule for the fall semester. You'll be taking mostly general studies, but those will also include a couple of the prerequisites that you'll need to enter the Business School."

Ha! Marcella had big news for this heifer. She'd already reviewed the requirements of the accounting program and had determined on her own which classes she'd be taking. "I've already figured all of that out, so that won't be necessary," Marcella said, feeling more tickled than she had in a long time.

"You do know that your financial-aid forms will have to be filed right away, since classes begin in less than two months," Mrs. Harrison said. And from the sarcastic look on her face, it was obvious that she thought she was telling Marcella something she didn't know. But Marcella had a surprise for her, the kind of surprise that was going to make her hair stand up on ends.

"Oh, didn't you know?" Marcella said, knowing good and well she didn't. "The partners of the accounting firm that I work for have decided to include part-time employees in their educational reimbursement program, which means they'll be paying-fifty percent of my tuition. And I've already applied and received approval from my bank for a student loan to cover the rest of my expenses," Marcella said with her head held high.

"Well, it looks to me like you wasted both my time and yours by coming in here," Mrs. Harrison said, rolling her eyes away from Marcella with an attitude.

Marcella had been waiting for the perfect opportunity to tell this wannabe bitch about herself, and the time was finally here. "To tell you the truth, I really don't give a damn about you or your precious little time.

And the next time you decide to talk about someone behind their back, you might want to close your door. Not halfway, like the first day I was in here, but all the way. I know you thought I was gone, but I wasn't. 'It really pisses me off when I see these welfare women getting over the way they do,' " Marcella said, mocking Mrs. Harrison's voice.

Mrs. Harrison gazed at her in total shock, and didn't open her mouth.

"Oh, yes, I heard every word you said. And what was that other comment you made about me thinking I was going to conquer the world? Well, I may not conquer the world, but I *will* graduate from this university with a four-year degree, pass the CPA exam, and become one of the best accountants Nicosia and Associates has ever had," she said, standing up from the chair. "Regardless of what you or anyone else has to say about it."

Mrs. Harrison continued looking at her with a damn-I'm-busted expression on her face, without speaking.

"What you need to do is learn some professionalism," Marcella continued. "And more than anything, you need to take a long look in the mirror, because somehow, someway, you seem to have gotten the idea that you're better than I am. And whether you want to accept it or not, *your* face is just as black as *mine*. And nothing is going to change that one bit. Not your little uppity attitude or that little desk you're sitting so proudly behind," Marcella said, pointing her finger at Mrs. Harrison.

"I refuse to be talked to in this manner, and I'd appreciate it if you would leave my office," Mrs. Harrison said, sounding nervous.

"What I should do, is report you to the president of this university," Marcella said, ignoring Mrs. Harrison's request for her to leave. "As a matter of fact, that's exactly what I'm going to do."

Mrs. Harrison looked at her with a scared-to-death look on her face.

Marcella wanted to burst out laughing. Especially, since she had no intention of reporting anything to anybody. But she still had to show this woman just who was running things when it came to her education. Had to let her know that she wasn't the naive little welfare girl she'd made her out to be. She was just as intelligent and professional as she was, and she wanted her to know it. Marcella stood up. "Well, it's been nice talking with you, Mrs. Harrison," she said with a smirk on her face. "You take care of yourself, okay?" she said sarcastically and left the office.

Marcella had conjured up at least a dozen more choice words for Mrs. Harrison, but like every other time she told someone off, she never thought of them until after the commotion was already over.

"Hey, can I help you find something?" a gentleman, standing to the right of her, asked.

Marcella jumped. She didn't realize she'd been standing there long enough for someone to recognize it. "Is it that obvious?" she asked, looking up from the map and feeling sort of awkward.

"Well, you've been standing in that same spot for almost five minutes, like you were in deep thought. And when someone does that on the first day of classes, it usually means they're lost," he said.

"Actually, I was kind of daydreaming, but I'm also having trouble finding Messner Hall," she said, slightly embarrassed.

"That's just two buildings down," he said, pointing.

She glanced in the direction of the building, and then back at him. She couldn't believe how handsome he was. Medium-brown complexion, wavy coal-black hair, beautiful dark-brown eyes, and lips to die for. The man was fine. "This is so embarrassing," she said, smiling. "Here I am searching for my class, and the building is practically sitting right in front of me."

"There's no reason to be embarrassed. This is a pretty large campus, and it's easy to get lost, until you learn your way around. But you'll know it like the back of your hand in a few weeks."

"I sure hope so."

"By the way, I'm Keith Howard," he said, extending his right hand to shake hers.

"Nice to meet you. I'm Marcella Jones."

"Nice to meet you, too. So, did you transfer here?"

She wished. She knew it was just a matter of time before she'd have to explain to someone that she was twenty-nine and just starting college for the first time. It was so humiliating. But then, the more she gazed at him, the more she realized he didn't look to be a day younger than twenty-six or twenty-seven himself. Maybe he'd started later than usual, as well. "No. As a matter of fact, this is my first time ever attending college. I worked full-time, but now I'm going to school full-time and working part-time until I graduate."

"What degree are you working toward?"

"Accounting. What about you?"

"This is my last year of law school. I started working right after I finished my bachelor's degree, but then I decided to apply to law school. I was twenty-eight when I finally enrolled."

Not only was the man fine, but he was intelligent, as well. Not to mention the fact that he wasn't as young as she thought, and had to be at least thirty. "That's wonderful."

"Well, I'd better let you get to class," he said, smiling at her.

"Okay. And thanks for pointing out my classroom building."

"No problem. Hey, maybe we can get together sometime, if you're not seeing anyone."

She couldn't believe what she was hearing, and she felt like grinning from ear to ear. "Maybe we can," she said in the voice of a schoolgirl.

"Why don't you write your number down, and I'll give you a call this evening."

She felt like screaming. No decent guy had shown any real interest in her in years, and she couldn't believe someone as well-educated and good-looking as Keith was asking for her phone number, let alone wanting to go out with her. She wrote her name and phone number down on one of her notebook pages, tore it out, and passed it to him.

"So, is there any special time I should call?" he asked, sliding the piece of paper inside his black leather book bag.

"Well, once I pick up my son and daughter from the baby-sitter, and get them dinner, I should be home around six." Usually she wouldn't be home until after nine, but this week she was only working from two to four in the afternoon.

As soon as she finished her sentence, the happy expression on his face went blank. "Oh, I didn't realize you had children. You don't look like the type."

Then what type did she look like? He'd seemed so interested, and now he was staring at her like he'd just seen a ghost. This was so typical. Guys were always doing this. They seemed so interested at first, but once she mentioned the fact that she had children, their whole attitude seemed to change. It was so amazing how quickly they could be turned on and off, without it even fazing them. She wasn't sure how to respond. A part of her wanted to set him straight, but another part of her was hoping that he didn't care that she had children, and that he was still going to call her. "Well, believe it or not, I have an eight- and an eleven-year-old. My youngest will be turning nine next month."

"Well, I'll give you a call around seven, if that's okay."

"That's fine," she said, glancing at her watch. "I'd better get to class."

"See ya later," he said, turning to walk in the opposite direction of where she was heading.

Whether he was going to call or not was a thousand-dollar question, and while she was hoping that he did, she didn't have any time right now to dwell on it, or be depressed about it. She walked inside the building and searched for her math class.

After picking up the children and stopping at McDonald's for dinner, Marcella was glad to make it home. She'd been running around ever since six o'clock that morning, and couldn't wait to undress so she could totally unwind. The children would be starting school again in a couple of weeks, which meant she'd have to rise no later than five A.M. to make sure they were dressed and had eaten before their school bus came to pick them up at seven-thirty. The summer wasn't so bad because she didn't have to iron their school clothes, or mess around with Ashley's hair. But during the school year, she had to monitor what they were putting on, making sure Ashley wasn't trying to dress too old for her age, and that Nicholas wasn't going out of the house mismatching. And although Nicholas always whined and sometimes cried when she told him to go to bed at night, he literally hated it when she woke him up in the morning. She had to call him two or three different times, and sometimes had to get downright upset with him before he finally started getting dressed. And that was the main reason she'd changed his bedtime from nine to eight-thirty. A half hour didn't seem like much as far as time was concerned, but it did make a world of difference when it came to waking Nicholas up. Ashley was more of a morning person, so Marcella never had too much of a problem with her. Plus, she was older, and it was only fair that she got to stay up at least a little later than her brother, anyway.

Marcella started toward her bedroom, and then turned when she noticed an argument heating up between Ashley and Nicholas. As usual, they'd drummed up another dispute over what they were going to watch on TV.

"I always watch the Cosby reruns, Nicholas, and you know it," Ashley said, jerking the remote control from her brother.

"Stop it, Ashley. I was the one who turned the TV on first," he said with tears welling up in his eyes.

"Look, you two. I'm not going to put up with this tonight. I've had a long day, and both of you are going to have to cut all of this out. Now, whose turn is it?" Marcella asked with irritation in her voice.

"It's Nicholas's, but they're going to celebrate their grandparents' anniversary tonight, and I want to see it. I told him I'd let him watch his little cartoon two nights in a row," Ashley said, rolling her eyes at him.

"If this is his night, you know what the rules are, Ashley," Marcella said, staring at her.

"Dog. That's why I wish we had another TV set. Everybody else does," Ashley said, throwing the remote control down on the sofa. She stood up and started to walk away, until Marcella stopped her.

"Go back and pick that remote control up and hand it to your brother," Marcella said angrily.

Ashley frowned, but obeyed her mother's orders.

"And I don't want to hear anything else from you about what we don't have. Your grandmother was nice enough to buy us that TV for Christmas, and you ought to be thankful, instead of complaining about it. I'm doing the best I can, and now I'm struggling to work, go to school, and take care of both of you, just so I can try to make things easier for all of us."

"But now you're only working part-time, so how are things going to be better?" Ashley asked, looking at her mother.

Marcella was stunned. This couldn't possibly be her daughter standing in front of her, because *her* daughter would have never spoken that way to her, or disrespected any adult in that manner. Especially when the adult was her own mother. "What did you say?" Marcella asked, squinting her eyes.

"Nothing," Ashley said, with her arms folded.

"Listen, Ashley. I don't know what's gotten into you, or where you got that little attitude from, but you'd better get rid of it. You're the child, and I'm the adult in this house. I don't owe you any explanations. And since your mouth is so smart, I don't want to see that phone up to your ear for the next seven days."

"But, Mom," Ashley begged.

"I mean what I said, Ashley."

"You already took Aunt Racquel away from us, so what difference does it make if you take the phone away, too," Ashley said boldly, without the slightest fear.

Ashley stormed into her room, and it was all Marcella could do not to snatch her up. For the first time since she'd been raising her children, she had to catch herself. Because if she didn't, someone was going to have to bail her out of jail tonight. Who did Ashley think she was talking to, anyway? If Marcella or Racquel had even thought about talking back to Corrine or their father that way, they would have found themselves getting up off the floor. And she knew her grandmother had never taken mess like that from her children, either, because Corrine and Aunt Clara had told them stories about it on more than one occasion. She just couldn't figure out what had gotten into Ashley. It wasn't like her at all, and something was wrong. She'd been warned over and over of what it was going to be like once Ashley turned eleven or twelve, and since she was turning eleven next month, Marcella was starting to see exactly what every other mother was talking about.

Nicholas gazed at her in silence, and it was obvious that he was just as shocked as his mother about the way Ashley had just shown out. Marcella turned and walked into her bedroom, shutting the door behind her.

She knew she had to nip this in the bud immediately, before it got too far out of hand. Marcella knew her mother was working, and usually when something as serious as this happened, she called Racquel. But since they still weren't speaking, she couldn't. She'd thought for sure this little spat between them would have blown over by now, but it hadn't. She'd never gone without talking to her sister more than two days before, and now it had been over five weeks. The thought of not having her sister to lean on made her feel sick. It was almost as if a part of her was missing, and she didn't know what to do about it. They'd had arguments before, but never to the extent of the one that had erupted on the Fourth of July. Marcella wished to God she could take back everything she'd said, because she knew how sensitive her sister was when it came to having a baby, and how seriously she took it. But, then, Racquel had said some nasty things to her, as well. As a matter of fact, she didn't know if she was ever going to forget what Racquel had said about her being ignorant enough to have two children by some fool like Tyrone. But still, they were sisters, and if they didn't have anyone else, they did have each other.

Corrine had been begging both of them to make the first move, but neither of them was willing to do it. She needed desperately to talk to someone. Anyone. It was times like these that she wished she had a husband, or at least a significant other who loved and cared about what happened to her. Someone to comfort her when she was feeling down, or going through trying times like she was now.

As she lay back across the bed, the phone rang. She looked at it and smiled when she realized it had to be Keith. He'd said he was going to call, but she'd thought for sure that her mention of two children had changed his mind completely.

She answered the phone. "Hello?" Marcella said, trying to sound as if she wasn't expecting anyone in particular.

"Marcella? It's me, Racquel."

"Hey," Marcella said, trying to disguise the fact that she was shocked that her sister was actually calling her, and disappointed that it wasn't Keith. But she knew she'd been fooling herself. She'd known the minute that funny expression crossed his face, but a part of her had still hoped he was going to call just the same.

"Don't you think this has gone far enough?" Racquel asked.

"It never should have happened in the first place, if you ask me," Marcella said, sitting up in the center of the bed.

"I said some things I didn't mean, and I'm sorry."

"We both said things we didn't mean, and I'm sorry, too. I've missed talking to you and seeing you so much, that it hurts."

"Girl, I've shed so many tears over all of this, till I don't know what to do, and I don't ever want to go through this with you ever again. It's silly."

"You're right. It is silly. We've both been going through some hard situations, and I think we, for whatever reason, took it out on each other."

"I'll tell you what," Racquel said, sniffling her nose, obviously crying. "I'm not going another day without seeing you, Ashley, or Nicholas. I'll see you in a little bit. Okay?" Racquel said.

"I'll see you, then," Marcella said and hung up the phone.

Marcella hated when Racquel cried, because it made her want to do the same thing. Except now she was feeling so many emotions that, instead of crying, she felt like screaming. Maybe changing her work schedule to part-time and going to school was a mistake. There was no doubt that they were going to have less household money, and starting next week, she'd be going to class full-time during the day, working four hours in the evening four nights a week, and then studying whenever she could in between. The partners at the firm had hired a new receptionist, and then more or less created a clerical position for her, so she could go to school and continue working for them simultaneously. And they'd already offered her a permanent position with them as an accountant as soon as she completed her degree. And while all that sounded good, it meant she would be spending hardly any time at all with the children. After begging and pleading with Tyrone, she'd finally talked him into picking Ashley and Nicholas up from the bus stop and then keeping them until she got off work. But with the way Ashley was acting, she was starting to wonder if this was the right time to be spending all of these hours away from her.

Marcella's head started to pound harder and harder as thoughts zipped through her mind, one right after another. If only she could make it through these next four years, everything would be perfect. She'd be able to give Ashley and Nicholas the lives they deserved, and she'd be the career woman she'd always dreamed of being. No, the more she thought about it, the more she realized she couldn't back out now. She had to make this work. And most importantly, what she had to do was double her determination.

Chapter 10

"**W**hy are you doing this, Tyrone?" Marcella said
with tears flowing down her face.

"Because I'm sick of you neglecting your children,
that's why," he said, yelling at her. "And if you want to
keep going to that little university, I suggest you find
another baby-sitter."

Another baby-sitter? How in the hell could Ashley
and Nicholas's own father call himself their baby-sitter?
Marcella had known all along that this agreement with
Tyrone wasn't going to work, but she'd been praying
hard all last semester that he would, for whatever reason,
do right by her just this once. He never had before, but
she'd hoped things would be different this time.

He watched the children faithfully from August to
December, but now that it was the end of January, and
she was two weeks into her second semester, he was
backing out of the deal that they'd agreed upon. Her

whole world was tumbling down around her, and she had no idea where to turn to next.

"Tyrone, you know I can't continue to go to school and work if somebody doesn't watch Ashley and Nicholas," she said, sounding as if her life was coming to an end.

"It's your responsibility to watch your own children, and I'm not doing it anymore. Here it is Saturday, and you've got my kids stuck up over at your mother's house. What kind of mother does some shit like that?"

"They're *your* children, too. And you have just as much responsibility when it comes to taking care of them as I do."

"You were the one who got pregnant," he said, pointing at her.

Marcella just stared at him. If she had a dollar for every time he'd made some stupid remark like that, she'd be filthy rich. This man was insane. Had to be, if he honestly believed she had spontaneously gotten pregnant two times without any help from him. He was trying to tear down everything she'd been trying to build up, and he made her sick. And for the first time, she wished she had a gun to blow his brains out. She hadn't felt pressure like this for as long as she could remember. Here she was trying to make something of herself so she could give her children a better life, and Tyrone was doing everything he could to sabotage all of her efforts.

"Can't you at least watch them until the end of the semester? Then I'll try to find someone else for this fall."

"I already told you. I'm not doing it. Not the rest of the semester. Not even next week. Hell, *I* don't have the privilege of going to school full-time, so why should you? I have to work my ass off every day, so I can pay that child support you keep whining about."

"Tyrone, please. You go to work for one reason, and one reason only: to wine that dizzy broad you call yourself messing around with. Yeah, I know all about her," Marcella said. Her tears were drying up, and she was starting to get pissed off.

"You don't know shit," he said, getting loud again.

"I don't know why you're trying to hide her from me, because you know I don't give a damn about who you sleep with, anyway."

Tyrone laughed sarcastically. "Yeah, right, Marcella. If you don't care, then why are you bringing my personal life up in the first place? Huh? Why is that?"

"So long as you're paying my child support, you can screw whoever you want to."

"Whatever, Marcella," he said, moving closer to the front door.

"So, you're not going to keep them?" she asked for the last time.

"I'll tell you what. If you reduce the child support to thirty dollars a week, maybe I'll think about it."

Was this jackass crazy? Or just plain brainless? She felt her blood pressure rising fast and furious, and she wasn't two steps from tearing into him. Physically. "Tyrone, get the fuck out! Now!" she said, walking toward him.

"That little university has turned you into a fool. But you'd better learn some sense when you're around me, because I'm not playing with you. Tryin' to put somebody out. Girl, you'd better wake up before I turn that dreamworld of yours into a nightmare."

"Fine. You just stay right where you are," she said calmly, and then walked as quickly as she could toward Nicholas's bedroom. She slid open his closet door and searched madly for his baseball bat until she found it. Tyrone had practically gotten away with disrespecting her mother one year ago, but now it was high time that he paid for that, and all the other shit he had done and said to her, as well.

She reentered the living room. "Now, what was that you were saying?"

"You crazy bitch," Tyrone said, struggling to open the door without taking his eyes off of her.

"Yeah, I am crazy, thanks to your no-good ass," she said, moving closer to where he was trying desperately to exit the apartment. He finally succeeded.

Marcella stood in front of the door in a daze, and she felt like she couldn't breathe. When was this situation with Tyrone going to end? Day after day, week after week, year after year, she'd been having to put up with this idiotic mess, and her patience was wearing thinner as time went on. She wasn't sure how much more she could take from him.

When she realized she was holding Nicholas's bat in her hand, she dropped it to the floor. She couldn't believe what she'd just done. She'd actually planned to strike Tyrone across his head. She'd even imagined how the brood would gush out all over her floor. This wasn't like her, and the whole idea of it all frightened her to no end. He brought out the worst in her, and now she was resorting to violence. Something had to be done before she ended up killing him.

And as much as she hated to admit it, she despised the fact that he was dating someone. Usually, it never mattered to her, because most of his women were in one day, and out the other. But this Priscilla had been hanging around for over four months, according to Nicholas and Ashley. Marcella didn't want Tyrone, but she couldn't help but wish she had someone to love her just the same. Someone who wanted to be with her *for her*. Someone who didn't have the slightest problem with the fact that she had two kids. It wasn't fair that Tyrone could get dressed and go out with whomever he wanted, whenever he wanted, while she had to stay home like some ninety-year-old woman, who was waiting patiently to perish. Why did it always have to be this way, when a woman had children by a man she'd divorced or had never been married to? She'd met four different guys since she started the university, beginning with that Keith on the first day of classes, and while they all seemed interested at first, their whole attitude changed when they found out she had two children. It was almost like they saw them as excess baggage. Which was strange because most women didn't seem to care in the least when they found out a guy had children by some other woman. But then, it was probably because they knew there would only be a few select times when they would actually have to have contact with them. Especially, since most men didn't have custody of their children, and didn't want it. It was sick. She knew all men weren't like that, but Tyrone had given her the lesson of a lifetime. And while she hated herself for thinking it, she couldn't help but wonder how her life would have turned out, if she hadn't had Ashley and Nicholas at all. She'd probably have a master's degree by now, and there was a good chance she'd be living in the same neighborhood as Sharon. The mere thought of it all was depressing.

What in the world was she going to do about the children? Her classes stretched daily from eight to noon, and she needed to study and complete her homework in the afternoon. And quitting her job wasn't even an option, because she needed the money so desperately. Not to mention the fact that they were paying a big portion of her tuition. If she had to drop out of school, it was going to kill her, but right now she didn't see where she had any other choice.

Marcella picked up the bat and carried it back to Nicholas's closet, where she'd found it, and went into her bedroom. A pastel-blue fitted sheet was covering the two ends of the mattress at the head of the bed, the way she'd left them when she'd heard Tyrone knocking at the door. She pulled the rest of the sheet across the bed, spread the top sheet across it, and tucked it under at the foot of the bed. She pulled on the pillowcases and then placed the burgundy comforter on top.

After vacuuming her carpet and dusting her dresser, she made her way into Ashley's room. When she arrived, she shook her head in disgust. She'd told that girl to clean her room before going over to her Granny's, but from the looks of it, she'd totally ignored her. Her bed was half straightened, the pair of jeans and T-shirt she'd worn the day before were lying on the floor, and her dresser looked like a hurricane had swooped right through it. Ashley knew better than this, and even when she was just a little thing, Marcella had never had a problem with her cleaning up like she was told. And most of the time, she didn't even need telling. Ashley simply did it on her own.

But now she'd become mouthy, irritable, and hard-headed. Marcella couldn't believe her grades were still intact. Ashley was still the same straight-A student she'd always been. But it was just that little attitude of hers. And she was so withdrawn. She spent most of her time closed up in her bedroom, and when she did decide to come out to the living room to watch TV, she was silent; acting as if no one was in the room except her. Marcella had tried being patient with her, but it wasn't going to be long before she put her foot down. All the way down. Ashley needed to be reminded who was boss, who was paying the bills, and more than anything else, who was still young enough to get her little behind whipped.

Marcella picked up Ashley's clothing and threw them in the hallway, so she could take them to the Laundromat later in the afternoon. She pulled Ashley's bedcovers until there were no wrinkles showing, and walked over to her white mirrored dresser. The more she gazed at the mess, the more disgusted she became. She had a mind to toss it all in the garbage, but figured that might be going too far. She pulled open the top right drawer and shook her head in disagreement again. This was junkier than the top of the dresser, and was filthier than anything she'd ever seen. She rustled through it to see what all the different papers were, and saw that most of it was old homework assignments that had been graded, and a few young-adult paperback books. As she continued rummaging through the drawer, she saw a loose sanitary napkin, and wondered where the box was. Now, what was she going to do with this? It was too dusty to use, so what was the point in keeping it? The whole idea of her starting her menstrual cycle at the ripe old age of eleven still gave Marcella the creeps. She'd started hers at twelve, but it still didn't seem right knowing her baby was actually having a period.

She shut the top drawer, and pulled open the one just below it. Marcella couldn't believe it, her underwear was actually folded. She'd been meaning to check and see if she needed to buy Ashley a few more pairs of panties, so she counted them. When she came to the bottom of the pile, she noticed a fuchsia notebook and pulled it out. There was no label on it, but from the looks of it, it was one of the ones she'd bought for school. When she opened the inside cover, she saw the words "My Diary, 1994" written in blue ink. Marcella lowered her eyebrows in total confusion. Ashley didn't seem like the type of girl who wrote her thoughts down on paper, but maybe that's why she no longer confided in Marcella the way she used to. This diary thing was a huge surprise, and Marcella couldn't help but wonder what was in it. She knew it was wrong, but since she'd come across it, she couldn't resist taking at least a small peek. She turned to the first page, and saw that it was dated January 1, which meant she'd just started writing in it three weeks ago.

Marcella skimmed through the first couple of weeks and laughed at most of it, because some of the things she'd written were so cute. But when she finished reading the entry for the fifteenth, which took up three whole pages, she covered her mouth with her right hand and sat down on the edge of the bed. There had to be some mistake. She read the entry again:

Today is Saturday, and as usual, Mom made us clean up again. I'm so sick of her telling me what to do. She can't even take care of her own life, and still she controls everything I do. That's why when she went to the grocery store this morning, I let Jason in. Mom can't stand him, but as soon as she left, he knocked on the door and I let him in. Nicholas said he was going to tell, but I know he won't, because I promised him he could have control of the TV for a whole week. So, when Jason came in, Nicholas was fine with it. Jason has been wanting to come over for a long time, but of course, with Mom breathing down my neck all the time, he couldn't. But lately she's been leaving us alone for a couple of hours to go to the grocery store on Saturday, so I told Jason yesterday to watch out of his window around ten, because I knew she'd be leaving around that time, and that's what he did. It was so much fun when he got here. He said he really liked me a lot, but that he would fall in

*love with me if I did something for him. At first he just
kept smiling, and then he finally said, it's something
that will make him feel good. He said that boys his age
(he's 13) had special needs. And that he was almost a
grown man. He said that he'd been liking me since last
summer, but he thought I was just a little girl. But he
said if I did this one thing for him, then he would know
I wasn't a little girl at all. He'd know for sure I was a
real woman. Finally, he pulled his pants down and told
me to get on my knees in front of him. At first I was
scared, but he kept saying how fine I was, and he kept
smiling at me. I'm in love with him, I just know it.
Finally, he told me that he wasn't like most guys who
went around making girls do stuff that would get them
pregnant. He said he cared about me too much to do
that. He told me to close my eyes and open my mouth,
and then he put his thing inside of it. I didn't know
what to do, so I just closed my lips around it. He told
me to suck it, so I did. But then this yucky white stuff
came out, and he made these really funny noises. I almost
choked on it, and I spit most of it out on the floor. I
hope he didn't think I was acting childish. But I must
have done it right, because he asked me to go with him,
and I said yes. I can't wait to see him again.*

Marcella quickly turned to the next Saturday, to see
what else Little-Miss-Fast-Ass had written, but that was
today's date. "Wait a minute," Marcella thought. "That
means this just happened one week ago." A feeling of
anger seized her every emotion, and she couldn't wait
until that little Ashley got home. Better yet, she was
going over to Corrine's to get her little butt, right now.
She'd leave Nicholas and bring Ashley back home with
her. And she was going to kill that little mannish-tail
Jason. And as much as she despised Tyrone, she knew

he'd kill that boy, too, if he found out about it. But then he'd also blame her for letting it happen.

Marcella dropped the notebook down on Ashley's bell, stormed out of the bedroom, threw on her coat, gloves, and boots, and headed out the front floor. She had to take care of this Jason business right now.

"Mom, why did Nicholas get to stay at Granny's?" Ashley asked as Marcella pulled out of Corrine's driveway.

Marcella didn't say anything.

"Mom," Ashley called out, trying terribly to get her mother's attention.

Marcella continued driving without turning to look at her even once, because she was afraid of what might happen if she did. The last thing she wanted to do was slap the crap out of her own daughter. She'd tried to calm herself down on the way over, so her mother wouldn't figure out that something was wrong. But now that it was just the two of them in the car, her anger was slowly starting to escalate all over again. She wasn't two inches from exploding.

"Mom, what's wrong with you?" Ashley asked.

Marcella glanced at her and then looked back at the road.

Ashley saw a look on her mother's face, like she'd never seen before, and decided that it was time for her to keep her mouth shut.

Marcella parked the car, opened the car door, stepped out of it, and then slammed it as hard as she could. Ashley stepped out on the passenger side in slow motion. As soon as they were in the house, Marcella removed her outer garments, and Ashley did the same. When Marcella saw that Ashley had taken off the last boot, she grabbed her by her wrist and dragged her into her bedroom.

"Explain this, Ashley," Marcella said, forcing the notebook into her daughter's hand.

"What?" Ashley said, looking down at the notebook.

"Girl, don't play dumb with me," Marcella said, yelling.

"It's just some notes, Mom, that's all," Ashley said in a shaky voice.

More than anything, Marcella hated to be lied to. This girl thought she was playing games, and she had to let her know how serious she was. "Notes? You call sticking your head between some little boy's legs, just some notes? Ashley, do you think I'm stupid?"

Ashley stared at her, scared to death, wondering if she should answer her, make a comment, or say something. But she decided to keep quiet.

"Did you let that little boy in here last week when I was gone, or not?"

Ashley wanted to lie. And bad. But she knew she was going to get the whipping and punishment of a lifetime if she did. She was going to get both of those anyway, but somehow if she lied, she hated to even think what would happen then. "Yes, Mom," she said, already crying her eyes out. "I'm sorry, Mom." She reached out to her mother to hug her.

"Don't touch me, Ashley," Marcella said, moving away from her. "You mean to tell me that you let that little ghetto boy in here, after I told you specifically not to open the door for anyone when I'm gone. And then you took him into your bedroom, left Nicholas all by himself, and then let him sweet-talk you into sucking his little mannish dick? Is that what you're telling me?"

As soon as the word "dick" crossed her lips, Marcella regretted it. She was pissed off as hell, but she'd always made sure not to use those type of words around either one of her children. Her parents hadn't talked that way in front of her and Racquel, and she had the same respect for her own children. But she was too upset right now to be concerned with any of that. And what Ashley had done to that boy was far worse than her using some trashy word.

"Mom, I didn't mean it."

"How could you *not* have meant it? You wrote right in there about how you'd told him the day before to be on the lookout around ten o'clock? Oh, yeah, you meant to do what you did. What you didn't mean was to get caught," Marcella said, making gestures with her right hand.

Ashley's face was flooded with water, and she was scared to move out of her tracks. With the rage on her mother's face, she didn't dare say anything.

Marcella took a deep breath and tried to get control of the situation. She was too angry to take a belt to Ashley, and decided against it. Like her grandmother used to say, she was "putting this one up on the shelf for later" because little Miss Thing wasn't getting away with this.

"I don't want you to even answer or use that phone until school is out in June. And as far as any sleep-overs at your aunt Racquel and uncle Kevin's go, you can forget that, too. For the next four and a half months, I want you to go to school, come home, do your homework, and go to bed. Do you hear me?"

"But Mom, I didn't mean it," Ashley said with her chest elevating up and down, crying harder and harder.

"I've said what I have to say, and I don't want to hear another word about it," Marcella said, walking toward Ashley's bedroom door.

Ashley fell on her bed, screaming and boo-hooing as

loud as she could, and Marcella was starting to become annoyed.

"Look, Ashley. I want you to cut out all that noise, and I mean cut it out right now, before I give you something to cry about," Marcella said.

The crying stopped instantly.

"I can't believe you, Ashley. For as long as I can remember, you've never given me any reason to be anything except proud of you. So what's wrong with you now? Why are you acting like this? You've been talking back, strolling around here with an attitude practically every day, and now this thing with that Jason. What's wrong with you? I've always been so proud of both you and Nicholas."

Ashley sat up on the side of the bed, and walked toward her mother. "I'm so ... sorry ... Mom," she said with her voice trembling. They hugged, and now tears were falling down Marcella's face.

"Baby, I know Mom hasn't been able to spend a lot of time with you since I started school, but I promise you, things will get better. I have to go to school, so I can get a better job. And when I get a better job, I'll be able to take care of you and your brother a lot better than I have been. And I have to work now, because we need to pay bills and buy food. Don't you understand that, honey? I know it's hard, but we can get through this. You're a big girl now, and sometimes I'm going to need you to look out for Nicholas. And when I ask you to do that for a couple of hours, I need to know that I can trust you. Okay?"

Ashley shook her head yes, without moving it away from her mother's chest.

"You really hurt me, Ashley, and I don't want you doing anything like that ever again. Regardless of what that boy says, all he wants to do is use you. When you're old enough to date, you'll find someone who really cares about you, but right now, you're too young to even be thinking about being with some boy. The next thing he'll be doing is trying to get you to go all the way," Marcella said, lifting her daughter's chin. "Remember what we talked about the day you started your period? You have your whole life ahead of you, and the last thing you want is to end up pregnant. You're still a baby yourself. And with AIDS spreading around like it is, you have to be even more careful. And you can still get it by doing what you did to Jason. Oral sex is just as dangerous as regular sex."

Marcella hugged Ashley tight. "What I want you to do now is think about what you did, and then I want you to straighten up this room. Then when I'm finished with cleaning up the rest of the apartment, we'll go back over to your granny's for dinner."

Marcella closed Ashley's bedroom door, and closed her eyes. This was all her fault. If she hadn't subjected Ashley to this run-down, low income, thug infested apartment complex, she never would have come in contact with Jason or anyone like him. And while Ashley was wrong for disobeying her in the first place, she was young, dumb, and naive like most girls her age. Wanting to feel like she belonged to the "in" crowd. Wanting to know what it felt like to be liked by some little boy. Marcella didn't know what she was going to do. This boy's mother seemed like the type who didn't care about anything or anybody, and if she went over there to confront her about her son, she'd probably cuss Marcella out like some sailor. If she told Tyrone, he'd rush right over to take care of the situation, but he'd probably take the whole thing too far, and would end up in jail instead. If she told her mother, she'd be worried sick, and would definitely tell Racquel and Kevin. And Marcella couldn't have that. Racquel was already convinced that she wasn't raising her children the way she should, and this disaster right here would be all the proof she needed. She had to talk to someone, though. And, like when every other major tragedy took place, that someone was Sharon.

Chapter 11

Marcella pulled on the jet-black pantyhose as carefully as she could, and prayed that she wouldn't tear a run in these, like she had with the previous pair just a few minutes ago. This was the last pair she had, and she had to make them work. It was already 9:30 A.M., and Sharon had phoned earlier saying she'd be by to pick them up around ten o'clock. Church services started at 10:45, and they needed at least fifteen minutes of driving time.

She slipped on a black knit ankle-length dress and then doubled back both of her arms to zip it. Then she slipped on her black pumps and put on her gold-toned hoop earrings. She wondered how far Ashley and Nicholas had gotten, and decided to check on them.

Ashley was completely dressed and was sitting in the living room flipping through the TV channels when Marcella came out of her bedroom. The TV was one of the few forms of entertainment that hadn't been included in her punishment, and she looked to be enjoying it. Nicholas was as slow as a hundred-year-old man whenever he did anything, so Marcella always had to help him along.

She walked into his room and saw him sitting on his bed with nothing except his dress pants on. He was flipping the pages of some *Star Trek* book Sharon had purchased for him a couple of weeks ago. It was filled mostly with pictures, and even though he'd already thumbed through the pages at least twenty times, he still looked just as interested as the first time. Sharon was always buying him and Ashley things like that. Between Corrine, Racquel, and Sharon, the children were spoiled rotten.

"Nicholas, why aren't you dressed yet?" Marcella said, picking up his navy-blue turtleneck sweater. "Your aunt Sharon is going to be here any minute."

"Okay, Mom," he said, still turning the pages of his book.

"Nicholas," she said with more authority than before.

He dropped the book down, stood at attention, and smiled at her. He knew she wasn't playing, but it was still funny to him.

She couldn't help but smile back at him. "Boy, you'd better get this shirt on, and put on your dress shoes."

"I wanna wear my boots," he said in a semibegging voice.

"Not today. There's not that much snow out there, and the sidewalks and the streets are clear."

"Aw, Mom. I wore them yesterday, and you didn't mind."

"That was yesterday, and this is today. Now put them on," she said, pulling his navy-blue blazer from his closet.

He obeyed her, but he wasn't happy about it.

After Marcella handed him the blazer, he pulled it on, and went out to the living room to sit with Ashley. Marcella knew there was going to be an argument about the television, so she intervened before it even got started.

"I don't want to hear anything about who's watching what on that television. Ashley was watching it first, Nicholas, so don't start with her."

"But, Mom, Ashley said I could have control of the TV for a whole week, if I didn't . . . ," he said and then cut the rest of his sentence off. He looked at his big sister timidly.

Ashley stared at him with anger. Even though her mother had already found out about her deep, dark secret, it was obvious that Ashley still didn't want him bringing it up.

He kept his mouth shut and looked straight ahead at the TV.

Marcella had forgotten all about the deal Ashley had made with Nicholas, if he didn't tell, but now that she'd been reminded of it, she was going to make her stick to it. She should have never put her little brother in that kind of situation anyway.

"Ashley, if you made some deal with Nicholas, then give him the remote control."

Ashley looked at her mother and then at Nicholas. "Here," she said, frowning at him.

Nicholas licked his tongue out and smiled at her. Normally, Marcella would have scolded him about that sort of gesture, but Ashley deserved what she was getting.

Yesterday she had cried herself to sleep and stayed in her room for the rest of the evening. It was obvious that she felt terrible about what she'd done, but she seemed more embarrassed than anything else. Instead of the two of them going back over to Corrine's for dinner, Corrine picked up a pizza, and then she and Nicholas came back to the apartment. Ashley finally dragged out to the kitchen after about an hour, but she couldn't look her grandmother in the face. Corrine knew something had gone on, but never said anything. Marcella knew it was just a matter of time before she started asking questions, though, and she'd either have to tell the truth or have some well-concocted lie ready. She didn't like lying to her mother, but she just didn't see how she could confide in her about what Ashley had done. She just couldn't. She'd played it in her head over and over and over again all last night, and she didn't see how anyone was going to understand any of this. Although, when she'd phoned Sharon and told her the situation, she'd understood, and had given her nothing except moral support. But she was different from the rest of them. Somehow, someway, they'd find a way to blame her for what happened, and she just couldn't take that chance.

As Marcella finger-positioned her curls, which were hanging loosely down the sides of her face, she heard a knock at the door. "Ashley, that's probably your aunt Sharon, but ask who it is first," Marcella yelled out to the living room.

She heard Ashley ask who it was, and then open the door.

Marcella walked out to greet Sharon. "Hey, girl. You're looking awfully nice this Sunday morning."

"So do you," Sharon said, dropping her purse down in the chair next to the sofa.

It was nice to know that Sharon always tried to make her feel good.

"So, how are my favorite niece and nephew doing?" Sharon asked the children.

"Fine," Ashley said with a look of embarrassment on her face.

Nicholas was so glued to the television set, that he hadn't even heard the question.

"Boy, didn't you hear Aunt Sharon ask you how you were doing?" Ashley said, pushing him on the shoulder. "You are so rude."

"What?" he said, coming out of a daze trying to figure out what he had missed.

Sharon laughed. "How are you, Mr. Nicholas?"

"I'm fine," he said, smiling, and then switched his attention back to the cartoon.

Sharon loved Ashley and Nicholas like they really were her niece and nephew, because Marcella's family was the closest thing she had to blood relatives. And that was the reason she helped Marcella out as much as she could, whenever she could.

"Girl, we've still got another twenty to thirty minutes, so come on in my room for a few minutes."

Sharon turned and strutted into the bedroom.

Marcella shut the door behind her and sat down on the bed. Sharon sat down on the other side facing her.

"So, how have things been with Ashley since I talked to you last night?"

"She's been pretty quiet, and she was scared to death that I was going to tell her granny."

"I'm not surprised, because she had a funny look on her face when I spoke to her a few minutes ago. She'll get through this, and I doubt that she'll even think about doing anything like that again."

"Girl, I hope so, because I can't have this. I mean, she's only eleven years old. And I don't know what that little no-good boy was thinking."

"Have you thought any more about talking to his mother?"

"Not really. It was like I told you last night, they're a rough-natured family, and I don't know if I even want to confront them about any of this."

"Yeah, you do have to be careful. You never know about these thirteen-year-old boys from this generation. When we were growing up, everybody's parents in the neighborhood were your parents, but now little thugs like him are liable to blow your head off, just for telling on him. You just don't know anymore," Sharon said, crossing her legs.

"That's what I'm talking about. I am going to tell him to stay away from Ashley, though. And we just have to hope and pray that he listens," Marcella said, folding her arms into her stomach.

"Girl, what about Tyrone? Have you told him?"

"There's no way in the world I would tell him anything about this. First, he'd jump all over me and tell me how terrible of a mother I am, and then he'd be after that boy. It's just not worth it. I mean, if it gets out of hand, and I can't stop Jason from bothering Ashley, then I won't have a choice but to tell him. But other than that, I'm not saying anything to him."

"I guess I can understand that. So, has he been staying on time with his child support?"

"For some strange reason, he has. But get this," Marcella said, anxious to fill Sharon in. "We had one of our usual falling-outs yesterday, and he had the audacity to say he's not baby-sitting the children anymore in the evenings, but that he might reconsider it, if I let him reduce the child support to thirty dollars a week. Can you believe that?"

"I know he didn't!" Sharon said in amazement.

"Oh, yes, he did."

"Thirty dollars? He's only paying sixty now, isn't he?"

"Yeah, and he's barely doing that. He's really starting

to get on my nerves, and I mean bad. I almost cracked his head with a baseball bat yesterday."

"You what?" Sharon said, laughing. "It's not funny, but I can't help it. And I can't believe you didn't tell me about that last night."

Marcella laughed with her. "Girl, I was so wound up about this thing with Ashley, that I didn't even think about it. And to tell you the truth, I still can't believe I did that."

"You used to be the scariest person I knew when we were in high school."

"Girl, I know, but my whole attitude is changing. I'm under so much pressure, that sometimes I feel like I'm going to explode. It's a wonder I haven't cracked up or something."

"What did he do to get you so upset?" Sharon said, stroking the back of her hair.

"I told him to get out after he made that comment about the child support, and he started talkin' some crap about the university turning me into a fool, and that he wasn't playing with me. So, I politely went into Nicholas's room and found his baseball bat."

"Did he leave?"

"What do you think? Girl, you should have seen him struggling to get out the door. I don't think he thought I had it in me. And to be quite honest, I didn't, either."

Sharon cracked up laughing again, and so did Marcella.

"I know I'm laughing, but I'm telling you," Sharon said on a more serious note. "Tyrone isn't worth it. And you need to keep your distance from that fool."

"How can I do that, when he's the father of my two children? There's just no way of getting around it. And I don't know what I'm going to do next week for a baby-sitter."

"Well, what time does your mother get off work?"

"She works second shift."

"Oh, yeah. That's right," Sharon said in disappointment. "Well, I can watch them for you a couple nights a week, and I know Racquel will, too. So, all we have to do is find someone to keep them from the time they get out of school to when we get off work."

"I think their school has an aftercare program, but even if they do, I can't afford to add another bill to our budget. It's stretched to the limit as it is."

"Don't worry about it, we'll work this out, even if it means that I have to pay for it myself. So, if you've been thinking about quitting school, you can just forget that,' Sharon said, raising her eyebrows.

"You can't be doing that. You have your own bills and your own life to live," Marcella said, feeling like a failure.

"Like I said, we'll work this out," Sharon said, ignoring her. "We'll all get together after church, so we can figure out what to do."

Marcella gazed at her in silence because she knew if she spoke one word, or so much as blinked, tears would fall down her face.

Sharon took notice, moved closer to her and hugged her. "Don't worry about it. Everything will work out fine. I promise."

"I don't know what I would do without you. Sometimes you understand me better than my own family does," Marcella said, wiping her face with her hands.

"I don't know about that, but I do know that I would rather die than see you and those little ones in there suffering unnecessarily. It's not like I'm rich or anything, but I can afford to help you from time to time when you need me to."

"But it seems like you're always doing things for me,

even though I'm never in a position to do anything for you."

"Marcella. You're my best friend, you love me like a sister, and that's all the payback I need from you."

Marcella sighed deeply. "Well, all I know is that these next three-and-a-half years are going to be rough, and I'm going to need you more than ever when it comes to emotional support, if nothing else."

"My grandmother used to say that anything worth having takes a lot of hard work, and then some. And she was right. When this is all over, you'll look back on it and laugh. Just wait and see."

Marcella stood up and walked in front of the mirror. "My face is a mess."

"Better fix it," Sharon said, laughing. "You never know who you might meet at church."

"I doubt that very seriously," Marcella said, walking out of the room and into the bathroom. "I really doubt it."

"Hey, Ashley," Racquel said, stepping inside the church door. "Hey, Nick."

"Aunt Racquel," Nicholas said, turning toward his aunt and hugging her. "Hey, Uncle Kevin," he said, hugging him, as well.

"Hi," Ashley said, barely looking at Kevin or Racquel.

Kevin spoke back to her, while Racquel was trying to figure out what was wrong with her.

"What's with that gloomy look on your face, sweetheart?" Racquel asked Ashley.

"Nothing," she said, lying.

"Well, then, put a smile on that pretty face," Racquel said, rubbing her finger softly under Ashley's chin. Racquel knew something wasn't quite right, though, and she couldn't wait to find out from Marcella what the problem was.

Corrine entered the church shortly after Racquel and Kevin, and all of the adults hugged each other and then proceeded toward the church vestibule, where two ushers were passing out the weekly church bulletins and envelopes for tithes and offerings. They each took the appropriate envelope, walked single file into the church, and sat down in the fifth row on the left-hand side of the church. Corrine, Marcella, Sharon, Racquel, Ashley, Nicholas, and Kevin. In that order. There were so many of them, they almost took up the entire pew.

Westside Missionary Baptist Church wasn't the largest church in the Chicago area, but it held about five hundred members if you included the balcony and the choir stand. And since they'd added on the educational center last year, the church looked a lot bigger and much more contemporary than it used to.

When Deacon James stood up to call the church to worship, Racquel looked at her watch, and saw that it was 10:45. Good, she thought. They were actually starting on time for a change. Before Deacon Thurgood passed away, he started devotion like clockwork, but ever since Deacon James had taken charge, they'd been starting anywhere between ten and fifteen minutes late. Which didn't make any sense to Racquel, but who was she to complain.

After the mass choir walked in two by two and spread throughout the choir stand, Deacon James and four other deacons stood up and faced the congregation.

"I love the Lord, He heard my cry," Deacon James sang as loud as he could without the use of a microphone, and it was sort of like follow the leader. Deacon James sang the words of each verse at normal speed, but when the congregation joined in, they sang the words in sort of a dragged-out way. When the hymn was finished, the second deacon read a scripture from St. John; the third spoke a meditational thought; and the fourth led the congregation in prayer.

By the time they'd finished the Lord's Prayer, morning hymn, and responsive reading, Nicholas was fidgeting back and forth in his seat, and Ashley's head started bobbing up and down like she was about to fall asleep. Marcella took notice to it, and gave both of them "the look," and they immediately turned their undivided attention toward the choir members, who were preparing to sing their first selection of the morning.

"If anybody asks you . . . where I am going . . . where I am going . . . soon. I'm going up a yonder . . . I'm going up a yonder . . . I'm going up a yonder . . . to be with my Lord," the choir sang, swaying from side to side and clapping in sync with the rhythm of the music, which was a lot more contemporary than when the youth choir used to sing it fifteen years ago.

When the song ended, the announcement clerk stood and walked into the pulpit to the right of the minister's podium, and asked all visitors to stand, to state their name and what church they were from, and then took up ten more minutes reading every announcement under the sun. By now, Racquel was starting to get a little restless herself. She'd been born and raised Baptist, and still Racquel never understood why the service always had to be prolonged. Some of the information was important, but a lot of it was unnecessary. They were going to have to sit for another ten minutes listening to Pastor Morgan put on the guilt trip for church members who didn't pay their tithes. "You're robbing God, when you don't pay your tithes," he would say. "The Bible says ten percent, and it don't mean take-home pay, either. God wants his off the top, before Uncle Sam or anyone else gets their hands on it."

Racquel had heard him beg the congregation so many times, until she didn't pay much attention to it anymore. And whether it was right or wrong, she just hadn't been moved enough to pay out ten percent of her gross earnings. And she felt even more strongly about it whenever she saw Pastor Morgan cruising around town in that brand-new Lexus. And those flashy rings he had on every finger didn't help much, either. And his wife, "the first lady," made it clear early on that she wasn't about to step inside of Westside Missionary Baptist Church, unless her suit, hat, purse, and shoes were all classily color coordinated.

Racquel just couldn't see it, but her mother thought differently about the subject. She paid her tithes every Sunday, and even made up for the Sundays that she missed if she couldn't attend service for some reason or another. Her mother was convinced that people were blessed tenfold whenever they gave from their hearts. And maybe Racquel would have felt that way, too, if she thought tithing would give her the baby she'd been trying so hard to have. And maybe someday she *would* change her whole way of thinking, but from the way things were going, it definitely wasn't going to be today.

Racquel scanned the congregation as she walked to the front of the church and placed her offering in one of the collection plates. There must have been at least ten women to every man. For the life of her, she couldn't figure out why more men didn't come to church. Maybe they were afraid to, or thought it might lessen their manhood somehow. Racquel didn't know, but she couldn't help but wonder about it.

After Pastor Morgan took his text, preached the first part of his sermon, and asked for a couple of Amens, he changed gears, and the organist played the music the same as he did for the choir when they were singing. Pastor Morgan took the microphone and strutted down the aisle. Then he went back toward the pulpit, but before he stepped up to it, he leaped up on the front pew, preaching as hard as he could.

Ashley and Nicholas jumped and looked around when the woman behind them leaped out of her seat and started shouting and dancing in place. They'd seen this time after time, but they still seemed just as frightened as they did the first time they'd witnessed someone being filled with the Holy Ghost. It was just too intense and too complex for them to understand, Racquel guessed.

When Pastor Morgan finished the benediction, Corrine, Kevin, Ashley, and Nicholas went to shake his hand. Racquel, Sharon, and Marcella stood in the middle aisle, close to where they'd been sitting, and discussed where they were all going to eat for dinner.

Marcella looked toward the back of the church and noticed an extremely handsome-looking man staring at her. And he was smiling. She turned her head back toward Racquel and Sharon, pretending to take part in their conversation, but it wasn't long before she looked again to see if Mr. Fine was still standing there. But he wasn't. Instead, he was making his way up the aisle.

"Marcella, right?" he said, stopping in front of her.

"Yes. Do I know you?" she asked, trying to determine how he knew her name.

"No, but I play ball at the 'Y' with your brother-in-law, Kevin, from time to time, plus I've seen you a few times here at church. I'm Darryl Johnson."

Marcella couldn't believe Kevin had put her on the spot like this without warning her, and she was going to kill Racquel if she'd been aware of this surprise meeting all along and had purposely kept it from her. If she had known she was meeting someone as gorgeous as this man, she'd have borrowed one of Sharon's professional-looking suits. She hoped she looked okay. "Oh," she said, not knowing what else to say.

Racquel and Sharon looked at each other and eased away from where Marcella and Darryl were standing. Marcella was going to murder both of them when this was all over.

"I hope this isn't making you uncomfortable. I told Kevin he should say something to you, so you wouldn't be caught off guard, but he said you wouldn't be offended by me introducing myself."

"Uh . . . no. I'm not offended," she said, eyeing Kevin as he walked down one of the outer aisles of the church. He was smiling, and Marcella wanted to hold up her fist to him. She'd take care of him later, though. The children and Corrine were walking behind him. Marcella saw Nicholas trying to slip through the pew, obviously wanting to come over to where she was at, but Corrine steered him down the aisle toward the back of the church.

Darryl noticed the same thing. "It looks like your son is getting anxious," he said, smiling.

"Yeah, he gets like that sometimes. He just wants to be nosey," Marcella said, wondering how he knew she had a son. Kevin must have told him, which was good because that meant he didn't have a problem with the fact that she had children.

"Well, I'll tell you what. Here's my business card, and my home phone number is written on the back. You can call me if you want, or you can give me your number and I'll call you."

Marcella wanted him to call her. At least when the man made the first move, it felt like he was the one pursuing the relationship. He'd already shown his interest by coming up to her right now, but still, she wanted him to dial her phone number first.

"I think I have a notepad in here somewhere," she said, fumbling through her purse.

"Here," he said, passing her another one of his cards. "Write it on the back of this."

"Thanks," she said, writing her name and number down.

"If you're not doing anything tonight, I'll call you then."

"That'll be fine," Marcella said, smiling at him as they walked out to the vestibule, where the rest of her family was waiting.

When he left, Racquel, Sharon, and Corrine started laughing.

"You guys think you're slick, but you're not," Marcella said, rolling her eyes playfully. "And you know I'm going to pay you back, Kevin," she said.

"I told you," Sharon said, cracking up. "You never know who you might meet at church."

Chapter 12

For the past four months, Marcella had been living in pure heaven, and life was better than ever. She still had to pinch herself whenever she thought about Darryl being a medical resident at Covington Park Memorial. A doctor. The man was actually a doctor. And he was interested in *her*. It was all so hard for her to believe, and no matter how many times he called, came to visit, or took her out, she still couldn't understand it. It was almost like she was living in some sort of fantasy world, waiting to be thrown back to reality. And he adored Ashley and Nicholas. The idea of her having two children didn't bother him at all, and sometimes he even planned outings that included all four of them. He was everything she could have possibly ever hoped for, and she prayed daily that this would never end. Intelligent, decent, caring, and while looks weren't the most important characteristic, he was fine.

He had features similar to that Keith-guy she'd met

a year ago on campus. Medium complexion, wavy jet-black hair. The only difference was, he was much taller. At least six-three. And whenever she looked up at him, she felt like melting.

Yes, life was good. And even Racquel seemed happier than usual, and wasn't nearly as obsessed with getting pregnant. She'd taken that infertility drug for more than six months, and then finally stopped when she began experiencing some weird side effect. She hadn't gotten pregnant, but she didn't seem to be depressed about it the way she used to be. Maybe the fact that she'd been keeping Ashley and Nicholas every evening while Marcella worked was making a difference. Sometimes the children even spent the night when Marcella had tons of studying or needed time to work on some paper she had due. Racquel was finally getting the opportunity to do what she loved most. Taking care of two children on a daily basis. And while Marcella was thankful for all that Racquel and Kevin had done to help her this past semester, it was now summer break, and the children wouldn't be spending nearly as much time with them. Racquel was on summer break from teaching and had offered to keep the children during the day while Marcella worked, but Marcella had found an all-day summer program designed for low-income families instead. It offered all sorts of educational activities, field trips, and other recreational activities, and it was only costing her ten dollars a week per child. She hoped the absence of the children wasn't going to cause Racquel to slip back into a severe state of depression, but Ashley and Nicholas needed to be in an educational atmosphere, because it was better for them. Maybe Kevin would reconsider the option of artificial insemination. He'd always said that it wasn't an option because of how expensive it was, but maybe if Racquel kept working on him in the right way, he might just change his mind.

Marcella washed the last of this morning's breakfast dishes and then waited for Darryl to arrive at her apartment. Her mother had taken a week of vacation and wanted her grandchildren to spend the night with her. Corrine had picked them up from the center, brought them by the apartment to get a change of clothing for the next day, and then took them to the park to watch her company's baseball game.

With school being out, she'd been spending as much time as possible with Ashley and Nicholas, and hadn't spent much time alone with Darryl. He didn't seem to mind, but she knew it was important for them to spend some quality time together when it was just the two of them.

It was 6:30 P.M., and since Darryl wasn't scheduled to pick her up for dinner until 7, she picked up the latest issue of *Essence* that Racquel had given her, and read through the various articles. When she finished it, she reached to pick up the previous month's issue, and heard a knock at the door. She stood up, strutted over to the door, patted her hair to make sure no strands were out of place, and opened it.

"Hey, sweetheart," he said, pulling her into his arms and kissing her.

"How's it going?" she said as they released each other.

"Tired. The hospital was a madhouse today."

"Did you just get off?"

"Yep. I worked a twelve-hour shift today, but I'm off tomorrow," he said, dropping down on the sofa.

"Then, you probably don't feel like going out to dinner."

"Not really, but we can if you really want to."

"It doesn't matter to me. We can order a pizza or something instead, if you want."

"That sounds good," he said, leaning back on the sofa with his eyes closed.

"You wanna pick it up on the way to your apartment or have it delivered?" she asked, walking toward the phone in the kitchen.

"We might as well pick it up, since it's on the way."

Marcella looked up the number in the phone book and dialed it. "Hi. I'd like to order a medium pizza with sausage, mushrooms, and double cheese," Marcella requested and then paused, waiting for the waitress to tell her how long it would be. Carl's was the busiest and best-tasting pizza place in the area, and it usually took thirty to forty minutes for them to prepare each order. And since today was Friday, it was probably going to take even longer.

"Thank you," she said and hung up the phone.

"How long?" Darryl asked.

"Forty-five minutes," she said, sitting down on the sofa next to him. "We might as well watch TV or something until then," she said, realizing that the pizza place was only about ten minutes away from her apartment.

"I promise you, things will be different when my residency is completed next year. No more long hours, and I'll finally have the money to take you out to nice restaurants for a change," he said, as if he felt bad because they were having pizza. They did have it a lot, but Marcella didn't mind at all. She was just happy to be with him.

"Don't worry about it. I'm happy just the way things are."

Darryl leaned his head into Marcella's chest and placed his arms around her waist, while she caressed the back of his head. It felt good to have him so close to her. So close to her heart. She'd been trying to contain her feelings for him for months now, but it was becoming more and more difficult to keep it up. She was in love with him, and wanted to tell him. Something told her that he was in love with her, too, but he'd never actually said the words, and the last thing she wanted was to take the risk of telling him how she felt and then getting her feelings hurt. Being with him was almost unrealistic, and she had to take some precautions. She didn't want to end up getting hurt the way she had with Tyrone. But then, Darryl wasn't at all like Tyrone because the two of them were as different as Black-folks dressing and store-bought stuffing. To put it plainly, they were different in every aspect.

She smiled when she heard Darryl breathing deeply. He was so cute when he slept, and she could have sat there holding him forever. She flipped through the channels on the TV set and didn't see anything interesting. She wasn't a frequent TV watcher, but on days like today she wished she had at least one of those overpriced pay channels. But, of course that wasn't even an option, since she could barely pay the monthly basic-cable rate as it was. And the only reason she had that, was because her mother had paid to have it installed for the children. And she helped out with the bill, as well, when times were rougher than usual for Marcella.

When she finally settled on CNN, she heard a couple of knocks at the door and frowned. It was probably some of those kids looking for Ashley or Nicholas, and since they weren't home, she decided to ignore it. But it wasn't long before there were more knocks, and this time they sounded a lot harder, like someone was pounding a fist against the door. The sound was so loud that Darryl sat straight up.

"What was that?" he asked with his eyes still half closed.

Marcella felt nervous, because she knew there was only one person crazy enough to beat on her door in that manner. "Someone's knocking," she said, standing up. She walked over to the door and opened it.

"What took you so long to answer the door?" Tyrone asked, brushing past her.

Now, who did he think he was bulldozing his way into *her* apartment?

"I should have known you had somebody up in here," Tyrone said, casting his eye at Darryl.

"Hey, man, what's up?" Darryl said, speaking to him cordially.

Tyrone ignored him. "Where's my kids?" he asked Marcella.

"They're with my mom," she responded.

"Damn. Do you *ever* keep your own kids. I mean, shit. You go to school nine months out of the year, and now that you're out for the summer, you mean to tell me, you're still throwing them off on your mother?"

"This is not the time for this, Tyrone. I told you where they are, and if you want to see them, you know where my mother lives."

"You barred me from going over there. Remember?" he said, laughing sarcastically.

He'd only been there for a few minutes, but Marcella had already taken as much of him as she could stand. "Please leave, Tyrone," she said, trying to see what expression Darryl had on his face. She was so embarrassed.

"Oh, now you want to be nice in front of your little company, when just a few months ago you told me to get the fuck out. Remember that? So don't be trying to put on that Little Miss Innocent act now."

Where was that baseball bat when she needed it? Darryl had never heard her use words like that, and she felt like crawling under a table or into a closet. Anywhere. Anywhere at all. Why was this fool doing this? He was supposedly so in love with that Priscilla, so it couldn't have been jealousy causing him to act so stupid. She had to get rid of him. "Tyrone, I'm asking you again. Please leave," she said as calmly as she could.

"I'll tell you one thing, you better not be screwing this punk when my kids are here," Tyrone said.

What? She'd known from the very beginning that it was a mistake in opening the door to let him in. And worse than that, she knew it was just a matter of time before Darryl broke his silence.

"Man, I think you'd better leave," Darryl said, standing up.

"I'll leave when I damn well please," Tyrone said, scanning Darryl from head to toe. "And if you ever try to put your hands on Ashley or Nick, you'll be dealing with me. Nicholas told me how you be hanging around over here all the time, but if you think you're about to play Daddy with my kids, you can forget that."

"If you spent more time with them, you wouldn't have to worry about it. Now would you?" Darryl said, just as pissed off as Tyrone.

"Don't let that little medical degree get your ass kicked," Tyrone said. "You might think you're this and that, but you don't mean shit to me."

"Tyrone, stop it!" Marcella screamed. Things were escalating higher and higher, and it was time to put a stop to all of this before it got physical.

"If you don't leave, Tyrone, I'm calling the police," Marcella said, opening the front door.

"Bitch, this isn't the end of this. I promise you that," Tyrone said, storming out the door.

Marcella closed the door behind him and dreaded
turning around to look in Darryl's face. How was she
going to explain all of this? Tyrone had known all along
that she was seeing someone because Nicholas had told
him about it shortly after they'd gone out on their first
date. He hadn't acted like he had any problem with it
then, so she couldn't understand at all what the problem
was now. He'd been slacking on his child support again
and was spending less and less time with the children,
but she hadn't made one complaint about it. She never
messed with him about anything anymore because she
didn't care. For the first time in her life, she was happy
and didn't have time to be worrying about what Tyrone
was or wasn't doing. She'd made it without his help the
first year, and now that she was starting her sophomore
year in the fall, she figured she could make it through
that one just as well.

"I am so sorry about this," Marcella said, looking at
Darryl.

"He's got a lot of nerve coming in here acting like
he owns the place," Darryl said in an angry tone.

"I don't know what's wrong with him. He knows I
spend as much time as I can with Ashley and Nicholas,
so I don't know why he's trying to make it seem like I
don't. This is the first night since the semester ended
that Ashley and Nicholas have spent the night anywhere
else. And the only reason they spent a few nights here
and there with Racquel and Kevin was because I had to
study or do research for one of my papers. And it definitely wasn't because I was out having the time of my
life."

"Well, he's got one more time to approach me the
way he did tonight. And I don't know who he thinks I
am, but I grew up in the same neighborhood that he
did."

"Darryl, look. You're a doctor, and I know you're not going to stoop to Tyrone's level. He's not worth it."

"I know he's not worth it, but I'm not about to let him walk over me like I'm some child, either. And I definitely don't appreciate the way he talks to you. If anything, you should be the one complaining. He doesn't do anything for Ashley and Nicholas. Hell, I do more for them than he does, and I'm not even their father."

"I know you do, baby, and I love you for it," she said, immediately wishing she could take every word back. This was the last thing she wanted, and now that he knew how she felt, it was probably just a matter of time before his calls and visits started to lessen, and then eventually ended permanently. She looked the other way.

"Hey," he said, turning her face toward him delicately with his hand. "What did you say?"

"Nothing," she replied, walking away from him. Her emotions were running wild, and she couldn't think straight.

"Well, unless something's wrong with my hearing, I could have sworn you said you loved me," he said, smiling.

"We have to pick up the pizza," she said, grabbing her purse. "Are you ready?" she asked, ignoring his last comment.

"Not until you tell me what you just said," he said, folding his arms, still smiling.

"I love you, okay. Now, are you satisfied?" she said, pretending to be mad at him.

"Oh, I'm very satisfied," he said, hugging her and laughing slightly.

Why wasn't he saying it back, she thought. That's what she got for getting herself all wrapped up in someone so sophisticated and as intelligent as him. She'd been fooling herself for months now, and it was finally coming to a head. What she should have done was leave well enough alone. In fact, she was starting to get a little upset at him because it was almost as if he was gloating about it. She pulled away from him. "By the time we get to the restaurant, the pizza is going to be cold," she said, walking toward the door.

"So what. That's what microwaves are for."

"I know you think you're funny, but you're not," she said without any sign of a smile on her face.

Darryl must have picked up on it. "Come here," he said, reaching out to her.

"No. I'm ready to go," she said, opening the door.

"Marcella, close the door, and come here. Please," he said, sounding serious.

"What?" she said, closing the door.

He pulled her against his body again, and then gazed down at her. "I'm in love with you, too, Marcella, and I have been for a long time now."

She felt paralyzed. These were the words she'd been waiting for, and now that she was actually hearing them, she wasn't sure how she should react.

When she didn't say anything, he continued. "For weeks, I've wanted to tell you, but I wasn't sure if you felt the same way or not, and the last thing I wanted was to end up hurt like I did just before I started dating you."

Just before? He'd never mentioned anything like this, and she didn't like the sound of it. For all she knew, he'd started seeing her on the rebound from some other relationship gone bad. Maybe he just *thought* he was in love with her. Maybe he just needed someone to ease his pain. Someone to keep him from being alone. And what was going to happen if this ex-lover came back into the picture and decided that she wanted to get back with him after all. Marcella had told herself from the beginning that this whole situation was too good to be true.

"I didn't realize you were just getting out of a relationship when we met," she said, trying to sound like she wasn't bothered by what he'd just told her.

"It was a terrible situation, and as far as I'm concerned, it's in the past. You're all that I care about now, so none of that matters."

She prayed that he was being honest with her. Some men had a problem when it came to honesty, and she hoped he wasn't one of them. "We'd better go," she said, glancing at her watch.

Once Marcella was securely seated inside the Volkswagen, Darryl closed her door and walked around to get in on the driver's side. He pulled his seat belt on, placed the car in reverse, and drove out of the parking lot.

After eating a few slices of pizza, Marcella and Darryl had ended up making love, and now they were in bed snuggling close to each other.

"Baby, I love you so much," Darryl said, stroking Marcella's hair.

"I love you, too," she said with her face leaning against his chest, and her eyes closed.

"And you make me feel so good when we make love," he continued.

"I'm glad," she said, wishing she could return the same compliment back to him. It wasn't that he made her feel horrible, but at the same time she really wasn't all that impressed with his performance in bed. She'd been hoping that it would get better as time went on, but so far it hadn't. And she was pretty sure that this mediocre lovemaking had a whole lot to do with the fact that he wasn't all that big. Sharon had complained about this very thing when it came to Marcus, and now Marcella knew exactly what she meant. But she still didn't see sex as being a good enough reason not to marry someone. As a matter of fact, she'd marry Darryl in a heartbeat if he asked her to, because there were far too many good things that more than outweighed this one deficiency. And anyway, nobody was perfect.

"So, what about you?"

"What do you mean?" she asked, opening her eyes, and was glad he couldn't see the guilty expression on her face.

"You know. How do you feel when we make love? I mean, do I satisfy you?"

There was no way she was going to tell him the truth about this. She wished like hell that she could, but she just couldn't. "I feel wonderful, and yes, you do satisfy me," she said, trying to sound as sincere as she could.

"Good, because your satisfaction is important to me."

Marcella didn't know what to say, so she said nothing.

"And if you have a certain desire, I hope you'll tell me, because otherwise, there's no way I'll know."

There *was* something he could do, but she was a coward and didn't have the nerve to ask him. Tyrone had done it all the time, and never thought twice about it, but some men had a problem when it came to going down on a woman, and she didn't want to push it. "No. I'm fine with the way things are between us. I'm fine with the sex and our relationship in general."

"You're sure?" he asked, holding her tight.

"Yes. I'm sure," she said, kissing him on his chest and wondering why he was asking her all these questions. She hoped he hadn't sensed her dissatisfaction, because the last thing she wanted was to hurt his feelings. And more than anything, she didn't want something like this to come between them.

They lay there for a while, enjoying the moment, and then Darryl finally spoke. "I still can't believe Tyrone tripped out the way he did earlier."

"Yeah, I know," Marcella said and wished Darryl would drop the Tyrone subject.

"I mean, how long is it going to take for him to realize that you and he are living totally separate lives, and that what you do with your life is your business?"

"Tyrone knows that what I do is my business, and all he's trying to do is mess up what you and I have with each other."

"Well, he needs to get over it, because you and I are going to be together whether he likes it or not."

"Look, let's forget about Tyrone," she said, looking up at him. "Because all that matters to me is you."

Darryl smiled and then kissed her passionately. Marcella knew he was preparing for round two, and she hoped that through some miracle, it was going to be much better this time. But then, even if it wasn't, she was still going to love him as much as always.

Chapter 13

"**W**e mortgaged our house for this, Racquel. Have you forgotten that?" Kevin screamed at the top of his lungs.

Racquel shivered. She couldn't remember Kevin ever being this angry, and he was scaring her. "Sometimes it takes more than one try," she said, changing her position on the side of the bed.

"More than one try? Hell, we did that artificial insemination thing six months in a row, paid almost ten thousand dollars for that in vitro whatever you call it, and now you think I'm going to agree to try it again? You must be crazier than I thought," he said, leaning against the wooden armoire.

"But Kevin . . . ," she cried.

"Do you realize how long this has gone on?" he asked, ignoring whatever she was going to say. "Ever since the day we got married, I've had to hear you go on and on about getting pregnant, but I still stood by you. Then you started buying all that unnecessary shit from I don't know how many different department stores for a baby we still don't have. Then instead of making love, we started having sex just to try and make a baby. Then you insisted that we go to an infertility specialist. And I did. Then you practically killed yourself trying to take that infertility medication, and when you found out that that wasn't going to work, you started hounding me again about all these other overpriced procedures. And for whatever ridiculous reason, I agreed to those, too. And now that we've spent all this money for nothing, you've got the audacity to ask me to take out another mortgage against the house? What's wrong with you?" he said, staring at her. "Huh? What's wrong with you, Racquel?"

She cried hysterically and didn't say anything.

And it was obvious that he didn't feel sorry for her one bit, because he kept on screaming at her. "How much more of this do you think I can take? We've been married for almost four years, and I've had enough of this. You said that if I went to the infertility specialist with you, and none of the options worked out, you would put this whole baby business behind you. That's what you told me, and I believed you. But now you're starting this all up again. Not to mention the fact that you were in so big of a hurry that you couldn't even wait for the insurance company to review our appeal. It's just not meant to be, Racquel. So why can't you just accept that?"

Why was he torturing her like this? And no matter what he said, it *was* meant to be. She'd read about women who went years without having a child and then ended up pregnant. And their babies were born healthy, too. He just didn't understand, and she couldn't believe he was blowing up at her like this. She was lost for words, but she wanted to say something. Anything. "One more try isn't going to hurt anything, Kevin. The success rate is a lot higher with the in-vitro-fertilization method. So, maybe all we need is a second try at it. I'll get a part-time job to help pay for it, if I have to. Just one more try, and I promise I'll never mention the idea of trying to have a baby ever again. I promise," she said, rising from the bed and walking toward him. She reached out to touch him.

"What are you? Deaf or something?" he said, pushing her hand away from him. "You haven't been listening to a word I've said, have you? Everything is always about what you want, and I'm sick of it. I've been as patient with you as I can, but things are getting worse instead of better. I used to think that our love for each other would outweigh all of our problems, but I was wrong. Love doesn't seem to mean anything to you anymore, and I'm starting to feel the same way. I'm too young to spend the rest of my life chasing some fantasy, and I'm not doing it anymore."

"So what are you saying?" she asked pitifully, with tears still rolling down her face.

"Exactly what I said, Racquel. I'm not doing this anymore. Either you give this up, or I'm filing for a divorce."

Her heart did a cartwheel, and her stomach turned in the same manner. "Honey, you don't mean that," she said, almost begging.

"I love you more than anything, Racquel, but I'm telling you, if you don't stop this obsession of yours, I'm moving out, and I'm divorcing you."

"How can you say you love me in one breath, and then threaten me with divorce in another? How can you do that?"

"First of all, it's not a threat. I'm telling you honestly

what's going to happen if you don't stop this. It's as simple as that. And no matter what you think, I do love you. If I didn't, do you think I would have spent these last four years arguing with you, putting up with your depressed moods, and paying all this money to some infertility clinic? And to think I let you talk me into taking out a second mortgage on this house—knowing good and well I didn't want to. Only a fool or somebody in love would do any of that. Especially, when you don't show any appreciation for any of it. So now I'm giving you a choice."

"How can you expect me to just give up? You know how badly I want a baby, and I can't believe you're doing this."

"I'm not going to spend the rest of the day arguing with you. I took the afternoon off so we could spend some time together, but if I had known you were going to ask me to spend more money on this infertility shit, I would have stayed at work. It's getting to the point where I hate being here."

"Well, then leave," Racquel said, raising her voice for the first time since the conversation started.

"So are you saying that you're not going to give this up?" he asked, waiting for an answer.

"What I'm saying is, if you don't want to be here, then leave," she said, calling his bluff. The last thing she wanted was to be without Kevin, but she wasn't going to keep begging him, either.

"What a waste," he said, and stormed out of the bedroom.

Racquel stood in the middle of the floor crying silently, yet uncontrollably. She wiped her tears with her hand and then held them across her face leaning her head back. She felt like dying. Like her whole world was over. This was all wrong, and she didn't have the slightest idea as to how she could fix it. She'd drawn a picture of how her life was going to be before she'd even met Kevin. She would graduate from college with a degree, find a job teaching small children, get married to the perfect husband, have lots of healthy, beautiful babies, and live happily ever after. But now, everything was going in the wrong direction. Kevin was actually threatening her with a divorce. What nerve. She'd been the best wife she could be, and then some. At least she thought she had. She was faithful to him, and she loved him. What more did he want? As far as she was concerned, he was getting everything he wanted, and it was she who had always gone lacking. All she wanted was this one thing, and she couldn't have it. And even worse, Kevin wasn't willing to go the extra mile to make sure it happened. Yes, they had paid a ton of money to the clinic, but it was worth it. Hell, they'd spent more money on each of the cars they drove than what they had on that. It was only money, and something as miraculous as having a child was far more important. Kevin just didn't get it, and she wasn't sure how she could make him see it. He was carrying on like she was some crazed maniac, and he kept saying she was obsessed, but she wasn't. She would have loved nothing more than to see him move out, so she wouldn't have to hear his complaints and ultimatums anymore. But she knew she was fooling herself. She loved him too much for that, and she needed him for more reasons than she cared to think about.

She pulled a tissue from the Kleenex box, wiped her face, and blew her nose. Before this argument had erupted between her and Kevin, they'd planned on going out for a late lunch, but now she didn't have an appetite. She never knew what to do with herself when they got into it like this. At least when school was in, she could tune all of her problems out by concentrating on the children in her class, but now that school was out, she didn't even have that to turn to. Maybe Kevin would come to his senses and everything would be fine. But, based on how enraged he was, she knew that was doubtful.

When she looked out the bedroom window and noticed that Kevin's truck was gone, she did what she always did after they argued: lay across the bed and fell asleep. After about an hour and a half, the phone rang and woke her up.

"Hello?" Racquel said in a muzzled voice with her eyes closed.

"Hey, girl. What's up?" Marcella asked.

Racquel cleared her throat. "Not too much. I must've dropped off to sleep for a minute."

"What are you doing sleeping in the middle of the afternoon?" Marcella said, sounding surprised.

"Kevin and I were at it again, and like always, he left."

"At it about what?"

Racquel hated even going into this with Marcella because she knew Marcella was going to have the same attitude as Kevin. What she needed now was some encouragement. What she needed was a vast amount of moral support. But there was no sense in trying to disguise the situation because chances were, Marcella already had a pretty good idea of what was going on anyway.

"I want to try that in-vitro-fertilization procedure one more time, but Kevin is totally against it."

Marcella paused for a moment to choose the right words. The last thing she wanted was to piss Racquel off or hurt her feelings. "I don't know what to say, except that, you did say you were through with trying if this last attempt didn't work."

"I know, but I just want to try this one last time. That's all. But all Kevin can see is how much money it's going to cost."

Marcella was lost for words and felt like her hands were tied. If she told Racquel that she agreed with Kevin, which she did, Racquel would probably hang up on her. But she didn't see where she had much of a choice. "Look, Racquel, don't take this the wrong way, but doesn't this in vitro fertilization cost close to ten thousand dollars? Maybe that's why Kevin is so concerned about it."

"I know it's a lot of money, but it won't hurt to take out another mortgage. And if it came down to it, we wouldn't even have to do that, because we already have enough to cover it in our savings account."

"Yeah, but do you think it's a good idea to spend your life savings on something you're not sure of?" Marcella asked. She'd tried not to side with Kevin, but Racquel was making it hard for her not to.

"But that's just it. I *am* sure it will happen. And I don't know how Kevin can put a price tag on the life of a child anyway."

"Well, I don't know," Marcella said, doing everything she could not to make any more negative comments.

"I don't either. And even worse, he threatened to divorce me. He's never done that before, so I don't know if he was serious or not," Racquel said and switched the phone from her left ear to her right.

"Divorce?" Marcella said in an upset tone of voice. "He actually said that?"

"Yes. He did. And I'm telling you, Marcella, I'm scared."

"Maybe he was just upset. We all say things we don't mean when we're upset."

"I don't know, but he sounded awfully serious to me."

"Girl, I know you don't want to hear what I'm about to say, but this isn't worth losing Kevin over. He loves you, and he practically worships the ground you walk on. And he's such a good husband. You've got to give this up, so the two of you can get on with your lives," Marcella said, and waited for Racquel to start yelling at her.

But she didn't.

"I know, but I want to have a baby so bad, and I'll never be able to forgive myself if I don't."

"Forgive yourself for what?"

"You remember that abortion I had when I was in high school."

"Racquel, you can't look back on that. You've asked God for forgiveness, and that's all you can do. You made a mistake, and you learned from it."

"But it was the biggest mistake of my life. And, God, Marcella," Racquel said, covering the mouthpiece of the phone and leaning her head back trying to fight back the tears. "I had another one when I was in college."

"You what? By who?"

"You wouldn't believe it if I told you."

"Wouldn't believe what?" Kevin asked, leaning inside the doorway of the bedroom.

Racquel jerked her head and looked at him in total shock. She shook her head slowly from side to side. She'd thought for sure he was gone. She had checked out the window before she laid down, and had only fallen asleep for a few minutes. At least, she'd thought it was just a few minutes. How was she going to explain this to a man who was talking about divorcing her? And even worse, she wondered how long he'd been standing there. Eavesdropping. She was speechless.

"Won't believe what?" Marcella asked.

"Hey, let me call you back. Okay?" Racquel said softly.

"Why can't you tell me now?" Marcella asked anxiously.

"I have to call you back. Okay?" Racquel repeated and hung up the phone.

"Answer me, Racquel," Kevin said with anger flowing through his voice.

"Baby, it's not what you think," she said nervously.

"Just stop it, Racquel," he said sternly. "How long do you think I've been standing here listening to your conversation? I'll tell you how long. Long enough to know that you've had two abortions, and that you never told me about them. We've even discussed this before, and you flat out lied to me. How could you do that?"

"I didn't know how to tell you," she said desperately.

"But you lied. And you've been lying all along. What else have you been lying about?" he asked.

"Nothing, Kevin. I swear."

"Nothing my ass, because I just heard you telling your sister that she wouldn't believe something. So what was that all about?"

Racquel was caught and felt like crawling under the bed. She'd never told anyone about the life she led while she was in college, and she just couldn't bring herself to tell Kevin now. If she did, he really would divorce her, and wouldn't think twice after doing it. But if she continued to lie to him, he would hate her even more, and she couldn't bear that, either. She felt like the walls were closing in on her.

"Tell me, Racquel!" he screamed when she didn't respond.

"Stop yelling at me, Kevin!" she said, screaming back at him.

"Well, then, you'd better start explaining," he said without any sympathy for her.

She stared at him, but didn't respond.

"Tell me!" he said, screaming at her again. "Tell me, dammit!"

"I got pregnant by a married White guy," she yelled. "Are you satisfied now?"

Kevin paused and then backed away from her slowly. He shook his head in denial. "No, you're kidding. Right? You've got to be?"

"I'm telling you the truth. I got pregnant by someone else's husband," she said with humiliation.

"So what you're telling me," he said, pausing, "is that I'm married to a tramp who kills babies."

Racquel just looked at him and figured it wasn't worth saying anything. And what could she say, anyway?

"Damn. If I hadn't interrupted your phone conversation, there's no telling what else I would have heard, is there?"

Racquel remained silent, but didn't take her eyes off of him.

"This is too much for me. I'm outta here," he said, walking out of the bedroom.

She wanted to call him, beg him, plead with him. She wanted to do something to make him come back. Maybe if she explained it better, he would understand. But realistically, she knew he never would. This was the last straw. And while she feared even thinking about the future, she knew her marriage was over.

* * *

Marcella waited by the phone for a whole hour, expecting Racquel to call her back, but she didn't. She wanted to know what Racquel was trying to tell her, and why she had to end their conversation so suddenly. None of this was adding up, and she couldn't wait any longer to find out what was going on. She picked up the receiver and dialed her sister's number.

"Hello?" Racquel answered.

"Why didn't you call me back?" Marcella asked impatiently.

"I was going to, but the longer I sat here, the more I didn't feel like talking to anyone."

"What's going on over there?"

"I thought Kevin was still out when you called, but he wasn't. I fell asleep for almost two hours and didn't realize how much time had gone by. So I didn't hear him when he came back in the house."

"So what does that have to do with anything?"

"Everything. He heard every word I said about the abortions, so I didn't have a choice except to tell him how I got pregnant that second time."

Marcella wanted to know the same thing. And even more, she wanted to know why Racquel had kept this from her in the first place. "Well, how did you?"

"This is so embarrassing," Racquel said, taking a deep breath. "Remember when Daddy moved out for good?"

"Yeah."

"And when Mom thought I was going to have to drop out of school because Daddy was acting iffy about paying my tuition?"

"Mmm-hmm."

"Well, I ended up meeting this White guy, who just so happened to be CEO of Trasco, Inc."

"Not Trasco, the huge electronics corporation?"

"Yeah. That Trasco."

"How did you meet him?"

"My roommate and I used to go to this elite bar and grill that a lot of businessmen went to after work. And of course, I ended up meeting all sorts of people."

"A White guy, Racquel?" Marcella asked, like maybe she'd misunderstood her.

"Yes, and on top of that, he was married and had three children."

"Married with three children?" Marcella said in total shock. "How come you never told me about this?"

"I couldn't tell anybody, and I've regretted it ever since."

"How long did this go on?"

"Right up until I graduated. He paid practically all of my tuition during my junior and senior years, and how do you think I got that apartment off campus?"

Marcella was flabbergasted. This couldn't have possibly been the same woman who was supposed to be her sister. And how could Racquel have been carrying on like this without her finding out about it. They knew each other like the back of their hands. At least, she'd always thought they had. "Girl, this is unreal."

"Don't get me wrong. I'm not proud of what I did in the least, but it happened just the same. I made a lot of mistakes back then, and I knew one day they were going to come to the forefront. Everything always comes back to you. Good or bad. And now I've probably lost Kevin because of it."

"Where is he now?"

"He left again, but I don't know where he went. He was pretty mad."

"Well, it's not like this happened while you were married to Kevin. As a matter of fact, you didn't even know him back then."

"It's the fact that I had two abortions, and messed around with someone else's husband. When it comes to family, Kevin has high standards. That's one of the main reasons why I was so attracted to him in the first place, and you know how much he despises any woman who messes around, including his own mother. He never forgave her for running off and leaving his father for another man, and he's never going to forgive me for this, either. Plus, I know he feels like I deceived him. And as much as I hate to admit it, I did lie to him when he asked me if I had ever had an abortion."

"Girl, you've got to talk to him as soon as he walks through that door."

"Hmmph. I don't even know if I can face him, let alone talk to him."

"You don't have a choice."

They were both silent for a few seconds.

"I'd better get off of here, so I can fix dinner for Ashley and Nicholas. But you call me if you need me, okay?" Marcella said.

"I will," Racquel said, grabbing the phone from her shoulder.

"And try not to worry. Everything will work out fine."

"Oh, and Marcella. Whatever you do, please don't say anything to Mom about this. I just couldn't take that."

"You know better than that. I would never tell her something like this."

"Then, I'll talk to you later," Racquel said.

Marcella hung up the phone without moving the rest of her body. Racquel had actually messed around with a married man. And not just any married man, but a wealthy White one who was probably old enough to be her father. What could she possibly have been thinking? And why couldn't she have taken out a student loan like everyone else did when they needed money for school? It just didn't add up. And it was so unlike Racquel. And even worse, she dreaded even thinking about what was going to happen to her sister's wonderful marriage.

Chapter 14

Washing, blow-drying, and curling her hair had taken Marcella longer than she'd planned. Darryl had phoned earlier to say he'd be picking them up at five o'clock sharp, so they could make the 5:45 P.M. showing of some Disney remake, because if they went after six o'clock, they'd have to pay full price.

Nicholas had been begging Tyrone to take him for the longest, but as usual he never had the time to do it, and now that he was finally going, he couldn't wait. Ashley, on the other hand, didn't see what the big deal was. As far as she was concerned, she didn't want to see this "baby" movie anyway.

"Are you guys ready?" Marcella yelled, pulling on her black jeans and sweatshirt. She wanted to wear the black sleeveless mock turtleneck that Sharon had given her last month, but the weather was just a little too nippy for it. Which was sort of strange, she thought, since it was only the first week in September.

"I'm ready," Nicholas said proudly.

Ashley didn't respond.

"What about you, Ashley?"

"I'm ready," she said with no enthusiasm.

Marcella didn't say anything back to her, but if she didn't lose that funky attitude by the time they made it to the movie theater, she was going to wish she had. She didn't know what was wrong with that girl. She was so moody. Not to the extent that she had been at the. beginning of the year, but she was still pretty bad with it. Everyone kept saying it was just a phase she was going through, but Marcella couldn't wait for it to end. She'd thought for sure that her worries were over the day Children and Family Services had taken that Jason and his little brothers away from their mother, but Ashley was still walking around acting like she was mad at the world and didn't want to be bothered with anyone except herself. But at least she was keeping her grades up in school. They'd only been in school for a couple of weeks, and already she was getting A's on all of her homework assignments.

Darryl picked them up a few minutes early, and they headed for the theater. When they arrived, Darryl stepped out of the car, and Nicholas pushed the front seat forward and then jumped out of the car filled with excitement.

"You wanted to see this movie bad, didn't you," Darryl said, shutting the door.

"Yep," Nicholas said.

"He likes to see any movie," Marcella said, holding the seat forward so Ashley could get out on her side. "Especially when it's at the movie theater."

They all walked toward the entrance, which had a long line winding from the ticket window all the way around the building. It was so funny how everyone always tried to beat the six o'clock cutoff, Marcella thought. It was still early, but maybe they hadn't gotten there early enough.

They walked to the end of the line and took their places in it.

"Mom. Isn't that Daddy's car?" Ashley asked, pointing toward the parking lot.

Marcella watched as Tyrone drove through the parking lot searching for a park. Oh no, she thought. Not today. The last thing in the world that she needed was a confrontation with him. And from the looks of it, he had that Priscilla in the car with him, as well. What luck.

"Yeah, I think it is," Marcella finally answered.

"Who are those kids with him?" Nicholas asked, stretching his neck to see who was walking through the aisle holding his dad's hand.

Marcella and Darryl looked at each other but didn't say anything because they knew what Nicholas was thinking. Tyrone was always saying he didn't have time to take Nicholas and Ashley anywhere, but here he was big as day bringing somebody else's children to the movies.

As Tyrone and his posse walked closer to the line, he recognized Ashley and Nicholas.

"Hey, Ashley and Nick," Tyrone said, pretending he didn't see Marcella or Darryl.

"Hi, Daddy," Ashley said with a quick wave.

"Hey, Dad," Nicholas said with an almost-sad look on his face, and kept staring at the little boy and girl.

Marcella was getting more pissed off as the seconds passed by. It was one thing for him to clown with her, but it was another when he did something to hurt her children. She hated to act ugly out in public or in front of Darryl, but if Tyrone said anything else out of the way, she was going off.

"So what are you here to see?" Tyrone said, patting Nicholas's head.

"He's here to see the same movie he's been begging you to take him to see for the last three weeks," Marcella said and wasn't whispering. "You know. The movie you didn't have time to take him to."

"I'm telling you now, Marcella. Don't start this stuff with me, because I'm not in the mood for it."

"I don't care what you're in the mood for. And you're not going to keep treating my babies like this and getting away with it," Marcella said and looked around when she noticed an immediate silence. All the people in line were now giving her their undivided attention, and she felt so ashamed.

Priscilla looked at Marcella like she was crazy, but didn't dare say anything.

"Why are you trippin' like this?" Tyrone asked Marcella with a frown on his face.

"Baby, it's not even worth this," Priscilla interrupted. "We can go somewhere else if you want to."

Marcella wanted to slap this synthetic-weave-wearing heifer more than anything, but she knew she didn't have a reason, because this woman hadn't done one thing to her. She hated Tyrone and everything he stood for, and she wished he would drop dead. Things would be so much easier without him.

By now, Nicholas was crying, but Ashley pretended like none of this was bothering her in the least.

"Hey," Tyrone said, squatting down next to Nicholas. "I'll come by and pick you and Ashley up tomorrow. Okay? And I'll take you anywhere you want to go," he said, hugging him.

Nicholas nodded his head yes, but Ashley just stared at him with no response and no expression on her face; obviously tired of his lies and unkept promises.

Tyrone and his extended family left the line, strolled over to his car, got in, and drove off.

Marcella placed her arm around Nicholas to comfort him and looked at Darryl for the first time since this whole fiasco had started, but he continued looking straight in front of him.

"Can you believe him?" Marcella asked Darryl.

He turned to look at her, and then turned his head away again without answering her. He was angry, and now Marcella wished she hadn't said anything to Tyrone. She didn't know what had come over her, but she just couldn't help herself. She knew she had embarrassed all of them, but when she saw the looks of disappointment on her children's faces, she didn't care about anything else. She was tired of Tryone getting away with murder. Tired of him acting as if Priscilla's children were more important than his own. Hell, she wasn't even aware that this woman had any children, and based on how Nicholas was acting, he and Ashley couldn't have known about them, either.

"What's the matter, Darryl? Why aren't you saying anything?" Marcella asked in a more soft-spoken tone.

"There's nothing to say," he said, still looking straight ahead.

Marcella felt nervous. Darryl had never been this upset with her before, and she could tell he was fed up with this Tyrone situation. Why couldn't she have kept her mouth shut? She had wanted to, but when she saw Tyrone entertaining his little girlfriend and her children, she'd lost it. But she had to make Darryl see that she didn't mean to cause any embarrassment or humiliation for him, and that she wasn't going to ever have another confrontation like that with Tyrone ever again. She couldn't lose him over something as petty as this. She just couldn't.

* * *

Racquel backed the Camry out of the driveway and drove out of the subdivision. After sitting in the house all afternoon, wondering where Kevin was, she'd finally decided to pay her mother a visit. She would have loved nothing more than to spend some time with her niece and nephew, but since they were going to the movies, that was out of the question.

She headed down Baxter Avenue, Covington Park's main strip, and debated as to whether she should stop at some carryout joint to get something for dinner. She'd wanted to spend the evening with Kevin at some nice restaurant, but he still wasn't speaking to her. She'd prayed all week that he would forgive her, but he hadn't. She'd thought for sure this whole situation would blow over in a matter of days, but now it was plowing into its second week.

She was so miserable, and while she knew Kevin realized it, he didn't seem to care. She'd seen him angry many times before, and they argued from time to time the same as any other married couple did, but eventually they always made up. As a matter of fact, they never even went to sleep without making up. They had always loved each other too much for that. But now their relationship was at its worst, and she didn't have the slightest idea as to what she should do about it. She tried to explain everything to him that night he'd overheard her talking to Marcella, but he had ignored her completely. Wouldn't even look at her for that matter. And he'd even had the audacity to move into the guest bedroom. Something he'd never done the whole time they'd been married. She'd thought they could work all of this out, but the odds were slowly piling heavily against it.

She continued down Baxter scanning each side of the street searching for a restaurant, but none of them sounded good. Then it dawned on her. Her mother usually fried fresh catfish every Saturday, and always had way too much left over when she finished. She was the only one in her household, but she always cooked a lot, just in case Racquel, Marcella, or some of her other relatives dropped by for dinner.

As she drove closer to her mother's house, she saw Kevin's truck parked in the driveway, so she parked on the street. A warm feeling came over her. Maybe he had come to his senses. Because if he hadn't, the last place he would want to be was at her mother's house. But then again, Kevin was the sort of man who didn't believe in falling out with the rest of the family, simply because he wasn't speaking to her. And he loved catfish more than Racquel did. Maybe he hadn't come to his senses at all, and had only stopped by there to eat dinner. When Racquel had spoken with her mother earlier, she'd asked about Kevin, but Racquel had played it off, like he was out running some errands. Corrine had asked about him earlier in the week, as well, but Racquel had made up some excuse for his absence that time, too.

She stepped outside her car, shut the door, headed up the driveway, and heard the back door slam shut. She felt nervous when she realized it was probably Kevin on his way out. She continued walking toward the back of the house, until she saw Kevin walking toward her. A part of her wanted to reach out and grab him, so she could hug him as tight as she could. It was near dusk, but she could already see the anger and the I-don't-give-a-damn attitude covering his face. When he was no more than three feet away from her, she opened her mouth to speak to him, but he walked past her without so much as glancing at her. She turned around with her mouth still wide open and watched him as he opened the door of his truck. He looked at her, shook his head, and stepped inside of the vehicle. This was no different than a nightmare. And how could he simply ignore her like that? She continued staring at him, until he turned the key in the ignition. After he backed out of the driveway, he pressed the accelerator to the floor as far as it would go.

Racquel felt like crying her eyes out, but she knew she couldn't. Because if she did, she'd have to explain this whole mess to her mother. And the more she thought about that, the more frightened she became. What if Kevin had told her mother everything? Maybe it wasn't dinner at all that he'd been looking for. Maybe he had come to tell Corrine how terrible her oldest daughter was. And what was she going to do if he had? She'd never be able to face her mother, or anyone else, if they found out what she'd done. Maybe it was a bad idea to visit her mother, after all. But, then, on the other hand, Kevin would never say anything to hurt his mother-in-law. He cared about her too much, and plus, he just wasn't like that. And on top of that, he had no business telling her mother anything that Racquel didn't want her to know. She'd made that clear since the day they got married.

Racquel felt better now that she'd thought this whole situation through. She walked up to the back door and knocked.

Corrine opened the door without delay and walked back up to the kitchen without looking at Racquel.

"Hey, Mom," Racquel said, shutting the door and walking up to where her mother was standing.

"Racquel, tell me it's not true," Corrine said without hesitation.

Racquel could tell that her mother knew everything, and she felt like dying. While she wanted to turn and walk back out the door, she knew it was better to confess so this could all be over with.

"It's true. Everything that Kevin told you is true."

"After all this time, I can't believe this is happening."

"Mom, what was I supposed to do?"

"I don't know, but you should have done everything in your power to hold your marriage together. I told you a long time ago that if you didn't get rid of this obsession about having babies, something bad was going to happen. But I didn't have any idea it was going to come to all of this."

Racquel couldn't believe Kevin had the audacity to tell Corrine about her abortions. It wasn't his place, and he knew it. This was *her* mother, not his. But now that the beans were spilled, she figured she might as well tell her mother all of it. From beginning to end.

"Mom, sit down," Racquel said, pulling a chair out from the kitchen table. Corrine sat down directly in front of her. "I know it was wrong to have two abortions the way I did, but I was young, dumb, and didn't know any better. And I couldn't bear the thought of dropping out of college . . ."

"What are you talking about?" Corrine interrupted with a worried look on her face. Racquel knew this was hard on her, but she had to tell her the truth.

"Mom, please. Just let me finish," Racquel continued. "I don't know what was going through my mind when I started messing around with Tom, but I know part of it was money. He took care of all my college expenses, and paid the rent for my apartment. I needed money so bad back then, and as time went on, it didn't seem to matter that he had a wife and three kids, or that he was White. I know it was wrong, but it just didn't matter," Racquel said, and it was all she could do not to run out of her mother's house.

"What abortions? And in God's name, who is Tom?" Corrine said, raising her voice.

Why was her mother acting as if she didn't know what she was talking about? Kevin had already told her everything, so why was she in denial about all of this? It didn't make any sense. "Mom, I know you don't want to believe what Kevin told you, but it's all true."

"All Kevin told me was that you guys haven't been getting along, and that you might be getting a divorce. So what are *you* talking about?" Corrine asked fearfully.

Divorce? Racquel stared at her mother in disbelief, and felt as though a dark shadow was surrounding her entire body. From the way her mother had been acting, she'd thought for sure that Kevin had told everything. But apparently he hadn't. And because of her assumption, she'd told on herself for no good reason. Why couldn't she have kept her mouth shut, until her mother had given her a better indication of what she knew. It was just like her to jump to conclusions, or become overly obsessed about everything, the same as she had been when it came to getting pregnant. She'd already ruined her marriage to Kevin, and now she'd ruined her mother's whole way of thinking. Her mother had always been so proud of her and her accomplishments, but now she knew the rest of the story. The part of the story that Racquel would have rather kept a secret.

Corrine stood up from the table. "Where did I go wrong in raising you girls?" she asked. "First, Marcella went and got pregnant during her last month of high school, and now you're telling me you needed money so bad, that you had to sleep with some married White man?"

Racquel remained silent.

"Why didn't you tell me that you needed money?

And what about the financial aid you told me you were getting?''

"I did get some grants, but it wasn't enough to cover everything. And right after I applied for a student loan, I met Tom.''

"What were you thinking? This is such a disgrace. No wonder Kevin wants to file for a divorce. Who could blame him?''

At first, Racquel felt bad about her mother finding out the truth, but now she was starting to become irritated with all these insults. Her mother was making it sound like she was stupid. Maybe if she'd been more concerned with raising her daughters instead of trying to keep their father from messing around with other women, her and Marcella's lives might have turned out a lot different. But Racquel decided not to point any fingers. Especially at her own mother. "Mom, I'm sorry for what happened, but there's nothing I can do to change it. I apologized to Kevin, and that's all I can do.''

"I told you to stop pressing him about this infertility thing, but you just wouldn't listen. And now that he knows about you having two abortions, that's even worse.''

"I know I made some terrible mistakes, but there's nothing I can do to change them now. I regret everything I did, and I'm sorry, but if Kevin can't forgive me, then that's just the way it is.''

"How can you say that? You should be at home begging him to forgive you. He's stood by you all these years, only to find out that you're not the person he thought you were. He was so devastated when he was here, but I had no idea, he knew about all of *this*.''

"I'm still the same person I was when I met Kevin. Plus, all of this happened before I met him. What's in the past is in the past, and this is now. And I'm not about to beg him or anybody else for anything, let alone forgiveness. We married each other for better or worse, but it seems like he's forgotten about that. And anyway, why are you taking sides with Kevin?" Racquel asked, getting angrier by the minute.

"I'm not taking sides with him. I'm just trying to get you to see how good of a husband you have, and how you need to do everything you can to keep him."

"I'm not like you, Mom. I'm not going to beg Kevin to stay with me simply because he's my husband," Racquel said, instantly wishing she could do some sort of disappearing act. She hadn't meant to say anything that would hurt her mother's feelings, but Corrine had pushed her too far.

Corrine gazed at her painfully.

"Mom, I didn't mean that, and I'm sorry."

"I didn't beg your father to be with me for my sake. I did it for yours and Marcella's," Corrine said, pointing at Racquel. "The only thing I ever wanted was for you girls to grow up in a two-parent household. I stopped loving your father a long time before I finally put him out that last time. So don't ever think I was some hopelessly-in-love wife who was willing to put up with anything just to keep a man, because I wasn't. And if I'd known you were going to resort to messing around with some wealthy married man for money, I would have never put your father out until after you finished college."

Racquel felt like crap, and didn't know what to say. This was the second time she'd disrespected her mother like this, and she wasn't sure how to make up for it. But she had to say something. "Mom, I know I've said this a lot tonight, but I'm sorry. I'm sorry that you had to find out about all of this, and I'm sorry for talking to you the way I just did. I know you did everything you could for Marcella and me, and I love you for it," she said, standing up from the table and walking toward her mother. She reached out to Corrine and hugged her.

"All I want is the best for you and Marcella, and right now, I think the best thing for you to do is go talk to your husband. It's hard to find a man like Kevin, and I just don't want to see you guys busted up over something that can be worked out."

"I know, Mom. I promise, I'll try to talk to him again tonight, when I get home."

"Everything will be fine," Corrine said, forcing a smile on her face. "Everything will be just fine."

Chapter 15

Marcella was happier than she had been in a long time. School was going well, Ashley had finally gotten her attitude back on track, and things couldn't have been better between her and Darryl. He'd been upset about the incident at the movies, but he eventually came around after a couple days had passed. She'd thought for sure that their relationship was going to end, but it hadn't, and she was glad. She loved him so much, and it was getting to the point where she didn't know what she would do without him. Ashley and Nicholas seemed to like him a lot, as well, and it was almost like they were attached to him. He was clearly the father that they wished they had, and she was glad that Darryl treated them as well as he did.

Tyrone had come by yesterday to drop off his child-support payment, and although it was the first payment he'd made in three weeks, Marcella had decided not to make any waves. Especially since she knew Darryl wanted her to avoid any conflicts or confrontations with Tyrone as much as she could. Darryl couldn't stand Tyrone, and Tyrone couldn't stand Darryl. She wished things could be better between the two of them, but she knew that was never going to happen. She loved Darryl, but Tyrone was her children's father, and there was nothing she could do to change that. And it was simply a fact that, from time to time, she was going to have to deal with him. Plus, things hadn't been so bad as of late because he seemed so wound up with that Priscilla. Which was a blessing, as far as Marcella was concerned, because that meant he didn't have as much time and energy to mess with her. He still didn't spend as much time as he should have with the kids, but Darryl took Ashley and Nicholas lots of places, and that made a world of difference. She never thought the day would come when she didn't have to argue with Tyrone, but now it actually had.

Ashley and Nicholas were on the sofa watching a long, lost episode of *Lassie,* so she sat down at the kitchen table to write out checks for this week's bills. This was the one thing she hated about Saturday mornings, but she knew there was no sense in complaining. She searched through the envelopes stacked on the table, and smiled when she realized that this was her "easy week" because the only bills she had to pay were the ones from the electric and phone companies. This meant she'd have a little left over for buying Christmas gifts. It was only October, but the children had already picked out everything they wanted in the Christmas catalog. Sharon had already assured her that she would take care of everything on their list, but still Marcella wanted to contribute at least a portion of it. It was her responsibility, and she wasn't going to feel right if she didn't.

After she finished writing out the checks and sealed the envelopes for each bill, she noticed a letter from the welfare agency and opened it. She read the letter twice, but she thought for sure her eyes were playing tricks on her. "That bastard," she said out loud, and then looked over at the children and saw Ashley staring at her with curiosity. She never used profanity in front of them, and she could tell that her daughter was surprised about what she'd heard her say. And while Marcella was livid about the contents of the letter, she had to explain herself. "That's a bad word, and I'm sorry for saying it," she said, looking at them with guilt shielding her face.

"What did Daddy do this time?" Ashley asked confidently.

Marcella wanted to tell her. She wanted to tell both of them how deadbeat and how terrible their father was. But she had vowed a long time ago not to bad-mouth Tyrone to the children, regardless of what he did. "He didn't do anything. It's nothing," she said, trying her best to convince Ashley that she was telling the truth.

Ashley looked at her in disbelief, and then turned her attention back to the television screen. Nicholas didn't seem to care one way or the other, and never even looked in his mother's direction. There was a chance that he hadn't even heard what she'd said, since he seemed so caught up in the television set.

She picked up the letter, went into her bedroom, and shut the door. Then she sat down on the side of the bed and dialed Sharon's number. Marcella was so furious, that she could barely wait for her to answer the phone.

"Hello?" Sharon said.

"Girl, you will never guess in a million years what that bastard did!" Marcella said quickly.

"Who? Tyrone?"

"Who else?"

"What did he do now?" Sharon asked, sounding prepared for almost anything.

"I got a letter from my caseworker today, and it says that my food stamps have been suspended until I report to their office. And that my case will be redetermined after they investigate how much child support Tyrone James has been paying me for his two children."

"What?" Sharon yelled.

"You heard me? Suspended because of the child support *Tyrone* has been paying."

"Where did they get that information from?"

"It's more like *who* did they get it from. He's the only one who would have reported anything like that. I can guarantee you that."

"You think he's low-down enough to do something like that?"

"Of course he is. And the worst part of all is that he barely pays me anyway. He brought over a check yesterday for the first time in three weeks, so I don't know how he had the gall to report anything."

"He actually writes you a check?"

"Yeah, he didn't start doing that until I started seeing Darryl, but now I know why. And the only reason he's doing this is because he doesn't like Darryl."

"I don't think it has anything to do with him liking Darryl. More than anything, he's probably pissed off at the fact that you're seeing someone as intelligent as Darryl. Tyrone is jealous. You can believe that."

"I don't know what for, because he and I were

through long before I met Darryl. And he's been going out with Priscilla forever."

"Still. I guarantee you, he's jealous."

"Tyrone makes me so sick till I can't stand it. Wait till I see him."

"If I were you, I wouldn't waste my time arguing with him. And you know how pissed off Darryl got the last time you had a run-in with Tyrone."

"I know, but I can't let him get away with this. He's gone too far this time, and I'm going to tell him about himself. Darryl will just have to understand."

"But what if he doesn't? I'm telling you, Marcella, you should leave well enough alone. Tyrone isn't worth it, and he's definitely not worth losing Darryl over. He's the best thing that has ever happened to you. You said that yourself."

Marcella was becoming more and more furious by the minute, and while she understood where Sharon was coming from, it didn't seem to matter to her. She had to set Tyrone straight once and for all. And she had to do it now. "Hey, let me call you back, okay?"

"Marcella. I know you're not going to confront him, are you?" Sharon said in a pleading voice.

"I'll call you back, okay?" Marcella said, ignoring Sharon's question as politely as she knew how.

"Look, Marcella, for the hundredth time, he's not worth it."

It felt more like a thousand times, and Marcella was a little fed up with hearing what Sharon had to say. She'd called Sharon for one reason, And one reason only: because she needed her support. But this was one time Marcella wished she hadn't. Sharon was supposed to side with her, but she was acting like she was trying to take up for Tyrone. The last thing she wanted to do was hang up on Sharon, so she tried to end the conversation again. "Sharon, I know you don't agree with what I'm about to do, but you're just going to have to understand. I have to get this off my chest, and the only way I can do that is by calling Tyrone," she said irritably.

And Sharon picked up on it. "Look, you're my best friend and the sister I never had. I love you more than anything in this world, and there's nothing I wouldn't do for you or Ashley and Nicholas. All I care about is your happiness. That's all. I'm not trying to tell you what to do, but I don't want to see you ruin things with Darryl, either."

Marcella knew Sharon was right, but she still couldn't let Tyrone get away with what he had done. She'd let him practically walk over her for years now, and this was the last time he was going to get away with it. "I know you're just trying to look out for me, but I have to do this. He's pushed me to the limit for the last time."

"I don't know what else to say, except that you're making a big mistake."

"Well, if I am making a mistake, then I'm the one who's going to have to live with it. Right?" Marcella said, surprising herself. She'd never spoken to Sharon in that manner before, but at the same time Sharon should have never tried to tell her what to do, either. And she was so persistent about it.

"Fine," Sharon said in a tone that sounded as though her feelings were hurt. "Do what you have to do."

"I intend to. And I'll talk to you later," Marcella said and pressed the button on the phone. As soon as she set the receiver down on the base of the phone, she cringed. She'd actually hung up on her best friend. She and Sharon had never had an argument. Maybe a disagreement or two, but never a full-fledged argument.

But, then lately, whenever the subject of Tyrone and her children came up, Marcella was in the habit of going off on whomever she came in contact with. She'd gotten into it with Racquel last year at the Fourth of July cookout, threatened Tyrone with a baseball bat, embarrassed herself in front of Darryl at the movie theater, and now she'd hurt Sharon's feelings for no reason at all. She didn't know what was happening to her. Sometimes she felt like she was losing her mind. One minute she was happy, and the next minute she was ticked off at the smallest little thing. She wanted desperately to call and apologize to Sharon, but she wasn't sure what she should say to her. Maybe it was better to let things cool down for a while. She'd call her later in the evening or possibly stop by her condo.

As she reached to lift the phone, preparing to dial Tyrone's phone number, it rang. "Hello?" Marcella said, not wanting to talk to anyone.

"Hey, we need to talk," Sharon said and sighed. "I'll be over in an hour or so, okay?"

"Okay, I'll see you then," Marcella said, smiling, and then hung up the phone. She felt better already. She needed Sharon in her life more than ever before, and she thanked God for giving her a best friend who was so loving, so caring, and so understanding. She couldn't wait to apologize to her, and she was never going to treat her this terribly ever again.

Marcella picked up the phone and dialed Tyrone.

"Hello?" his mother said.

"Hey, Ma," Marcella said in a surprised voice. She'd expected Tyrone to answer the phone, and not his mother. "How are you doing?"

"Oh, I'm fine, honey. Working hard every day, but I'm fine. How's my grandchildren?"

"Oh, they're fine."

"And how's your mother?"

"She's fine. As a matter of fact, I just spoke with her earlier this morning, and she asked how you were doing, too."

"You tell her I said hello when you talk to her again."

Marcella didn't want to be rude, but she needed to talk to Tyrone now. "Is Tyrone there, by chance?"

"He sure is. I'll get him for you," Tyrone's mother said and yelled for him to pick up the phone.

He picked up another extension, and his mother told Marcella to take care and that she'd talk to her later.

"Hello?" Tyrone said, sounding sarcastically pleasant.

"All I want to know is one thing. Did you or did you not report your child-support payments to the welfare office?"

"I told you if you kept clownin' on me what was going to happen. You thought you were the shit when you had your little boyfriend over, but who's getting the last laugh now. Huh?"

"You no-good bastard. You make me sick," Marcella said, tightening her face. "Why don't you just make it easy for everybody and die?"

"I told you to stop messing with me, but you kept talking to me like I was nobody."

"So, because your little ego got hurt, you decided to take food away from your own children?"

"You can manage. You do still work, don't you? And I know the Housing Authority dropped your rent to zero when you went back to school. Hell, I'm not stupid."

"Maybe if you paid your child support like you were supposed to, I wouldn't have to worry about food stamps or anything else."

"Hell, I'm not paying you so you can spend it on

yourself. And for all I know, you might be spending it on your little doctor friend."

"Tyrone, you are really something else. I knew you were a lowlife, but I had no idea you would stoop low enough to do something this dirty. But what goes around comes around."

"Oh, so now you're threatening me again. Marcella, please."

She slammed the phone down so hard that she felt a vibration move up her arm. She felt like screaming at the top of her lungs. She took a deep breath and tried to calm herself down. She would get through this. Tyrone was doing everything he could to make her miserable, but she wasn't going to let him succeed at it. She was in love with a wonderful man; she had two beautiful children; she had a mother and sister who loved her; and a best friend who would move mountains if it meant helping her. No, Tyrone wasn't going to bring her down. One day he would regret not spending time with his children the way he should have, but it was going to be too late.

During the next three hours, Ashley and Nicholas cleaned up their bedrooms and did whatever else Marcella told them, while she cleaned up her bedroom, the bathroom, and finished her homework assignment for Accounting II. She'd been working on this same problem set for the last hour, but she just couldn't seem to make it balance. Her eyes were starting to get tired, so she laid her pencil down and pushed the ledger sheets to the side. She glanced at her watch and wondered where Sharon was. She'd said she'd be over in about an hour, but now it was almost four hours since she'd spoken with her. It was unlike her to be late for anything, and if she couldn't help it, she usually called. Maybe she and Marcus had decided to do something at the last minute. It was Saturday, and they did usually spend the whole day together. She wished she could spend time with Darryl, too, but he was pulling a double shift at the hospital. She wondered how Racquel was doing and decided to call her.

"Hello?" Raquel answered.

"Hey, girl. What's up?"

"Not much. What's up with you?"

"The kids have been cleaning up and watching TV, and I've been working on my accounting homework. That's about it. So how are you and Kevin?"

"There's still some distance, but at least he's talking to me again. I guess it'll take some time before things get back to normal."

"I'm so glad to hear that. You two belong together."

"Yeah, I know, and I can't believe we came so close to ending our whole marriage. And you'll be glad to know that I've finally decided to consider adoption. I still don't feel completely comfortable with the idea of it, but I promised Kevin I would think real hard about it."

"That's wonderful. I really think you're making the right decision."

"I sure hope so, because I'm telling you, there's no way we would have made it, if we hadn't come to sort of a compromise."

Marcella heard the call-waiting signal in her phone "Hey, hold on for a second," she said, pressing the button inside of the phone receiver. "Hello?" she said to whoever was calling.

"Marcella," Darryl said sadly. "I don't know how to tell you this, but . . ."

"But, what?" she said, sounding alarmed.

"Sharon was in a serious car accident."

"Oh, no, Darryl, no. I'll be there in a few minutes.'

"Marcella, wait," he said, pausing.

"Wait for what?" she asked, confused.

"She didn't make it."

"Noooo, Darryl. Please," Marcella said, dropping down to her knees on the kitchen floor, still holding the phone, and slowly shaking her head in denial. "Not Sharon, Darryl, please tell me it wasn't her."

"Baby, I'm leaving the hospital right now, and I'll be there as soon as I can. I called your mother, and she should be there any minute."

Marcella dropped the phone to the ground, curled her body in a ball, and cried loudly. Ashley and Nicholas ran to her and kneeled down beside her.

"Mom, what's wrong?" Ashley asked and put her arm around her mother.

"Mom, you're scaring me," Nicholas said with tears in his eyes.

Marcella was crying hysterically by now, and felt like her heart had been yanked out. She folded her arms and rocked back and forth. Ashley heard a knock at the door and ran to answer it, while Nicholas sat next to his mom, trying to hold on to her as best he could. When Ashley opened the door, she saw that it was her grandmother.

"Granny, something's wrong with Mom," she said, leading her over to where Marcella was.

"I know, baby," Corrine said, hugging her granddaughter and walking with her through the living room and then into the kitchen.

"Sweetheart," Corrine said, kneeling down to the floor, pulling Marcella into her arms. "I know it hurts, but you have to believe that everything is going to be all right," she said, stroking Marcella's hair.

"Granny, what's wrong with Mom?" Ashley asked in a worried tone of voice.

Corrine blinked quickly as tears began to fall from her eyes. "Your aunt Sharon was killed in a car accident."

"Oh, God, Mom," Marcella screamed out. "I killed her. I killed her. I killed her," Marcella said quickly.

"No, baby. Don't say that." Corrine tried to calm her daughter down.

"Yes, I did. If I hadn't treated her so badly on the phone, she never would have tried to come over here . . . It's all my fault," Marcella moaned.

"Look, baby, no matter what you think, it's not your fault, and there's nothing you could have done to stop this from happening. All of our times are set, honey, so don't blame yourself. What you have to do now is ask God for strength, so you can get through this."

Ashley and Nicholas looked at their mother and it was obvious that they didn't understand why this was happening. Corrine saw the look on their faces and wanted to console them, but right now she had to do everything in her power to help Marcella. Because if she didn't, there was a chance her daughter might have an emotional breakdown.

Chapter 16

For the next two days, Marcella stayed in bed and refused to discuss anything that had to do with Sharon's funeral. She knew it was her responsibility, since Sharon had no family, but she just couldn't bring herself to make the arrangements. Since the day of the accident, Racquel and Corrine had tried to talk her into it, but she still wasn't ready to face the fact. A part of her wanted to believe that this was all just some horrible nightmare. But the hours and the days were starting to pass by, and she was starting to realize that this wasn't some nightmare at all. That it was as real as the sun rising in the east and setting in the west.

She still regretted that she'd been so rude to Sharon when they'd had the conversation regarding Tyrone, and she kept playing a mental tape of it over and over again. She wanted so desperately to turn the time back, so she could apologize to her and take back everything she'd said, but it was too late. Sharon had said she was on her way over, and Marcella had thought for sure she'd have the opportunity to tell her how sorry she was when she got there. But Sharon had never made it more than a few miles from her apartment when some reckless teenaged driver swerved in front of her on the expressway. She was thrown from her seat, and her head had crashed straight into the front windshield. She suffered severe head injuries and other deep lacerations as a result of the glass shattering all over her body. She'd died on arrival at Covington Park Memorial Hospital. Her car had been totaled, and when they transported her to the hospital, the police had searched through her purse trying to find information concerning next of kin, but they hadn't found anything. That was the reason why it had taken so long for someone to contact Marcella. And if Darryl hadn't just so happened to go down to the ER, there's no telling when Marcella would have been notified. Sharon had always been so well organized and so well put together, and it surprised Marcella that she didn't have something in her wallet or purse to indicate who should be called in case of an emergency. And it surprised her even more when the investigating officer said that Sharon didn't have her seat belt on. It was so unlike her.

Marcella felt numb, and she wished she could close her eyes, fall off to sleep, and never wake up again. This was such a tragedy, and she honestly didn't know how to deal with any of it. Ashley and Nicholas had gone to school today, and she was glad, because it wasn't good for them to see her in such bad shape. She usually tried to be strong in front of them whenever something bad happened, but this was one time she hadn't been able to. She still had her family, but at the same time she felt so alone. So empty. It was a feeling that she hadn't experienced before. She and Sharon had both just turned thirty this year, and she'd thought for sure that they had their whole lives ahead of them. That they had so much more time to spend together. There were still things she needed to tell her. Things she needed to do with her. It just wasn't fair. And while she knew it was wrong to question, let alone blame God for what had taken place, she didn't understand why this had to happen. Sharon was such a wonderful and giving person, and here murderers, drug dealers, child abusers, and the like were running around doing whatever they pleased. Life was so confusing. She'd known all along that no one could live forever, but she never expected that Sharon's life would end before her thirty-first birthday. Tragedies like this only happened in the movies, and even if it did happen in real life, things like this never happened to her. Her grandparents had passed away a few years back, but she'd had plenty of time to prepare because they'd both suffered from long-term illnesses. But Sharon had died almost instantly and without warning.

Marcella lay in the bed for another half hour and then dragged herself into the shower. She stood under the hot water so long, her body shriveled up like a prune. After she dried herself off, she put on a pair of stone-washed jeans and a black wool sweater. She usually lotioned her body down, especially in the fall and winter to keep her skin from becoming so dry, but she didn't care about any of that today. She brushed her hair back and wrapped a thick beige rubber band around it. The people from the funeral home had called the evening before saying she could come to their office around four o'clock, so they could prepare the obituary for the newspaper, pick out the casket, and make the final funeral arrangements. It was now nearly noon, and Corrine had said she'd be by to pick Marcella up at 12:30

P.M. She'd taken off work, so that she and Marcella could go over to Sharon's condo to search for any insurance policies, which she may have had, and to look over her will. Marcella had thought Sharon was too young to make out a will when she'd had her attorney draw one up two years ago, but now she had to admit, it did make things a lot easier when someone died. Tomorrow wasn't promised to anyone, and Marcella was more of a witness to that theory now than she cared to be.

Corrine arrived at Marcella's apartment on schedule, and they immediately drove over to Sharon's. When they entered the condo, they went directly up to the guest bedroom, which Sharon had turned into a home office. Inside the closet was a safe, which Sharon had given Marcella the combination to, so Marcella pulled it out, opened it, and spread all of the documents across the oak-wood desk. She and Corrine sat facing each other. The first item she noticed was Sharon's will. She skimmed through the first page of it, which was mostly a bunch of legal jargon, and finally turned to the second page, which began to list her assets and who she'd left them to. Marcella hated doing this. Two weeks ago, she would have liked nothing more than for someone to leave her some luxuries or money in general, but now she didn't care about any of that. As a matter of fact, she was starting to realize how messed up her priorities had been over the last few years, because what good was money if you didn't have the people you loved to share it with?

She moved her finger down the page and read through the paragraphs carefully. From the looks of it, Sharon had made her executor, which she already knew. But what she didn't know, was that she had left everything to her and her family. She knew Sharon didn't have any living relatives, with the exception of her father, but she didn't know where he was anyway. She'd made Marcella, Ashley, Nicholas, and Corrine the beneficiaries on the life-insurance policy provided by her employer, which was worth one times her base salary. And Marcella was sure that Sharon earned just over sixty thousand dollars annually.

"Mom, can you believe this?" Marcella said, teary eyed.

"Sharon loved you so much," Corrine said, smiling at her daughter.

"She loved all of us," Marcella said, turning her attention back to the will.

"She left twenty-five percent to each of us. There's a lot of legal terms here, but it basically says that Ashley's and Nicholas's portions are to be placed in trust and used to pay toward their college expenses, but should they decide not to attend college, the monies will be kept in trust until they reach twenty-one years of age. And should something happen to Ashley, then her money would transfer to Nicholas for his education, and vice versa," Marcella said and paused for a moment. "But it also says that if her death results from an accident, the policy will pay two times her salary. And it sounds like we'll each still get twenty-five percent of the first fifty percent, or fifteen thousand dollars, but the remaining amount will also go toward the children's education. Except, if they don't go to college, then that portion of their money will revert back to me."

"What does all that mean?" Corrine asked, obviously confused by what Marcella had just said to her.

"I'm not completely sure, but I think it means that since she died accidentally, her policy will now pay one hundred twenty thousand dollars. Which means that we'll all still get twenty-five percent of the first sixty thousand, but the other sixty thousand will be divided equally between the children. But, if they don't go to college, then that portion of their money will revert back to me. So, from the way it looks, they each have forty-five thousand for school."

"It sure sounds like she really thought this all out, doesn't it?"

"That's just how Sharon was, and she knew that one of my main worries was how I was going to put Ashley and Nicholas through college."

"Is there a policy for her funeral and burial expenses?" Corrine asked. "That's what we need more than anything else."

Marcella searched through the pile. "I don't see anything. Maybe there's something else in the will," Marcella said, turning the page. She scanned down the page until she came to the word "burial." "Here it is. It says that her savings account at Bank First is to be used for her funeral and burial expenses."

"Did you see any bankbooks or statements?" Corrine said, gazing down at all of the paperwork.

Marcella shuffled through the documents again and found a bank statement. She opened it and then reviewed the information contained in it. "She has a little over five thousand dollars in the account, but if that's not enough to cover it, I'll pay the difference from what she left me."

"No," Corrine said. "You have two babies to take care of, and you know that car of yours isn't going to outlast these winter months. I'll pay the funeral home and the cemetery, and whatever else they need. And we still have to go by the flower shop to order the blanket for the casket."

Marcella knew she should be happy to have such an inheritance, but suddenly, she felt sad again. She just couldn't shake this, and it felt strange sitting inside of

Sharon's condo when she wasn't there. And even worse, knowing that she wasn't coming back. And it seemed wrong to be sitting here discussing what she'd left for everyone else, but Marcella knew it couldn't be helped. Her grandmother had made sure that all of her burial expenses had been taken care of before she passed away, too, and when her grandfather had died, she had even purchased a headstone with both of their names on it. Her grandfather's birth year and the year he died were engraved under his name, and her grandmother's birth year was printed under hers with a dash after it. It was almost like she was waiting to die. Marcella had thought putting your own name on a headstone while you were still living was the weirdest thing she'd ever heard of, but now she realized how much stress it took off the family. It was hard enough trying to come to terms with the loss of a loved one, but it would be an even greater disaster if the family didn't know where they were going to find the money to pay for a decent funeral. Marcella could still hear her grandmother's words: "Baby, we all have to leave here one day, so we might as well get ready for it. And there's no sense in leaving a burden on the family, when we can help it."

Marcella gathered together all of the documents from the safe and placed them in a large envelope. She went to turn off Sharon's computer, which must have been running since Saturday afternoon. When she moved the mouse by accident, the screen saver vanished, and she saw a document that Sharon obviously had been working on. The heading said "Five-Year Goals," and she'd listed two of them. The first said that she wanted to find out who her father was, and the second said that she wanted to meet the perfect guy and get married to him. Marcella had thought Marcus was the man of Sharon's dreams, and she was sure that Marcus thought the exact same thing, or at least had been hoping he was.

She exited WordPerfect without saving the document, because the last thing she wanted was for Marcus to find out that Sharon hadn't *ever* planned on marrying him. Chances were, he'd never go through her computer files anyway, but Marcella still didn't want to take the risk. He loved Sharon more than anything, and it wasn't worth hurting his feelings.

Marcella and Corrine walked back down the stairs, checked things over, and then left.

"You do know that we're going to have to clean all of her belongings out, don't you?" Corrine asked Marcella.

"Yeah, I know. But I don't even want to think about any of that right now. Maybe in a couple of weeks."

"I'm sure Marcus will want to help, and there might be some things he wants to keep."

"I'm sure there will be. He's supposed to meet us at the funeral home and then come by my apartment later this evening, so maybe I'll mention it to him then," Marcella said, sliding into her mother's car.

Corrine turned the ignition and drove away from the condo.

It was nine o'clock, Ashley and Nicholas had just gone to bed, and Marcella was lying in Darryl's arms on the sofa with her head against his chest. She was glad that the day was finally coming to a close, and with the exception of a couple of items, all of the funeral arrangements had been made.

She, Corrine, and Marcus had decided to have the funeral on Wednesday, with a three-hour visitation prior to service time. The funeral director had shown them each of the caskets that he had in stock, and they'd all agreed on the deep cobalt-blue one, which had mixtures of silver in it. He'd also informed them that they needed to select something for Sharon to wear, so Marcella told him that she would bring everything he needed by the funeral home tomorrow morning. And the only thing they had left to do was deliver a photo of Sharon, and the order of service information, to one of the local desktop publishers, so the programs could be printed.

Marcella closed her eyes.

"What's the matter, baby?" Darryl asked.

"I feel so exhausted, and I can't knock this guilty feeling that I have."

"What do you feel so guilty about?"

"If I hadn't spoken to Sharon so rudely, she never would have gotten in her car to drive over here. I should have apologized to her when she called back, but I didn't, and I'll never forgive myself for it."

"You never told me that you guys were upset with each other, so what happened?"

Marcella opened her eyes immediately, and it was a good thing Darryl couldn't see the expression on her face. She'd never told him about the argument because she hadn't wanted to explain why she and Sharon had been exchanging words in such a disagreeing manner. He'd made it pretty clear that he didn't want her confronting Tyrone anymore, and she wasn't sure how he was going to react if he found out that she'd gone against his wishes. But there was no sense in keeping it from him now. "I found out on Saturday that my food stamps have been suspended, until the welfare office determines how much child support I receive from Tyrone, so I called Sharon to tell her about it. And then one conversation led to another."

"But why would something like that cause you and Sharon to get into an argument?"

Marcella paused for a second. Maybe it would be better if she told him something other than what really happened. But, on the other hand, they had a truthful and trusting relationship, and she didn't want to jeopardize it by lying to him now. It wouldn't be fair to him or her, and she knew one lie always led to another. And then it usually got to the place where a person couldn't keep track of which lie he or she had told last. As far as she was concerned, it wasn't worth all of that. Besides, she felt bad enough as it was for not being truthful with him about their sex life. And anyway, she'd only called Tyrone, which was a lot different than seeing him in person, so Darryl probably wouldn't be nearly as upset as he was that evening they'd taken the children to the movie theater. "Because I wanted to call Tyrone and tell him off about what he did, and she kept telling me I shouldn't."

"What do you mean, what he did?" he said, lifting her upper body away from him.

"He's the one who called my caseworker to report his child-support payments."

"How do you know that he's the one who did it?"

"Because I just know, and anyway, he admitted it when I called him."

"So, even though you knew how I felt about these run-ins between you and Tyrone, you called him anyway?"

"Baby, I was upset, okay? I know how you feel, but I just couldn't help calling him," she said with an innocent look on her face.

"When is this going to end, Marcella?" he asked, staring at her angrily.

"There's nothing *to* end," she said nervously, because the only time he called her by her first name was when he was extremely serious or wasn't happy with her about something.

"You know, I'm getting real sick of hearing about Tyrone. And why can't you just leave him alone? I mean, he's never going to change, and you know that."

"I know, baby, but when I read that letter from the agency, I lost it. I know I shouldn't have called him, but I just couldn't help it. Tyrone knows that I depend on those food stamps, and he only did it because I'm seeing you. I just couldn't let him get away with doing that."

"Well, after you called him, did that change anything?" he asked sarcastically. "I mean, come on."

"That's not the point."

"Then, what is the point?" he asked, folding his arms and waiting for an answer.

She was at a loss for words, and decided not to answer him.

He shook his head in confusion. "Look, Marcella. I love you and I want to be with you, but I can't keep dealing with this Tyrone situation. I told you before that the best way to handle Tyrone is by ignoring him. He only pays you child support when he feels like it anyway, and it's not like you need him for anything else. This is going to have to stop, and that's all there is to it."

"How can you expect me to cut off all communication with Tyrone, when he's the father of my children? You know that's not possible."

"What do you need to talk to him about, Marcella?" he asked, raising his voice. "He doesn't do shit for Ashley and Nick, and he treats you like a dog."

"I know that, but there are still going to be times when we have to cross each other's paths."

"Why? Just give me one good reason why."

"You just don't understand," she said, rising from the sofa.

"I just don't understand what?" he asked, moving his body to the edge of the sofa.

"He calls over here to talk to Ashley and Nicholas, and he comes by to pick them up from time to time, so there's no way I can avoid seeing or talking to him completely."

"I never said that. What I'm saying is that you don't have to keep arguing back and forth with him. Ashley and Nick are old enough to talk to their father without your help, and when he comes to pick them up, the most he should be doing is honking his horn for them to come out. He doesn't need to be coming in here for any reason I can think of."

"I don't see why you're so upset, because it's not like I went to his house and confronted him."

"If you don't see why I'm upset, then we have a bigger problem than I thought," he said, standing up.

"Darryl, you knew I had two children when we met, and you had to know that there would be times when I would have to talk to their father."

"Yeah, when it came to their well-being, or something like that. But I'm not about to keep putting up with these arguments you and he keep having. It's almost like the two of you still have feelings for each other, or something."

"Darryl, please. You know good and well that I don't have those kinds of feelings for Tyrone. I'm in love with you, and I've told you that over and over again."

"I'm really starting to wonder if, in fact, you do, and it's getting to the point where I feel like I'm in some sort of competition with Tyrone."

What was he talking about? She loved *him*, and she couldn't care less whether Tyrone lived or died. And she couldn't understand at all why he was so upset about something so petty. He was acting like he was jealous of Tyrone, and that didn't make any sense to her. She spent all of her time with him, not Tyrone, and that was the only thing that should have mattered. She couldn't just pretend like Tyrone didn't exist. Like they didn't share two children together. So what was she supposed to do? "I don't know what to say," she finally said.

He stood in front of her. "Look. I don't want to upset you any more than I already have, and I don't want to keep arguing with you about Tyrone, so maybe I should leave."

"Darryl, my best friend just died, and I need you now more than I ever have. So, can't we just put this Tyrone thing behind us? At least until after the funeral?"

"I'll tell you what. I'll come by after work tomorrow afternoon. Maybe by then, both of us will have cooled down," he said, pulling her into his arms.

They hugged, but it didn't feel the same. He was more distant than he usually was, and she could tell that he'd only made the effort to hug her because he thought she expected it. And not at all because he wanted to.

"I'll talk to you tomorrow," he said, and kissed her on the forehead. Then he turned and walked out the front door.

First she'd lost her best friend, and now it felt like she was losing Darryl. She felt like her whole world was crumbling into a million pieces, and her heart ached violently. For once, she wished it could rain without pouring when it came to the problems in her life.

She turned off the television set, switched off the lamp on the faded brass end table, walked into her bedroom, dove facefirst on her bed, and wished for this night to be over.

Chapter 17

"It's hard to believe she's gone, isn't it?" Marcus said to Marcella. It had been four weeks since the funeral, and they'd both chosen today as the day to sort through Sharon's condo. They'd already packed up the office, and now they were in her bedroom.

"It really is. But it does seem like it's becoming more and more of a reality as the days continue on. At first, I didn't think I would ever accept the fact that she was gone, because I depended on her for just about everything. She always gave me a shoulder to lean on whenever I needed it, and a lot of people wouldn't have done half the things she did for my children."

"But she loved those kids like they were her own, and every time she referred to Ashley and Nicholas, she would always say her 'niece and nephew.' "

"I know, and they loved her like she was their biological aunt," Marcella said, taking some of Sharon's suits from her closet and laying them on the oversized wrought-iron canopy bed.

"Hey," Marcus said, unplugging the off-white floor lamp. "Do you mind if I ask you something personal?"

"Go ahead," Marcella said, wondering if he wanted to know something about her, or something about him and Sharon.

"Do you have any idea why Sharon wasn't that thrilled about marrying me?"

Oh, no! She'd been afraid that the subject of his and Sharon's relationship might come up, and she had no idea how she should respond to him. Especially, since she *did* know why Sharon didn't want to marry him. Or at least part of the reason why anyway. "I think maybe she just wanted to be sure that getting married was the right thing for her to do. I mean, I know she loved you, because she told me so on more than one occasion, but you know how careful she was when it came to making major decisions," Marcella said, hoping she had convinced him that Sharon really did adore him.

"But what could have made her second-guess whether marrying me was the right thing to do? I mean, she knew how much I loved her and how dedicated I was to our relationship. So that's why I don't understand it."

Now what was she supposed to say? He was making her feel uncomfortable, and she wished he would change the conversation to something else; something that had nothing to do with him and Sharon. "Well, all I know is that she loved you, Marcus, and no matter what, you should never think differently."

"Look, Marcella, you and Sharon were like sisters, so I know she confided in you about everything. And if you know something more, then I wish you'd tell me. Even if it's something you don't think I want to hear.

Because at least then maybe I can add some closure to all of this," he said, leaning against the wall with his arms folded.

Why did he want to know about this so badly? And why was he acting like his life depended on it? She wanted to help him, because she knew how hurt he was over losing the woman he practically worshiped, but she just couldn't hurt him, and she didn't want to betray Sharon's confidence in her, either. "Sometimes people love each other more than anything else in the world, and still never get to the point of wanting to get married. It doesn't mean that there's something wrong with you, or that there was something she didn't like about you. But it simply means that she wasn't ready to take such a huge step in her life," Marcella said, standing in front of the armoire with a pile of sweaters draped over her arm.

"Yeah, maybe," he said doubtfully.

"You've got to get on with your life, Marcus. I know it's hard, but you have to do it. You're intelligent, you're an attractive guy, and you have your whole life ahead of you."

"You're right, but just answer me this one question."

"What's that?" Marcella asked curiously.

"Did it have anything to do with our sex life?"

"What do you mean?" Marcella asked, trying to sound surprised about the question.

"Was she happy with it? Did I satisfy her? You know, did she enjoy making love to me?"

Marcella couldn't believe what she was hearing. She'd always felt like she and Marcus were pretty close because of Sharon, but not once had she ever imagined him asking her something so personal. Something so embarrassing. She'd thought asking Marcus over to help clean out Sharon's belongings was a great idea, but now she wasn't so sure. As a matter of fact, she was starting to see just how much of a mistake it had been. "As far as I know, everything was fine," Marcella said and was sure she was going to be struck down with lightning any minute now.

"You're sure?" he asked, staring straight into Marcella's eyes.

"Really, I am."

"Well, if there wasn't a problem with that, then I don't know what was wrong with us."

"Nothing was wrong with either one of you, and who knows, maybe Sharon would have married you in time."

"I really doubt that, because whenever I brought the subject up, she always tried to avoid talking about it. She just wasn't interested in making a commitment to me," he said, pulling out each of the drawers to the dresser and placing them on the floor one by one.

"Well, like I said, you have your whole life ahead of you, and as time goes on, you'll be fine."

"I know, but it's hard when you love someone as much as I loved Sharon, and then you start to realize that the person obviously didn't feel the same way about you."

Marcella didn't know what else to say, but she couldn't help but wonder if maybe Darryl was suspecting the same thing about her. She never gave him any reason to believe that he wasn't satisfying her, but now after listening to Marcus, she really couldn't be sure.

She pulled two handfuls of lingerie out of one of the drawers Marcus had set on the floor and then placed them inside one of the cardboard boxes. For a while she and Marcus worked in silence, then they reminisced about all the good times they'd shared with Sharon. Over the next few hours, they finished packing everything in every room. Then they walked outside to their respective automobiles.

"Well, I guess this is it, until Kevin and Racquel pick up the U-Haul truck tomorrow morning," Marcus said, pulling the collar up on his brown leather jacket.

"Yeah, I guess it is," Marcella said and then turned back to look at the beautiful brick building they'd just exited.

Marcus did the same, took a deep breath and looked back at Marcella. "Marcella, if you ever need anything for the children, yourself or anything at all, I hope you know that you can call me the same as you would if you had a brother."

"I know that," she said, smiling at him. "And I will. I promise."

"Now, don't just say that, and then don't do it, because I'm serious."

"I'm telling you, I'll call you if I need you. And you do the same. Even if you just need someone to talk to."

"Okay, then, I'll see you guys in the morning," he said, hugging Marcella.

"We'll see you then, Marcus. And thanks for coming over to help me with all the packing."

"No problem. No problem at all," he said.

They sat in their cars, and shortly after, they both drove off.

Chapter 18

It was one week before Christmas, so Racquel and Marcella decided to drive downtown on Michigan Avenue to do some last-minute shopping. It had always been sort of a tradition for the two of them to spend the last Saturday before Christmas strolling the busy streets, admiring all the fancy decorations, but this year they'd changed the traditional day to Friday, since they both were on Christmas break; Marcella from the university and Racquel from the elementary school that she taught at. It was so beautiful this time of year, especially with the newly fallen snow, that they both hated when the holiday season ended.

They'd just left Filene's Basement, where they'd found some wonderful bargains, and were headed South on Michigan Avenue searching for a cafe that wasn't too crowded. When they found one, they went inside. The instrumental version of "Santa Claus Is Coming To Town" was playing, and a petite Italian-looking hostess seated them near the front window. After she advised them of the day's specials, she handed each of them a menu and asked if they wanted to start with something to drink. They'd gotten kind of cold from all of the walking, so they each ordered a cup of hot chocolate.

"Who would have ever thought that Sharon would never see another Christmas?" Marcella said, gazing out the window toward the sidewalk, where a group of happy-looking senior citizens was passing by.

"I know," Racquel said, switching her attention to the direction Marcella was looking.

"I get so sad every time I think about her. And even though I finalized the sale of her condo last week, it still doesn't seem real. She had so much promise, and she was such a good person."

"They always say that the good die young, and with the way this world is nowadays, you have to wonder if maybe she isn't in a much better place than we are, anyway."

"You do have a point there. Life is so strange. It seems like you're up one minute and down the next. And based on the way my life has been going, I don't think there's ever going to be a time when everything is going good all at the same time," Marcella said, scanning the menu.

"I've always wished for that, too, but to tell you the truth, I don't think it's possible. It seems like the things we want the most, are the things we can't ever have."

"All I've ever wanted was a decent job, and even though I'm about to start the second semester of my sophomore year, it seems like I'm never going to finish."

"Well, you wanted a good man, too, and Darryl is all of that and then some."

"Yeah, but things haven't been the same since we

had that argument about Tyrone two months ago. He still calls and comes by, but not nearly as often as he used to. And he seems distant."

"Well, I'll tell you like you told me when Kevin and I were having all those problems. You need to sit down and have a serious talk with him. Because if you don't, things will get worse before they get better."

"I don't even know if it will do any good. I think the idea of having to deal with a woman who has children by another man is a bit more than he's willing to put up with. He doesn't have a problem with Ashley and Nicholas, but he can't stand the sight of Tyrone."

"Forget Tyrone. What you need to do is cut that jerk off completely. He doesn't mean the children or you any good anyhow. And he sure as hell isn't worth losing Darryl over."

"I know, but you know I can't do that. Ashley is getting to the point where she could live with or without him because he's always lying to her, but Nicholas adores everything about him. Regardless of what he does or doesn't do for them."

"Good it's you. Because I'm telling you, men like Darryl are hard to find. And on top of that, he's a doctor, too? There's no way, Marcella."

"You're only saying that because you've never had to be in this situation. It's just not that easy," Marcella said, closing her menu.

"I don't understand you and Mom. It's almost like Tyrone has some spell over both of you. First, Mom accepts his apology for showing out on her in her own house, and now you're prepared to give up Darryl for him."

Marcella didn't say anything.

The waitress set down two cups of hot chocolate and two glasses of water, and then prepared to take their orders. "So, have you decided on what you're going to have?" Racquel asked Marcella, realizing that she'd crossed the line with her previous comment.

"Yes, I'll have the bacon, cheddar, and onion quiche," Marcella answered and watched the waitress jot her selection down.

"And you?" the waitress said, smiling at Racquel.

"I'll have the California pie," Racquel responded.

"Is that it?" the waitress asked, reaching for their menus.

"I think that'll be it for now, but we might want dessert later," Racquel said.

"That'll be fine," the waitress said and then left the table.

"So, have you decided what you want for Christmas?" Racquel asked Marcella.

"No. Not really. And anyway, you've already bought most of Ashley's and Nicholas's gifts, and that's enough."

"Well, that's the least I could do. I know Sharon had planned to buy some of them, but I'm their aunt, and I wanted to get them some things, too. But that still doesn't have anything to do with you."

"I know, but I got the biggest gift ever last month when I bought that Grand Am. It was a couple of years old, but it feels like a new car to me."

"That was so wonderful of Sharon to leave her insurance policy to you, Mom, and the kids, especially since you've been needing another car for a long time now."

"I know. That Cutlass was on its last leg, and I don't know how much longer it was going to be before it gave out. And there's no way I could have gotten to work and school without a car. It was such a blessing."

"Yeah, it really was. So what happened with Sharon's car since it was totaled?"

"Her insurance company paid it off because the boy that caused the accident didn't have any insurance on his car."

"That is so ridiculous. And I can't believe people actually ride around here without insurance. It's so inconsiderate to everybody else."

"It really is," Marcella said, looking toward the kitchen of the restaurant, checking to see if their food was coming.

"That's a cute gold bracelet," Racquel said, admiring what she saw on Marcella's wrist.

"Oh, thanks. This was Sharon's. And so was this sweater I've got on. She willed all of her personal items and furniture to me, too. Plus, we got both of her TV's and her entertainment center."

"Girl, you have really been blessed. I mean, you have nice furniture in your apartment, you're two years away from getting your degree, you're driving a nice car, and you've got money in the bank."

"Yeah, my life is a lot better in some ways, but not much better financially because I spent almost ten thousand on the car. And I put the other five thousand in the bank for living expenses and my auto insurance."

"But at least you have more things than you had before. I know Sharon is gone, but I'm so grateful that she loved you enough to do what she did. Friends like her don't come along every day, because I know I've never had a friend like that. Of course, you're my best friend, but I still don't have one that I'm not related to," Racquel said as the waitress set their entrees down on the table. She asked if she could get them anything else, they both said no, and then she turned and left.

"This is so good," Marcella said in the middle of chewing a forkful of the quiche.

"They have a different type of quiche daily, and

they're always real good," Racquel said, sprinkling pepper inside of her California pie. "So how's Marcus doing?"

"I spoke with him two days ago, and he seems to be doing okay, but he really misses Sharon a lot. He was so in love with her."

"Gosh, it's a good thing he never found out that she didn't feel the same way about him, because I remember when you told me about what she'd written on her computer."

"Yeah, I know. It's hard when you love someone, and then you find out they don't feel the same way. He would have been devastated."

"I was so shocked when you told me she wasn't happy with the sex, because not only does Marcus look good, but he also has a decent job."

"I know," Marcella said, sipping some water from a long-stemmed glass. "And she told me more than once that she really loved him. But, regardless of how good someone looks or how much money he has, if he's not the one, he's just not the one."

"You know I know that better than anyone. Remember Cecil from high school. He used to hound me every day during my entire senior year. Actually, he was one of the nicest guys I ever met, but I just couldn't make myself like him."

Marcella laughed. "Maybe he was *too* nice, because those are the guys nobody ever wants for some reason or another. It's stupid, but that's usually how it is."

"Maybe. But I still did okay by marrying Kevin. He's always treated me one hundred percent, and we never had any real problems until this thing with me trying to get pregnant came about. He was downright cruel with some of the things he said to me, and he walked out on me practically every time we had an argument.

All of that really took a toll on our marriage, and I wish none of it had happened."

"But all that matters now, is that you finally got things worked out."

"Somewhat. Because we still aren't the same, and I'm starting to wonder if we ever will be. He spends a lot of time at work and at the 'Y,' so we haven't spent a whole lot of time together during the past two months. I mean, it doesn't seem like he has an attitude, or like he doesn't love me, but he just isn't the same as he used to be. I can't put my finger on it, but something's different. And we only make love once or twice a week."

"Maybe you need to ask him what's wrong."

"I've wanted to, but I don't want to stir things up if I don't have to."

"Well, making love once or twice a week is a milestone compared to what's going on with me. It's been over a month since Darryl and I have done anything like that. He's usually working, and if he's not, the kids are always around."

"Well, that's no reason. Because you know Ashley and Nicholas can always spend the night with us."

"I know, but I've been trying to spend as much time as I can with them. They miss Sharon almost as much as I do. She did a lot for them, and they loved her like she was their blood aunt. Plus, Darryl loves being with them, too."

"But, still, you need to spend some time alone with him. I'm sure he doesn't mind being around Ashley and Nicholas, but you can bet he'd like to spend at least some of his time with *just* you. Every relationship needs that. I know you have a responsibility to your children, but you have to balance your time between doing things with them and doing things with him. That's the very reason why most married couples grow apart after they have children. They don't spend enough quality time together. I mean, how romantic can you be when two crumb snatchers are looking directly in your face."

They both laughed.

"I know. I know. But it's just that they don't have anybody else. Tyrone is never there for them, and I hate putting them off on you and Mom all the time."

"Putting them off?" Racquel asked, frowning. "Please. We love those children, and we love you."

"I know you do," Marcella said, smiling.

"Look at those cute little twins," Racquel said excitedly as she looked out the window and saw two adorable little girls dressed in red wool coats and matching hats.

Marcella smiled.

"What I wouldn't give to have two beautiful little girls like them."

Marcella wasn't sure what to say. Racquel was so wishy-washy when it came to the subject of having babies, and she didn't want to say the wrong thing. Maybe she should say something encouraging about adoption. "So what have you finally decided as far as trying to adopt a baby?"

"I've thought about it objectively, and we've met with a lady from the adoption agency once, but I haven't decided for sure. Kevin thinks it's a great idea, so I'm sure we'll go forward with it, if . . . ," Racquel said, cutting the sentence off.

"If what?" Marcella asked curiously.

"My mouth is so big. I promised myself that I wouldn't say anything to you, Mom, or Kevin, and now look," Racquel said with disappointment.

"Racquel. The cat is out of the bag now, so you might as well tell me whatever it is you're trying to hide," Marcella said, laughing, but deep down she felt uneasy. She hoped Racquel hadn't gone and done something behind Kevin's back. She didn't know what it could be, but what if she'd bypassed Kevin and used some donor's sperm? It sounded far-fetched, but Racquel was so desperate, there was no telling what she'd done.

"You promise you won't say anything to anybody?"

"Do I ever?"

"Girl, I'm serious. You can't tell anybody."

"Okay, what?"

"I missed my period at the beginning of this month."

"You what?" Marcella said, smiling.

"At first, I thought I was late, but then when three weeks passed by, I started wondering if maybe I might be pregnant. So this morning I took a sample of urine to the infertility clinic."

"Girl, that's great news. I can't believe you didn't tell me."

"I didn't want to get anyone's hopes up. Especially Kevin's. And there's a chance he would have gotten angry if he thought I was still holding on to some fantasy."

"Why didn't you just go and buy one of those home pregnancy tests? Because I don't know how you can stand waiting."

"I don't trust those. I know it's silly, but I feel more comfortable when it's done professionally. Not that it's ever helped me in the past, though."

"Girl, I am so happy for you," Marcella said, grabbing her sister's hand.

"Don't get too happy, because we don't know anything yet. It could be just another false alarm. Lord knows, I've gotten enough negative pregnancy results to last a lifetime."

"Kevin will be so excited. And Mom will be thrilled when she hears about it."

"Marcella, what did I tell you?" Racquel asked, squinting her eyes.

"I mean, after you find out."

"Okay. Because you did give me your word that you wouldn't say anything."

"How come you're so calm about all of this? You've wanted this for as along as I can remember, and now you're acting like it's no big deal."

"Because I've been disappointed too many times. So if I am, I'll be happy; but if I'm not, then that's fine, too."

"When will they have the results?"

"Later this afternoon, I'm sure."

"Why don't you call the nurse on your cellular phone right now?"

"No, I'm not going to worry about it until I get home, and if she hasn't called me by then, I'll give her a call."

"I don't believe you," Marcella said, shaking her head.

"When I was overly obsessed with the idea of getting pregnant, you guys didn't understand, and now that I'm nonchalant about it, you don't get that, either. How can a person win?" Racquel said, laughing.

"I know, but it's just that I'm so excited, and I don't understand why you're not."

"I am excited, but not to the extent that I used to be. I mean, even though it took me forever, I do finally realize that it's time for me to stop being so selfish and to just be thankful for all the good things that I do have in my life."

"I guess," Marcella said. Actually, she was glad that Racquel had come down to reality and was willing to accept whatever the outcome was, because it was better for everyone involved. Especially, when it came to Kevin. At first, she'd thought Racquel was just pretending when she said she'd given up on trying to get pregnant and was considering adoption, but now Marcella was starting to believe that she was telling the truth. Marcella hoped that Racquel was pregnant, but more than anything, she was glad to know that if she wasn't, her sister wasn't going to crack up over it.

They finished their lunch, ordered two slices of chocolate cheesecake, which was too rich in taste, and chatted a little while longer. When they'd eaten the last of their dessert, Racquel left money on the table to cover the check and tip, and soon after they left the cafe. They went to a couple of department stores, a number of specialty stores, and then headed back home.

As Racquel pressed the garage-door control, she turned into the driveway and saw Kevin's truck already parked inside. More than anything she'd wanted to beat him home, just in case the nurse called from the clinic, but the backed-up traffic on the expressway had made it virtually impossible. She turned the ignition off, gathered together the shopping bags in the backseat, stepped outside the car, and then pressed the garage-door control a second time. She opened the door leading to the kitchen as best she could, since both of her hands were full, and then stepped inside the house. She dropped all of the bags on the floor, removed her black wool hooded jacket, matching scarf, and black leather cowboy boots. Kevin was nowhere in sight, and since he usually never played the messages on the answering machine, she figured she'd ease into the bedroom and play them herself. He was probably already lying on the sofa in the family room watching television, so she doubted that he would notice anything. This was good, because that way, if the results were negative, she'd have plenty of time to settle herself down before going in to speak to him. She'd thought this was no big deal like she'd told Marcella, but her nerves had been running wild ever since they started on their way home two hours ago. She'd tried not to get her hopes up, but the truth was, she was more excited this time than she ever had been before.

She walked up the stairs as quietly as she could, and then slipped into the bedroom. She could hear the theme music from *Family Matters* playing, so she quickly stepped into her bedroom and shut the door. But to her surprise, Kevin was sitting in the plush-textured lounger over in the corner by the window with his legs crossed masculine-style. She jumped when she saw him.

"What are you so jumpy for?" he asked with a serious look on his face.

"Nothing really, I just wasn't expecting you to be in here, since I heard the TV playing in the other room," she said, trying to play off the fact that he'd caught her trying to sneak into the bedroom.

She walked over to him and they kissed.

"So how was work?" she asked, glancing on the sly at the answering machine, praying to God that it wasn't blinking. When she saw that it wasn't, she felt relieved. It was too late to find out now, but at the same time, it was much better to wait until Monday, when Kevin would be at work.

"Almost everybody took the afternoon off since it's so close to the holiday, so I took off the last two hours, too."

She felt like suffocating. What if he'd gotten home in time to answer the phone call from the clinic? Maybe that was the reason the answering machine wasn't blinking in the first place, and even worse, maybe that's why he'd been sitting in the bedroom waiting for her to get home. He didn't look upset, but he was probably going to confront her any minute now. She breathed deeply, pretended like she was searching for some important item on the dresser, and waited for him to say something. Anything.

"So when were you going to tell me?" he finally asked.

Her body felt like it was on fire, and while she tried, she couldn't look at him. He'd known about this from the very beginning, and he'd done nothing more than string her along. She could kill him for doing this to her, and she was never going to forgive him for being so cruel. Especially about something like this. She was pissed off now, and decided to play right along with the program. "When was I going to tell you what?"

"That you were pregnant. That's what," he said, rising from the chair.

What was he talking about? She just knew she hadn't heard him right. There was no way. She didn't know what to say, but babbled out something off the top of her head. "I didn't know."

"Well, I know you didn't know, but you had to think you were, or you wouldn't have taken a pregnancy test. Why didn't you tell me?"

She could feel her pulse beating faster and faster and faster, and she felt the same as John Amos had in *Coming to America:* like break-dancing. Could it actually be true, she thought. "Are you telling me the test was positive?"

"The nurse called a couple of hours ago, and said that you were definitely pregnant."

"Oh, Kevin, can you believe this?" she said, and then did what she always did when something major happened. She cried. Except, this time, it was because she was happy.

He grabbed her, laid his cheek against hers, and it wasn't long before she felt tears dropping from his face and onto her neck. This was the happiest day of their lives, and she couldn't believe it had actually come to pass. God was good, life was great, and America was a wonderful place to live as far as she was concerned. She wasn't sure what living in America had to do with any of this, but for some reason she was thinking it. But right now a thousand thoughts were cruising through her mind, and she didn't know what to do next.

"Baby, I'm so sorry for the way I've been treating you," he said, crying louder and louder.

"I know, sweetheart," she said, caressing his back as they continued holding each other. "But we've been under so much stress because of all of this."

"I know, but I had no right treating you so badly," he said, and then cried so hard that if they'd been in public, it would have been humiliating for both of them.

She pulled him over toward the bed and sat down on the edge of it. He kneeled in front of her, laid his head to the side on her lap, and then wrapped both of his arms around her waist. Usually she was the one who always needed consoling, but here she was having to comfort Kevin for the first time since they'd been together.

"Baby, it's okay," she said, trying to convince him that everything was going to be fine.

He cried for a few minutes longer and then raised his head up. He stared at her in the same manner that he used to, before all the arguing and confusion had started. "Baby, I love you so much, and I promise you, I'll never turn against you like I did ever again. I mean that," he said, and kissed her passionately. She felt chills shooting through her entire body, and wanted him as badly as she could tell he wanted her. She'd promised Marcella that she would call her as soon as she found out whether she was pregnant or not, but that particular phone call was going to have to wait. Because nothing, absolutely nothing, was going to interfere with the feelings she and Kevin were experiencing at this very moment.

Chapter 19

"Okay, now, it's time to settle down," Racquel said to her extremely active, and rather loud, second-grade class. It was 8:35 A.M., and time for the day to begin. The children were always hyped up when they entered the classroom, but it was even worse when they came in on Monday because they were always so excited about the items they'd brought in for show-and-tell. Even Racquel enjoyed this part of the class period because she knew her students were liable to bring in anything, from household gadgets to vacation souvenirs. One never could tell, and anything at all was possible.

"One . . . two . . . three," Racquel said in a serious tone, so they knew she meant business. Which worked, because now they were all sitting in their seats giving her their total attention.

"So who wants to go first?" Racquel asked, smiling,

because she knew everyone's hands were going to rise at the same time. It was the one time when they all longed to go first. But, of course, the response was just the opposite when it came to answering questions in relation to their main subjects.

"Pick me, Mrs. Wilson, please," most of them begged, waving their hands through the air.

"Why don't we start with Jeremy this time," she said.

Jeremy left his seat and walked on his heels to the front of the class, licking his tongue out at the rest of his classmates on the way. He was going first and was proud of it.

"That's enough of that, young man," Racquel said to Jeremy in response to his tongue problem.

"These are the two Power Rangers that my foster dad bought me this weekend," Jeremy said, holding one in each hand.

"So what," Christopher said. "My mom bought me *all* the Power Rangers a long time ago. So what's so big about that?"

"Christopher!" Racquel yelled. "You know better than to say something like that, and I've told you over and over again that it's not nice to be rude. Now tell Jeremy you're sorry."

"Sorry," Christopher said as low as he could but still loud enough for the class to hear him. And of course now he was pouting.

Racquel saw the sad look on Jeremy's face and felt bad for him. He wasn't as fortunate as most of the kids in the class, and he didn't get toys on a weekly basis, like some of the other children. He didn't even wear clean clothes all the time, for that matter. But it wasn't his fault, and Racquel wasn't about to allow any of his classmates to hurt his feelings. It wasn't right, and she wasn't going to have it.

None of her students came from wealthy homes, but most of their families were considered middle class. Jeremy, however, fell in a different category altogether. He lived in the projects not too far from the school, and his mother was barely able to put food on the table, let alone buy extras like toys and clothes. Not to mention the fact that he'd been taken away from her and placed into a foster home on two separate occasions, thanks to her leaving him at home for days all by his lonesome. So, Racquel understood exactly why Jeremy was proud of his Power Rangers, but at the same time she also understood clearly that seven- and eight-year-olds really didn't know any better.

"Those are very nice, Jeremy. Aren't they, class?" Racquel said, trying to smooth Christopher's comments over.

"Yes, Mrs. Wilson," they all said in unison.

"Okay, Jeremy, you can have a seat. Tiffany, you can go next, please."

Tiffany skipped from her desk in the last row all the way to the front, but didn't have anything in her hand to show the class. She stood there smiling at first, and then began speaking. "This is my new jean outfit that my mom bought me," she said, grinning from ear to ear.

Most of the boys frowned at her, and some of them watched her with no expression at all. But the girls pursed their lips together and then rolled their eyes at her because they couldn't stand her. Tiffany was a beautiful little girl with a light-chocolate complexion, who wore two thick jet-black braided ponytails, with a part down the center of her head to separate them. And really the fact that she was beautiful wouldn't have been so bad, but the problem was, she knew it. The rest of the girls in the class always complained that Tiffany

thought she was cute, and that she bragged too much.
And while Racquel would never have agreed with them
openly, she knew exactly what they were talking about.
She was only a second-grader, but she hardly ever wore
the same thing twice. Which was ridiculous, because
that was the very reason her attitude was so messed up.
She didn't have any values, and it was obvious that her
parents weren't making the slightest effort toward teaching her any. And there was only so much Racquel could
say and do. So mostly she just put up with her, so long
as she wasn't criticizing any of the other children about
what they didn't have.

"That's very nice, Tiffany," Racquel said, hoping
she'd take her seat immediately. But she didn't.

"It's made by Guess?, and my mom bought it from
Marshall Field's, " she said boastfully.

"Okay, Tiffany. Thank you," Racquel said as politely
as she could, but the rest of the children still laughed
out loud. They hated Tiffany's guts. That was for sure.

Tiffany strutted to her seat with her head high in the
air, ignoring all of them. She didn't have any friends,
and from the way she acted, it didn't seem like she really
cared one way or the other. She'd cried a couple of
times at recess when some of the other girls wouldn't
let her play hopscotch or jump rope with them, but
her feelings didn't stay hurt for too long. This girl was
something else, and Racquel didn't even want to think
about how sad her life was going to be once she became
an adult.

Racquel chose the rest of her students one by one,
so they could each have a turn showing and telling, and
then she had them take out their spelling workbooks.
After that, they saw a science film about birds, went to
lunch, did their math, worked on their reading assignments, and then prepared to go home.

"Tonight, I want you all to start studying your spelling words, so you'll be ready for the test on Friday," Racquel said, leaning her behind against the front of her desk. She set both of her hands on top of her stomach, and after a few seconds she felt the baby moving. She continued holding her stomach because the baby was kicking in an extremely rough manner. "Whoa," she said before she realized it.

"What's the matter, Mrs. Wilson?" Christopher asked with concern in his voice.

"Mrs. Wilson, what's the master with your tummy?" Cynthia wanted to know.

Miss Tiffany sucked her teeth the way people do when they're irritated about something. "Don't you know anything? It's the baby kicking. My mom's stomach used to do that all the time before she had my baby brother, and she used to let me and my dad touch it."

Miss Thing was way too grown, and too far beside herself, and Racquel just looked at her. "Yes, it's just the baby kicking," Racquel confirmed for the rest of the class.

"Now, when did you say it was coming again?" Brianna, a cute little biracial girl wanted to know.

"In August, while you guys are enjoying your summer break," Racquel said and then felt a little awkward. Nowadays the whole concept of getting pregnant was discussed with children a lot more openly than it had been when she was growing up. She could still remember overhearing her grandmother whispering to her mom whenever they discussed the fact that someone had gotten pregnant or was just about to deliver a baby. Her grandmother didn't think that that particular "grown folks" topic should be brought up in front of anyone who wasn't over sixteen years of age, and her mother pretty much still felt the same way today. But

Racquel had learned early on in her teaching career that these little elementary-school students knew so much that they could almost teach their elders a thing or two.

After the explanation of her due date, the bell rang, and the students grabbed their spring jackets, and hurried outside into the hallway. Racquel sat down at her desk and took a deep breath. Teaching second grade had always been a challenge—an enjoyable one, but still a challenge. But now that she was six months pregnant, it really wore her out. But on the other hand, since she had already gained thirty pounds, maybe that had more to do with her being tired than anything else. She couldn't believe she still had three months to go and was already wobbling around like she was ready to deliver at any time.

She leaned back in her chair and closed her eyes, trying to relax her mind, but it wasn't long before she started thinking about the baby and everything that had to do with it. The ultrasound had shown almost conclusively that she and Kevin were having a little girl, and she couldn't have been happier. Especially, since she'd bought tons and tons of pink clothing. She'd even decorated the nursery in pink and mint green. She'd bought everything from cloth diapers, Pampers, and receiving blankets to crib sheets, stuffed animals, and sleepers. She'd even purchased the car seat, stroller, and baby monitor. She hadn't missed a beat, and that was the main reason she didn't see a reason for her mother and Marcella to waste money on giving her a baby shower. She didn't know what people could bring that she didn't already have. She'd bought most of it over the last few years, but the day after she'd found out she was pregnant, she'd shopped for the baby every single weekend thereafter. And sometimes she shopped on weekdays, if she felt good and was in the mood for it.

She opened her eyes and turned to the next day's lesson plan, so she could mentally prepare herself for what the class would be covering. As she started to review it, she remembered that she was supposed to remind Kevin to pick the clothes up from the cleaners. Some of the cleaning was his, but most of it was hers, and since she only had a few professional-looking maternity outfits, she was almost out of things to wear. She pulled out her cellular phone and dialed his work phone number.

"Kevin Wilson speaking," he answered.

"Hi, baby. How's it going?"

"I'm fine. And how are you and my daughter doing?"

Racquel loved when he said that. His daughter. It had sort of a nice ring to it, and it made her feel good all over. "We're both fine. I'm about to get out of here after I finish up a couple of things, but I wanted to call and remind you about the cleaning."

"And it's a good thing you did, too, because I definitely hadn't thought about it anymore."

Of course he hadn't. How many men remembered any of what they were supposed to? Unless, of course, it had something to do with what time and what day of the week the football, basketball, or baseball games came on. But she was used to his forgetfulness, and after all these years it really didn't phase her.

"Okay, then I guess I'll see you at home in a couple of hours," she said, holding the phone with her shoulder so she could arrange the piles on her desk.

"I love you, baby," he said in a caring voice.

"I love you, too."

After she finished organizing her desk, she turned the lights out and left the room. As she drove along in her car, she passed Ashley and Nicholas's school and smiled. Usually she picked them up on the way home, but after Sharon died, Corrine switched her job from the night shift, so she could work days instead. She had wanted to leave that shift for a long time, and there was no better time than now, when Marcella needed all of their help the most. So, Corrine and Racquel shared the responsibility of keeping them every other week, but this week just so happened to be her mother's.

She continued driving down the road and felt a sharp cramp in the lower part of her stomach. *Shoot!* She could just kick herself for eating those leftover baked beans at lunchtime. But they were so good that she couldn't help herself. As a matter of fact, she couldn't help herself when it came to eating anything. She practically ate and drank everything she came in contact with, and she couldn't think of too many foods that she didn't like. Everything tasted good so long as it filled her stomach up, and lately, that's all that mattered to her.

The pain was slowly starting to subside, and she felt a lot more at ease. She drove down the street that led to her subdivision, entered it, and then drove into the driveway. After she pulled into the garage, she pressed the control to close it, swung her legs outside the car, closed the door, and then inserted her key inside the lock of the door leading into the kitchen. Once she was in, she set her purse down, kicked off her one-inch pumps, proceeded through to the living room, opened the front door, and grabbed today's mail. But, when she went to close the door, she felt another sharp pain in her stomach, except this time it was ten times sharper than the one she'd experienced earlier. She held her stomach and made her way to the plush chair to sit down. She'd thought it was just gas again, but now she was doubling over with excruciating pain, and it didn't seem like it was going to let up. She'd never felt pain like this before, and it sort of scared her. She was only six months along, but based on what Dr. Reed had told her, and what she'd learned in Lamaze class, she knew a baby could come at anytime; even if it was way too early. She struggled to stand up, forced herself into the kitchen, and pulled the cordless phone down from the wall. Her first instinct was to call Kevin, but for some reason she didn't think she had time to wait for him to drive all the way home and then take her to the hospital, so she dialed 911 and waited for them to answer. She moaned and groaned, and the pain was getting worse instead of better.

"Nine-one-one. What's your emergency?" a lady answered.

"I think I'm going into labor," Racquel said, straining to get the words out.

"Okay. Is anyone there with you?"

"No, my husband is still at work," Racquel said, breathing harder.

"Do you have any idea how far apart your contractions are?"

"No. My stomach started cramping a few minutes ago, and it still hasn't stopped."

"I think we'd better get an ambulance over to you right away," the 911 lady said without delay. "Is your address 2222 Holly Lane?"

"Yes," Racquel said, tightening her face with pain.

"I'm dispatching an ambulance to you right now, but I want you to stay on the line with me until the paramedics arrive, okay?"

"Can you call my husband?" Racquel asked with a groan in her voice.

"I sure can. What's his number?"

Racquel recited Kevin's work number to the 911 representative and then waited for the ambulance to get there.

Kevin had been sitting and waiting on pins and needles for what seemed like ten hours, and he felt like he was about to go insane. He'd paced up and down the hallway next to the surgical waiting area more times than he cared to think about, and his nerves were running wild. Corrine and Marcella had tried to settle him down, but nothing they said to him seemed to make a bit of difference. He couldn't understand why it was taking so long. Dr. Reed had come out close to an hour ago saying that they were going to perform an emergency C-section, but he hadn't given any specific details as to what was going on. Kevin was starting to get worried, and while Corrine and Marcella had been trying to hide their fears, he knew they were just as concerned as he was. He tried to be positive about the whole situation because lots of babies were born when the mother had only carried them for six months. They were usually premature, but with time, they turned out just as healthy as normal children.

He sat down across from Corrine, Marcella, and her children, but it wasn't more than sixty seconds before he'd stood up again and walked back out into the hallway. Corrine and Marcella looked at each other.

"Mom, what's going to happen to Racquel if she loses her baby?" Marcella asked Corrine in a whisper.

"I really don't know, but I do know that we have to keep our faith strong."

"I'm trying to, but you know she already had one miscarriage."

"I know, but that time she only carried the baby three months."

"Maybe you're right," Marcella said, glancing across the room at Nicholas, who was sitting at a small round table trying to put a jigsaw puzzle together. Ashley was doing her math homework.

Kevin walked slowly back into the waiting room, sat down in the chair closest to the doorway, and laid his head back with his eyes closed. But right when he did, Dr. Reed walked in and closed the door.

"Is everyone in here part of your family?" Dr. Reed asked and sat down in the seat adjacent to Kevin.

"Yes, this is Racquel's mother and sister. And her niece and nephew," Kevin responded nervously. "Is Racquel okay?" he asked fearfully.

"Racquel is fine. It took awhile for us to get her stabilized because her blood pressure shot up so high, but she'll be fine."

"And how's the baby?"

"I'm sorry, Kevin, but she didn't make it. Her lungs just weren't strong enough to survive such an early delivery."

Kevin gazed at him without any movement, tears slowly streamed down his face.

"Lord. Lord. Lord," Corrine said, making her way across the room to Kevin. She sat down in the chair next to him, rubbing his back.

"No," Marcella said in a grunting voice with her hand over her mouth.

Ashley looked at her mother, set her math book down in the next chair, and walked over to sit with her. Nicholas followed behind her.

"Your wife is in recovery right now. You should be

able to see her in about an hour or so. Someone will let you know when she's been moved to a private room," Dr. Reed said and stood up. "I'm really sorry," he said again, and patted Kevin on his knee. Then he left the room.

Tears were flowing from Kevin's face at a more rapid pace, and both of his hands were balled into tight fists. They'd gone through all of this for nothing, and he couldn't understand why things had turned out the way they had. He tried hard to think back to what he might have done to deserve such harsh punishment, but he couldn't think of anything. He had always tried to lead a decent life ever since he could remember, and he went out of his way to treat people with the utmost respect. This whole ordeal had turned into a complete disaster, and he wanted to run outside the hospital, so he could scream in peace with no one around so he wouldn't have to feel embarrassed. But he knew he had to be strong for Racquel because she was going to need him more now than she ever had before. She was going to need all of them. He sniffled a couple of times and wiped the wetness from his face with the two tissues Corrine had given him.

"Everything will be all right," Corrine said, trying to convince Kevin, but more than anything, she was trying to convince herself.

"I know, Mom," Kevin said. "But you know how badly we wanted this baby. And how am I going to tell Racquel?"

"Racquel will be fine. It will take some time, but she'll be fine," Corrine said, trying to give him peace of mind, and she hugged him. "It might not seem like it now, but God knows best."

Marcella wiped the tears from her face and walked across the room to where her mother and brother-in-law were sitting. She sat down on the other side of him. "We *will* get through this, Kevin."

Kevin closed his eyes and thought a thousand thoughts. But there was one thought that stuck out in his mind the most: What was going to happen to their marriage now?

Chapter 20

A whole month had passed since they'd buried their beautiful daughter, Karlia Renee Wilson, but Racquel was still acting as if her own life was over. She really didn't see a reason for living, and she did nothing except mope around the house day after day. And sometimes she didn't even bother to do that.

She'd gone into total hysterics when Kevin had told her the news about the baby, and for a while the nurses had thought for sure they were going to have to sedate her and strap her down to the bed. Everyone in the family had known that the loss of the baby wasn't going to be easy for her to deal with, but they'd never guessed that her reaction was going to turn out as bad as it had. Dr. Reed had kept her in the hospital for three days; partly because of the C-section, but mostly because of her extreme emotional state. Corrine and Marcella had been worried sick the entire time. When she finally did come home, she walked straight through the front door

and into the bedroom without saying anything to anyone. It was almost like she was a zombie and had lost
her mind. And the most she'd said during the ride home
from the hospital was that she wanted to go up to her
own bedroom and not the guest bedroom on the first
floor. But eventually Corrine convinced her that it
wasn't good for her to climb stairs so soon after having
surgery. Racquel hadn't argued with her about it, but
it was obvious that she wasn't happy about it, either.
And to prove it, she hadn't spoken to any of them the
rest of that afternoon.

Racquel dragged her legs out of the bed and started
toward the master bathroom until she heard the phone
ringing. Her first thought was to ignore it, but since it
might be Kevin, she decided to answer it.

"Hello?" she said in a monotone voice.

"Hey," Kevin said enthusiastically. "Are you up yet?"

"If that's what you want to call it," she said dryly.

"So how are you feeling?"

"Okay, I guess."

"Do you feel well enough to meet me for lunch?"
he asked optimistically.

Racquel hated going through this with him every day,
and he was starting to get on her nerves. Couldn't he
see how hurt she was? She hadn't even gone back to
work before the school year ended, like he'd suggested,
so she couldn't understand at all why he thought she
wanted to go out to some restaurant. "I don't feel like
it today. But maybe some other time."

"Okay, then when?" he said irritably.

"I don't know, but not today."

He paused for a minute and then spoke. "What do
you want me to do, Racquel?"

"What do you mean, what do *I* want you to do?"

"Exactly what I said. I've gone out of my way to try

and help you overcome the loss of the baby, and I don't know what else to do.''

"Overcome the loss of the baby? Is that what you're waiting for? Well, I'm sorry to disappoint you, because that's never going to happen. I don't even know how you can expect something like that. Hell, I don't even know how you can just pretend like nothing happened. Just because you've been waltzing around here like everything is back to normal, I hope you don't think I'm about to do the same thing."

"I didn't say everything was back to normal, but, Racquel," he said, pausing, "life goes on."

"Maybe for you it does, but not for me."

"I knew this was going to happen. We're back in the same old rut we were in before you got pregnant, aren't we?"

"Look, Kevin. My baby just died, and regardless of how you feel, I can't just sit here and pretend that she never existed."

"I'm not pretending, either, but maybe if you at least try to put forth some kind of an effort, we might be able to get through this a lot easier."

"Kevin, who are you to tell me about putting forth an effort, when you never even so much as said hello to your mother when she came here for the funeral?"

"Racquel, you know the situation with my mother, and you know why I don't have anything to say to her. And I didn't invite her to come here in the first place. You did."

"She had a right to be here the same as your father did because Karlia was her granddaughter, too. At least she thought enough of us to come. Something my own father didn't even have the decency to do."

"Racquel, what does all of this have to do with us?" Kevin said in a fed-up tone.

Racquel was steaming and felt like slamming the phone on the hook, but she didn't.

"So, you don't have anything else to say?" Kevin asked angrily.

"As a matter of fact, I don't."

"Well, then, I guess this conversation is over."

"Whatever, Kevin," she said and slammed the phone down. And for some reason, she didn't feel bad about it, because right now she was pissed off at everyone involved. Her mother had been coming by every single day trying to get her out of the house; Marcella had been talking some crazy mess about adoption; and Kevin was acting as if he didn't care whether Karlia had lived or died. And she was never going to show her face back at Westside Missionary Baptist Church for as long as she lived. Those women at the church had come over each day claiming to bring food for the family and to pay their respects, but all Racquel saw them doing was filling up their own plates and spreading a lot of gossip. It was almost as if they were celebrating the fact that someone had died. She'd heard one of the deacons' wives saying, "We've got it backward. We're supposed to be sad when a child is born into this sinful world, and happy when someone passes on to their glory." The fact of the matter was: Nobody understood how she felt. *They* hadn't lost their own flesh and blood. *They* hadn't lost the only thing that mattered to them the most. And she could bet *they* didn't feel like dying the way she did.

She walked into the master bathroom, pulled out a medicine bottle, opened it, and dumped two sleeping pills into her hand. She ran some water in a paper cup, threw the tablets in her mouth, and swallowed two gulps of water behind them. Then she crumpled the cup up, threw it in the forest-green wicker wastebasket, and walked back out to the bedroom.

She picked up her purple satin robe from the chair, tied the belt, and walked over to the dresser. She pulled the top-right drawer open, pulled out an envelope, and sat down on the bed. When she turned the envelope upside down, a stack of photos came tumbling out. They were the photos that the church photographer had taken at the funeral. Her mother and Marcella hadn't thought it was a good idea for her to have pictures of the baby lying in a casket, but Racquel had made it clear that her mind was made up, so they'd had no choice except to go along with it.

She gazed at the first one, and then moved it to the bottom of the pile. Then she did the same with the second, third, and fourth. But when she came to the fifth one, she paused for a minute and then dropped the rest down on the bed. Most of the photos were similar to each other, but for some reason this one stood out in the crowd. And now she knew why. Karlia was smiling at her. Or at least it looked like she was. And it seemed like she was trying to say something to Racquel.

"What is it, sweetie?" Racquel asked, smiling at the photo.

"It's scary in here, Mommy," Racquel heard Karlia say.

"I know, honey. Mommy's going to come get you from that dreary old funeral home just as soon as she can get dressed," she said in baby talk. "Your daddy is going to be so happy when he gets home from work," she said joyfully.

Racquel closed her eyes tight and held the photo against her chest with both hands. Maybe Karlia wasn't dead after all. Maybe Kevin had made a huge mistake when he'd told her that the baby's lungs hadn't been strong enough for her to survive. Yeah, that had to be it, she thought with a smile.

She opened her eyes and pulled the photo away from her body, so she could tell Karlia that everything was going to be fine. But what she saw this time, was her worst nightmare. It was her beautiful baby girl lying in a gory-looking, miniature off-white casket. And she wasn't smiling, and her eyes were no longer open.

Racquel dropped the photo on the floor and screamed at the top of her lungs.

"I don't know what we're going to do with that girl," Corrine said to Marcella, and then folded the last of Nicholas's underwear.

Corrine had worked ten hours at the factory and had decided to stop by Marcella's for a little while to see the children. But since the children were occupied with their usual summer-evening activities, she was helping Marcella fold the clothes that she'd washed at the Laundromat earlier that afternoon.

"Kevin called me this afternoon at work saying that Racquel hung up on him. And I'm telling you, Mom, he sounded like he was completely fed up with her," Marcella said, folding Ashley's red short set.

"If she doesn't stop this, he's going to leave her. I just know he is," Corrine said worriedly.

"And then, she'll really lose her mind."

"Maybe you can try to talk to her again."

"Every time I try to talk to her, she makes an excuse to get off the phone, and if I drop by the house, she pretends like she's sleepy or doesn't feel well. And the few times she has talked to me, she usually says something like 'You don't understand' or 'You're just taking Kevin's side.' And to tell you the truth, I'm getting a little sick of it. Racquel's my sister, and I love her, but she's taking this too far."

"Maybe she needs to see a psychiatrist or something. Maybe this is worse than we thought."

"Even if we found one for her and made the appointment, she'll never go."

"No, she probably wouldn't," Corrine said disappointedly. "I'm telling you the truth—if it's not one thing, it's another."

Marcella didn't say anything because she knew her mother was worried sick about Racquel. And who could blame her? Racquel was her daughter, and she had a right to be concerned about her well-being. But Marcella was starting to wonder just how long Racquel was going to carry on like this, because enough was enough.

"I called her this morning when I took my first break, and she sounded okay," Corrine continued.

"Well, I didn't call her today at all. I thought about it, but I knew she was going to have the same attitude, so I didn't. And when Kevin called and said she'd hung up on him, that *really* made me not want to call her."

"I know you're a little irritated, but she's still your sister, and she's still my daughter. And it's up to us to try and understand what she's going through."

"But that's just it, Mom. We *don't* understand what she's going through. I mean, we both know what it's like to have children, but at the same time we've never lost any. And that's why when I talk to her, I don't know what to say. So, I don't know, maybe you're right. Maybe we really should try to get her some professional help."

"But it's like you said before, she probably won't go." Corrine patted down the stack of Nicholas's T-shirts that she'd just finished folding.

"Well, at this point I don't think we have a choice because Kevin isn't going to put up with her too much longer. Their marriage was barely hanging by a thread before she found out she was pregnant, and I don't think he's going to keep putting up with all this rejection from her.''

"You know what? I'm going over to talk to both of them right now, because this doesn't make any sense at all," Corrine said, picking up her purse and standing up.

"I really hope you can talk some sense into her. Because if you don't, she and Kevin don't have a chance."

Shortly after Corrine left Marcella's apartment, Darryl showed up. With all the crazy hours he'd been working at the hospital over the last two months, they'd hardly spent any time together, and she missed being with him. And this was as good a time as any, since Ashley was in Marcella's room on the phone with her little girlfriend, and Nicholas was playing with the Nintendo that Tyrone had bought for him two weeks ago. A purchase that had surprised everyone. And to top it all off, he had even bought him a remote-controlled television set to go along with it. Nicholas wasn't turning eleven for three months, but Tyrone claimed that since Nicholas had been begging for it for so long, he wanted to give him his birthday present early. And that was the main reason why Marcella hadn't gone off on him for not paying his child support for the last two weeks. She knew he still had a responsibility to pay her, regardless of what he bought extra, but for some reason she didn't mind going without it, after she saw that huge smile on her baby's face. He'd never had anything that expensive before, and his happiness was important to her.

She walked into the living room and sat down next to him.

"So what's up for this weekend?" she asked, caressing his fade haircut.

"Work, of course."

"Not again," she said with a disappointed look on her face.

"I know, but I really don't have a choice."

"Well, when are you going to have a day off again?"

"I barely glanced at the schedule on the way out, but probably next Monday and Tuesday," he said, staring straight at the television.

He was acting strange, and Marcella was starting to feel uncomfortable. "Well, maybe I can get the partners to give me one of those days off, so we can do something. Shoot, we haven't gone anywhere together in months." Or made love, either, for that matter. At least that's what she wanted to tell him because truth was, she had needs just like every other woman in America, and it was time he realized it. But she didn't want him to think she was some sex-craved animal, so she kept her thoughts to herself.

"Hey, Nick," Darryl said, ignoring what Marcella had said.

"Hi, Darryl," Nicholas said, smiling and giving him a high five. "You wanna play a game with me on the Nintendo?"

"You mean, do I want to beat you at a game on the Nintendo?" he said, standing up.

"No way. Nobody can beat me at any of the games. Not even you," Nicholas said excitedly.

"Well, we'll see about that," Darryl said, dragging him playfully into his bedroom.

What, Marcella thought. They hadn't seen each other in over a week, and now he was going to play some game with Nicholas? None of this added up, and she was starting to get upset. She'd known for a while now that their relationship wasn't the same as it had been in the beginning, but she'd thought things had gotten a lot better since the Tyrone situation. But maybe it had just been her imagination. And just maybe she'd been fooling herself, because now he was acting like he didn't want to be with her at all. And if he didn't, then why did he bring his tired ass over to her apartment in the first place? She wasn't going to be treated like this without some sort of an explanation.

"Darryl," she said, standing inside Nicholas's doorway.

"Yeah," Darryl said, keeping his attention on the game. Nicholas was so engulfed that he didn't hear a word she said.

"Can I see you for a minute?" she said without smiling. The last thing she wanted was to clown him right in front of her children. But, if he didn't have a good reason for acting the way he was, all sorts of fireworks were about to shoot off.

"Let me finish this game, and I'll be in there."

She wanted to tell him to put the stupid game control down now, but she decided to stay calm. She walked into her bedroom.

"Ashley, you're going to have to switch to the kitchen phone, or call your little girlfriend back."

"Girl, hold on a minute," Ashley said, blowing with disgust.

"I just know you're not blowing because I told you to get off my phone, are you?" Marcella asked, raising her eyebrows as high as they would go.

"I wasn't blowing at you," Ashley said, lying as best she could.

"Of course you were. Just for that, I want you to hang that phone up and stay off of it for the rest of the night."

"What did I do?" Ashley asked, raising her voice. She was clearly irritated.

"Get out of here, Ashley, before I make it a whole week."

"Dog," Ashley said under her breath while storming out of the room.

"What did you say?" Marcella said, walking behind her daughter.

"Nothing," Ashley said fearfully because she knew she'd gone too far.

Marcella grabbed her by her collar. "I don't know who you think you're playing with, but I'm the mother in this house," she said, pointing her finger so close to Ashley's nose that she almost touched it.

Tears were rolling down Ashley's face, but she didn't dare say anything.

"You can just sit in here for the rest of the evening, and I don't want you using that phone until I tell you to. Even if it's next year. With your little fast self," Marcella said, angrily slamming Ashley's bedroom door.

"What's going on with you two?" Darryl asked, following Marcella back into her bedroom.

Marcella ignored his question and slammed the door as soon as they both entered the room. She'd planned on talking to him in a decent manner, but she was too fired up now to control herself. "So what's up, Darryl? I mean, why are you acting like this?"

"Acting like what?" he asked.

"You know exactly what I mean. A few months ago, you told me that you were in love with me, but now I hardly see you at all."

"That's because I've been working so much. And until this past month, you were going to school and working a lot of hours yourself."

"So what? I've been doing that the whole time that we've been dating, and it's never been a problem before."

Darryl sat down on the bed and took a deep breath "Sit down."

"Sit down for what?" she asked angrily.

"Marcella, please sit down."

She finally did what he wanted, but she sat as far away from him as she could.

"I've been trying to say this for the longest, but I didn't know how."

She didn't like where this conversation was going, but she didn't have a choice now except to hear it.

"I've been offered a position in California when my residency is up next month, and I've decided to take it."

She was stunned. "You're what?"

"I'm taking a position in California."

"Did it ever once occur to you that maybe we should discuss a decision as important as that?" she said, raising her eyebrows.

"No, because you and I both know our relationship hasn't been working out the way we thought it would. In the beginning, things were great between us, but Tyrone was always in the background. And you allowed him to be."

"Tyrone? You know good and well Tyrone doesn't have anything to do with this."

"Maybe not as far as you're concerned, but I told you from the start that I couldn't deal with my woman continually getting into heated arguments with some guy she used to go with."

"But you knew what those arguments were about, and it wasn't like we still had feelings for each other."

"To tell you the truth, I didn't know what was going on between you and him."

He was pissing her off more and more by the minute

and she was close to kicking him out. "So, then, that's it? You're moving away, just like that?"

"I really don't have a choice. It's the best offer that I have, so have to take it."

"It wasn't more than a year ago that you said you were pretty sure Covington Park Memorial was going to offer you a good position. So what happened to that?" she asked, crossing her arms.

"Their offer wasn't even close to the one I'm taking in California."

"You really had me fooled, Darryl. You know that?" she said, standing up.

"Look. I hope there're no hard feelings behind this, because I really think this is better for both of us."

"How can you say this is better for me? Because I sure as hell don't see how I'm going to benefit from any of this."

"But it's still better, because you deserve someone who can spend more time with you. Someone who can deal with your particular situation."

"What do you mean *my* particular situation?" she asked, placing her right hand on her hip.

"You know how it is, Marcella, when a woman has children by another man. It takes a very special person to deal with that, and I just don't think I could ever handle it. I love Ashley and Nicholas, but I think we'd both be fooling ourselves if we started thinking that we could all live happily ever after. And even if we tried, Tyrone would find some way to mess everything up."

Tyrone. Tyrone. Tyrone. She was sick of all of his whining about Tyrone. Here he was supposed to be a doctor, but he was acting like a jealous schoolboy who was having problems with his first teenaged girlfriend. This was ridiculous, and while she hated not having anyone in her life, she didn't need someone consumed with all these insecurities. And if she'd said it once, she'd said it a thousand times. She, Ashley, and Nicholas were a package deal, and any man who couldn't deal with that might as well move onto his next victim.

"I'm not even going to acknowledge that stupid comment you just made, because if I do, I'll end up cussing you out in a way like you never have been before. So, just get out," she said, opening the bedroom door.

"Marcella . . . ," he said. "I don't want to leave until you calm down. I mean I wouldn't want you to slice my tires over something like this," he said, laughing.

This Negro was something else. And she couldn't believe he had the nerve to actually be standing there laughing in her face. Like this was some joke of the week. And who did he think he was anyway? Denzel Washington or somebody? Hell, he wasn't *that* good. And now that he was rising so far above himself, she decided that this was the perfect time to fill him in on a few things. "Slice your tires?" she said, closing the bedroom door, hoping her children wouldn't hear what she was about to say. "First of all, I wouldn't even stoop low enough to do anything like that, and secondly, your sorry ass isn't all of that, anyway. And the sex wasn't that great, either. Oh, I know you thought you were really doing something whenever we supposedly made love, but I've got news for you, sweetheart. You need to buy some books, watch some videos, take some classes, or do whatever it is men do when they can't fuck. And while you're learning how to do that, I suggest you grow a dick big enough to back up all of that huffing and puffing you used to be doing."

He laughed, but she could tell from the strange look on his face that he was embarrassed. But he tried to pretend like this newfound information wasn't fazing him the least little bit. "Yeah, right, Marcella. You sure weren't saying all of that a few weeks ago."

"Oh, you mean a few weeks ago when you went down on me? Yeah, you're right, that was good, but the rest was just as pitiful as it's always been. I just never told you because I didn't want to hurt your feelings. But now I don't give a damn."

"Women always get like this when they get dumped," he said, opening the bedroom door.

"I've never had a reason to tell any other man how terrible he was in bed, because I've never experienced anyone as pathetic as you. Shit, you're in a class all by yourself, and I feel sorry for you. And I'll tell you another thing, if someone does marry you, it'll be for one reason, and one reason only. That medical degree that you have, and the salary that goes along with it," she said, following him to the front door.

"Well whoever it is, it won't be you," he said, walking out the door.

"You worthless bastard," she yelled and slammed the door.

What nerve. When she'd first met him that day at church, she'd felt like melting. He was gorgeous, polite, and intelligent. Shoot, by her standards he was everything a woman could hope for, and then some. She'd been thinking all along that someone like him wouldn't be with her forever, but in the back of her mind she'd been hoping that things just might work out. She wasn't even that in love with him anymore, but he was good with her children. And until lately, he treated her like royalty. And she was even willing to accept the terrible sex he was dishing out as a trade-off for all of his other good qualities. And the fact that he was going to earn over one hundred thousand dollars a year had made him a lot more attractive than any other man she knew, too. She never dated men for their money, but at the same time it didn't hurt when they had it.

She didn't want to be alone, but for the first time ever, she'd been "dumped" by a man and wasn't the slightest bit hurt over it. Well, maybe a little hurt, but not to the extent where she couldn't get over it. And one thing was for sure. If she'd survived all the other trying times in her life, this one wasn't going to be any different.

Chapter 21

"**K**evin, what am I supposed to do for money?" Racquel asked, following behind him from one room to the next.

"I'll help you out until the divorce is final, but after that, I suggest you go back to work like everybody else does when they need money," he said sternly.

Kevin had begged and pleaded with her in every possible way he knew how, but it hadn't made any difference, and nothing had changed between them. She refused to go out of the house, she still didn't want to make love to him, and she'd made it clear that she wasn't going back to work at the elementary school when classes started at the end of this month. Her mother and sister had tried to convince her that she needed professional help, but in so many words, she'd told both of them to mind their own business. And they'd done just that.

But now Kevin had waited as long as he could, and

since another month had passed since the death of the baby, he decided that their marriage was over. Racquel didn't seem to care about anything but herself anyway, and he had to move on. Even if it meant without her.

"Kevin, why can't you understand what I've been going through? I'm your wife, and you're supposed to be here for me—no matter what."

"That's the whole problem. I've been here for you all along, but you've been so caught up in your own little selfish world, that you couldn't see it. We've been together, what? Five years? And we've done nothing except try to have a baby. And now I'm emotionally drained from all of it," he said, carrying another load of suits down the carpeted stairway.

She followed behind him out to his utility vehicle. "If we talk this over, I know things will get better," she said, looking around the neighborhood. From what she could see, there was no one in the vicinity standing outside or peeking out their window. She was glad it was dark outside. Because the last thing she wanted was for her neighbors to see Kevin moving his things out of the house.

"I'm all talked out. And even when I did have something to say, you allowed it to go in one ear and right out the other. Even when your mother came over here last month to talk to both of us, you pretty much ignored everything she had to say. And you've gone out of your way to hurt her and Marcella every time they've called or come by to see you."

"I lost my little girl, Kevin. How many times do I have to keep saying that, and when are you going to understand how painful that was for me?" she asked as they both walked back up to the bedroom.

"Why is everything always about you?" he yelled. "Hell, I lost my little girl, too. But life doesn't end just because something bad happens. I mean, just look at you. You've been off work all summer, and you've barely been out of the house more than ten times in the past two months. I remember when getting your hair and nails done was one of your top priorities, but now you don't even do that anymore. And worse than that, it's pretty obvious that you don't even take a bath or get into the shower on a daily basis. You're a complete mess, and I hope for your sake that you do something about it."

"How can I worry about any of that when I'm still mourning the loss of my child?"

"You just don't get it, do you?" he asked, shaking his head. "You really don't."

"I can't believe after all we've been through, you're going to just walk out on me like it's no big deal."

"But that's just it. We've been through too much, and I'm tired of going to hell and back every time something doesn't turn out the way you want it to."

She leaned against the wall by the armoire and looked on as he continued packing his underwear, socks, and ties in the black nylon suitcase. He'd been threatening to leave her for the longest, but she had to admit, not once had she ever believed he would actually go through with it. It crossed her mind from time to time, but that was pretty much it. And he was right when he said she'd hurt everyone else's feelings, because she could still remember every single one of the times that she'd been downright rude to her mother and sister. And now she realized that all they'd been trying to do was help her; but to her, they'd gone about it the wrong way. And that was the very reason why she'd reacted the way she had. They'd tried to force her into seeing some psychiatrist, but she didn't see a reason to waste money on something that she didn't need. She'd had a few hallucinations about the baby being alive, but that had only happened a couple of times, and she'd tried to tell them that. But they hadn't listened and still insisted that she needed to talk to someone about her emotional well-being and her very serious marital problems. But she tried to make them see that all of her problems would eventually work themselves out without the help of some overpriced shrink. Her mother had warned her time and time again that one day Kevin was going to do more than just talk about leaving and was actually going to do it. And while Racquel really hadn't paid much attention to her advice before, right now, that's all she could think about. She had to stop him. That was all there was to it. Even if it meant she had to pretend about how she really felt.

"Okay, okay, okay. You win. I'll go to a counselor, I'll go back to work next month, and I'll make love to you every night if that's what you want," she said confidently.

"What do you think this is, some kind of game? Hell, it's too late for a bunch of promises that we both know you're not going to keep. I've given you chance after chance to come to your senses, but you never took me seriously. And now nothing, and I mean nothing you say, is going to stop me from moving out."

She couldn't believe what she was hearing. She'd said all of the right things, and she'd thought for sure he'd change his mind about leaving. It had always worked in the past whenever he talked about ending their marriage, but this time he didn't seem to care about what she had to say. "But, Kevin, how can you just throw away five years of marriage?" she asked fearfully.

"It was more like five years of hell. Things were good the first year, but you and I both know it's been tumbling downhill ever since. You didn't care, and now I feel the same way," he said, zipping the suitcase.

"Are you saying you don't love me anymore? Because you know I love you more than anything in this world." Tears were rolling down her face.

At first he tried to ignore what she'd just said, but it was obvious that he felt sorry for her just the same. "Racquel. Sit down," he said, sitting on the side of the bed.

She sat next to him.

"I do still love you, but the problem is, I don't know if I'm *in* love with you. We've had a lot of problems, and our relationship has been terribly damaged because of them. When you found out you were pregnant this second time, I thought for sure our marriage was going to get back on track. But when you lost the baby, things got worse than they had been before. Instead of just accepting things the way God obviously meant for them to be, you became more and more obsessed with chasing this fantasy of yours. And although I wish I could look at you and say that we can work this out, I can't. Too much has happened, and I doubt very seriously if we can do anything to fix it," he said holding her hand.

"But, Kevin . . . ," she said bawling.

"I'm sorry, Racquel, but that's how I feel." He gazed at her for a few seconds and then stood up. "If you need me for anything, I'll be at The Waterstone. Their number is in the phone book." He picked up his suitcase and then walked over to the doorway. She sat on the bed staring at him, and although he stared back at her, neither of them said a word. Finally, he walked down the stairs, and it wasn't long before she heard him drive off.

Kevin had actually left her. She kept playing the whole idea of it over and over in her mind, but it didn't seem real. All she'd ever wanted was a family, but now she had nothing. She didn't have a baby, and now she didn't have a husband to love her. She felt like the walls were closing in on her, like she was cracking up. And how on earth was she going to face her mother and Marcella when they found out about all of this? They'd both seen this coming for some time now, and the last thing she needed to hear were a bunch of I-told-you-so's. Especially since they'd tried to warn her on more than one occasion. But what hurt her the most was that she hadn't paid enough attention to her own situation to foresee any of what was happening. She knew they had problems and that Kevin was unhappy with the way their marriage was going, but she never thought things were bad enough to cause a separation. Or even worse, a divorce. But then, he would never go as far as filing for a divorce. Not Kevin, the man who said he would always love her, no matter what. But on the other hand, she hadn't thought he would just walk out on her like he had, either, so she really couldn't be sure of what he was going to do.

She sighed deeply and swallowed hard. She had to figure out a way to get through to him. She had to make him see that this could all be worked out. Because if she didn't, there was no doubt that she was going to lose the best thing that had ever happened to her.

As soon as Racquel opened her eyes, she shut them quickly, trying to avoid the sunlight that was beaming down from her bedroom window into her face. She'd tossed and turned most of the night, hadn't dropped off to sleep until around 5 A.M., and she felt like she'd been run over by a train. Her whole life was in a rut, and she honestly didn't know what to do to make things better. She'd wanted to call Kevin last night, but since he probably needed some time alone, she'd decided against it. But now she needed to talk to him. She needed to hear his voice. She picked up the phone on the nightstand and dialed his number at work. It rang four times and then finally his voice mail answered. "Hi, this is Kevin Wilson at Whitlock Aerospace, and I'll be out of the office until Monday, August twentieth. However, if you have a situation that needs immediate attention, please press zero when you hear the tone, and someone will help you. Thank you."

Racquel waited for the tone, but didn't see any sense in leaving a message since he was going to be out for a whole week. Which sort of surprised her because he hadn't mentioned one thing about taking time off from work. And she couldn't help but wonder what was going on.

She reached inside the bottom drawer of the nightstand, pulled out the phone directory, searched through the Yellow Pages for the number to where Kevin was staying and dialed it. The phone rang five times before there was an answer.

"Thank you for calling The Waterstone. How may I direct your call?" answered a Black woman with a very distinctive voice.

"Could you please ring Kevin Wilson's room?"

"One moment," the woman said and then transferred the call.

After three rings Kevin picked up. "Hello?"

"Hey," Racquel said softly.

"How are you?" he asked in a groggy tone of voice, sounding like he'd just woken up.

"As well as can be expected, I guess, considering the fact that you left me the way you did."

He didn't say anything.

"I didn't wake you up, did I?" she continued.

"As a matter of fact, you did. I didn't get to sleep until sometime early this morning."

"Is that why you missed work today?"

"No. I decided to take the rest of the week off yesterday."

"Well, I didn't know what was going on when I called your number at work because you never said anything about taking a vacation."

"This whole thing with us has taken a toll on me, and I needed a break. That's all."

"I can understand that, but why did you have to move out?"

"I explained that to you last night."

"But I still don't understand it. I mean, I know we've been going through a rough time, but I never thought you would actually walk out on me like this."

"I didn't want to, but things were getting worse every day. And for three months you've acted like I don't even exist. And I couldn't take that anymore."

"I realize that now, and I know I was wrong for treating you the way I did. But I swear if you give me another chance, I'll do everything in my power to make this all up to you," she said pleadingly.

"But just last night, you were still trying to make it seem like I was wrong for having a problem with the way you've been acting. So how can you just change your whole way of thinking in one night?"

"Because I had all night to think about it. And regardless of what I said, or how I may have been acting the last couple of months, I know now that you're the most important thing in this world to me, and I'll die if I lose you," she said, stroking her hair.

"But it's not just the things that went on over the last couple of months. It's all the crap that I had to put up with for the last five years. I mean I went out of my way to make you happy, and I gave you all the love that I knew how to give. And it still didn't make a difference to you because all you ever cared about was making a baby. I don't think you ever went one day without mentioning it, and that's not normal. And all of this is partly my fault, because I never should have let it go on for as long as I did."

"But we loved each other, and that's all that mattered."

"No, that's not all that mattered to *me*, because a marriage is based on a lot more than just feelings. What about trust?"

"What do you mean, trust?" she asked, frowning.

"Racquel, you know what I'm talking about."

"No, I don't," she said, knowing good and well that he was referring to the abortion issue.

"I'm talking about those abortions you had."

"All of that happened before I met you, and since I knew how you felt about abortions, I was afraid to tell you. Can't you understand that?"

"No, because I asked you if you'd ever done anything like that, and you flat out said no."

"But you wouldn't have understood then, just like you don't understand now."

"How do you know? I mean, I could have gotten over the fact that you had two abortions, but what really pissed me off was the fact that you lied to me. And on top of that, you slept with a married man for money. Shit, that's no different from being a prostitute, if you ask me," he said angrily.

She couldn't believe he was actually comparing her to a prostitute. Her relationship with Tom hadn't been anything like that because they'd had real feelings for each other. They hadn't been in love. Or at least she hadn't. But they still enjoyed being together. And while she knew they were wrong for playing around behind his wife's back, not a day went by when she didn't feel sorry for it. But there was nothing she could do to change it now, and she wished Kevin would stop harassing her about something that had nothing to do with him.

"It wasn't like that, Kevin," she said, trying to convince him.

"Whatever," he said, sounding irritated. "And regardless of what that doctor said, I'd be willing to bet that those two abortions are the real reason you can't carry a baby to full term."

"Oh, so now you're the doctor, right?" she said furiously. She'd tried to be nice ever since the conversation started, but now he was tapping into the wrong subject.

"No, I'm *not* the doctor, but I do know that having two abortions at such a young age couldn't have helped you any."

"Kevin, if that had been the problem, Dr. Reed would have figured it out when he ran all those tests on me. There was nothing wrong with me, and you know it."

"See," Kevin said, laughing sarcastically. "You're still obsessed with that same old shit."

"You're the one that brought it up. Not me."

"Look, I'm not even going to keep arguing with you about this. And anyway, I need to get ready for an appointment, so I'm going to have to talk to you later."

"What appointment?" she asked with deep curiosity.

"With my attorney."

Attorney? Why did he need to talk to an attorney so soon? Surely not about divorce proceedings. He just couldn't be. She dreaded asking him what this was about, but she had to know. "What are you seeing an attorney for?"

"I'm filing for a divorce."

"You're what?"

"I've thought about it from every angle, and I just don't see any chance of us working this out."

She wanted to beg him not to do it, but she could tell that his mind was already made up. "Well, I guess there's nothing else I can say."

"Look, no matter what you think, I never wanted things to end this way. And to be honest, I thought being in love with you was enough, but I realize now that love doesn't mean anything if your wife doesn't appreciate you."

"But I did appreciate you. I might not have shown you as often as I should have, but I did appreciate you. And I loved you."

"But you didn't love me or make love to me the way your sister Marcella does now."

Racquel sucked her breath in as hard as she could, popped her eyes open, and sat straight up in her bed all at the same time. She moved her eyes back and forth around the room trying to familiarize herself with the surroundings, and then it finally dawned on her that she was sitting inside of her own bedroom. Her face was covered with thick layers of sweat, her heart beat rapidly, and her nightgown was soaked to no end.

She peeped over at Kevin, who was still asleep, and closed her eyes for a few minutes. Then she smiled when she realized that this marital separation had been nothing more than a terrible dream.

Chapter 22

"Mom, my head hurts," Nicholas said, walking into his grandmother's kitchen.

"It's probably just from all the excitement, because I know you hardly slept a wink last night, and you don't feel like you have a fever or anything," Marcella said, removing her hand from his forehead. "The party isn't going to start for another two hours, so maybe you should go lie down for a while." Marcella hugged him close to her.

"You can go get in my bed if you want to," Corrine said, smiling at him, because she knew how much her grandson loved lying in her bed.

Nicholas left the room without any argument.

Marcella was sitting at the kitchen table trying to figure out which games the children were going to play; Racquel was mixing some pop and punch together;

Corrine was finishing the hors d'oeuvres for the adults who were coming; and Ashley was in the dining room setting up the paper products on the table. Nicholas was turning eleven today, and the family was giving him a birthday party. He'd had small ones before at Chuck E. Cheese, and places like that. But this year they'd decided to give him one at home, so they could invite all of his little friends from school, as well as all their relatives. Which was sort of a tradition, since they'd done the same thing for Ashley when she'd turned eleven two years ago. Marcella wasn't sure why they'd chosen such an oddball year like eleven to give the children their first family birthday party, but for some reason that's just the way it had turned out.

"Has Nicholas been complaining about any headaches before?" Corrine asked.

"Last week, he said he had one, and I gave him some children's aspirin. He was fine after that, though," Marcella said.

"Well, if it keeps up, maybe you should take him to the doctor," Corrine said.

"I know. And I should probably go ahead and make an appointment now because his pediatrician only takes welfare patients on certain days."

"But you're not on welfare, are you?" Racquel asked, looking at Marcella.

"Well, not really, since I don't receive any cash, but we're still covered by the medical card," Marcella said.

"But what does that have to do with what days you can see the doctor?" Racquel asked.

"I don't know, but there are a lot of doctors that do that."

"That's stupid, and it's almost like they're discriminating against people who don't have some high-class insurance carrier."

"That's a shame," Corrine commented.

"So whatever happened with your food stamps getting cut off?" Racquel asked.

"They're deducting ten percent from my allotment every month until the overpayment has been recouped. But I thought I told you that already," Marcella said.

"You might have, but you know how out of it I've been for the last few months. Sometimes it feels like I lost a whole year of my life," Racquel said shamefully. "And I never did apologize to either of you for acting the way I did," she said, looking from Marcella to her mother.

"Baby, don't even worry about that," Corrine said. "We know you were going through a hard time, and all that matters now is that you and Kevin are trying to work things out, and that you're getting on with your life."

"That's right," Marcella said, looking up from the game materials. "Nobody's even thinking about any of that."

"I know. But I don't know what I would have done if both of you hadn't been there for me, because I really was about to lose my mind. Having those hallucinations and all those nightmares was starting to scare me," Racquel said.

"Yeah, they were starting to scare me, too, when you told me about that crazy dream you had," Marcella said, laughing.

"Oh, don't even bring that up," Racquel said, feeling a little embarrassed because it was that very dream that made her realize she couldn't live without Kevin. She hadn't been the least bit worried that her sister was really having an affair with him, but it definitely **had** painted her a vivid picture of how awful it would **feel** losing him to some other woman. And it was **the reason** why she'd taken a semester's leave of absence from work, so she could be the wife she should have been to him a long time ago.

"I mean, just think. Kevin and I in love with each other," Marcella said, cracking up.

"Girl, I don't even know what made me dream some crazy mess like that," Racquel said.

"I don't know, either," Corrine said, laughing.

"I mean, don't get me wrong, I would love to find someone like Kevin, but that's about as far as it goes," Marcella said.

"You will," Racquel said.

"I doubt it. When I first started seeing Darryl, I thought he was the perfect guy, but you see how that turned out. And the worst part about it was that I really wasn't expecting it when he broke up with me that night, and some of the things he said really hurt me."

"Poor man," Racquel said. "I don't even want to think about what you said to him."

"You know how it is when your feelings get hurt," Marcella said. "A person is liable to say anything."

"Oh my goodness," Corrine said, laughing.

"Shoot, you'd have thought I had Filthy Mouth Disorder with the way I went off on him," Marcella said, laughing.

"Filthy Mouth Disorder?" Racquel said, laughing. "What's that?"

"It's the illness I always get when men like Darryl need to be cussed out," Marcella said.

"You're terrible," Racquel said, and they all laughed.

Ashley stuck her head into the kitchen and shook her head at all of them. Marcella looked at her and felt guilty, because even though Ashley's and Nicholas's bedroom doors had been closed, she knew the children had heard almost everything she'd said that night. And the last thing she'd wanted was for them to hear her cuss a man out like that. Or anyone for that matter. But Darryl had hurt her, and she hadn't been able to help it.

"Oh, shoot," Marcella said, covering her mouth. "I forgot to bring the cake."

"I thought you picked it up this morning from the bakery?" Corrine asked.

"I did, but it was so early that I put it in my refrigerator and then forgot about it," Marcella said, standing up from the table. "I'd better run home real quick and get it."

"You want me to ride with you, Mom?" Ashley asked.

"Only if your aunt and your granny don't need you to help with anything else."

"We've just about got everything done, so go on ahead, baby," Corrine said to Ashley.

"We'll be right back," Marcella said, heading out the back door with Ashley following behind her.

"I'd better go and check on Nicholas to make sure he's all right," Corrine said, placing the last appetizer on one of her silver relish trays.

"He's probably long gone to sleep by now," Racquel said, pulling four packages of hot dogs from the refrigerator.

Corrine walked through the dining room to the hallway that led into her bedroom and saw Nicholas tossing from side to side like he couldn't get comfortable.

"Baby, what's the matter?" Corrine asked him.

"My head hurts, Granny. It hurts bad," he said, holding his head on each side with both of his hands.

"Where is it hurting?" she asked, sitting down beside him on the bed.

"It hurts all over," he said, still curling his legs up to his chest.

"Racquel," Corrine yelled into the kitchen.

Racquel dropped the hot dogs on the counter and rushed into her mother's bedroom. "What is it, Mom?"

"There's something wrong with Nicholas, and I think we need to take him somewhere."

"Owwwww," Nicholas said, screaming and crying as loud as he could. "Owwwww."

"Honey, call an ambulance," Corrine told Racquel.

Racquel grabbed the phone and dialed 911 as fast as her fingers allowed.

"Nine-one-one. What's your emergency?" a man answered.

"We need an ambulance right away. My little nephew is complaining of a severe headache, and he's in a lot of pain."

"When did this start?"

"What?" Racquel said angrily. "It started earlier, but there's no time for all of that. We need an ambulance, and we need one right now because he's about to go into a fit."

"Is your address 3331 Hampton Avenue?"

"Yes, it is."

"An ambulance will be there shortly."

"Nicholas!" Corrine yelled as she watched him stop moving.

"Mom, what's wrong with him?" Racquel said, dropping the phone to the floor and leaning her head down to his chest to see if his heart was still beating.

"Oh Lord have mercy, I don't think he's breathing!" Corrine said loudly and grabbed him into her arms.

"Nicholas?" Racquel called to him. "Nicholas?"

But he didn't answer, and he didn't move.

"Lord have mercy on this child," Corrine said, rocking him back and forth.

Racquel picked the phone back up. "Hello?"

"Yes, I'm still here," the man said.

"He's not moving, and he's barely breathing.'

"But he is breathing, though?"

"Yes, I think so," she said nervously.

"Okay, just stay on the line until the paramedics arrive. They should be there any minute."

Racquel watched her nephew in terror.

"Nicholas is going to be so happy when he sees that new bike his aunt Racquel and uncle Kevin bought him," Marcella said, turning down Baxter Avenue, which was about three miles from the apartment.

"They got him a bike?" Ashley asked in amazement.

"Yep, they sure did."

"That same dirt bike he's been looking at in that catalog?"

"Uh-huh," Marcella said, pulling up to a four-way stoplight.

"Are Uncle Leroy and Aunt Clara coming?"

"You know they wouldn't miss a family get-together for nothing in the world."

"Mom, is Aunt Racquel ever going to have a baby?" Ashley asked hesitantly, because even though she was thirteen, it was obvious that she didn't know if she should be asking such a grown-up question.

"Probably not, but why are you asking?" Marcella asked, wondering why Ashley had brought this subject up out of nowhere.

"Because she seems so sad all the time, and Nicholas and I hardly ever get to spend the night with her and Uncle Kevin anymore."

"They've been through some really rough times trying to have a baby, and now they're trying to spend as much time together as they possibly can. I know it might be hard for you to understand, but sometimes when a husband and wife have problems, they grow apart and need to spend time alone with each other."

"Is that why you and Darryl broke up?"

"What do you mean?"

"Because you hardly ever got to spend time alone together."

Marcella wasn't sure where Ashley was going with all these questions, but she had a feeling she wasn't going to like it. "We spent lots of time together when he wasn't working."

"I know, but I heard him say that it takes a special man to deal win a woman who has children by someone else. Or something like that."

"When did you hear him say that?" Marcella asked, knowing exactly when Ashley had heard him make those horrible comments.

"That night you and him got into that argument, and he walked out."

Marcella pulled into the parking lot, parked the car in front of their apartment building, turned the ignition off, and turned toward her daughter. She'd already figured that Ashley had heard some of the argument between her and Darryl, but she had no idea that Ashley had heard his comments about her and Nicholas.

"Darryl and I broke up for one reason, and one reason only. We weren't right for each other. So don't you think for one minute that you and Nicholas had anything to do with it. And if he had had a problem with either one of you, I would have stopped seeing him a long time ago. You and Nicholas mean everything in this world to me, and the three of us will always be together no matter what. I know since I started school, I haven't been able to spend as much time with you like I used to, but it's only because I'm doing everything I can to make a better life for all three of us."

"We know that, Mom," Ashley said, like Marcella had told her all that a hundred times before. "I missed you a lot when you first started, but now I understand why you have to work and go to school at the same time."

"We owe your granny, your aunt Racquel, and your uncle Kevin a lot for taking care of you guys the way they do, and I promise when I graduate a year and a half from now, we'll spend a lot of time together, and we'll do all the things normal families get to do."

"It would be even more normal if Dad could be with us, too," Ashley said, looking straight ahead.

Marcella felt her stomach turn, because lately she'd been under the impression that it didn't matter to Ashley one way or the other if her father came around or not, but apparently that wasn't so. "I know, sweetheart, but sometimes things don't work out like that for every family. And that's why I struggle every day trying to be a mother and a father for both you and your brother. Someday when you and Nicholas are older, you'll understand better why people can't be together when they're not right for each other. Now do you have any other important questions before we get out of the car?" she asked, smiling at Ashley.

"Nope. That was all," Ashley said in a mature tone of voice.

When they walked into the apartment, Ashley headed straight for the bathroom, and Marcella made her way into the kitchen. She set her purse down on the table, pulled the cake out of the refrigerator, and set it on the counter. Then the phone rang.

"Hello?" Marcella answered.

"Marcella," Racquel said in a shaky voice.

"What's wrong?" Marcella asked worriedly.

Racquel tried to speak but couldn't. And after a few more seconds, she broke down in tears.

"Racquel, what's wrong?" Marcella asked swiftly.

"Baby?" Corrine said to Marcella after taking the phone from Racquel.

"Mom, what's wrong with Racquel?" Marcella asked anxiously.

"Honey, it's Nicholas."

"What about him? Is he all right?" Marcella asked nervously.

"Kevin is on his way over, so he can bring you to the hospital."

"Why, Mom? What's wrong with my baby?" Marcella said, clamping the phone in her hand as tight as she could.

"He had an aneurysm."

"I'm on my way, okay?" Marcella said, preparing to hang up the phone.

"No, baby. You wait for Kevin because you're too upset to be driving anywhere."

"But he needs me, Mom. What are the doctors saying? Are they going to do surgery? What?"

As Ashley walked out of the bathroom, she heard a knock at the door and looked at her mother to see if she wanted her to answer it or not.

"Mom, that must be Kevin at the door, so I'll see you in a few minutes," Marcella said and hung up the phone. She walked swiftly through the living room and opened the front door. Ashley followed behind her, trying to figure out what was going on.

"I'm ready, Kevin," Marcella said, ready to walk out of the apartment without her purse, keys, Ashley, or anything except herself.

"Marcella, wait," Kevin said, stepping into the apartment.

"There's no time for that. Mom said Nicholas had an aneurysm, and we have to get over there right now."

"Marcella, I promise you I'm going to take you to the hospital, but I need to tell you something first."

"What?" she said impatiently.

Kevin hesitated and took a deep breath.

"What?" she said frowning at him.

"Nick passed away a little while ago."

Marcella felt a knife slice through her heart. "What do you mean he passed away a little while ago?" she asked in disbelief.

"He's gone, Marcella." Kevin stared at her with tears rolling down his face. "Little Nick is gone."

Chapter 23

Marcella gazed out the window of the black limousine as it cruised down Orchard Avenue behind the hearse. They'd just left the funeral and were on their way to the cemetery for the burial services. Marcella's eyes were bloodshot red from all the crying that she'd been doing over the last five days, and the pounding in her head was unbearable. She was numb and heartbroken, but more than anything, she felt guilty, because she was convinced that Nicholas would still be alive if she hadn't spent so much time away from him. He'd had a couple of headaches, but she hadn't paid much attention to them until the day of his birthday party. And not once had she even considered that he might have something as serious as an aneurysm. Especially since he was just turning eleven years old, and had never been sick with anything except maybe the flu or a cold.

And it had all happened so fast. One minute she was

picking up his cake, and the next minute Kevin was at her door telling her he was dead. She hadn't even gotten a chance to say goodbye or to tell him how much she loved him, and she was never going to forgive herself for that. Her mother and sister had been with him right up until the moment he took his last breath, but she was his mother, and it was her responsibility to be there for him whenever he needed her. If it hadn't been for her stupid goals and selfish determination to succeed, she never would have spent all that time taking classes at the university and then working all those hours at the accounting firm in the evening. She tried to be with him and Ashley as much as she could during the summer, but that hadn't been enough, and now she knew it. And what right did she have anyway going back to school at twenty-eight? She had two small children who depended on her, and it was her duty to take care of them until they became adults. She'd made her bed, and it was her responsibility to lie in it. When Sharon had suggested that she go back to school to get her degree, she'd thought it was a wonderful idea, but now she could clearly see how big a mistake it had really been.

Marcella looked across the limo and saw Ashley buried deep inside her father's arms. She cursed the ground that Tyrone walked on, but she was glad he'd been there to comfort Ashley over the last few days when she couldn't. Especially since he'd practically bawled his eyes out when they'd called him to the hospital. And while she couldn't believe it, it was because of him that Nicholas had a decent life-insurance policy. It wasn't like he had gone out and purchased one on his own, but it was his company's policy to cover all employee dependents, and it had made a world of difference as far as the funeral costs. As a matter of fact, if it hadn't been for that policy, she and her family would have had to scrounge up the money to cover whatever the welfare department wouldn't.

When they arrived at the cemetery, they parked and then walked over to the tent that hovered over the burial site. Marcella, Corrine, Ashley, Tyrone, and his mother sat down in the five chairs positioned directly in front of the body, and Racquel and Kevin stood behind them. Marcella saw her father and his wife standing to the side and tried to force a smile on her face. Everyone else gathered around them accordingly.

When the pastor had finished with the prayer and announced that food was being served back at the church for the family, the funeral director removed roses from the bed of flowers covering the casket and passed one to each of the immediate family members. After that, everyone except Marcella stood up. She knew it was time to go, but she couldn't stop staring at the monstrous-looking hole that the yard men had dug for Nicholas. And the thought of them lowering him down into it made her skin crawl. She just couldn't bear the idea of leaving him out there all by himself, and she wanted to take him back home where he belonged.

After Corrine shook hands with a few people, she gently pulled Marcella up from the chair and started walking her in the direction of the limo. But as soon as she did, Marcella pulled away from her.

"What am I going to do without you, Nicholas?" Marcella said, leaning over the casket, crying. "What am I going to do?"

"I know, baby," Corrine said, trying to ease her away from the tent. "You don't have to worry about him because he's resting now."

"Oh, God, Mom, why?" she said, laying her head

against her mother's chest with her hands balled up in front of her face.

Her father and Kevin noticed Corrine struggling with Marcella, and rushed over to help her. Both of the men held Marcella on each side and escorted her over to the limo. When everyone was seated and the doors had been shut, the driver headed back to the church.

A couple of hours had passed since they'd arrived back at Corrine's house from the church. She, Ashley, Racquel, and Kevin were now sitting in the den watching a moment-of-truth movie on Lifetime. Marcella hadn't felt too good on the way home and was now lying down in the bedroom.

"Ashley, you can go lie down, too, if you want," Corrine said.

"I'm fine, Granny," she said, sadly leaning back in the cocoa-brown recliner.

Corrine's heart went out to her granddaughter because she could tell that Ashley was in a lot of pain. But she also knew that there wasn't a whole lot she could do, and that only time could improve the way she was feeling.

"Granny, do we have to go back home tonight?" Ashley asked.

"Not if you don't want to. You and your mom can stay here as long as you need to," Corrine said, wondering why she didn't want to go back to the apartment. She figured it was probably because they'd spent every night with her since the day Nicholas passed away, and Ashley was starting to get used to it.

"If we are, then we need to go get some more clothes," Ashley said.

"You're not going to school tomorrow, are you?" Corrine asked.

"I might," Ashley said, looking at her grandmother.

"Maybe we can go get them when your mom wakes up," Racquel said, looking over at Ashley.

Ashley nodded in agreement and turned her head back toward the television. Then the doorbell rang.

"I wonder who that is?" Corrine said, preparing to stand up from the love seat.

"I'll get it, Mom," Racquel said, rising from the sofa.

"It's probably your dad," Kevin said, glancing at Racquel.

Corrine looked at Racquel, but didn't say anything.

Racquel strutted through the living room, pulled the front door open, and smiled when she saw her dad standing on the steps.

"Hey, Daddy," Racquel said, hugging him.

"Hi, pumpkin," he said, hugging her the way distant relatives do when they haven't seen each other in a long time.

"So how come you and Theresa didn't come back to the church for dinner?" she asked, referring to her stepmother as she closed the door.

"We were kind of exhausted from the flight this morning, so we went back to the hotel to get some rest."

"Why didn't she come with you over here?"

"She doesn't feel comfortable around your mother, so she decided not to. You know how that is."

"Oh, she could have come," Racquel said, knowing good and well she was glad the witch hadn't. Because the last thing she wanted to see was her hanging all over him like some teenager. And that was the same reason she hadn't offered for them to stay with her and Kevin when she'd found out they were flying in for the funeral.

"I'm really glad you came, Daddy," Racquel said and then hugged him again.

"I know, pumpkin, and I'm sorry I wasn't here for you when you lost the baby a few months ago," Mitchell said, kissing her on the forehead.

"Oh, I understand," Racquel said, trying to pretend that his not coming hadn't bothered her, when in reality, it had practically killed her. But she wasn't about to give him the satisfaction of knowing it.

"Where's everybody at?" Mitchell asked.

"Marcella is lying down in Mom's bedroom, and everyone else is in the den," Racquel said, heading down the hallway. Mitchell followed behind her.

"How's it going, son-in-law?" Mitchell said, extending his hand to Kevin.

"Fine, Mr. Jones. How are you?" Kevin said, standing to his feet, shaking his father-in-law's hand.

"And how's my favorite granddaughter?" Mitchell said, grinning at Ashley, obviously wanting to hug her.

But Ashley remained seated because she'd only seen this man two other times in her life, and she really didn't know him all that well. "Hi," she said, smiling the way people do when they first make an acquaintance.

"Corrine," he said acknowledging his ex-wife after he saw that Ashley wasn't interested in hugging him.

"Mitchell," Corrine acknowledged in a cool tone and then switched her eyes back to the tampon commercial on the television screen.

Racquel noticed it and spoke up. "Sit down, Daddy."

"Well, maybe just for a little while," he said and then hesitated when he realized that the only seat available was the one next to Corrine on the love seat.

"You can sit down," Corrine said surprisingly.

Mitchell grinned a funny grin and sat next to her.

"So how long are you here for?" Kevin asked.

"Until tomorrow morning," Mitchell answered.

"How come you're leaving so soon?" Kevin asked.

"I thought we would at least get to take you out to dinner or something."

"We've got some things to take care of at home, so we have to get back."

Racquel looked at her father and thought, Yeah, right. Because she knew the real reason they were leaving was because his wife hadn't wanted to come in the first place.

"You mean to tell me, you only flew in here for one day, knowing full well that your daughter just lost her child?" Corrine asked him.

Racquel didn't like the look on her mother's face, and she prayed that she wasn't about to go off on him. They'd gotten into it during every other one of his visits, but she'd thought for sure that things would be different this time, given the circumstances.

Mitchell looked at Corrine and pretended like he hadn't heard her, obviously not knowing what to say.

"I'm telling you the truth, some things just never change," Corrine said, standing up and walking out of the den.

Ashley watched her grandmother leave the room, glanced at her long, lost grandfather, and then looked over at her aunt Racquel, waiting for her to say something.

"She's just under a lot of stress right now, Daddy," Racquel said, trying to butter her mother's comment. "That's all."

"Maybe I should go," he said.

"But you just got here," Racquel said, partly wanting him to stay and partly wanting him to go before her mother blew up completely.

"I know, but I really should be getting back to the hotel."

Her mother was right, Racquel thought. Some things

didn't ever change. Or some people for that matter. Here her father had messed around with one woman after another the entire time she and Marcella were growing up, and now that they were older, he still didn't see a reason to spend any quality time with them. It just didn't seem to be the most important thing on his agenda, and it was starting to piss Racquel off.

"Well, at least look in on Marcella before you leave," Racquel said as nicely as her emotions allowed her to.

"Oh, definitely," he said, standing up and walking toward Corrine's bedroom. He opened the door.

"Baby girl?" he called out to Marcella, checking to see if she was asleep.

"Hi, Daddy," Marcella said, raising up in the bed. "I thought I heard your voice in there. Come on in and turn on the light."

Mitchell flipped the light switch on and shut the door halfway. "How's my baby girl doing?" he asked, leaning down to hug his youngest daughter, and then sat down beside her.

"It hurts so bad, Daddy. And I miss him so much."

"I know you do, but you'll get through it."

"I don't know if I can or not, and I wish I never had to leave this house ever again. I know it sounds strange, but every time I think about him taking his last breath in this room, I feel so close to him when I'm in here."

"It might not seem like it right now, but things will get better as time goes on. You'll see," he said, rubbing her back. "And you've got a beautiful little daughter out there who needs you more than anything."

"I know, Daddy," she said sadly.

"And while I'm not a churchgoing man, the best advice I can give to you is to pray for strength."

"I have been, but the pain isn't getting any better."

"But it will in time," he said, smiling at her.

"Well, I'm going to be leaving out first thing in the morning, so I'd better get back to the hotel."

"I thought you were going to stay until the weekend?" she said, obviously disappointed.

"I wish I could, but I've got some things I need to take care of at home," he said, barely able to look her straight in her eyes.

"Well, I guess if you have to go, you have to go."

"I'll try to get back here to see you around Christmas, if I can," he said, hugging her again and then kissing her on her cheek.

"Thanks for coming, Daddy," she said, feeling like she was talking to some stranger.

"You take care of yourself, and I'll call you this weekend." He eased out the door.

"Bye, Daddy," she said, smiling with tears in her eyes because she knew it was going to be a very long time before she saw him again.

Mitchell stepped back into the den, shook Kevin's hand, and hugged Ashley whether she wanted him to or not. Racquel walked him to the front door and hugged him. She watched as he drove the black rental car out of the driveway.

Right after their father left, Racquel finally convinced Marcella to take a ride with her so she could get some fresh air. Marcella still wasn't happy about leaving the house, but since Ashley needed a change of clothing for the next day, she reluctantly agreed to it. She couldn't care less if they went to pick up a change of clothing or not, because she wasn't going anywhere anyway. But Ashley was acting like she was going to have a fit if they didn't. Kevin was still at Corrine's watching some special on ESPN.

"I never had a full understanding of how you felt

when you lost Karlia back in May, but if it's anything like the way I feel now, I don't know how you survived it," Marcella said, leaning her head back against the headrest.

"It was one of the hardest things I ever had to go through, and I wouldn't wish it on even the most terrible person," Racquel said, pressing on the accelerator, leaving a four-way stop sign.

"My heart aches so bad."

"And it will for a long time, but I promise you, it will get better."

"It just doesn't seem fair. First it was Sharon, then Karlia, and now Nicholas. I mean, if anything else happens to me, I'll probably go insane."

"Believe me, I know exactly how you feel," Racquel said, slowing down at the stoplight. "And I want you to know that I'm here for you day or night, and that I'll always be here for you and Ashley, no matter what," she said, squeezing Marcella's left hand with her right one.

Tears streamed down Marcella's face, and Racquel did everything she could to hold hers back. Because for the first time in her life, she wasn't so concerned about her own problems, and she knew she had to be strong for her sister. The sister that meant everything to her.

"Mom?" Ashley said when she thought her mother had settled down. "Can we stop at Henry's to get a hamburger?"

"I know you're not still hungry after eating all that food at the church," Marcella said, turning to look at Ashley.

"I felt sick, and I didn't eat that much."

"I guess we can stop on the way back to Mom's if your aunt Racquel doesn't mind."

"You know I don't mind," Racquel said. "We can

stop wherever she wants to. So how long are you planning to be off work?"

"I don't know. To tell you the truth, that's the last thing on my mind," Marcella said, gazing out the window.

"Well, I'm sure they'll understand, and since you're only working part-time because of school, they can probably make it without you for a while."

"Who knows?" Marcella said like she had no interest in the conversation.

"I know you probably don't feel like it, so if you want, I can call your professors to find out what your assignments are. At least that way you won't get so far behind."

"I have a course syllabus for every class, so all I have to do is follow that. But I'm not going to worry about school anyway until sometime next week, because I'm just not in the mood for it right now," Marcella said and then leaned her head back on the headrest and closed her eyes.

Racquel knew it was too soon for Marcella to think about anything or anybody except Nicholas, but at the same time she was trying to keep the conversation on a more positive level. Because if she didn't, not only was Marcella going to break out in tears again, but she was going to do the same thing herself. But since she could tell Marcella wasn't interested, she figured it was better to drop the school and work subject altogether.

"Ashley, have you decided whether you're going to school tomorrow?" Racquel asked.

"I still don't know if I want to or not," Ashley said.

"Tomorrow is already Friday, so you might as well wait until Monday," Marcella commented.

Ashley didn't say anything and continued looking out the window.

They drove the rest of the way in silence, and when Racquel turned into the apartment complex, she parked. Then they all stepped out of the car and walked inside the building. But as they approached Marcella's apartment, they noticed that the door was cracked partially open.

"Did you forget to close the door?" Racquel asked.

"No, I don't think so," Marcella said as they walked closer to it.

"Mom, what if somebody's in there?" Ashley said, staying close behind her mother.

They moved closer to the door and stood there for a minute trying to see if they could hear any noise or movement going on inside. And then finally when Marcella saw that all the lights were on, she pushed the door open slowly. But when they walked in, all three of their mouths fell wide open. Everything was gone. Sharon's navy-blue leather furniture. Sharon's brass and glass coffee tables. Sharon's twenty-five-inch color television. Sharon's glass dinette set. Sharon's Pentium computer. And from the way it looked, the list was only going to continue, once they made their way through the rest of the apartment.

Marcella stood in a complete daze. Racquel and Ashley did the same.

Chapter 24

"**I** know I asked you this last night, but do you have any idea who could have robbed you like this?" Corrine asked. She'd just dropped Ashley off at school, and now she and Marcella were sitting at the kitchen table having coffee.

"No, I don't have the slightest idea," Marcella said, shaking powdered creamer into her cup. "But with all the thugs and delinquent boys that live in the complex, it could have been anybody. And that's the very reason why when we moved my old furniture out and Sharon's in, we did it late at night. But apparently that didn't make any difference."

"I think it would be better if you and Ashley stay here for a while. At least until you're able to get back on your feet."

"I really hate to burden you like this."

"Honey, you and Ashley are not bothering me one

bit by staying here, and as long as I have a place to stay, so do the both of you."

"I can't believe the only thing they left were our bedroom sets, and that was probably only because they didn't want to bother with taking the beds apart. And to think that they took my living-room furniture and my dinette set. I mean, it had to have taken a lot of time to do that, because it's not like you could just move all of that out of the apartment and out of the building in a few minutes."

"Yeah, but thieves have been known to rob people when they know a funeral is going on because they know more than likely no one will be home."

"It's just not right, though. Sharon worked hard to buy those things, and now they're gone. And it just doesn't make sense."

"I know, but you know how roguish some of these fools can be here in Covington Park. Some of them would steal the clothes off a dead man if they thought it would benefit them in some way."

Marcella glanced at her mother with a hollow look on her face. She knew her mother's reference to a dead person was just a figure of speech, but it still reminded her of just how lost she felt and how depressed she was over losing Nicholas.

As soon as Corrine realized what she'd just said, it was obvious that she regretted it. But she didn't say anything.

"Mom, why did I have to lose my baby like this? I've always tried to be a decent person, and I've always tried to be a good mother. So, why did God just take Nicholas the way He did? I keep trying to understand it, but I can't."

"Honey, God has His reasons for doing the things He does, and even though we might not understand them, He doesn't make mistakes. And He never burdens you with any more than you can bear."

"I've been struggling all these years trying to take care of two children all by myself, living in a low-income housing complex, and trying to go to school. And then on top of all that, I lost the best friend I ever had, watched my sister almost have a nervous breakdown, lost my little Nicholas, and now practically everything I owned is gone, too."

"Things will get better. You may not think so right now, but they will."

"But things aren't getting better, they're getting worse!" Marcella yelled. "So why does everyone keep telling me that?"

Corrine stared at her daughter, but didn't speak.

"I'm sorry, Mom," Marcella said, pushing her chair back from the table with tears streaming down her face. She walked out of the kitchen without looking back.

Corrine watched her until she was out of sight and wondered what was going to happen next.

At twelve o'clock Marcella woke up, left her childhood sleeping quarters, and strutted into the den hoping to find her mother. But when she arrived, Corrine wasn't there. She continued through the house, calling out her mother's name, but there was no answer. Finally she walked into the kitchen and saw a note lying on the counter next to the microwave oven. It was from her mother saying she'd stepped out to the grocery store, needed to run a few errands, and would pick Ashley up from school on the way home.

Now Marcella felt even worse about the way she'd yelled at her mother. She hadn't meant to, but it was just that she was fed up with hearing about how everything was going to be all right. How everything happens for a reason. And how things get better with time. They were all nice words of encouragement, but at the same time they weren't making her feel any better. As a matter of fact, she was starting to see exactly why people committed suicide. Before last Saturday when Nicholas had passed away, she'd thought it was the sickest thing a person could do to themselves, but now the whole idea of it didn't sound so bad. Especially now when she really didn't have anything to live for. And she could kick herself a thousand times over for not understanding what Racquel was going through when she'd lost Karlia. She'd known that losing a child had to be painful, but never in her wildest imagination had she thought it would hurt this severely.

She paced back and forth through the house, sat down for a minute in the den, stood up again, and paced the floor some more. She was a nervous wreck, and she wanted this day to end. She wanted all this suffering to go away. Some of the women at the church had promised her that things would start to look up after the funeral, but now that it was one day past, she felt worse. And she was starting to realize that it wasn't ever going to get better.

And she couldn't understand at all why Ashley had gallivanted off to school the first day after her brother's funeral, like nothing had happened. Like it was just another normal event that had taken place and wasn't a big deal. Didn't she know that Nicholas was her brother? Didn't she know how much he loved his big sister? And even worse, didn't she love him back?

Marcella decided that she needed to lie down again and headed into the bedroom. But as soon as she stretched out across the bed, the doorbell rang.

Who could that be, she thought and frowned. She hoped it wasn't someone from the church dropping by for a friendly visit because she wasn't in the mood for it. She went into the living room and peeped out the window. It was Tyrone.

She opened the door wide enough to speak through it. "Ashley decided to go to school today, so she won't be home for at least another three hours or so," she said, wishing he'd go away.

"Well, is it okay if I come in and talk to you for a few minutes?"

About what? He'd never wanted to talk to her about anything before. And whenever they did try to communicate with each other, they always ended up arguing. And she wasn't about to go there with him today. "This really isn't a good time, and I was just about to lie down. Maybe I'll feel better later, and you can call me then."

"I know things haven't been the greatest between us, but all I'm asking is that you let me come in for a few minutes. That's all," he said sincerely. Or at least it sounded sincere to Marcella.

"I'm really having a hard time dealing with everything that has happened, and I'm just not in the mood for any heated debates," she said, stroking her hair from front to back. "I just can't handle anything like that right now."

"I'm having just as hard a time dealing with this as you are, and that's why I want . . . no, that's why I need to talk to you," he asked with both his hands stuck inside the pockets of his black leather jacket. It was barely the second week in October, but it was already windy and starting to get a little nippy outside.

Marcella wasn't sure what to do now. His words seemed genuine, and he'd never been this cordial with her for as long as she could remember, but she just didn't know if it was a good idea to let him in or not. Plus she didn't feel right inviting him into her mother's house knowing how horribly he'd disrespected her two years ago. But on the other hand, she needed to be with someone, or there was a chance she was going to lose her sanity. And as much as she hated to admit it, she really didn't mind if that someone was Tyrone. "Come on in," she said, holding the door open so he could pass through it. Then she closed it and they walked into the den.

"So what did you want to talk to me about?" she asked, sitting down in the recliner.

He sat on the edge of the love seat. "To tell you the truth, I really don't know where to begin. I guess the first thing I want to say is that I'm sorry."

"Sorry for what?" Marcella asked, staring at him. He'd never apologized for anything before, and she couldn't wait to hear this.

"For treating you the way I have for the past few years, and for not being there for Ashley and Nick the way I should have been."

Marcella couldn't believe what she was hearing. Tyrone James was actually sitting there saying the words "I'm sorry." Now that was a new one. And she couldn't help but wonder what the catch was. There had to be something. She was sure of it. "So why are you telling me this now?" she asked curiously.

"Because I woke up this morning feeling like I owed you an apology, and I've been thinking about our situation a lot lately. Maybe it's because of what happened to Nick," he said sadly.

Oh, that's exactly what the reason was. And the only reason he'd come over to talk to her was because he was feeling guilty. The kind of guilt that adult children feel when their elderly parents die and they haven't done one single solitary thing to help take care of them. But now that he'd made this wonderful discovery, she wondered what he wanted from her. Surely not her sympathy. She was becoming slightly miffed at the whole idea of him apologizing because really, it was too late for any of that. And since she was starting to become a little irritated, it was probably better if she didn't make any comments. So she didn't.

"Don't you have anything to say?" he asked, gesturing with his hands, almost begging for her input.

"What is it *for* me to say? I mean, I never did anything to cause you to treat me the way you did, and I never kept Ashley and Nicholas away from you. You had every opportunity to be with them whenever you wanted, but you didn't. And on top of that, you wouldn't even pay your child support the way you were supposed to or watch them in the evenings while I worked."

"I know. I know. I know, but I promise you, things are going to be different now. You can believe that."

Promises, promises, promises. He'd made a lot of promises to her when they were in high school, too, but he hadn't made good on any of them. So why on earth should she believe any of what he was saying now? "Well, for Ashley's sake, I hope you do start acting like her father, because she needs both of us."

"I'm telling you, Marcella, things are going to be different. I swear they are."

She gazed at him doubtfully.

And he obviously picked up on it. "I'm serious. Things are going to be different. And to tell you the truth, the situation never would have gotten like this in the first place if it hadn't been for me messing up my knee the way I did."

Why did the father always have an excuse when it came to the reason why he didn't spend time with his children? Mothers were never allowed any privileges like that. And if they did neglect their children to that extent, they were labeled unfit. And it wouldn't be long before Children and Family Services came knocking at their door snatching the children away so they could place them in some foster home. No, he could believe what he wanted, but the truth of the matter was, his knee injury had little, if anything, to do with him being irresponsible. But she still wanted to see what his reasoning behind all of this was. "What did your knee injury have to do with anything?"

"You know how bad that messed me up. My whole life depended on football, and when I lost my scholarship, I couldn't afford to go to college."

"But you still got a high-paying job through that apprenticeship program. So it's not like you haven't been making good money. Some people who have college degrees don't even make the kind of money you make."

"But playing college ball was my dream, and you know I had a good chance of going to the Pros, too."

"So what are you saying? Because you didn't get to live out your dream, you thought it was okay to take your frustrations out on everybody else?"

"No, that's not what I'm saying at all, but I did build up a lot of anger because of what happened, and I've wanted to blame everyone except myself. I've been talking to my mother about it a lot lately, and she thinks I should talk to someone professionally."

"Well, all I can say is that I hope you start trying to build a better relationship with Ashley as soon as possible because she seemed so distant this morning, and she's acting as if none of this has really affected her, but I know it has."

"I want to start building a better relationship with you, too," he said seriously.

She wasn't sure where he was going with that comment, but she hoped he wasn't thinking that there was some small chance for them to get back together, because there wasn't. "If you had paid your child support and spent time with Ashley and Nicholas like you should have, we never would have had any problems with each other. And this thing with you trippin' out whenever I date someone has got to stop, too. I don't have a problem with your and Priscilla's relationship, and I think it's only fair that you give me the same respect with mine."

"I know, but it just makes me crazy when I see that you have feelings for someone else. I know I don't have a right to get angry, but I do."

"But why? You and I broke up for good over eleven years ago."

"I know, but it still bothers me. I guess I'm just jealous," he admitted.

"Well, my main concern is not about me dating anyone, it's about Ashley's welfare," she said, changing the subject.

"Maybe we should spend time with Ashley together. Maybe we should try to be more like a family."

After all those times he'd called her out of her name? After all those times he'd missed paying his child support? After all those times he'd tried to cause problems with her and Darryl and any other guy she'd ever dated? He couldn't have been serious. She could never fall in love with him again, and the only feelings she had for him were the kind a woman has for a man when she has children by him. And that was it. "I really wish things could have worked out between us years ago, but now too much has been said and too many incidents have taken place."

"So, you don't think there could ever be a chance with us getting back together?" he said regretfully.

"No, I don't," she said and actually felt sorry about it because he seemed so humble. She wanted to know what had happened with Priscilla, but since it wasn't her business, she shied away from asking him about her.

He looked at her and forced a partial smile, obviously trying to pretend that he was okay with her response.

"I don't know when I'm going back to school or work, but I do know that Ashley and I will be staying here with Mom for a while, so this is where you'll have to come see her or pick her up," she said, trying to steer clear of the getting-back-together subject.

"Why are you going to stay here?"

"Somebody came into the apartment yesterday and took almost everything we had."

"No way," he said in a surprised manner.

"Yeah. They did."

"Did you report it to the police?"

"Yeah, but you know they'll never find out who did it."

"Well, if you need anything, let me know."

With Tyrone acting this nice, the world was definitely coming to an end. Marcella just knew it. "If you really pay your child support and spend more quality time with Ashley like you said earlier, we'll be just fine."

"I'll be by to get her this evening," he said, standing up.

"Okay," she said, rising from the recliner. They walked into the living room.

"When are you going back to work?" he asked, opening the front door.

"I don't know. One minute I'm having a normal conversation with someone the way we are right now, and the next minute I'm crying my eyes out, or feeling like I want to die," she said, leaning against the entryway wall. "I'm just not ready yet."

"I can understand that. Well, I guess I should go. Tell Ashley to call me, alright?" he said, gazing at her.

Marcella gazed back at him, examining his face. She hadn't paid much attention to his physical characteristics in years, but today she couldn't help but notice his gorgeous hazel-brown eyes. The same eyes that her sweet little Nicholas had been blessed with. And while she'd always tried to convince herself that Nicholas hadn't resembled his father in the least, now she could no longer deny the fact that he was his father's son. He was the spitting image of him. And she wished she could stand there admiring Tyrone's face for the rest of all eternity. She missed Nicholas so much, and the only connection she had with him was Tyrone. She felt weak and she could feel the pressure building inside her eyes as she tried to resist shedding any more tears. She'd wept so much over the last few days that her eyes felt permanently swollen. She felt so alone, and she wanted to beg Tyrone to stay with her until her mother came back home. She knew it wasn't the logical thing to do, but she needed someone to hold her. Someone to make her feel safe. "Tyrone," she said, swallowing hard while tears rolled down her cheeks. "What am I going to do without my baby?"

Tyrone closed the door and pulled her into his arms.

Chapter 25

Racquel sprayed Windex across the dining-room table, and then cleaned it with the front section of yesterday's newspaper. It seemed strange using something other than a paper towel or a rag of some kind, but the newspaper kept the glass spotless and left no smearing. When she finished with that, she pulled out black linen place mats, matching linen napkins, two off-white plates and placed them at each end of the table. Then she wrapped the silverware inside the napkins, inserted black candles inside each of the two brass candleholders, and placed everything on the table the way she wanted it for dinner. She and Kevin hadn't shared a romantic dinner like this one all year. And she couldn't wait to see his face when she surprised him with his favorite dish, broccoli-and-cheese lasagna.

Their marriage was still on shaky ground, but she was hoping that after tonight, things would start looking up. She'd neglected him in every way, and it was time to do something about it. She'd thought for sure that things would return back to normal when she'd finally given up on trying to have a baby, but it hadn't. And when her nephew passed away, their love for each other had seemed like it was becoming stronger. But now that the funeral was over, Kevin was distancing himself from her again, and it was obvious that he'd only been affectionate with her, trying to make it easier for both of them to deal with Nicholas's death.

She left the dining room, walked back into the kitchen, washed the glass-cleaner residue from her hands, lifted the covered lasagna filled baking dish from the counter, and set it inside the preheated oven. Then she removed the lettuce, cucumbers, and tomatoes from the refrigerator, sliced them, mixed everything together, and poured a mixture of oil and vinegar over the entire salad.

She glanced at her watch and saw that she still had plenty of time to shower and get dressed before Kevin got home from work. She wasn't sure what she was going to wear, but she wanted it to be something sexy. Something that would make him stand up and take notice. Something that would complement the elegant after-five hair-style she'd received at the hair salon earlier that morning. Something that would make him lose all control the minute he saw her. Especially since they rarely made love anymore, and when they did, Kevin no longer bothered with any foreplay and simply went straight for the kill. And it was clear that all he was interested in was satisfying himself. He'd never been like that before, but Racquel knew that his actions had a lot to do with the fact that making love had become nothing more than a dreadful routine. He'd told her that months and months before, but she hadn't listened, and now she was paying for it.

After Racquel showered, lotioned her body, and rolled deodorant under her arms, she went into the kitchen and removed the lasagna from the oven. It had taken an hour to bake, but now she needed to let it cool for at least a half hour. When she returned back to the bedroom, she slipped on a black lacy bra, matching bikini panties, and ebony-black pantyhose. Then she pulled a black sleeveless crêpe-wool dress from the closet, stepped into it, and zipped it. She replaced the makeup that she'd washed off before showering, stepped in front of the mirror attached to the dresser, and smoothed the sides of her hair with both hands. Kevin was going to be there any minute, so she slipped on a pair of plush black slippers and went into the kitchen so she could warm the garlic bread. When the bread was ready, she went into the dining room, pulled out two wineglasses from the server, and lit the candles. Then she dimmed the dining-room lights and flipped on the CD player so she could listen to some jazz while she waited.

She sat patiently for ten minutes and wondered if maybe she should call to check on Marcella. She hadn't sounded like she was doing too well when Racquel had spoken with her this morning, and she was hoping that things might have gotten better for her as the day went on. Their mother was starting to become worried, but it had only been a week since the funeral, and Racquel knew better than anyone that it took time to overcome the loss of a child. And in all honesty, one never overcame it, but simply learned to live with it.

When Racquel heard Kevin enter the house, she went to meet him in the kitchen.

"What's all this for?" he asked, dropping his black leather briefcase down on the kitchen table.

"It's for you," she said, kissing him.

"I know that's not my lasagna over there?" he said, looking in the direction of the stove.

"As a matter of fact, it is," she said.

"What's the occasion? And why are you all dressed up?"

"There's no occasion really. I just thought it would be nice to surprise you with dinner."

"Well, is it ready? Because I'm starved," he said, slipping off his suit jacket, laying it on the back of the chair. Then he loosened his tie and opened the top button of his shirt.

"It's ready, but I want us to have a drink first so we can talk."

"Baby, I don't mean to mess up what you have going here, but if it's okay with you, I'd rather we talk while we're eating. I haven't had anything to eat since noon," he said, grabbing an everyday plate from the dish rack.

No. No. No. This wasn't at all how she'd planned for the evening to turn out. He was supposed to walk through that door, grab her into his arms, kiss her erotically, and then sit down with her for a glass of wine. And couldn't he see that she'd already set plates on the table from their good china set? And she could just kill him for loosening his tie and undoing the button on his shirt like they were sitting down to eat pizza. What did he think she'd gotten all dressed up for anyway? She wanted to yell at him, but since she didn't want to argue, she decided against it. "I already have plates on the table," she said, moving the bowl of salad to the dining-room table.

"Oh," he said, replacing the plate back in the rack.

When they sat down in the winter-white high-back chairs, Kevin forked a hefty amount of salad onto his plate, and Racquel poured herself a much-needed glass of dinner wine.

"So how was work?" she asked.

"Okay," he said, chewing a mouthful of lettuce, and didn't elaborate any further.

"Kevin, what's wrong with us?" she asked, setting the empty wineglass down on the table.

"What do you mean?" he asked, looking at her.

"I mean, what's wrong with our marriage?"

"It's not so much what's wrong with our marriage, but more like what happened to it than anything else," he said, sipping some wine.

"But we've gotten past all those problems."

"But it still caused a lot of distance between us."

"Well, what do you think will make it better? I mean, tell me what you want me to do."

"To be totally honest with you, I really don't know what you can do. I used to think that all our problems had to do with the infertility situation, but now . . . now I don't even know if I'm in love with you anymore," he said, taking another sip of wine.

She swallowed hard and stared at him. She'd heard him say those same exact words in her dream, but this time she was wide awake, and the pain was much more real than it had been then. "So what are you saying?" she asked hesitantly.

"Hey, why don't we finish eating first, and then we can talk after that," he said, scooting the high-back chair away from the table.

She wanted to object, but she was hurting so bad that she decided to go along with his idea of delaying the conversation.

When Kevin chewed the last forkful of lasagna, he leaned back in his chair. Racquel sat in her chair waiting for him to speak.

"That was good," he said, referring to the meal.

She didn't acknowledge his appreciation and continued to wait for him to resume their discussion.

"Look," he said, pausing. "It's not that I don't love you, but it's just that we don't have that same passion between us like we used to. And I know it's because of all the problems we've had."

"Well, I don't know what to do to make things better. I mean, I took a leave of absence from teaching with the hope that I could spend more time trying to satisfy you. But that doesn't seem to be making any difference at all."

"I know you did, but something still isn't right. And the last thing I want to do is end our marriage without trying to make it work, but it seems like the more we try, the worse things get."

"Is there someone else?" she asked and regretted it as soon as she closed her mouth. Because if there was, his confession was going to kill her.

"No. There's not. You know I'm not like that, Racquel. Or at least you ought to know by now."

"Kevin, I don't know what to think with you sitting here saying that you're not in love with me."

He sighed intensely. "Maybe that wasn't the right choice of words."

"Well, that's what you said."

"And I also said that I do still love you, but it's just that the passion isn't there."

"Well, what do you suggest we do?" she asked disgustedly.

"Maybe what we need is some time apart," he said, clasping his hands together on the table.

"You're not serious?" she said, frowning.

"It's not what I want, but maybe a separation would allow us to rethink our priorities."

"*My* priorities are straight," she said, elevating the sound of her voice.

"But they weren't always," he said matter-of-factly. 'I suggested a long time ago that we give up on trying to have a baby because I knew how much tension it was causing between us. And although you said you would consider adopting a child, you haven't said much else about it."

Is that what this was all about? Adopting a baby. She'd said she would consider it, but this was a very serious move, and she needed to be sure that this was the right thing for them to be doing. "So, are you saying that adopting a baby will solve all our problems?"

"No, I'm not saying that at all because now I'm not sure if it would be smart bringing an innocent child into our lives when we're having all these problems, anyway. So, I guess what I'm trying to say is that I don't think it's doing either one of us any good to keep living the way we're living. I'm not saying that we should just separate and cut off all ties, but I do think we need some time apart so we can try to work this out."

"You sound like you've been thinking about this for some time now, so when were you planning to tell me?" she asked and pursed her lips because she was sick of hearing those same romantic jazz songs playing repeatedly on the CD player. Especially since there wasn't anything romantic about what was going on with her and Kevin.

"I hadn't thought about it seriously until the last couple of weeks."

"Well, is that what you're going to do? Move out?" she asked nervously.

"I really think it would be best."

"What about seeing a marriage counselor?" she said hastily.

"I don't know, because the last thing I want to do is blow a bunch of money on something that isn't going to help."

"You didn't think it was a waste of money when you and my family tried to get me to see a psychiatrist after the baby passed away."

"But that was different."

"How was it different, Kevin?" she asked, leaning back in her seat.

"I don't know," he said, obviously confused about his feelings. "Okay, maybe we *should* see a marriage counselor."

"Well, if that's the case, I think we should see one before you move out. I mean, maybe moving out isn't the right thing to do, because it might push us further apart instead of closer together."

He didn't say anything.

"I'll call your benefits office tomorrow to see if your insurance covers seeing a counselor," she said, ignoring the fact that he hadn't fully agreed on not moving out.

"Fine," he said, rubbing his hands down the front of his face like he was exhausted. "Make the appointment."

Racquel stared at him with tears in her eyes, not knowing what to say or what move to make next. Her romantic, candlelight dinner had pretty much been ruined with all this talk about separation, but she still wanted to make love to him. Because strangely enough, it seemed like she craved him more after they argued, or like now, when she was sad about something. It didn't make much sense, but that's how she always felt. And she had a feeling that Kevin felt the same way, because it was during those times that they made the best love of all. Although now, he was just sitting there watching her without any expression on his face, and she couldn't tell if he desired her, or if he was dwelling on the problems in their relationship. She wanted to seduce him, but decided that it wasn't worth risking the chance of him rejecting her.

She slid her chair back, stood up, lifted her partially empty plate and wineglass from the table, and walked toward the kitchen trying hard not to look in his direction. But he stopped her as she passed by him.

"Hey," he said, smiling at her. "Set that down for a second, and come here."

She did what he asked and sat on his lap. "What?" she asked, trying to appear emotionally grounded, but knowing full well that what she really wanted to do was burst into tears.

"You know, I do really love you," he said, wrapping his arms around her waist. "And whether you believe it or not, I do want us to work all of this out."

She rested her hands on his shoulders and cried silently.

"And regardless of what I said about us separating or me moving out, it's not what I want. But it's just that I get so frustrated when I think about how in love we were when we first met and how good we were together. And for the longest time, you didn't seem to care about what happened between us one way or the other, so I decided that I might as well take the same attitude."

"I know, but I promise you, all of that is over," she said, placing both of her hands on the sides of his face. "And all I want to do is show you how much I love you and how much I need you in my life," she said and pecked him on his lips.

He wiped the tears from her face and kissed her fiercely. And her heart felt like it was going to explode. Then without even realizing it, she pulled off his tie, removed his dress shirt and then his undershirt. She kissed him passionately around his neck and on his chest. He unzipped her dress, pulled it up over her behind and then over her head. Then he unsnapped her bra, tossed it on the carpet, grabbed her breasts in each of his hands and sucked both of them wildly, switching back and forth from one to the other. She dropped her head backward and screamed with total enjoyment.

But when the foreplay was over, they both stood up. Then he removed his trousers, and undershorts, and sat back down in the chair. She stepped out of the rest of her undergarments and straddled herself across his thighs. He eased inside her and followed her rhythm as she swirled her body toward him and then away from him in repetitive motion. The moans grew louder; the groans grew deeper; and the movement accelerated to another level. And finally when they couldn't hold back any longer, they entered complete ecstasy.

Chapter 26

"**H**ello?" Marcella answered in a groggy voice, her eyes still closed. "Hi, I'm looking for Marcella Jones, please," the voice said on the other end of the phone line.

"This is she" Marcella said, raising up in the bed when she realized the voice sounded like Bob's, one of the partners at the accounting firm.

"Marcella, this is Bob Jenkins."

"Hi, Bob, how are you?" she asked, wondering why he was calling her.

"Did I wake you?"

"No," she lied. "I'm not feeling well." She realized that today was the day she'd told him she'd be returning to work.

"Oh, I'm sorry to hear that. Are you back in school yet?"

"Yes," she lied again. And she couldn't help but

wonder if he knew she was lying, since he was calling her at a time when he knew she should be at school.

"So, are you still planning to come back to work this week?"

"To be honest with you, Bob, I'm still not feeling up to it." Although she didn't dare tell him, she didn't know when she was going to be ready.

"Well, I know you're going through some difficult times right now, but we've been without a part-time clerical person for over two months, and we really need you to come back this evening."

Now what was she going to do? She'd put them off for more than eight weeks, and they'd been more than understanding about her situation. But now it sounded like he was giving her an ultimatum, and she wasn't sure how to respond to his request. "I missed almost two whole weeks of school, and it's been hard these last couple of months trying to get back into it. But I really think I'll be ready to come back to work by next week or the one following. Especially since by then, I'll almost be finished with my semester course work, and I'll be getting ready to take my finals." She hated lying to Bob the way she was, but there was no way she was going to tell him that she'd withdrawn from all her classes.

"Well, we've got some extremely important projects that we're working on, and as much as I hate saying this, we're going to have to hire someone in your place if you're not able to come in."

Hire someone in her place? Was this some nice way of telling her that she was going to be fired? It was only a part-time position, so why couldn't they simply hire someone through one of those temporary agencies until she returned? She'd been with the firm for over five years, and she couldn't believe they'd get rid of her just like that. "Do you think you could give me until next week?'' she asked fearfully, because she really needed her job, but at the same time she wasn't ready emotionally or physically to go back, either.

Bob paused for a few seconds and then spoke. ''Although I know Martin isn't going to be too happy about me doing this, I'll give you until day after tomorrow.''

What good was two more days going to do for her? ''Thank you, Bob,'' she said, pretending to be relieved. ''And I really appreciate you doing this for me.''

''Well, I hope you feel better, and I'll see you on Wednesday.''

''Okay, I'll see you then,'' she said, preparing to hang up the phone until she heard him say something else.

''Marcella?''

''Yes.''

''If for some reason you don't make it in on Wednesday evening, we'll have no choice but to let you go. We'll still consider hiring you when you graduate, but we won't be able to keep you on part-time or pay any more of your tuition,'' he said regretfully, and Marcella could tell that his decision was strictly business, and nothing personal.

''I understand,'' she said, moving her legs from under the comforter to the side of the bed.

''Take care.''

''Thanks for calling,'' she said, hanging up the phone.

She'd known for some time that this day was coming. She'd tried to force herself into going back to school two weeks after Nicholas's funeral, but it hadn't worked out. No matter how hard she tried, she just couldn't grasp onto what her instructors were trying to teach, and most of the time her mind drifted off in a thousand directions. Which is why she'd finally gone to the admis-

sions and records office and had withdrawn from all
her classes. She hated doing it, but she promised herself
that it was only for this term and that she would reenroll
next semester. Of course when her mother and Racquel
had found out about it, they'd thrown a complete fit.
That is, until she informed them that *her* life was *her*
business, and that her dropping out of school really
didn't concern either one of them.

But if she lost her job—well, that was going to be a
whole different story. Because then she'd have no choice
except to surrender her apartment, and she'd be forced
to move in with her mother on a permanent basis. The
Housing Authority had already dropped her rent to
zero due to her part-time employment, but without a
job at all, she wouldn't have nearly enough money to
pay her utility bills. As a matter of fact, the only money
she would have to depend on was Tyrone's child support. The same child support that he'd so conveniently
gotten lax with again.

She could kill herself for sleeping with him that afternoon he'd come by her mother's house to see her, but
for some stupid reason, she hadn't been able to resist
him. She was lonely, and she'd allowed him to play
on her vulnerability to the fullest extent. She'd always
known that he couldn't be trusted, but he sounded so
sincere when he said he wanted to do right by her and
Ashley, and that he wanted them to be a family. But
now he spent even less time with Ashley than he had
before Nicholas passed away. Marcella didn't now—and
wasn't ever going to—have any genuine feelings for
him again because there was far too much history
between them, but a part of her had wanted to believe
that he was still in love with her. Not because she wanted
a relationship with him, but because she needed to be
loved. She needed to be loved by man.

But, then, who was she kidding? Because Tyrone was far and apart from even resembling a real man, let alone actually being one. He acted more like an immature little boy than anything else. So she knew all those thoughts about needing to be loved were basically just a bunch of excuses and a bunch of wishful thinking. And while she hated admitting it, she could no longer deny the fact that she'd had sex with him for one reason and one reason only: He knew how to rock her world. As a matter of fact, she'd never even been with another man who could compare to him. He was that good, and she hated him for it.

The more she thought about Tyrone and how trifling he was, the more she despised herself for allowing him to skip payment after payment. She should have turned him in right after he caused that reduction in her food-stamp allotment, but whenever she thought about it, it reminded her of the day Sharon was killed in that car accident. Because it was that whole Tyrone incident that had caused them to disagree in the first place. She had wanted to tell Tyrone off, and Sharon kept advising her not to.

"Well, I'll tell you one thing, you didn't die for nothin'," Marcella said out loud to Sharon, picked up the beige receiver and dialed 411.

"Directory assistance, what city, please?" the directory operator answered.

"Covington Park. Could you give me the number for Child Support Enforcement, please?" Marcella asked, waiting to take a mental note of the phone number.

"Thank you, here's that number," the operator said and played a computerized announcement.

Marcella pressed the button inside the phone and dialed the number.

"Good morning, Child Support Enforcement, how

may I help you?'' a younger woman, probably in her early twenties, answered.

"Yes, I'd like to speak to someone concerning the issuance of a child-support order,'' she said, switching the phone from her right ear to her left.

"Do you know where the father lives and where he works?''

"Yes, he lives and works right here in Covington Park,'' Marcella said guiltily because she'd always known where he was, but she'd told her caseworker from the very beginning that she didn't, so they wouldn't cut her money off when she'd first gotten on welfare and wasn't working.

"Good, because that'll make the process go a lot faster. Now what I'll need to do is take your name and phone number, so that I can assign you to a caseworker, and then he or she will call you back with a time to come in for your initial intake interview.''

Marcella told the woman her name and recited her mother's phone number instead of her own, because she knew her telephone was on the verge of being shut off. Plus, she probably wasn't going to be moving back to her apartment any time soon, anyhow. "How long will it take to get into court once I have my interview?''

"Oh, probably anywhere from six months to a year. It just depends on your particular case.''

"Six months to a year? But that's such a long time.''

"I know, but with the number of cases we have in this county, compared to the small amount of caseworkers, it's the best we can do.''

"Okay. When do you think someone will call me to schedule my appointment?''

"Probably sometime this week, but if not, definitely by the first of next week.''

Marcella felt like telling her to just forget the whole

thing, but she knew she needed this money more than ever, since there was a good chance she might be losing her job. And she'd spent the rest of the money from Sharon's insurance policy on miscellaneous bills. "Well, thank you for your help," Marcella said.

"Goodbye," the woman said and hung up.

It just wasn't fair for her to have to wait this long to get what was rightfully hers, and now she wished she'd taken him to court a long time ago. Everyone had begged her to, but she just hadn't been motivated enough to do it. And she wasn't sure why she hadn't, except that back when she wasn't working, she'd been worried about them cutting her check off completely. And even now she wondered just how long it was going to be before they calculated an overpayment for that. Then when she started working she had become worried about them eliminating her food stamps. She knew she'd been cheating the government by concealing Tyrone's whereabouts, but it was the only way she had sort of made ends meet.

Marcella stood in front of the old-style wooden dresser and stared at herself in the mirror. Her hair was wild and scary and she hadn't done anything with it in over a week. And she wasn't going to do anything with it today, either. She walked outside the bedroom, went into the kitchen to find a few snacks, and looked up at the clock on the wall. It was almost ten o'clock, so she had to hurry if she wanted to get back into the bedroom before *The Price Is Right* came on. She pulled down an unopened bag of tortilla chips from the cabinet, pulled out a jar of medium salsa and a can of Coke from the refrigerator, and grabbed a partially filled bag of Chips Ahoy. Then she headed back into the bedroom, set the phone down on the floor, and piled all of her food on top of the nightstand. She picked up the remote, turned on the twenty-inch color TV set, and turned it to the network hosting her favorite game show. As the commercials flashed across the screen, she positioned a deep-turquoise backrest against the wooden headboard, leaned back on it, and then opened her chips and salsa dip.

Her day began and ended pretty much the same way every day. First she watched *The Price Is Right, The Young and the Restless,* then the area news, followed by *The Bold and the Beautiful, Days of Our Lives,* a local talk show, and then *Sally,* and finally *Oprah.* And it was these television shows that allowed her to keep at least some sanity because she really didn't care about anything else. And it was fine with her if she never left the house ever again. Her mother was taking care of Ashley and was doing a good job with her. And since it seemed like Ashley enjoyed spending all this time with her grandmother, Marcella really didn't have any important responsibilities anymore. And why should she care about anything anyhow? She'd tried to do all the right things, she'd tried to treat people the way she wanted to be treated, but where had all of that gotten her? From what she could see, nowhere.

She watched all of her programs as planned, and with the exception of a few sales calls over the phone, there hadn't been any other interruptions. But now she heard her mother laying her keys down on the kitchen counter, and Marcella knew it was just a matter of time before she burst into the room with her usual fussing.

"Have you been sitting in this room watching TV all day?" Corrine asked as soon as she stepped inside the doorway.

"Pretty much," Marcella said nonchalantly.

"Where's Ashley, and why isn't she home yet?" Corrine asked with her hand on her hip.

She's gone, and that's why she's not home *yet*, Marcella thought sarcastically, but didn't dare say it. "She's probably over at that Patrice's house," Marcella said without taking her eyes off Oprah and her guests.

"Ever since the school district switched her bus route to the one over here, she's been going somewhere else every day after they drop her off," Corrine said, pausing. Then she continued. "You know, I've been taking care of Ashley like she's my own child for weeks now, and even though I don't mind it, she's your daughter and it's time for **you** to start acting like it."

Marcella looked at her silently and wished her mother would stop drowning out the talk show.

"Don't you have anything to say?" Corrine asked irately.

"Mom, what do you want me to say? I'm barely taking care of myself, so how am I going to take care of Ashley? She acts like she prefers being around you instead of me anyway."

"That's because you don't give that girl the time of day. You don't say more than two words to her when she's here, and you don't do anything with her."

"I don't have any money to do things with her."

"I'm not talking about those kind of things. I'm talking about sitting down with your daughter to see how she's doing in school, or even just to see how she's dealing with her brother's death."

"She's barely even shed any tears since the day of the funeral, so I'm sure she's fine."

"Marcella, I don't know what's gotten into you, but this isn't like you at all. You used to be such a good mother, and I was always so proud of that."

"Well, if I was such a good mother, then why did God take Nicholas away from me? Huh, Mom? Tell me that?" Marcella said, slightly raising her voice.

"Girl, we've been through that over and over again, and I'm tired of trying to explain the facts of life to you. And whether you understand what happened or not, that still doesn't give you the right to just give up or to neglect your daughter the way you're doing. She's thirteen years old, and a girl that age needs her mother."

"Ashley knows that I'm here for her if she needs me."

"No, she doesn't. And what type of an example do you think you're setting for her by lying up in this filthy room like you've been doing?" Corrine asked, shifting her eyes around the room.

"Mom, I'm depressed. Why can't you understand that?" Marcella said, trying to make her mother comprehend.

"Do you remember when Racquel kept singing that same song when she lost her baby, and you told her that it was time for her to accept what happened so she could get on with her life? Do you?" Corrine asked, folding her arms.

"This is different."

"Different how, Marcella?" Corrine asked sternly.

"Racquel never even got to know her baby, and she only held her for a few minutes. But I was with Nicholas for eleven years."

"Losing a baby, is losing a baby, and it doesn't matter how much time you got to spend with it. And I sure hope you don't say anything like that to Racquel."

"Mom, why are you doing this?" Marcella asked, wishing she would leave her alone.

"Because I want you to get up off of your behind and start living again. I've tried to be as patient with you as I can, but enough is enough. And it doesn't make any sense how you just dropped out of school in the middle of your third year. All that time and work for nothing."

"Mom, how do you expect me to go to class or study feeling the way I do?"

"Because you're strong. I raised both you and Racquel to be strong Black women, and I refuse to accept anything less than that. I went through a lot with your father. Lord knows I did. But I started on my job when Racquel was barely two months old, and I've been there ever since. And even when your father left, I took care of you girls, and I made sure the bills were paid. So, you tell me what would have happened to you if *I* had fallen into some deep state of depression. What would you and Racquel have done then? Both of you were a lot older than Ashley, but you were still only teenagers."

"Mom, losing a husband is not the same as losing a child. You have to know that."

"I'm not saying it is the same, but what I am saying is that life has to go on. And you need to go back to work before those people end up firing you."

Marcella looked straight at the television set because the last thing she wanted was for her mother to find out that she was only two days away from losing her job with the firm. "What sense does it make for me to go back to work when I can't even concentrate on anything else for more than two minutes."

"You at least have to try," Corrine said, and then the phone rang.

After the second ring, Marcella reached down to the floor to pick it up. "Hello?"

"Ms. Jones?" a woman said.

"Yes, this is," Marcella said, trying to figure out the voice.

"This is Mrs. Johnson, Ashley's counselor at Covington Park Junior High."

"Yes, what can I do for you?" Marcella asked curiously.

"Ashley seems to be having some problems with not getting her homework done in just about every one of her classes, and a couple of the teachers have reported that she's been sassing them whenever they ask her a question or tell her to do something."

"When did all this start?" Marcella said, glancing at her mother reluctantly and wishing she would I go away.

"It started about a month or so ago, and we've mailed a couple of letters to your house. I even tried to call you a couple of times, but I didn't get an answer."

Marcella wasn't surprised about the unanswered phone calls, because there were lots of days when she didn't even bother to look at the phone, let alone answer it. But she did think it was strange that she hadn't gotten the letters, since she'd had all her mail forwarded to her mother's address. "Well, I'll have a talk with her as soon as she gets home this evening," Marcella said in a frustrated manner.

"We just wanted to let you know because Ashley was a model student when she started here last year in seventh grade, and she always got straight A's, but this year, things aren't going well for her at all. I don't know if it has something to do with her brother's death or if something else is bothering her."

"Well, as I said, I'll speak with her this evening, and I'll try to give you a call sometime tomorrow afternoon."

"That will be fine."

"Thank you for calling," Marcella said and hung up the phone.

"What was that all about?" Corrine asked without delay.

"That was Ashley's counselor calling to say that she

hasn't been turning in homework, and that she's been sassing some of her teachers."

"Mmm. Mmm. Mmm. See, that's exactly what I've been trying to tell you. That girl needs you, and it's your responsibility to know what's going on with her."

"She always says that she doesn't have any homework, or that she did it at school. So what am I supposed to do?"

"You're supposed to be her mother, Marcella," Corrine yelled.

Marcella was getting fed up with all this harassment, and she wished her mother would stop it before this whole conversation turned uglier than it already was.

"The next thing you know, she'll be sneaking around here seeing some little mannish boy, and I'd hate to see her end up pregnant."

"Pregnant?" Marcella said, frowning. "Mom, Ashley is only thirteen years old. And she's way too smart to let something like that happen anyway."

"Nowadays, these girls are getting pregnant earlier and earlier, and being book smart doesn't mean she won't get caught up with some boy."

"Ashley is not messing around with some boy."

"How do you know?"

"Because I do," Marcella said and heard the back door shutting.

Corrine looked at her and walked out of the bedroom without saying anything else. Marcella followed behind her. When they arrived in the kitchen, Ashley was setting her book bag down in a chair.

"Ashley, what is this I'm hearing about you not turning in your homework assignments?"

"I don't know," Ashley said, shrugging.

"What do you mean you don't know?" Marcella said, raising her voice.

Ashley stared at her with an I-don't-see-why-you're-trippin' look on her face.

"Your counselor called here this afternoon, and not only did she say you weren't doing your homework, but she also said that you've been talking back to a couple of your teachers. So is that true, too?"

"No," Ashley said, looking at her grandmother.

"Oh, so what you're saying then, is that your teachers are lying on you," Marcella said in an I-know-better-than-that tone of voice.

Ashley looked at her grandmother again, like she was expecting Corrine to defend her.

"Don't look at me," Corrine said. "It's your mama who's talking to you."

"I'm really disappointed in you, Ashley. You know I've been going through a rough time, so why are you trying to do things to worry me like this?"

"You don't care about me anyway, so why should I waste my time doing some stupid homework?"

Marcella raised her eyebrows in shock. "What do you mean I don't care about you?"

"You don't. And all you ever talk about is how much you miss Nicholas."

"That's because I do miss him."

"But he's *dead*, Mom," Ashley said in a hostile tone. "And *I'm* still here."

"Ashley!" Marcella said, shaking her head in disagreement.

"Can I be excused now?" Ashley asked, looking away from her mother and folding her arms.

"Ashley, what's gotten into you?" Marcella asked, realizing for the first time that something was seriously wrong with her daughter.

"Nothing," Ashley said, scowling.

"What I want you to do is go to your room," Marcella said, feeling angry and hurt at the same time.

"You're just like . . . ," Ashley mumbled as she left the room.

"What did you say?" Marcella yelled out, walking behind her.

"You're just like my no-good daddy."

Marcella's heart fell to the floor.

Chapter 27

"I just don't understand what's gotten into Ashley," Marcella said, leaning back on the sofa in her sister's family room. "She's so ornery and disrespectful."

"For one thing, she's hurting over Nicholas," Racquel said, curling her legs under her behind.

"I realize that, but I'm not going to keep putting up with that little attitude of hers. And do you know what she said yesterday before she stormed her little self out of the room?"

"What?"

"That I was just like her no-good daddy. And if I hadn't caught myself, I would've strangled her."

Racquel looked away from Marcella like she was suddenly interested in what was on TV.

"Can you believe that?" Marcella continued.

"Maybe she didn't mean it exactly like it sounded."

"How else could she have meant it?"

"Maybe it's because you haven't spent as much time

with her lately. I know you've been going through a hard time, but she probably needs you right now more than she ever has before."

"But I *have* been there for her, and so has Mom," Marcella said defensively.

"I know, but I'm telling you from experience. Sometimes we get so caught up in ourselves that we forget about the needs of everyone else. I mean, take me for example. I was so obsessed with getting pregnant, that I neglected the most important person in my life. And I almost lost him because of it."

"I'm not obsessed with Nicholas's death, I'm just having a hard time accepting it."

"I know you don't see it that way, because I didn't, either. But it does seem like you've gotten to the point where you don't care about anything or anybody."

"That's not true, and I love Ashley more than anything else."

"I know you do, but since Kevin and I have been going to see that marriage counselor, I'm finally able to see how selfish I was. All I cared about was having a baby, and everything else was second. Including my marriage. So, I'm telling you, Marcella. Don't make the same mistakes did."

"Well, I don't know what to do."

"Do exactly what you used to do before Nicholas passed away. Even though you were in school and working, you still used to spend a lot of time with them when you could, and I'm sure Ashley misses that."

"Maybe if I hadn't started school in the first place, none of this would be happening."

"What does your going back to school have to do with anything?"

"It kept me away from them so much. I was so busy worrying about how much more money I could make by going back to school, that I didn't even notice how sick Nicholas was."

"Marcella, I know you're not still trying to blame yourself for Nicholas's death, because there really weren't any warning signs, so there was nothing you could do."

"But maybe if I had been around him more, I would have noticed something out of the ordinary. Something that would have made me take him to the doctor."

"Mom and I watched Ashley and Nicholas all the time when you worked, and we never noticed anything. As a matter of fact, until you said he'd had a couple of headaches, we weren't even aware of that. So you have to know that there wasn't anything any of us could have done. God knows, I wish we could have, but there wasn't."

Marcella acknowledged her sister's comments with a slight nod.

"I know losing a child is difficult," Racquel said. "Believe me, I do. But you have to move on. Not just for your sake, but for Ashley's. Because if you don't, she's going to end up in trouble. And you know what kind of trouble I'm talking about."

"Mom was saying the same thing yesterday, but I really doubt it because Ashley is too sensible for that," Marcella said and then suddenly remembered what Ashley had done to that little Jason when she was just eleven years old. But Racquel still didn't know about that.

"Well, just the same, you'd better watch her a lot more closely than you have been. Especially since she's got that I-don't-care attitude and thinks that nobody cares about her. Because believe it or not, your childhood can affect you for the rest of your life. That's part of the reason why I have such a huge desire to have children."

"What do you mean?" Marcella asked in a confused tone.

"Because with Daddy and Mom arguing all the time and then getting a divorce, it's almost like I'm wanting to give my child the type of home I thought I should have had. It's almost like I'm hoping that I'll be able to relive my childhood the right way through my own son or daughter. At least that's what the counselor has been saying."

"You were having those same thoughts yourself two years ago. Remember when we talked about it that day we were driving home from Michelle's baby shower?"

"I know, but I still couldn't change the way I was feeling. So, maybe I needed to hear it from a professional before I could finally do something about it."

"Well, if that's what it took, then that's all that matters," Marcella said, glancing at the television.

"I'm just glad for Kevin's sake, because I was really taking him through a lot of changes."

"So, are you guys doing okay?" Marcella asked, leaning the side of her head into the palm of her hand, and resting her elbow on the back of the sofa.

"A whole lot better than we were, that's for sure. And it seems like we've both benefited from the counseling sessions, because we've learned more about each other in the last two months than we have the whole time we've been married. And even though we still have a long way to go, it seems like we're a lot closer. Almost closer than when we first met."

"I'm really glad to hear that, because you and Kevin deserve to be happy," Marcella said, smiling at her sister.

"You and Ashley deserve to be happy, too, and you will be as soon as you two start doing more things together," Racquel said, gazing directly at Marcella.

"Well, now that I have to go back to work tomorrow,

it's going to be even harder for me to spend time with her."

"I thought you said you were going back in a couple of weeks?"

"That's what I wanted, but one of the partners called me yesterday and said that if I don't come in tomorrow evening, they're going to replace me."

"It's probably a good idea for you to get back to work anyway, but maybe they'll let you work during the day now that you're not in school."

"That's just it, they don't know about me dropping out of school, and I don't want them to. Especially since they paid half of my tuition, and I withdrew from my classes too late to get a refund back."

"But maybe you should tell them anyway, because there's a chance that they'll understand."

"I don't know. And to be honest, I really don't feel mentally or physically ready to go back to work anyway. It took everything I had just to take a shower, get dressed, and drive over here after I dropped Ashley off for school. And if I hadn't needed to talk to you so badly, I'd probably still be in bed."

"I know how you feel because the main reason I took this leave of absence from teaching was so I could concentrate on Kevin, but part of it was because I was still so messed up emotionally and didn't feel comfortable being around my students."

"All I know is that things have got to get better," Marcella said with a deep sigh.

"They will," Racquel said, smiling and rubbing Marcella's back in a circular motion. "Don't even worry about it."

"So how was school?" Marcella asked Ashley as she walked through the back door.

"Okay," Ashley said with no enthusiasm.

"What homework do you have for tonight?" Marcella asked, removing a package of ground beef from the refrigerator. Since Corrine had gone directly to the salon after work to get her hair done, Marcella had decided to cook some spaghetti.

"Algebra."

"Well, I think you should start working on it now, while I'm cooking dinner."

Ashley blew her breath louder than usual and headed toward her bedroom with her book bag hanging from her shoulder.

"Why don't you sit in here and do it at the kitchen table?" Marcella asked, wanting to keep her in the same room with her so she could make sure she was really doing her schoolwork.

"It's more comfortable if I do it on Granny's desk in the bedroom," Ashley said, looking at her mother.

"Fine, but if you have any trouble with those math problems, I want you to come out here and ask me."

Ashley left the room.

After about thirty minutes the phone rang. Marcella knew it was for Ashley, but she decided to pick it up anyway to tell whoever it was to call back later when she was finished with her homework. But when she lifted the receiver, she heard Ashley saying hello and some boy asking her what was up. Marcella's first instinct was to hang up, but instead of doing that, she reached her finger toward the base of the phone on the wall and pushed the mute button.

"Hi, Jason," Ashley said in a cutesy voice.

"So when did you move in with your grandmother?" Jason asked, sounding like a twenty-year-old.

"A couple of months ago after my brother died."

"Oh, yeah. I heard about that when we moved back in with my mom."

"You and your brothers live across from our apartment again?"

"Yeah. We moved back right before your brother died, but I never did get a chance to see you."

Marcella felt her blood pressure skyrocket. She wanted to go off right then and there, but she had to wait a few minutes longer to see where this ghetto-boy conversation was going.

"What were you doing up at our school today?" Ashley continued.

"Me and my boys hang out at a lot of different schools every day."

"What high school do you go to?"

"I don't. I threatened to kick this teacher's ass if she didn't raise up off me about some crazy homework assignment, and when the principal told me to apologize to her, I told him I wasn't hearing that noise, and that I wasn't tellin' her nothin'. So they suspended me, and I never went back."

"Man. So you don't go to school at all?" Ashley asked in a shocked tone of voice.

"Nope. And my uncle says it's a waste of time for any Black person to go to school anyway because no matter what you learn, the White man is still going to keep you down."

"Not if you get a college education, he can't."

"Girl, that piece of paper doesn't mean anything. You'll see."

Ashley didn't say anything, and Marcella was getting more upset by the second.

"So when are you and me gonna hook up? With your fine self."

"I don't know. We hardly ever come back over to

the apartment since all of our stuff got stolen," Ashley said, sounding sad.

"Well, why don't you skip school tomorrow so we can hang out?"

"Skip school?" Ashley said, sounding confused.

"Yeah. You ride the bus to school like you always do, and then I'll meet you on the school grounds."

"I don't know, Jason. . . . I mean, sometimes my mom takes me and drops me off."

"So what. She doesn't sit there watchin' you until you get inside the school, does she?"

"No, but if she finds out, she'll kill me."

"How is she going to find out? Look, Ashley, I know you're not going to start acting like a little girl, are you? Because I really like you a lot. Shoot, ever since we were together that one day in your apartment, I haven't wanted to be with anyone else but you. And I cried when your mother threatened to call the police on me if I kept messing with you. I wanted to be with you so bad."

"I don't know, Jason," Ashley said, sounding scared.

"Look, Ashley, I'm fifteen, and I have certain needs."

Marcella released the mute button. "I'll tell you what you need, you little low-life thug, you need to be locked up in jail somewhere. And if you ever call this house again, you'll live to regret it."

"Aw, man, Ashley. I just know your moms isn't threatenin' me again," Jason said, laughing sarcastically.

"No, I'm not threatening you. I'm telling you exactly what I'm going to do if you ever contact my daughter or go near her again."

"Look, bitch, my *mama* don't even tell me what to do, so who in the hell do you think you are?"

"Just call back over here again, and you'll see," Marcella said and then wondered why she was actually sitting here arguing back and forth with some illiterate fifteen-year-old.

"That's why all your shit got stolen out of your apartment."

"Boy, what are you talking about?" Marcella asked, scrunching her face.

"You heard me. And if you keep messing with me, more than that is gonna happen to your smart ass."

"Ashley, hang up the phone!" Marcella yelled, waiting to make sure she did, and then she slammed the kitchen phone on the hook as hard as she could.

"Ashley! Get out here!" Marcella screamed.

Ashley dragged into the kitchen as slowly as she could.

"Are you crazy, giving that boy this phone number?"

"I'm sorry, Mom," she said, trembling.

"Don't you remember the talk we had when you snuck that little mannish boy into our apartment two years ago? Huh?"

Ashley shook her head yes, but didn't make a sound.

"Well, what were you thinking now? That since you were two years older, it was okay to see him?"

"I just wanted to talk to him. That's all."

"I told you that you could talk to boys on the phone when you turned thirteen, but I think you know I didn't mean somebody like Jason. That boy is headed for trouble, and anybody that has anything to do with him is headed in the same direction," Marcella said, pausing. "Ashley, what am I going to do with you? I mean you're messing up in school and now you're giving out your grandmother's phone number to some thug. For all you know, he could be in some Chicago gang, or something."

Ashley stood in front of her mother, looking as if she was holding her breath, and her eyes were filled completely with water.

Marcella took a deep breath. "Ashley, don't you know how much I love you? Don't you know that you're the only thing I have left in this world besides your granny, your aunt, and your uncle?"

Tears gushed down Ashley's face, and her feet stayed glued to the floor.

"Honey, I know I haven't been myself lately, but when Nicholas died, I just didn't know how to deal with it. Sometimes I still don't know how to deal with it, but I'm going to try a lot harder to. I know it wasn't fair for me to ignore you the way I have, but I really wasn't able to see it, until your granny came down on me yesterday. And I'm sorry. But at the same time, you're old enough to understand some of these things, and just because I'm going through some changes, doesn't mean you should stop doing your schoolwork, or that you have the right to talk back to your teachers. Because you know I didn't raise you that way," Marcella said, pulling her daughter into her arms.

Ashley sniffled continuously with her eyes closed and hugged her mother like it was her last opportunity. Marcella held her until she calmed down.

"You do know that I love you, don't you?" Marcella asked, looking down at her.

Ashley looked up at her and said, "Yes."

"And you do understand how important it is for you to do well in school, right?"

"Yes."

"Well, then, why did you suddenly think it wasn't worth doing your schoolwork anymore?"

"Because *you* didn't. I heard you telling Granny one night that you just couldn't go to your classes anymore and that it wasn't worth all the trouble."

Marcella paused, closed her eyes for a few seconds, and then spoke. "But I was wrong, honey. And don't you ever let anyone lead you to think that it's not worth getting an education. Okay?"

"Yes," Ashley said, laying her head back on her mother's chest.

Marcella hadn't held her daughter this much since Ashley was a toddler, and she couldn't remember the last time Ashley had ever wanted to hug her as tight as she was right now. And she felt a closeness with her, like she never had before. The kind of closeness every mother and daughter alive needed to have if they wanted to survive all the troubles in this world.

And it was at that moment that she knew she was going to work tomorrow, that she was going back to school in January, that she was going to graduate from college, and that she was going to be the best role model and mother she could be for Ashley.

And that's all that really mattered.

Epilogue

MAY 14, 1998

Not once will I ever forget that day I found Ashley's diary, and not once will I ever forget what I read in it. It's been years now, but it still makes me cringe whenever I think about it. And while I thought the whole idea of writing my thoughts down on paper was kind of silly, for some reason I purchased this journal and decided that this would be the day I made my first entry. I'm not really sure where to begin, except with what's going on today. I'm actually graduating from the university! And on top of that, I'm graduating with high honors. I mean, who would have ever thought it? If only Sharon and Nicholas could be here to witness the ceremony, or just to even share this special time in my life. It's been almost three years since I lost Nicholas and almost four since Sharon passed away, but I still have a hard time accepting any of it. Well, maybe I have accepted it, but I still have my days when I can't help but shed a few tears. It seemed so unfair to lose both my *child and my best friend in the same twelve-month period. But I do realize that that's just how life is, and that we weren't put here to stay here forever. But at least I have my little Ashley. Although since she's turning sixteen next month, I guess she's not really all that little anymore. But no matter how old she gets, she'll always be my baby. And I couldn't be prouder when it comes to all of her accomplishments. She's a straight-A student in the college preparatory program at Covington Park High, a member of the cheerleading squad, vice-president of the Afro-American Club, and from the way it looks, she'll be graduating a whole semester early. She's such an intelligent young lady, and I couldn't be happier that she's decided to pursue a medical degree and wants to specialize in infertility. At first I wasn't sure why she chose that particular field to go into, but then I realized that it probably had something to do with Racquel and Kevin not being able to have a baby. And I don't think it made things any easier for her when she saw how many changes they went through because of it. But, thank God, their marriage is finally back on track and couldn't be better. And on top of that, they became foster parents to a beautiful two-year-old little girl. A little girl whose mother dropped her off at the nursery one morning and never came back to pick her up. She's been with Racquel and Kevin for some time now, and we all love her to death. She's such a little sweetheart, and Racquel and Kevin are planning to adopt her just as soon as the agency allows them to. And I really hope that the adoption agency doesn't take as long as the Child Support Agency took when it came to ordering Tyrone to take care of Ashley. It took a little over a year, but instead of sixty dollars a week, that wonderful female judge ordered him to pay me one hundred forty dollars a week. Of course, he started his usual slacking on the payments, and it wasn't long before I had to take him back to court. And this time the judge ordered that the money be taken directly from his paycheck. Needless to say, he barely speaks to me now, but he has been spending a fair amount of time with Ashley.*

Which is all I want from him anyway. It's amazing how things work out, though. Once upon a time, I didn't know how I was going to put food on the table, or how I was going to keep the electricity on in my apartment. And all I ever dwelled on was what I didn't have and how I was going to get it. But now things have finally changed. I'm getting over five hundred dollars a month from Tyrone; the partners at the accounting firm are starting me off with thirty-five thousand dollars a year as an accountant, and the thirty thousand dollars that Sharon left for Nicholas was issued to me a few months after he passed away. Which will make all the difference in the world when I make the down payment on the house Ashley and I have been looking at. It's been wonderful living with Mom, and even though we're closer than we've ever been before, it's still not the same as having my own place. Plus, now that she's dating a really nice guy from church, I'm sure she needs more privacy. She'll never admit it, but I know she does just the same. And Mom isn't the only one who met someone recently, because Marcus told me that he thinks he's met the woman of his dreams, and he's bringing her to my graduation today, so I can meet her. I'm really looking forward to it, and I'm extremely happy for him. So anyway, that's pretty much it for now, except I do have one last thing to say. Life wasn't always good for me, but right now I truly couldn't be happier. And if I never learn another lesson for as long as I live, I've definitely learned this: When it rains, it pours; but when the sun does shine, it really shines brightly.

BOOK YOUR PLACE ON OUR WEBSITE AND MAKE THE READING CONNECTION!

We've created a customized website just for our very special readers, where you can get the inside scoop on everything that's going on with Zebra, Pinnacle and Kensington books.

When you come online, you'll have the exciting opportunity to:

- View covers of upcoming books
- Read sample chapters
- Learn about our future publishing schedule (listed by publication month *and author*)
- Find out when your favorite authors will be visiting a city near you
- Search for and order backlist books from our online catalog
- Check out author bios and background information
- Send e-mail to your favorite authors
- Meet the Kensington staff online
- Join us in weekly chats with authors, readers and other guests
- Get writing guidelines
- AND MUCH MORE!

**Visit our website at
http://www.kensingtonbooks.com**

More Women's Fiction From Kensington